Requiem for
A
BLACK AMERICAN CAPITALIST

Requiem for
A
BLACK AMERICAN CAPITALIST
by
BILY Wms-FORDE

TROISIÈME CANADIAN   New York, Montreal, Paris.

TROISIÈME CANADIAN/WILLIFO ASSOCIATES, INC.
Cathedral Station, #325, New York City 10025

To The *Harlem Writer's Guild* and all
the novels yet to come, and to the
Writers For Our Times and the *Frederick
Douglas Creative Writing Center;* to the
Producer and Friends of *Black Journal,* and
the helpful people of *Fiction Collective;*
but mostly to all the *Foxes* and then to the *Cats.*

one

The flight bringing in Cal Winston was already twenty minutes over-due. Watching the planes circling, dipping, swooping towards the earth, Donald and "Wheeler Dealer" Gru waited behind the terminal's great glass enclosure. Passengers and those waiting for passengers bustled about them.

Donald caressed his cheek nervously. A trip to the first class shops of Fifth Avenue, to the grand and almost intimidating restaurants atop 666 and the Empire State building were special occasions. The bright mechanical world within a world of the airport was also somehow special, existing beyond the simple boundary that normally defined his day-to-day existence.

A few minutes ago he had left Gru for a moment for the bathroom, but then had hesitated before rejoining Gru, and walked into a cocktail lounge to have a drink. Instantly he had become keenly conscious of every face in the lounge, and it had seemed to him that the faces were equally conscious of him. Outside, of course, he had noticed that nearly all the sky caps were black and there were a few black clerks and a sprinkling of black passengers moving briskly amid the other passengers. But inside the lounge he was alone. . . .

If he had been dressed in a suit and tie rather than the old sport shirt he had hastily thrown on, he might have lingered at the bar a little longer. Instead he found himself quickly downing his scotch and soda and starting out. But just before he got through the door it struck him: he had picked up all the change and hadn't left a tip. The brightly-colored, and perhaps even gaudy-looking sport shirt seemed to press against his skin, attract all the light in the bar. What was the bartender thinking,

1

the others? —serve *them* and treat *them* right and they don't even leave a tip! But he seemed to be frozen at the door, unable to keep going on out or to come back in. For wouldn't it look even more stupid if he returned to the bar now and left a tip? All the sonofabitches staring at him . . . Yet how could he go out without tipping?

Finally he scowled almost angrily and avoiding the eyes he knew must be watching him, went back to the bar and left all the change in his pocket. This he certainly hadn't meant to do. At a glance he saw that it was eighty-five cents, at least a tip of thirty-five cents too much. But wouldn't he look rather cheap picking some of it back up? He turned in agitation and hurried out the door. Stupid! Goddamn stupid! But every sonofabitch in the bar had seemed to have their eyes glued on him, maybe even thinking: where was the broom, the goddamn mop, or, worst still, where had he hidden *his* sky cap.

Back at Gru's side, gazing at the planes zooming towards the sky, plunging towards the earth, he sought to take on some of Gru's assurance. Except that he suspected that Gru, deep down, was not as cool and collected as he appeared to be. Unless Gru was a fool. Which, when you really thought about it, Gru was. . . .

Maybe so foolish he wasn't even worried about what Winston was going to do when he got off that plane. You didn't lose—as close as Donald could figure it—maybe as much as fifty thousand dollars belonging to another man and then act as if there was no real reason for that man to be angry with you. Unless, of course, you were Wheeler Dealer Gru! Most often than not, Gru had a way of not looking at those unpleasant realities he didn't wish to see. Some one had once said you could flush a toilet all over Gru, and he'd come up out of the bowl talking about some great deal he'd just spotted, so magnificent in scope and possibility that only a couple of bucks were needed and a little "know-how" and before you knew it he, Gru, would have everything smelling like perfume again!

So the only thing that might be troubling Gru right now, rather than Winston's imminent arrival or the alien and dazzling world of the airport, would most likely be the fact he hadn't yet figured out how a "piece of the action" could be gotten at the airport, the *dream* of getting that action, of pulling off some grand and astounding coup, exciting him even more than if the realization of it became suddenly real.

"Maybe he missed his flight, or something?" Donald said, massaging his chin vigorously. "Them things crash, too, you know. And you never know what kinda lies them folks is announcing on them loud speakers."

Gru's dreamy brown eyes behind horn-rimmed glasses briefly clouded his nut brown face. He hitched up his pants over a stomach that was just beginning to bulge. But with his short-cropped prematurely grey-speckled hair and small pointed beard that gave him a sort of professorial air, he still looked rather calm and collected.

"Take it easy," Gru said. "Man, you're more nervous than I am. Hell, you worried I can't handle Winston?" Gru even chuckled, but suddenly the chuckle seemed forced rather than that there was anything really funny. "Man, the little money Winston invested, the big boys lose that kind of bread every day. What I keep telling you is, if Blacks hope to get a slice of the cake in this country, they got to accept risk. They got to quit thinking about opening up hot dog stands and barbecue joints and go *big*. Get into the banks, Wall street, wherever the real action is. Look at those jets out there. . . . Man, if I canvassed this whole country I wouldn't find ten niggers with guts enough to invest in a propeller! And all that bread in transportation . . . tours to Africa, Asia, Europe. Naw, Man, rather than invest, niggers have been programmed to work for somebody else. And, Man, you're never going to get anywhere punching a clock and working eight hours a day."

Donald stared at Gru almost angrily.

"Yeah? Well, what am I supposed to do, just drop my gig, starve?"

Gru chuckled in exasperation.

"Aw, Man, don't take everything so personally. I'm speaking . . . well . . . generally. I'm telling you what the folks got to do . . . to catch up. Look at Rockefeller, Ford, they didn't get all of their bread without taking risks, did they? And, besides, you doing okay; you're not just a mailman anymore. You're in the streets with me now, and if you keep on learning I'll show you how the big boys operate."

"Sure," Donald said. "If Winston don't kill us first."

3

Gru glanced at his watch.

"Let me worry about it."

Donald was pleased to do that. In fact, his attention had just then been diverted. Someone in the crowd had pushed rudely against him and kept right on going. Couple of the whites that had been in the bar. The big guy with the crew cut and dark shades and the blonde in pink sweater. Now he saw that the guy was even bigger than he had seemed in the bar and that the girl wore slacks that matched her sweater. It also appeared as if the girl must be wearing something rather skin-tight under the sweater and slacks; otherwise there was the possibility she wasn't wearing anything at all.

She was a very attractive girl, but before Donald could feel any particular desire for her as a woman, something in him got blocked. Women like her were so removed from the world he knew, he looked at her as though she wasn't quite real. Long ago he had probably adjusted to the fact that there were many things in life he'd never get, and that perhaps he wasn't even entitled to, and to allow himself to keep alive desires for what he knew to be unobtainable was simply to frustrate himself.

"Listen!" he heard the big man suddenly hiss to the girl. "Listen, whore, you getting paid. Now I don't want anymore shit out of you!"

The man's tone had meant to be a whisper, but the anger had rendered the voice clearly audible. Donald was somewhat stunned at the man's complete lack of respect for the girl. At the same time, he breathed a faint sigh of relief. Just two seconds ago he had been ready to turn on the big man and call the man a couple of motherfuckers. Knocking against him like that. Not even saying, excuse. Go up side the cracker's head, but . . . but . . . well, the cat was pretty big, and solid-looking to boot, and if the cat acted like he was ready to slap the girl right here in the airport, well . . . you never could tell what the bastard was capable of doing.

Now the man had lowered his voice, but Donald still caught a part of the one-sided conversation.

" . . . go easy on the photographers, Okay? Last thing Vanderpool need is another scandal."

Photographers? Donald wondered, as the man and the girl continued to push themselves through the crowd and away.

4

Maybe the woman was a movie actress and if so he had heard enough about Hollywood to know that they were all freaks and whores out there anyway.

He turned to Gru, wondering if Gru had noted the couple, heard the way the man spoke to the girl, but Gru had his notebook out. His horn-rimmed glasses had slipped towards the tip of his nose and he was writing feverishly. What? Notes on how niggers were going to get some of this action at the airport? Maybe the concession to run the toilets! You couldn't beat Gru at dreaming up ways to make a fortune. But the trouble seemed to be it was never going to be anything more than a dream.

The announcer came on again and Donald listened intently to the metallic voice. Seemed as if Cal Winston's flight had just been mentioned, that the plane had landed, but that instead of debarking as scheduled there would be another few minutes delay.

Donald looked out upon the field and saw a couple of planes taxiing in. He also now noted that a band had begun playing out there, and that a number of men, some in uniform, had lined up to meet one of the planes. Going into motion were several cars that looked like they were loaded with TV equipment. Everyone was trying to get in closer to the plane.

"Must be some VIP coming in," Gru said, impressed. Then joked: "Maybe the President." Though Gru had ceased writing, he held the notebook in his hand for a moment in case another good idea popped up.

Donald didn't always have the greatest sense of humor.

"Don't the President have his own plane? I mean, that looks like the plane the announcer just said Winston would be on. Man, you reckon while over there in Europe Winston done cut into something so great they got a band out there playing for him and TV and. . . . "

For a split second Gru wondered too. You really couldn't predict Winston. But then he shook his head.

"Naw. Impossible. Winston would've called me or something. Besides, look at that line up down there. Must be something big, really big!"

Three limousines had now pulled up, the one in front decked out in American flags. The TV men from the different networks were jockeying to get into position.

People pushed forward to get a better view of the scene

below and Donald and Gru were swept along with them. Some people had pulled out cameras of their own, aimed at the plane that had now come to a standstill.

Down there in the crowd, pushing their way closer to the plane, Donald was surprised to see the big man and the blonde girl. Men in dark suits allowed the two of them to pass through the line as though both the girl and the big man were somebody special.

The girl had donned a jacket and looked a little less flashy than when seen up close. The big man was all reserve and cool and appeared to be every bit a gentleman, disguising the thug Donald had been amazed to see in him earlier.

The door of the plane opened and a distinguished-looking man stepped out, smiling and waving. Donald had seen pictures of him in newspapers and on TV. Cameras were going off everywhere and the TV men were busy.

Then there was some kind of commotion. The man had descended several steps and was speaking into the microphones held towards him, when back up in the door-way of the plane a black face appeared, and then disappeared and then appeared again.

"Winston!" Gru said, his mouth hanging open.

Donald didn't know what to make of it either.

The big-shot guy speaking into the microphones was surely the one all the fuss was about, but what was Winston doing up there in the door-way? A couple of dark-suited men were now on either side of Winston, and it was clear from Winston's expression that he was mad as all hell.

Then Winston must have realized that the reach of the TV cameras could be getting him, too, and he relaxed, even wearing a faint if somewhat uncomfortable smile. In these recent years, never very far out of style, Winston looked pretty cool himself: white slacks, blue blazer, with a powder blue top coat thrown over his arm. Except that his skin was black, topped by a conservative Afro, he looked about as cool as the white VIP who now moved down towards the limousines. Like the white man, Winston was in his early forties; like the white man, Winston had instantly begun to pose for the cameras. Both, much like born actors.

However, the dark-suited men still seemed confused. They stood there flanking Winston as though not certain of their next

6

move. Then they seemed to decide to allow Winston to leave the plane.

In the meantime, the VIP was about to step into the limousine. When the blonde girl came rushing towards him, astonishment could be seen in his face. For a second it appeared as if the VIP would turn away from the girl altogether; but then his lips formed a smile and he embraced her and shook hands vigorously with the big man. All three of them got into the limousine.

The minute he was down the steps and through the crowd and was sure he was away from the cameras, Winston was no longer smiling.

"He looks pretty angry," Gru conceded, chuckling nervously, despite himself. "But, Man, did you see who that white cat was!" "Sure," Donald said, offended. "I ain't illiterate. I keep up with the world events, too, you know."

"Man, I didn't mean to imply you were illiterate and . . . "

"Besides, I seen him on TV a million times. Anybody knows that he is . . . er . . . er . . . " But Donald suddenly couldn't remember the man's name and he frowned. A warm wave of embarrassment began to flood his body, he felt so ignorant.

Gru chuckled condescendingly, tapping Donald on the shoulder affectionately.

"Forget it. You still my nigger."

"Goddammit," Donald said bitterly, but the bitterness turned against himself. "How come I can't remember when it's right here on the tip of my tongue?"

"Well, you just ain't ready," Gru joked.

"Shit, I'm ready as anybody!" Donald grated.

"Well, don't tax your brains," Gru persisted. "Might throw something out of whack!"

Donald shook Gru's hand off his shoulder. His red-rimmed eyes glared at Gru.

"You got so much brains, what it ever get you? You wouldn't be shit without Winston or them Jews you used to work for. Well, I still got my gig at the post office and I been there fifteen years and in five more years I can retire. I got that to fall back on if Winston fires both of us, but what you got? Nothing!"

Gru had developed a conviction so strong in his ability to charm, "handle" people, that he was amazed when control

7

slipped and someone broke out in anger against him, attacked him. And even more unnerving, as now, was to glimpse that Donald probably didn't like him, admire him, as much as he had thought Donald did or should.

"Hey, Baby!" he said, his tone syrupy, conciliatory, as he tried to bounce back not only in Donald's esteem but his own. "This is me, Gru. We're buddies, Man. What are you blowing your top at me for? I'm on your side. We going to win this thing together, beat this fucking system together. I mean, I'm the guy who's going to get you out of that post office, remember? Besides, instead of you and I fighting each other, we got to deal with Winston. Man, you saw how mad that cat was, and if we don't hang in there together, how we going to deal with him?"

Donald refused to be mollified. Normally Gru conned him into doing whatever he wanted done. But he could see the way the wind was blowing. Winston was certain to toss Gru aside, and if he kept hanging in there with Gru he could get tossed aside, too.

"Don't put that 'we' stuff on me. I ain't the one who's been messing up Winston's business. You got so much brains, you deal with Winston."

Gru seemed to wilt again, grow more flabby, but then he suddenly chuckled. Why waste time on a dumb nigger like Donald, whom he couldn't teach anything, no matter how hard he tried? Save his energy. Winston might prove a bit more difficult than he had anticipated.

"Aw, Baby," Gru said. "Take it easy. We'll sit down and have a drink later and work it out. But right now Winston should be getting through customs. We better shake a leg and get to him."

A porter was placing Winston's luggage atop a truck. Gru rushed forward and threw a great bear hug around Winston.

"Winston, Baby! Man, it sure is good to see you! You looking great, Man!"

Winston remained neutral for a moment and then eased off and shook hands with Gru. He wore a pair of those glasses that darkened the instant the sun touched them and cleared when he entered a room, but the glasses hadn't quite cleared yet and Donald couldn't tell what Winston was thinking by looking at his eyes. Also, Donald was again impressed by the ease with which Winston carried himself, cool, aloof, almost unapproachable. But now he remembered he had never felt comfortable those few times he had been in Winston's presence. Even more, he wasn't sure he had ever liked Winston or Winston him. How could you figure out a guy that though he looked at you, you always got the impression he really didn't see you, or had already seen you instantly and quickly, calculated everything you had going for you or didn't, and then raced on away from you with an impatience far greater than any sympathy? There was about Winston an air, even when he had it under control, of almost not living in the moment, but of always looking at some secret clock and rushing ruthlessly towards tomorrow. To slow him, you just knew you were stepping into a path of collision.

Shit, Donald thought. I didn't take no crap off of Gru and I ain't gonna take none of Winston either. I'm just sick and tired of everybody trying to fuck over me!

He even noted with some satisfaction that he was built heavier than Winston, perhaps more solidly, though Winston appeared younger, the full mustache and Afro not showing a touch of grey. He already knew that if Gru ever crossed him seriously, he could silence him with a single blow to the guts. He realized now with a sudden strange and confused anger that though it might be a little more difficult, he could take care of Winston too if he got pushed around and it came right down to anything physical.

What I mean is, Donald thought, trying to break through confusion, I don't mean to take no shit!

Then Winston was shaking his hand.

"Donald. Glad to see you, Man."

The hand-shake seemed warm, like Winston was genuinely happy to see him and Donald caught himself flushing deeply, as much from embarrassment as pleasure. He couldn't understand why a few seconds before he had felt a wave of almost pure hatred for Winston.

As they followed the porter, Gru was talking a mile a minute.

". . . . over a drink Winston, Baby, we can relax and I think you will see that things are not as bad as they seem. In fact, Man, why bore you with a lot of business crap right off. I mean, how were the broads over there, gay Paris, the Eiffel Tower, and . . . and . . . all that?"

9

"You said we now have another car?" Winston was almost abrupt.

"Er . . . yes. A Caddie no less. Pat is waiting in it."

"Pat?" Winston seemed surprised.

"Minute she heard you were returning, couldn't stop her from coming. Man, like I say, all of us have been doing our best to look out for your interests, even Pat. A good girl. I may still end up marrying her if I can break her resistance down."

The doors popped open electronically and they went through.

"Why a Caddie?" Winston asked.

"Well, Man, I picked it up for a song, a steal. Owned by this doctor who never drove it, in perfect condition except for a couple of er . . . minor details. Right, Donald?"

"Right," Donald mumbled. Except that the minor details were the fucked up transmission, the exhaust pipe, and the probable need of a complete brake job. Except that there were always these doctors or some old ladies who had these cars ready to sell you in "perfect" condition. Well, one thing, he hadn't been with Gru when Gru bought the car, so that was certainly something nobody could blame him for.

"Cross the street," Gru said, pointing with pride to the maroon Caddie sedan. "Four years old, but like new."

"Well," Winston laughed dryly. "If it is not taken in a bankruptcy proceeding, at least I'll have a place to sleep."

Gru started to laugh also but ceased abruptly when he saw that Winston wasn't joking.

"Baby," Gru said. "Trust me. Hell, though Real Estate is a thousand times safer, it can sometimes be as unpredictable as the stock market, that's all. But relaxed over a drink I can show you the figures. . . . "

"Sure," Winston said.

In the car sat a girl with perhaps the biggest Afro in the world. The fantastic and bushy sweep of her hair dominated her tiny oval face, a beautiful face, as dark as night, with large warm moon-bright eyes. Her gaze had not left Winston since she saw him coming across the street.

"Patricia," Winston said. "Wow, you looking good!"

"Hi, yourself, world traveler!" she said, in a tone of such tremendous gaiety it somehow rang false. "You looking pretty good yourself!"

10

No one was helping the porter to get the luggage into the trunk of the car, and Donald found himself stuck with the chore. He unlocked the trunk and loaded the bags, then he noticed that Pat and Winston were in the back seat and that Gru was about to climb into the back seat also. He had a bit of difficulty keeping a sudden anger out of his voice.

"Hey, folks, I ain't exactly the chauffeur, you know! In fact, maybe I can borrow you Pat to sit up front with me, since you the prettiest!"

Gru was annoyed. But perhaps it was better to humor the stupid bastard. "Okay, Home," Gru said. "Damn, I'll sit up front. Winston, you see how spoiled Donald has become since I got him out there working with us? But he's coming along. I'm trying to teach him now how to pass the Real Estate Board and get his broker's license."

Gru climbed in front next to Donald and Donald eased the car carefully into gear to cut down on the transmission noise. Still there was an angry ripping sound before the car shuddered forward and finally began to roll smoothly.

"I suppose Gru is pushing both Donald and me," Pat said. She hadn't moved over very far and Winston was conscious of their bodies pressed close together. "I meant to keep it a secret for awhile, but guess what? I'm back in school. And I'm happy about it. I'm really very happy about it."

Gru leaned back in his seat and intoned, "Ah'm gon help git dese darkies educated if it kills me! But no kidding, Pat is doing fine. First semester out she got herself an A and a B—but she also got a couple of C's. I told her she got to do better than those C's, same as I'm sure you'd have told her, like, Man, our women got to get qualified, help us to beat this goddamn system! She's doing fine but she still can't write a decent letter, take dictation. Man, it ain't no honeymoon trying to get these niggers ready!"

Pat tensed.

"Gru, please. Don't be insulting. I'm doing the best I can." She turned to Winston. "I really am. And I don't think I'm doing too bad, either."

"I'm sure you're doing great," Winston said.

"I made them C's," Pat explained, "Because ... because ... well, I've been worried. ... And I couldn't study properly

11

... plus my job. And it just ain't easy for a woman almost thirty to readjust to the class room routine."

"Hey," Winston said. "Don't get upset. The fact that you're back in school is good news. And I am very happy about it."

"Are you?" Pat said, still looking at Winston, none of the early gaity in her voice anymore, nothing in her voice except a sort of desperation. "Are you really?"

Donald couldn't understand why Gru didn't hear what was in her voice. But maybe because Gru didn't wish to hear it, he didn't.

Gru had snapped on the radio. New outbreak of fighting in the Mid-East; the missing witness hadn't yet been found and the Senate hearings had been suspended temporarily; a national poll indicated that there had now been a reversal in public opinion and ... Gru switched the dial till he got a black station with music. The sound was almost as good as stereo.

"Radio like new," Gru said. "Man, there's nothing very much wrong with this car. Now if there was no speed limit, Donald could show you what this baby could do."

"What's the hold up?" Winston asked, but meaning more why they had slowed to a crawl than that he was interested in seeing how fast the car would run. Donald thought he detected a note of impatience in his voice.

"Well, I can't run over the cars up ahead," Donald stated as calmly as he could. "Traffic piling up. Looks like there's been an accident or something."

"Say," Gru pointed. "Isn't that Mr. Big Wheel up ahead?"

Donald, too, had just noticed the limousine. Possibly one of those that had been at the airport—but where were the other two? He remembered there had been three limousines.

Near an exit a yellow Mustang had flipped over on its back. Cops were directing the traffic around the wreckage. An ambulance could be heard screaming in the distance.

One thing Donald prided himself on, he was a good driver. Every car was fighting to get into the single lane the policemen were waving traffic through. Adeptly, Donald cut off a couple of cars and advanced in line. He was almost up to the limousine, but the driver of the limousine, a young black guy in a blue uniform, proved to be even more aggressive than Doanld. Though Donald sped forward, the guy seemed to be completely

12

indifferent to a crash and cut the limousine arrogantly in front of him, forcing Donald to slam on the brakes.

"Sonofabitch!" Donald grated.

"Yeah," Gru said, trying to spot the occupants of the limousine. "I think it is the same Big Wheel that had you messed around on that plane, Winston." Gru leaned back, chuckling, but then almost couldn't stop laughing. "Man, for a minute I thought they were telling you, if you white you right and you can come on down to the ground, but if you Black get back till there're no more whites around!"

"Funny," Winston said. "Yeah. Something like that." A hard core of outrage was suddenly in his voice. "Seem like the bastard was due here in New York before going on to Washington and there was some kind of problem with his plane. Security cats came on and asked me if I'd mind moving back into the Economy class. Well, maybe I would've moved, but they weren't really asking. It was more like an order. And on a French air-line! So I decided to stay right where I had paid my good money to sit. As you can imagine, it wasn't a very pleasant trip, especially with these security guys walking up and down the aisle, guns bulging, as if I was some kind of a goddamn assassin or something!"

"My God," Pat said. "You could have gotten hurt!"

"I wouldn't of moved either," Donald said furiously. "The sonofabitches!" The limousine had cleared the narrow lane and was now on the open highway, diminishing.

"I don't know" Gru cautioned. "Man, it might be wise to be careful and watch your step from now on. There is a lot of crap going on in the Capitol these days and nobody knows yet what it's all about. . . . I mean, Man, if your name gets put on a list where you have crossed the wrong people, who in the hell knows what could happen?"

"But Winston was only standing up for his rights," Pat protested.

"Rights!" Donald snorted. The limousine was doing at least ten miles over the speed limit and Donald found himself doing the same and even more, trying to catch up. And it was Mr. Big Shot, all right. A couple of times now he thought he spotted the blonde girl sitting between the two men.

"Ain't she sweet?" Gru agreed. "Power determines what is

right, Baby. Pure dee power and nothing else. And, that's real power when you can commandeer airplanes and get the bands to come out and meet you and a whole slew of TV cameras. . . . Goddammit, that's the kind of action we got to get into, but niggers too busy drinking booze on the week-ends and buying fat cigars!"

"It's not that easy," Pat insisted. "Look how far down at the bottom we got to come from!"

Winston looked at her. His tone was harsh, almost angry. "Don't waste your time looking back at the bottom. Keep your eyes on the top."

"My God," Pat said, wounded by the lack of understanding in Winston's tone. "What can a little person like me really do? Gru is always saying I still seem like somebody who just escaped the cotton fields. Well, if that is true why is everyone so disappointed . . . you . . . you and Gru . . . that I'm not yet ready to be the First Lady at the White House?"

"I'm not criticizing you." Winston frowned.

"You are. You always do."

"Say, what are you two fighting about!" Gru said. He leaned over and slipped his hand over Pat's slim knee. Then, gazing at her and trying to hold her eyes, he suddenly allowed his hand to move up her thigh.

Pat's body coiled and her small dark face glowed with outrage.

"Gru, you got some goddamn lousy nerve!" Her blood-red fingernails zeroed in after his hand, and Gru barely had time to withdraw.

So sure was Gru of his mastery over women and over Pat in particular, he was more than a bit surprised at her violent reaction. He chuckled uneasily.

"You wouldn't believe it," he told Winston. "Pat and I are practically on our honeymoon and she still gets uptight if I even want to hold her hand in public! Man, Black women are just never going to learn to get with it! I don't blame you for taking off for Paris. I hear over there the gals grab you and throw a foot of tongue down your throat right in the middle of the streets. I tell you, sometimes I don't know what I'm doing in this goddamn country. Well, one day, when my luck changes, I could just pack up and be long gone."

"There they is," Donald said, triumph in his voice. He nodded towards the limousine he had caught up with.

Gru gazed into the back of the limousine and whistled softly. "Wow! Dig that broad that guy has got! And it really is Vanderpool. But who is that other guy? Security? Must be. He sure is big and mean-looking enough."

Winston was also staring into the limousine. Clearly, he still hadn't gotten over the humiliation he had suffered on the plane.

"He wasn't on the plane. But another bum it wouldn't be safe to meet after dark—unless you were also ready."

"He was at the airport," Donald informed everyone. "With the girl. He was so mad with the girl I thought he was going to slap the hell out of her or something."

"Slap that pretty thing," Gru said. "He must have been stone out of his mind!"

Winston nodded.

"Not bad. I suppose Vanderpool sees no reason why business shouldn't be mixed with a bit of pleasure."

"Pretty?" Pat said. "Not bad? With that dyed hair? And look how tight her skin is around the eyes. I bet she has had her face lifted fifty times!"

"Listen to her," Gru laughed. "Beware of sour grapes, Baby!"

"My God," Pat said, beginning lightly but almost ending bitterly. "If that is the kind of thing that can hang you guys up, please let me out of this car this minute. I'll walk."

"Don't hang me up," Donald said. "To me she's just another er . . . white bitch, if you'll excuse the expression."

"Well, let's throw Winston and Gru out, Donald," Pat said. "And let them walk. You and I will ride together."

"Right," Donald said. "Any time!"

Winston slipped his arm around Pat playfully.

"What's the matter?"

"Nobody loves me," Pat pouted. "Nobody." She didn't mean for it to get quite so serious, but when Winston only glanced at her, then stared again at the people in the limousine, she swallowed, "Nobody gives a damn about me."

Gru acted as if he wanted to touch her, to reassure her, but in the end he kept his hands to himself. "What do you mean, sweetheart? You know I'm crazy about you and ready and

15

willing to marry you, even if I'm not able, any time you want to break down."

"Yes, so that you will have a dictation machine and somebody to wheel and deal with you when . . . when . . . maybe that isn't what I want at all."

Once more Winston's arm tightened around her shoulder, but again playfully. He was still only half listening. It was as though the people in the back of the limousine were some kind of a great puzzle to him, especially Vanderpool. How did you ever get power like that, where you could walk into any Capitol of the world and shake hands with Kings and Presidents?

As for the blonde girl, her eyes flicked briefly towards the black folks, then flicked away again. She sat as stiffly and as frozen as a statue, almost as though there was something to be afraid of.

Vanderpool himself, a finger pressed against one of his silver temples as if in the deepest of thought, leaned wearily back against the car's plush leather. He didn't seem like a happy man. Apparently with the power and authority you also had to carry the weight of the world around in your brains.

For the life of her, Pat couldn't understand how Winston could envy someone like Vanderpool. Yet Winston's gaze reflected a terrible hunger as he stared at the man. In a moment Winston lifted his arm from around her as though she had never been there.

Closing his eyes briefly, he leaned back and then in a tone so strained to maintain control it came out cold, almost metallic, he told Gru, "Let Donald drop us off. He can take Pat on home. You and I might as well have that drink as soon as we get to Manhattan and, Man, maybe we can get into this business of how goddamn far I've slipped back to the bottom of the totem pole."

Gru adjusted his glasses, stroked his beard nervously.

"Today?"

"Why not?" Winston said harshly. "What's the point of putting it off?"

"I just thought . . . well . . . you might want to relax . . . get readjusted."

"Today," Winston stressed.

"How come I got to go home?" Pat asked. "After all, you guys keep saying you want me to learn, don't you?"

Gru had been searching Winston's face for some hint of warmth, understanding. He saw none. It was as though Winston had just taken a psychological step away from everyone in the car, and now sat there utterly alone, surrounded by nothing except his own cold and ruthless inner world. It was a Winston mood Gru didn't like being alone with.

"Well, you got my vote!" Gru told Pat. "And say, Donald, you can come along also if you want to. Hell, let's all of us have a drink! Celebrate! Nothing is ever as bad as it seems. But, of course, it is up to Winston."

Listening to Gru already caving in at the first sign of pressure from Winston, annoyed and disgusted Donald. His attention had been temporarily diverted. The limousine had jumped ahead again and though he attempted a wild maneuver around a Volkswagen to catch up, he failed. A low-built foreign sports car blocked his path.

By now he wanted to give up the race, but he wondered had either of the others noticed how the chauffeur of the limousine kept out-smarting him? Despite himself, he kept his foot on the gas, angling for an opening around the sports car.

"Do you mind if I tag along?" Pat asked.

Winston shrugged.

"It's up to you."

"But you'd rather I didn't?"

"Listen, come along if you like."

Pat sighed. She got a cigarette out of her purse and hurried up and lit it, as though afraid to risk waiting to see if anyone was going to light it for her. Winston made some vague move but seemed incapable of coming out of the stony world he had retreated into. Gru kept turning the dial of the radio, listening to the news, or pretending to.

" . . . Washington . . . Mystery witness . . . found . . . Site of a plane crash. . . . Body charred almost beyond recognition. . . . "

A little laugh bubbled up in Donald. He was great behind a wheel, didn't give a fuck what anybody said. He had zipped around the sports car, intimidated the Volkswagen and now he was moving in on the limousine again. He caught up at the bridge, joining the traffic flowing into Manhattan. In the distance the great glass and stone buildings were outlined against the evening sun. Whereas the sky had been bluer, clearer,

17

now a thick greyish mass seem to float atop the City, fed by black and blue curls of smoke.

Donald had figured out his strategy. Instead of coming in to the left he slowed a little and came into the right side of the limousine. Up ahead would be the exit to Manhattan where you had to get into the two inside lanes to make the turn. The chauffeur was stupid. . . . He'd be trapped out there in the third lane, and Donald intended to keep him squeezed out, unable to make the turn. . . .

Donald pulled up alongside the limousine, looked across at the chauffeur, grinning, thinking, you such a wise guy, now what you gonna do? But the chauffeur didn't even look around. Hell, it looked like something was wrong with the chauffeur, too. Scared? But of what? Or maybe that was the way it was when you worked around big-shots. Scared of losing your goddamn job. In any case, Donald didn't intend to bend an inch. He wasn't going to allow the limousine to get ahead of him and cut into the second lane, no matter what happened. To make the turn, the punk would have to admit defeat, slow down, and come into the lane *behind* him.

They were nearing the turn off, running neck and neck, when Winston said, "Where in hell are we going? To a fire?"

The tone of voice grated against Donald, threatened his concentration. He almost slammed into the side of the limousine. He fought the wheel and righted the Caddie as a burst of anger flared against Winston. Speaking to him as if *he* was a goddamn chauffeur! But he suppressed the anger. The limousine still had his attention. Also, he still wasn't sure how far he'd have to go if he ever let his anger go against Winston as he had against Gru. And after all, if he was going to learn how to make money and get out of that post office he was going to have to work for somebody like Winston.

Still, Donald couldn't keep all the anger out of his voice.

"It's not my fault! That dude keeps hogging the road!"

"Sure," Winston said. "Just slow it down, will you?"

"How can I when. . . ." Now it was against every fiber in his body to slow down and allow the car to get into the lane in front of him. But he didn't have to defy Winston directly. The double line was suddenly there. The chauffeur would either have to slow or keep on towards the Bronx and Upstate. Then it

18

was too late for the chauffeur to even slow; to make the turn he would have to stop stone still . . . or crash into the divider. Donald tensed up, waiting for the chauffeur to do one or the other. But the chauffeur did neither. Looking neither to the left nor right, the chauffeur kept moving towards the toll booths that led to the Bronx and Upstate. Donald had to ride the brakes of the Caddie and fight the wheel again to make the curve around the divider himself, so sure he had been the limousine would have to turn.

"Sorry," he mumbled, getting the car under control, feeling unutterably stupid. How in the hell had the chauffeur out-maneuvered him again . . . ? Didn't all the big-shots live down-town in Manhattan? So why the hell had the dude headed towards the Bronx and Upstate? Also, now that he thought about it again, what had happened to the other two limousines he had seen at the airport? He couldn't figure this shit out. Well, forget it. It simply looked as if it was going to be another one of those days. Nothing going right. And with this guy, Winston, ordering him around, maybe the worst hadn't even begun yet. . . .

two

Right in the middle of Bedford-Stuyvesant, sometimes known as the Harlem of Brooklyn, a woman lay dying. The boy knew it. He had known for several months that she was dying. The small apartment smelled of decay and death.

He had locked himself into the bathroom. The basin didn't work, so he had had to use water from the toilet bowl. Not long ago he had keeled over and fainted. Now he held onto the basin for support, trembling, vomiting. As he tried to stand, the old cracked mirror revealed a surprisingly young and sensitive face, about fifteen, but with eyes that were both haunted and terrified, and that seemed as old as forever. He was bean-pole thin and already almost six feet tall. His slim fingers gripped the basin, leaving a trail of sweat and blood.

He vomited again, the smell pushing against the scent of roach spray. Just before he passed out he had known he was dying, too—like Mama. Like Mama lying in the other room. He had been so sure he was dying he was surprised that he was still alive. And as he looked at himself in the mirror, he felt no joy that he hadn't died after all.

What was it that had aroused him? Sounds coming after him as he sank into . . . sank into something like the bleakness of a vacant lot, where tin cans and broken bottles and other refuse had been thrown, where cranes and bull-dozers waited, standing unmanned, deserted, and as silent as the cry he tried to get out, but nothing heard except his breathing. Dying to be found like that? Yet it had almost been beautiful to keep sinking down into the bleakness. He hadn't even attempted to arouse himself, to

20

fight anymore, until the sound from the other room became much like a scream, coming down into the pit after him, reaching desperately for him, and he had thought, "Mama."

If he fell all the way down, what about Mama? Who would lift her from the bed, hold her hand, clean the rooms and fix breakfast for her in the mornings? Who would lie to her and have her believe he was still in school, and tell her she was looking better and better every day and that there was no reason she shouldn't live forever?

He took a towel and mopped his face and tried to clean away the blood. He thought he heard her still calling and he leaned against the wall, breathing deeply, listening.

Nothing except a faint sound of scratching outside the door. Couldn't be a rat because he had sprayed and killed everything in sight and put down so much poison he had to always be careful what he touched. Then he had painted everywhere, the rooms over and over, bright frantic colors, as much to ward off bugs and rodents as to discharge torrents of young energy he otherwise wouldn't have known what to do with.

"Junior?" The voice on the other side of the door was so faint he could hardly hear it.

He froze. Mama! Lord, Lord, she had crawled outta bed!

He lurched towards the door but was clear-headed enough to stop himself from flinging the door open too fast. If she was leaning against it he'd be certain to hurt her.

"Mama," he said. "Move back a little please. Move back a little!"

Then he heard her weeping. He could hardly restrain himself, easing the door open with her weight against it. Lying there in her frayed night-gown. Her black face, skin tight, already looked like that of a skeleton. From a woman who had once weighed 135 lbs. she had dropped to 87 lbs. The smell of her dying fought with the odor of roach spray and paint and vomit. He cleared the door and though he stumbled, he got her up into his arms, where her bony fingers gripped him with a desperation even greater than usual, as though she somehow knew she had almost lost him.

He stumbled again but righted himself, carrying her across the room to the bed, her wet cheek pressed against his face. Though he fought against it, he suddenly realized that he was

21

also crying, saying, "Mama. Mama. I told you don't never be trying to git around without some help!"

He got her under the blanket, avoiding the touch of her left hip. It would make both of them self-conscious, as though neither of them could accept even yet that nothing flowed from her hip. She'd flinch and become speechless for a moment if she sensed that his hand was near the empty space. Or she'd begin speaking so rapidly it would embarrass both of them.

"You was in there so long," she said. "I thought . . . I didn't know. . . ." She sniffled and he gave her a kleenex. He used a kleenex himself, but turned his head and blew his nose so that she wouldn't know he had been crying.

He hesitated. Then lied.

"I was studying. Gitting my homework. . . ."

Her eyes in her cavernous face looked at him hard, always trying desperately to believe him. Her eyes even brightened a little.

"Lord have mercy, it sure ain't that far to June and if it's one High School graduation I'm going to hop out of this bed and git to, it sure is going to be yours. Show folks what a son can do even when his Mama never got beyond the eighth grade!"

"Yes M'am," he said. He averted his eyes, fixed the pillows around her.

"All them other young 'uns," she went on. "Turning out to be dope fiends and such, but I always say it is how you raise your children, give them the back-bone to resist temptation no matter how hard life gits."

He got the medicine bottle, didn't even have a label on it, and poured out nearly a half a glass full for her. He still didn't say anything. There wasn't very much he could say anymore.

She, too, had abruptly ceased, staring at the ceiling vacantly, sighing sadly, all the light running from her face.

"Mama?" he said.

He pushed the glass towards her and lifted her head and she groaned once but drank all the liquid in the glass.

In a minute she looked at him again, but her voice was tired.

"I saw your daddy," she said.

He stared at her. Had she gone completely out of her mind again?

She was always seeing his daddy, somewhere, somehow, even

before she got sick. Or someone who looked as she remembered his daddy had looked.

Now she frowned in genuine puzzlement.

"Didn't I tell you? That's how come I first started calling you. . . . Right there on TV I saw you daddy's face, plain as day. The announcer had it on one of them bulletins and said the same news is supposed to come back on at the hour news."

"Aw, Mama," he said.

"I ain't talking no nonsense," she said, almost vehemently. "Son, I saw him! Just turn the set up a little so I can hear cause it ought not to be long before that newscast comes on again."

His legs felt wobbly as he stood and took the few steps and turned the set up. The muscles of his stomach had coiled so tight, he was conscious of every breath he took. He held himself rigid against a momentary need to vomit again.

Before leaving the TV set he gazed at it for a moment, as he had looked at it yesterday and other TV sets the days before, not at the bright colorful picture, as bright and colorful as the walls he had painted, but at the set itself. Finally he looked away, frowning at himself in disgust, but aware of the intense craving ache in his stomach. No, he thought, not the TV set today, not today. It was all she had left here in the house to keep her company if he went out this evening.

"There he is!" she suddenly exclaimed, a hoarse shout. "Lord God Almighty, that's him! Every bit of him!"

Junior looked at the tube and saw a white man getting off an airplane. He stared at the man. Mama had really gone out of her mind. . . .

A rising excitement trembled her voice

"Lord have mercy, look at him! Riding airplanes and all the way over there in Europe! Told me over and over and over he wasn't going to let nothing on this earth keep him down and poor and nobody, and Lord God it sure looks like he told the Gospel truth!"

"That whitey? Mama, you all right?"

"Lord, I was never better. There he is! There he is again!"

Then Junior saw the man, not the white one but the black one at the door of the plane, who had been frowning as though in annoyance, but who now wore a faint almost mocking smile.

Without warning Junior felt his heart beginning to do crazy

things in his chest. It seemed to swell against the other pressures, knocking out aches and fears and self-disgust, lodging itself in his throat. He stared at the man. Never before had he gotten this kind of reaction when Mama pointed out someone who looked like his father or that she had mistaken for his father.

—Something about the way the man smiled, the way he moved—

Or maybe the man just fitted the handsome picture of someone he, too, had invented. . . ?

"Yes, Lord. . . ." he vaguely heard his mother rambling on, practically sitting up in the bed in her excitement. "Don't tell me I ain't right! I been telling you over and over you the spitting image of him. And he didn't leave me because he wanted to. He . . . he . . . just said he wasn't going to let nothing hold him down and bury him down here at the bottom. Now you can see where you got your talent from, how you can paint pictures and draw better than some of them folks working for magazines. And . . . and . . . Lord, God, limousines out there! Looks like he done gone and got himself an important job with the United States government itself!"

Junior had sunk down, sitting upon the floor gazing at the set, even though the cameras had now panned away from the man to the limousines. He tried to make sense out of the commentator's words:

". . . . at a happier occasion . . . upon arrival . . . airport today . . . forty-five minutes before tragedy struck . . . Vanderpool . . . said that . . . success of Paris . . . Washington . . . and that . . . as far as he was concerned . . . nothing to hide . . . from the American public. . . ."

". . . . the car carrying Vanderpool . . . and his companion . . . found 27 miles beyond . . . though the chauffeur, Leroy Brown . . . had not yet gained consciousness to give a statement . . . Miss Trina Swan, former Miss America runner-up and . . . an actress in . . . still being sought . . . Police said that. . . ."

But where was the man? Junior found himself changing channels wildly. But everything was dominated by the whitey, Vanderpool. Had the man Mama pointed out gotten into one of the limousines?

Yeah. Not quite so much a big shot as the white guy, but still all the way up there in the sky somewhere . . . Riding airplanes and limousines and palling around with rich whites while Mama and him. . . while Mama and him had nothing. And if Mama was right, though he couldn't really believe it, he was the man Mama had talked about all these years, loved all these years, but who hadn't sent but one post card during the fifteen years, from some faraway place in California, saying: "I received your letter and believe me I am sorry, Lydia. But I didn't make the world I am just trying to live in it."

Junior had looked at that writing on the post card over and over. All that he had of his father; no pictures, no other memories, nothing. Looked at the writing and hated even the writing, hating so much the unseen person who had written those words, who had left Mama to die and him in confusion, left without a backward glance no matter how Mama sought to rationalize it.

He turned the TV channels furiously, but caught only a brief glimpse of the man one more time, cool-looking with the top coat over his arm, and that strange smile that was stranger because it somehow seemed so familiar, and then it was all about the white guy Vanderpool again and the girl who had been with him.

"Dirty rotten bastard!" Junior thought, as though beginning to believe Mama when he knew he shouldn't. "I hope something happened to the car he was riding in, too! He ought to be dead! If I ever run into him I'll . . . I'll. . . ." And in a vision that had belonged to him when he was much younger and that he still hadn't rid himself of, he saw his father's face again, hacked, beaten, stomped, shot, pleading for mercy, forgiveness.

His hands had begun to tremble again, sweat popped out on his face. Suddenly the ache in his stomach lanced up and watered his eyes. "Bastard!" He gritted his teeth. Then he whirled towards Mama who had a dreamy, serene look upon her face. "How come, Mama, you didn't go to a doctor and just let the doctor kill me when that . . . that . . . that dirty rotten bastard left you!"

The woman was startled.

"Hush your mouth! If you'd been triplets or even more I'd kept all of you! And don't talk to me no more about him leaving me. I left him! I . . . I . . . mean I let him go. Yes, I know he was gon to go anyway, gon on up there where he was trying to git, and seemed to had to git to or kill himself, so . . . so . . . I just made it easier for him. The little money he took from me, he needed more than I did. I had my day-work with Miss McAllister to keep me going. But when he quit them low-paying jobs, he had nothing else, nowhere to go. He saw you, yes, Lord, saw you only that one time, just when you were beginning to walk. . . . I was so lonely I had to write him. I can't be blamed for that. He looked at you and seemed like he was doing everything in this world to keep from crying. Wanting to stay with you and yet maybe wanting even more to go on back out in the world and keep on trying to git what it seemed he had to git. . . . So . . . so . . . I just let him go again."

Junior's face was stormy with hatred.

"Let him go on up there to the skies and play the big shot while you die here in this rat hole! Mama, you ain't talking no sense!"

Mama shook her head from side to side as though to push away all threats to her memories, but her lips pursed and she sniffled. In a moment tears formed in the deep caves that were her eyes and began to roll down her cheeks.

"You . . . you . . . just wait. I let him go because . . . be-cause . . . I knew one day he'd find me again. I'd look out the window and he'd be coming down the street, fast as he could to git to me . . . and . . . and . . . he'd say, Lydia, Lydia, I'm back! I beat the devil outta them crackers and everybody else and now I'm back to git you and take you with me!"

"Aw, Mama," Junior said. "For Christsakes!"

She flared, the tears still flooding her cheeks.

"And he'll come! You wait and see! As the Lord is my Saviour, one day there's going to be a knock on that door and . . . and . . . he'll be standing there, plain as day!"

"Yeah," Junior said.

Trembling, he got up and stood between her and the medicine bottle. Concealing his intent as best he could, he poured out nearly a full glass and drank it down. The liquid almost cut off his breath. Perhaps even she knew now that the so-called medicine was nothing but cheap gin with a bit of coloring. She believed the doctors at the hospital had betrayed her and now she was being betrayed again. But at least now she had faith and maybe that was all she was going to ever have anymore.

"Sure," he said, more like a gasp. The gin still burned his throat, but as he had known it did hardly anything to quiet the craving trembling his body. "You might be right. Maybe drive up in a big limousine and take both of us away. I mean, if he's got any heart at all, he just can't forget us. And yet . . . look at all these years . . . and he ain't even turned around and looked back our way."

Mama's voice had tired. She wiped her eyes.

"Well, son, I guess he's been fighting so hard out there, couldn't afford to look back, less somebody run over him. I guess it just ain't easy for a poor man to fight his way up to the top. But now, thank God, looks like he done won and the Good Lord ain't gon let me down and one day. . . ."

Junior grimaced, walked to the window. He pressed his forehead tightly against the pane. Building tinned up next door, waiting to be ripped down. Younger children yelling in the distance, then abruptly ceasing. Beyond the grimy brick walls there was a tiny view of the teaming streets below. Three black men, one almost comically plump, were running after a taxi. But though the men yelled, the taxi sped on, as though fleeing the neighborhood.

He heard Mama sigh again and when he turned around she had sunk into sleep, the dreamy expression recapturing her dark bony face.

He pushed his fist into his hand, pacing. Bastard! Rotten bastard! Leaving her to dream he'd be coming back for her when nothing would be coming for her anymore.

Unless. . . .

He stood stone still for a moment. Unless the man getting off the plane really was his father. Again he saw he wanted to believe it. But it was almost too difficult to believe. Somebody starting down here and becoming so important he could ride airplanes all over the world. . . .

And yet . . . suppose it was true?

Wasn't it easy enough to find out? Perhaps the newspapers would have the full story of what had happened at the airport and the man's name. And address. Then what? Confront the goddamn bastard! Finish this crap once and for all!

He became a bundle of motion, pulling on his tennis shoes, flicking a comb through his hair, but at the closet he paused, uncertain. Then he grimaced again, angrily. He searched in the back of the closet until he found the small bundle he had hidden there. Unwrapping the bundle he stared at the tiny gun. He hadn't taken it with him now for two months, since he had almost used it. Why take it now? But he was already thrusting the gun into the pocket of his jeans.

The TV was something else again. No matter what, it had to be left here for Mama to watch, in case she woke up. He was sure to borrow or bum or hustle a couple of bucks once he hit the streets. The question was simply how long was he going to last out there before the cramps bent him over until he couldn't move anymore? Any other time he could think about pawning the gun, but not now. Not now. So maybe he really could take the TV, that is, if he could quickly replace it, as he had done a few times before. . . . Except how could he replace it by the time she woke up, maybe expecting to get a glimpse of the man again?

Naw. Sick to his stomach or not, he wasn't going to let her wake up without something to keep her company. Get out of here now and tell Miss Johnson next door to keep a close check on her as usual, and that he wouldn't be out too long.

He got his keys, mopped the sweat off his face and went out the door. His fingers were still trembling on the door-knob, his knee-caps feeling as though they were suddenly being drilled and filled with ice water, when he realized he hadn't quite yet closed the door.

A wave of bitterness and self-hatred attacked him, but he was already going back into the apartment. Without looking at Mama, he unhooked the TV.

He sniffled, snot running from his nose, tears from his eyes.

"You just wait, Mama. I'll make it up to you. You wait and see!"

Bending, stumbling under the weight of the set, he went out the door.

three

Ten minutes ago Winston had left the girl inside the room and come out upon the terrace. He was exhausted, his body still sweaty beneath his robe. Some women you needed a telephone pole or a prick like an elephant to make love to! The small world between her legs so minuscule, so fragile, and yet what a vacuum of hunger! At one point in there with her, he had gotten the impression he could throw in sticks of dynamite, lawn mowers, and perhaps even a couple of moving vans and she'd still lie there—passive, waiting, unimpressed. . . . But then he must have done *something* right, because suddenly she jumped alive, gasped, bloodied his back, whispered, "Freddy! Freddy!" collapsed, and then promptly went to sleep.

Now he could hear her snoring. If he looked around he knew he'd see her still sprawled white and graceless upon the rumpled bed, her body twitching occasionally as though still troubled.

But he didn't look around. An almost unutterable sense of frustration had moved back in and captured him hardly had he disengaged himself from the girl and left the bed. It was nearly as if he had not made love and there had been no warmth of embrace, touching of bodies, smells, taste, nothing—except the strange snores of a woman back in the room who was still a stranger; except the nagging unsettling question: why had she called him Freddy, and who in the hell was Freddy anyway?

But even the question of Freddy did not stir any real anger. Instead he caught himself thinking briefly of Patricia Wallstone, and the contrast in love-making. The tiny desperate black body, clinging to him, always eliciting from him tenderness, an almost frightening closeness, a longing to protect her, but at the same time a guilt that he still did not love her, and perhaps never would—or could.

That Pat was Gru's girl had little or nothing to do with it. He didn't give a damn what happend to Gru anymore. When he got off the plane it had been either break Gru's neck or force Gru to help him salvage something of what Gru had messed up. Tomorrow he'd find out if he had been correct to take another chance on Gru.

Winston moved to the rail of the terrace and stared out over the City. From twenty floors above it was a beautiful view. To the left, Central Park's green darkness flowed towards Fifth Avenue, ending at Central Park South in the distance. Beyond he could see the tip of the Empire State building and an approaching plane, blinking its lights, proceeding towards Kennedy or La Guardia airport. To the right was the Hudson river and the Palisades and New Jersey. Directly below, traffic grumbled and sped through the night.

Sometimes he still experienced a sense of safety up here. The bottom was below: Muggings in the park, people without air-conditioners in hot tenement apartments, poverty often so obscene and intense you could taste it. A world of proverbial crabs, squirming, lashing out within their narrow confines, but the lid was on. A world where he had once existed. And where it seemed he could get flung back to again. . . .

He shuddered. The thought of being pushed back down to the bottom of the City left him nauseous. Again it was clear why he must stop seeing Pat Wallstone, break the relationship once and for all, even if the deal with Bernie Stein went well tomorrow. It was going to be a long hard climb to recoup his losses, and then to keep on going up as fast as he still had to go. He needed a woman beside him that could climb as swiftly as he could. Pat simply wasn't equipped to make the climb. He could find himself stopped, slowed, not at his level, but a level dictated by *her* limitations. And nothing, nothing on this earth must stop him this time once he began moving again. He had too far to fall.

He would also have to phone his own landlord's management office Monday and ask why in the hell there wasn't greater security around the goddamn building? Or was he being paranoiac? Everyone was getting mugged, ripped off in the City. But he had gotten caught right in front of the building and look how much goddamn rent he paid! Young punk approached him hardly had he stepped out of a cab. Staring at him strangely. Tall skinny boy, eyes bright with drugs. Not saying anything yet, simply staring at him. Not even competent to pull off a professional stick-up.

"Yeah?" Winston demanded, staring back into the boy's face, not even really frightened of the boy yet, just intensely exasperated, thinking: I put up with a lot of Gru's shit all day and Donald's stupidity and Pat clinging to my goddamn back, and the Jew Bernie Stein trying to fuck me before I fuck him and I got to get to court Tuesday and a tenant complaining there hadn't been hot water in a building for six weeks and her toilet didn't flush either . . . and . . . and now this punk . . . escapee from some goddamn ghetto—looking like he had a gun sticking in the waist of his levis, but too fucking scared to pull it out and use it! Went back to the old thing, Black people, his own goddamn people, didn't have enough guts yet to tackle banks, Wall street, rather stick up some crummy grocery store, poor and defenseless old people, or some lone stranger like himself. Go after the goddamn banks, why didn't they!

"Yeah?" he repeated, glaring at the boy, still not afraid yet, just outraged.

The boy mumbled something incoherent, face beaded by perspiration, desperately trying to get words out, trying to touch his sleeve, or grab his wallet, which? As if, in a way, begging to be given money when he should have the fucking guts to pull out the pistol and demand it. My folks, he thought. We don't even learn anything from the Mafia. Washington.

Contempt was in the slap. He drew back and struck the boy beside the face, hard. The skinny frame buckled and the boy went down, banging his head against the lamp-post. Winston snatched the pistol and put it into his own pocket.

"I ought to kick your ass till you can't stand!" he told the boy furiously. He considered calling one of the guards that patrolled the grounds with the huge threatening police dogs and having the boy hauled off to jail. But what the hell good would it do? Another boy would break out of the ghetto tomorrow, scale the invisible walls, guns and knives in hand, and there was never going to be any safety in the City unless he climbed so high nothing from the bottom could ever reach him again.

Also, the boy lying there groggy against the lamp-post seemed so helpless, hopeless, that he almost felt a stir of pity. The face not even criminally hardened yet, but terribly young, even sensitive with the big dark brown eyes, shocked and humiliated almost to tears at having been slapped.

Winston had to force himself to keep the full edge of anger in his voice. "Get the hell on your feet and beat it, and don't let me catch you around here anymore!" Then he turned and walked off, but not before he glimpsed something else in the eyes of the boy: a stare of naked hatred. A hatred that seemed bottomless following him as he went up the steps and into the building. He frowned uneasily. But ain't that a bitch, he thought. Young punk attempts to stick me up but hates me for looking out for myself and stopping him. Twisted fucking world! But maybe kids like that see you looking successful and they are automatically envious . . . Hate you because you appear to be so high when they are trapped in a life that is so low. Well, Goddammit, he thought, he didn't get up off the bottom by luck or sitting on his ass or by hating those on top. He simply decided it was better to be a winner than a loser, better to live on the fortieth floor than in the basement, and then he made the necessary sacrifices to get where he wanted to go. Or rather where he was still trying to go.

Looking out over the City now, the peaceful looking park, the bright tips of skyscrapers pushing towards the sky, he found himself still annoyed just remembering the attempted hold-up, frowning, thinking: Trouble was, some of these kids these days thought they could *start* at the top, didn't know you had to work yourself to the bone and sacrifice to get ahead. In fact, what would that kid have thought if he knew that he, Winston, had once cleaned shit houses, worked as a nightwatchman, porter, bus boy, waited tables, and drove taxi cabs fourteen and fifteen hours a day, worked at everything and done many more humiliating things to get his start? It most certainly hadn't been easy, and sometimes the higher he climbed the tougher it got.

A breeze fingered his robe and he pulled it tighter about his sweaty body. From down below the sound of a crash followed by angry voices suddenly rose up and assailed him. Two cabs had smashed into each other at the intersection. Apparently they had been racing to pick up a fare. The couple who now moved away without even looking back were taking a third cab. The drivers of the other two cabs were a Black and a Puerto Rican. They had jumped out of the cabs and their voices were violent against each other. A crowd had begun to gather. Staring down at the men yelling stupidly, trading insults, Winston was suddenly willing to bet his life that the driver who had escaped with the fare had been neither Black nor Puerto Rican. . . .

Suddenly the Black man leaped at the Puerto Rican with a pipe and the sound of the blow could be heard all the way to the twentieth floor. The Puerto Rican man went down but almost instantly Puerto Ricans began jumping out of the crowd, seemed to pour out of buildings, to come up out of the very sidewalks. They all pounced upon the lone Black man.

Winston frowned in both outrage and annoyance, struggling with himself to keep from identifying with the lone Black man being beaten to the pavement.

"Stupid bastard!" he thought. "Why in hell had he struck the Puerto Rican in the first place, another poor man like himself, out there hustling for a living! In fact, made more sense if they had caught the third driver and beaten the hell out of him!"

Mercifully the guards from his building and the police dogs and two cops from the area moved in and began dispersing the crowd, arresting the slaughter. An ambulance arrived. In a moment there was the illusion of peace and quiet down below again.

Had he, too, been as vicious and desperate as those two drivers in those days when he had driven a cab? Winston wondered. Perhaps more so. On a slow night he had been prepared to do anything to get a good fare, and once he had the fare he had been ready to go the limit to exploit it. All the tricks of the trade. Short change, the long ride, ride the meter "stick-up," put on the most obsequious and humiliating act to get a goddamn twenty-five cent tip. His ass, his balls, sweaty and funky after the many hours behind the wheel, his nerves rattled, legs aching, constipated, his mind numb, dizzy from exhaustion, but already desperately counting the quarters, the dimes, the nickels he had managed to accumulate.

He had given himself a quota of banking $100.00 a week. Then he had raised that quota to $125.00 a week. He had even a couple of times banked as much as $150.00 in a week, but his budget was already so over strained he had begun to suffer from malnutrition. Eating the cheapest meat, the cheapest bread, the cheapest of everything to bank a dollar. In this manner he had accumulated his first five thousand dollars.

What a miracle! That day when he stared at his bank book and there had been a grand total of $5000.00! He couldn't believe it. He, Winston, who had never had anything and who now had so much money. Incredible! He had crossed a line that millions of people, poor people all over the world would never cross in all their life-time. A great day. Now he was safe, wasn't he? All he had to do was invest his $5000.00 wisely, right, and slow down and take it easy?

It took him several months to discover that $5000.00 was but a drop in the bucket. You couldn't even start a decent hot dog stand business with it. In the rich and powerful and expensive market-place of the United States of America you could buy almost nothing with it—but trouble.

As he did.

And in less than one year he was nearly flat broke again.

Bank account reading $1,116.00. Almost all the way back down there from where he had started. At first he was paralyzed by depression, then he had plunged back into the battle more desperate than ever to replenish his bank account, to increase it. Now it was to hell with malnutrition. He couldn't think of his health. He ate less, lost weight, sleep, lived on raw nerves, stumbled from behind the wheel of taxi-cabs like a zombie to his other jobs. The only thing that mattered was to see an increase in the figures on his bank book each week, for now he knew—he knew he had to have at least ten thousand dollars ($10,000.00) to begin to go where he wanted to go. And where he wanted to go was up off the bottom of America to the bright beautiful top of it.

It had been a very intense and most often humiliating period in his life. But nothing had been more depressing than the evening when he nearly ran over an old lady in his desperate effort to obtain twenty-five cents, and the encounter that same night with Marty Gero.

Old lady, no doubt on Welfare, or Social Security, half blind, arthritic, partly illiterate, taking a taxi because she couldn't walk the few blocks she had to go. Flagging down his taxi, where he sat a bundle of tension behind the wheel, already consumed by outrage before she got in, a fierce and bitter hunger to win, to become un-buried, to emerge, sweaty and angry but faking a smile. . . .

"Evening, M'am."

"Sho glad I caught you, Son. Some of these ole cab drivers won't stop in this neighborhood and pick up a soul."

Trying not to listen to the warm, sad, motherly tone of her voice. As hard and ruthless as the concrete City, sizing her up for what he could take from her, for what she could contribute to his bank account, another foot in the face of this sad old mother crab, too old to run, climb anymore, his foot, too, in her face but do not look back; climb faster; those screams, those pitiful cries from below were from the world of the defeated. One day he might not hear them anymore.

"Son, I don't care if you don't put your meter down. Go right on. Don't blame you for making all you can. I'm just going a few blocks anyhow."

"Thank you, M'am," he said, moving at top almost reckless speed, watching out for inspectors. Get where he was going as fast as he could before he got busted. "They got more than we got anyway."

"Sho do. Millions of dollars they spend on just going to the moon, where they ain't got no business. Then they spend millions and millions more running in these here elections, promising us poor folks everything, but once they is elected they don't keep no promises to nobody!"

"A bunch of gangsters," Winston agreed.

"Sho the God is. Now I hear-tell they using rifles and poison gas and killing each other. Don't know what it's all coming to."

"Me either," Winston said. "Which corner, M'am?"

"Right cross the street will be fine, Son. And it sure is a joy to talk to somebody nice like you."

Winston braked the cab.

"That will be . . . er . . . er . . . ." He cursed himself. He was about to over-charge her twenty-five cents but suddenly couldn't bring it off.

"Here's a dollar," she said. "The fare is usually seventy-five cents. Keep fifteen cents more for yourself, Son."

"Thank you, M'am," he said politely, but deep down he was frustrated. If he had cheated her, she would have known. She was a very nice old lady and even if she hadn't known he was cheating her, he would know. It would have taken him a couple of hours to get over the depressing fact that he had cheated her. Goddamn confusing! But what the hell, it was dog eat dog and he shouldn't hold himself in anyway responsible for her!

Then he noticed that the bill she gave him was a ten instead of a one. He was already making change, giving her ten cents and retaining fifteen cents for himself. Had she caught her error? Something deep inside himself urged him to go ahead and give her the balance of nine dollars that she was entitled to. It was always this other self deep inside himself that he had to fight. Sometimes he knew, like now, that it was the best part of himself, wanting to be honest, human, but another part of himself, like now, too, was already adding the nine dollars to his bank account.

If she finally noticed the mistake, he'd give her the money. . . . But if she didn't. . . .

She had closed her purse and was trying to maneuver her sad heavy body out of the cab. He noted that she had dropped an additional quarter. It glittered bright and silvery upon the back seat as she strained to get out of the door. Now his mind was torn between giving her the nine dollars and simply and quickly getting her out of the cab so that he could also grab the twenty-five cents and add that to his collection.

"Lady. . . ." he started, but ceased, instead pushing the door open so that she could get on out.

She was still talking, apologetic because she couldn't move faster. "Lordy, these poor ole bones. . . . Take life easy, Son. Ain't no fun when you git old and can't no longer git around good."

Then she was out. He locked the door quickly, already reaching and straining and picking up the bright silver quarter in one swift motion. He didn't know the car was still in drive. His foot had come up off the brake as he strained to reach the quarter. To cross the street, the old lady shuffled past in front of the car. The car jumped forward. For one terrifying instant he knew he wasn't going to be able to stop the car before he ran her down. Frantically his foot sought the brake, while his mind already imagined her crumbled and crushed and bleeding beneath the wheels. And the cops coming. And crowds gathering. Man-slaughter if not murder. Everything over, finished. . . .

As it were, he couldn't believe she was still standing as the car jolted to a stop. Continuing across the street, she didn't realize the danger she had been in. She even paused once, her wrinkled face creased in a heavy smile, looking back and waving at him as he sat stunned behind the wheel.

It took some time, hands trembling, his whole body trembling, before he put the car into gear again and sped away.

No, he hadn't encountered Marty Gero that night. Encountered no one except himself that night. Went home and puked his guts out. Took the cab to the garage and didn't drive for two days. Stared at himself in the mirror. Who? Who in the hell are you Winston? What is it you wouldn't do for money? He kept seeing the sad kindly old lady's face over and over, flooded by disgust at himself. But after a couple of days her face receded somewhat, pushed aside by his own desperation to keep moving, to win at all cost, and the stone walls finally began erecting themselves again around what seemed like his weaker and more sensitive self. By Monday morning he went to the bank and the nine extra dollars looked good added to his account.

But no, Marty Gero came later. Perhaps as much as a week later. A slow night. Drivers all over the city were hustling hard to find a decent fare. Heard a doorman's whistle blow, cruising the East Side, and rushed to answer, beating out two other cabs.

Waiting before the canopy, the doorman's white gloved hand holding the cab's door, the fare emerging from the bright shiny copper trimmed building entrance. Majestic building, the stone blasted white and clean and shiny, where people must live surrounded by all that money could buy, where you didn't know or think there could be a bottom to the City anymore, where you could be secure and safe and *somebody* at last. But a building where he, Winston, would have to use the servant's entrance to get inside of.

The doorman bowed and scraped, ushering the man into the cab, a plump soft-looking man, with a clean-shaven pink bald head, and round white silver glasses. A bold red tie gave life to an otherwise conservatively cut grey suit worth at least three-or-four hundred bucks. The man settled into the seat, grunting discontentedly, as though he had just eaten something disagreeable or broken away from an encounter with people who had rubbed him the wrong way.

A whiff of cologne or shaving lotion rose in the air, something of a mixture Winston couldn't remember having ever smelled before. It was pleasant and no doubt very expensive and maybe, Winston thought, rich sonofabitches like this had their scents made to order. But a little thing like smell, the sound of a fare's voice, the instant vibrations of one human being in contact with another, were only as important as they gave him a clue to what kind of fare he had. A cheap fifteen cent tipper, or a thirty center? Or was this one of the night's long-shots that he could really get something extra out of?

The voice came at him harsh, imperative, aimed at just another cab-driver, servant; he, Winston, the unknown entity behind the wheel, the unknown nobody, whose value hadn't even reached five thousand dollars again yet. Absolutely nothing and nobody except a pair of black hands to guide the wheel of the cab. An address in Riverdale was barked at him and then he was abruptly dismissed, as though chopped completely out of the man's consciousness.

Ah, but Riverdale? A perfect *arm job*. Once he got to the highway he could ride the meter "stick up" all the way.... Small chance of a hack inspector spotting him, riding in their white cars, taking his number and forcing him to appear before the Hack bureau, where he would be suspended again, where he had already been suspended so many times he really couldn't risk many more before he'd lose his license to hack altogether.

Should he politely ask the man to allow him to "make the trip for himself" or should he drive off and not turn the meter on and later pretend he had forgotten the meter? For some reason the man's arrogant tone had irritated him. He couldn't bring himself to effect humility and ask the man to do him a favor. He left the meter off and took a side street and then turned and headed for the East Side highway, thinking: goddammit, if I'm going to rob somebody, let it be the cab company or somebody like this bastard in back, not some poor old woman, never anyone like that poor old woman again.

The man grunted a couple more times, hawked, spat out the window, but said nothing.

Said nothing until they were near the East Side Drive, then the man whose name he found out later to be Marty Gero, lit a cigar and chuckled softly, disgustedly.

"Driver," he said. "I guess you know I'm not going to pay you."

Both Marty Gero's tone and meaning stabbed into Winston and left him numb. He didn't quite know how to react at first.

"If you got nothing on the meter, you get nothing," Marty Gero said, emphatically, almost with a strange bitterness. "Who you trying to con? Me?"

Winston controlled himself.

"I forgot the meter, Sir."

"Like shit you did. No. No. Don't put it on now. Simply take me to Riverdale. Don't give me any problem. I get a free ride and I'll allow you to go free to find yourself a real sucker. What the hell, do you think I was born yesterday!"

Winston flung the meter on anyway.

"You going to pay me whatever comes on this meter, Mister!" Anger had jumped into his voice and he had trouble getting the words out. Who in the hell did this sonofabitch think he was!

Marty Gero was silent for a second, as though amazed at the rage and tension he detected in Winston. Black hands on the wheel belonged to a face after all, nappy uncombed hair covered a brain; the cold blood-shot eyes staring from the rear-view mirror were desperate, furious, perhaps even dangerous.

Marty Gero caressed his cigar, puffing on it slowly, watchful, alert. Suddenly he seemed to be amused. When he spoke his tone had noticeably softened, "You got big balls, eh? Forget honesty is the best policy and all that shit, right? Well, everyone is forgetting, so why not you? The whole world is becoming a pile of crap and who really gives a damn anymore."

Winston said nothing. Frustration and anger still consumed him at losing what had seemed like an easy eight or nine bucks. Now he only wanted to get rid of the fare, hoping his luck would be better the next person he picked up.

Marty Gero leaned back, another cloud of cigar smoke wafted through the cab.

39

"Yeah, big balls. . ." he repeated. "But the question is, how big? I tell you, make a U turn here. I don't wish to take the East Side Drive. I want the West Side. Also. I'd like for you to make a stop on the way. Forty-Second Street just across Seventh Avenue."

"Listen, you out of your mind. I can't make a U turn here. Traffic violation, a sure ticket and. . . ."

"Well, if you get a ticket, I'll pay for it" Marty Gero said promptly. Then he pulled out his wallet and extracted two dollars and threw them upon the front seat. "Here. Beginning of your tip. Drive like I tell you and you got more coming."

Before he could get his thoughts together, Winston found himself slamming on brakes and whipping the cab around in a U turn, almost scraping a bus, straightening with the wheels still screaming, heading back in the opposite direction, suddenly even angrier than he had been before. Two lousy fucking dollars and he had almost wrecked the cab, risked a ticket, his mind suddenly going blank, pride disappearing at the idea of getting an even bigger tip!

"Good, boy," Marty Gero said. "I'll tell you when to stop."

Winston gripped the wheel, swallowing frustration. The only consolation was that he had glimpsed the guy's wallet when the guy pulled out the two dollars. And the wallet had seemed quite fat, twenties, a fifty. . . . O.K., then, play along with the bastard. Maybe pick up another couple of bucks, at least.

He approached Times Square, Forty-Second and Broadway, stopping for the light. Just across the street the very sewers of the City seemed to have opened up, disgorging people: Pimps, prostitutes, homosexuals of every variety, pick-pockets, drug addicts, muggers, young boys not yet ten years old dressed up like their elders in cheap gaudy finery, their bodies for sale, already schooled to cater to any and every degenerate sexual need, climbing into cars like the female whores for a quick whirl through a dark City street, blow jobs in the back and front seat of cars, in doorways, standing up, lying down. . . . A movie marquee showing a big busty but frightened blonde shackled to a tree being whipped by two men, RAPE OF A VIRGIN. Another marquee, a group of handsome boys embracing, TOM, JACK AND PAUL—and EDDIE! Tourist and squares and johns threading their way through the crowd, frightened, uneasy, titillated, or searching, their own faces flushed with some nameless desire, while the night people observed them from door-ways, lurking in shadows, searching for weaknesses, in the face, in the eyes, before approaching, pricks standing out stiffly against tight trousers, skirts covering needle-marked buttocks, the younger boys hesitating, but smiling, hoping, waiting.

"Disgusting!" Marty Gero snorted. "This used to be a nice beautiful safe area, now look at the bums! Scum of the earth! What did I tell you, this city, this country is sinking into hell, and who cares anymore? No one!"

Winston was silent. Many of the degraded people, defeated people, left out and perverted people were black, and he didn't quite know yet where this bastard was coming from. He pulled across Seventh Avenue, the snarled traffic moving slowly.

"Stop right here," the man said, staring out the window in disgust. "I'll only be a minute. Here," he extracted another buck and threw it on the seat. "You got more coming. But watch me—if any of these punks approach me on the street, blow your horn, call a cop."

Marty Gero clambered out, swiftly for a man of his bulk, hesitated and then hurried into one of the brightly lit stores.

Winston stared at the store-front, puzzled. The shop window advertised a twenty-five cent peep show, as well as a live show of girls on stage. Also displayed was an assortment of wax and rubber phalluses, false breasts, a complete and outfittable female sex organ—apparently to be blown up like a rubber tube, French ticklers, jellies of all color for vaginas, pictures of women with their eyes closed in rapture, in various processes of giving blow jobs. . . . Why had the guy gone in there? Possibly the Landlord. . . . A number of so-called nice people owned Times Square. Took the profit from the vice but were ashamed of it. Probably this guy was in there to pick up his night's take. . . . Then home to a clean, vice free area like certain sections of Riverdale, where guards, dogs, and police patrolled, hostile to strangers. . . .

Winston pushed it out of his mind. He thought of two things only: on second glance the wallet had seemed even thicker, the other thing was that he was both hungry and needed to urinate. In fact, just allowing himself to think that he needed to urinate made it worse. Suddenly he had to clinch his body tightly to keep from urinating in his pants. But use the bottle? In order to keep driving, make every nickel he could, he usually brought with him not only a sandwich he could eat in the car without stopping but a ginger ale bottle he could piss into as he drove. Or into which he could pause and relieve himself quickly and keep moving. But he was sitting in a bus stop now and the bright lights were all around him. If he began using the bottle someone was certain to spot him, if not a cop, then one of the creeps along the streets. . . . Creeps pounding on the window to get into the cab. Maybe thinking that he was some kind of pervert, asking for something. . . .

It was getting worse. He had tensed up and it had become painful to keep his bladder from over-flowing. Did he dare leave the cab and dash into a toilet somewhere? Where? Most of the businesses along the streets, except the movies, had closed their toilets, cut out both toilets and telephone booths. Junkies had been using them to shoot-up. Queers to do their thing. Whores to turn tricks. . . . And if he dashed into a movie he'd have to spend precious money to get in, and once he was in there fight off the homos to get out. . . . Take a chance, use the bottle? But his bladder had eased a little. . . . Maybe he could hold out? If he didn't think about it. Fifteen or twenty minutes to Riverdale and he could either make some pretense and stop on the way, or once he dropped the fare he could go and have himself another sandwich and relieve himself at the same time. Seemed like this guy was going to tip well, so he will have earned himself a half hour's rest.

It got better and he relaxed a little. He turned on his tiny transistor radio to distract himself, keeping an eye on the door of the store to be sure the fare didn't duck out and leave him unpaid.

A newscaster's voice crackled over the cheap transistor: . . . prices had risen another 9 1/2 % . . . fear . . . depression . . . a two hundred billion dollar shift to the Mid-East . . . 13th. victim . . . Central Park . . . for the week . . . Washington: . . . Giorgio DeBasko . . . former labor leader with alleged ties to the underworld . . . loan-sharking . . . etc. . . . after receiving an Executive Pardon . . . said at Waldorf today . . . proud . . . justice . . . had prevailed. . . .

But a depression, he thought. My God, was it possible? Just when he was getting organized to. . . . Well, he just had to move faster.

Then a smile came into the newscaster's voice: . . . Had anyone noticed . . . latest fad . . . sweeping the country? Well, little lady responsible . . . had once been . . . lowly paid beautician. . . . It was she who had come up with . . . modest idea . . . of drilling an extra hole in the ear . . . accommodating a second ear-ring. . . . Not since the Bikini . . . or should we . . . er . . . say . . . The String . . . or the Hoola Hoop, had an idea created so much excitement. . . . Some women weren't stopping at two holes, but drilling holes all around their ears. . . . Some even in their nose. . . . The little lady had become a millionaire over night. . . . Jewelry and allied industries were . . . raking in thousands of dollars. . . .

Tension? the newscaster said. Worried? Can't sleep at night? Well, use DOZOFF and. . . .

Marty Gero hurried out of the store, clutching a black plastic hand-bag, mopping his face, round white-rimmed glasses twinkling like tiny silver moons against his pink skin.

"All right, Driver," he clambered into the back of the cab, puffing heavily. "Keep going down Forty-Second. Stop at the first liquor store you see. God, I could use a drink! Every time I pass this scummy street I wish to vomit!"

Marty Gero got out at the liquor store and when he came out of there stopped at the delicatessen next door. Still puffing heavily he climbed back into the cab, carrying a fifth of Courvoisier and a package of cups. Sudden charges of anxiety seemed to be propelling him. He ripped open the package of cups, tore the seal from the brandy, poured generously, then downed the liquor. After that, he gasped, "Here, have a drink."

"Not on the job," Winston said, speeding the cab towards the Drive. Get this guy home and out as soon as he could. Shouldn't take over fifteen minutes.

Marty Gero relaxed a bit.

"I needed that. But wait until I show you what I picked up in that goddamn store! It is a crime. There should be a law against what's going on in this city. Can you imagine it, right there in one of those stalls in the store, a fellow peeping at two broads

43

screwing each other, while a young kid was down on his knees giving him a blow job! And did anyone protest? Did anyone kick that door down and beat the hell out of that bastard, corrupting that kid? No. Nothing. The customers in there pretended they didn't see it, though the door to the stall was clearly open wide enough for anyone to see what was going on. No, they kept on looking through those filthy books themselves. At least fifty men and a couple of women, secretly watching each other, ready themselves to pick up another degenerate and go into one of the stalls. Makes you want to vomit your guts out! If you will not have a drink, I'll have another. I need it."

Against his better judgment, Winston decided to have a drink. After all, he could fake it somewhat, sip from the cup, let the bastard back there blow off steam. What was wrong with the City, the Country, the World—drunker the bastard got perhaps the better he'd tip.

Winston accepted the cup, but a sip of the Courvoisier burned into his brains, attacked his stomach and he realized how very hungry he was again. He took a second sip to steady himself, speeded up now that he was on the highway, but finally slowed a couple of miles. He definitely couldn't afford an accident, a sure way to get fired.

Marty Gero had opened the plastic bag. Leaning towards Winston an edge of even greater indignation was suddenly in his voice. "Look at this," he said. "This is the crap I picked up in that store! Selling it over the counter. No law against it! Nothing!"

Breathing angrily, Marty Gero held the multicolored sex pictures where Winston could see them. A man pushing his huge penis into the anus of another man. A woman caressing a penis while it spouted its orgasm upon her nostrils, eyelids. Four women rooting between each other's legs. A brutish looking black man forcing his huge rod into a delicate looking blonde who seemed to have fainted. . . . Picture after picture, more of the same, if different positions, partners. . . .

Marty Gero shuffled the pictures like playing cards. Each picture feeding his indignation.

"Did you ever see anything so abominable? And there are

bastards that will tell me that all is well. Don't worry, Marty, we're simply going through a lousy period in history, that's all. People will rise up, vote, act, clean out the shit. The country will return to decency, law, where a man can earn a clean honest dollar again. Yeah, well, maybe I am somewhat pessimistic. . . . But then no one knows what I've been through in the last few years. The sheer agony of watching . . . watching myself, the irresolution, others folding before the wind. . . . But that's still another story. What I mean is, how is it the FBI can knock out the communists and yet can't give us any relief, clean up the rest of this crap, cesspools like Forty-Second street, loan sharks walking into your business and beating the hell out of you unless you give them part of the action? And what about the local cops? Surely they know what's going on. Think these pictures are disgusting, then look at this! Look at this." Marty Gero took from the bag a very large rubber penis, straps and all, normally used by lesbians; and a rubber vagina, hairs and all, excreting its own jelly, giving off a faint mint odor in the interior of the cab.

"God in Heaven!" Marty Gero shook his head. "And there are people who will tell me there is something to be optimistic about! And that isn't all. Tell you, when I get to my place, I'll put a couple of films on, women fucking dogs, can you imagine that? I invite you in. It is my house to do with as I wish. Black people are just as good as white. If my neighbors wish to move, it is their fucking problem. Me, I've never been prejudiced. I've invited a couple of colored fellows to my house before. . . ."

Winston mumbled something about taking a rain check. "I got to keep working," he said. Besides, a relief to get rid of this nut, who was so indignant about filth, but who would keep wallowing in it. And it was always beware when whites started talking about how non-prejudiced they were. Plus, he needed to piss as soon as possible. The Courvoisier had stimulated him, made him aware of himself again. Or had it been the pictures?

They passed the toll. Trees soon bordered the highway. The air became fresher, cleaner.

"No. No." Marty said. "I really invite you into my house. Status means nothing to me. I paid one hundred and fifty thousand dollars for it, but so what? If the country keeps sinking, the house isn't going to be worth a nickel either. My wife and kids are in Florida. Her side of the family got a small place down there—well, they call it small. But when I had my little trouble, I couldn't get twenty cents from the bastards. They didn't like my associates. Imagine, *now* they didn't like my associates! Why? Because the Do, Re, Mi had slowed, stopped rolling in? Except for the scandal, I finally realized that nothing would have made them happier than to see me with a bullet in the back of my head."

The house was more or less what Winston expected: circular drive, water fountain indirectly lit sitting amidst a vast green lawn and shrubbery. Windows white and green trimmed. Gas lights flickering before the entrance.

Winston was determined to keep moving, but as he brought the cab to a halt Marty Gero seemed to become more determined not to be alone. The brandy had thickened his voice, weakened normal controls. He gripped Winston's shoulder. "Listen, forget the meter! Let it run. Or cut it off. I don't care. Take this ten. Will that cover the bill? I treat my friends right. When you leave, you got another five bucks coming. I'm inviting you into my house. I'm not the kind of fellow who stands on ceremony. What does it matter that you are a cab driver and I am a business man? We are all the same in the sight of God, right? Come in, have a drink. I must show you this goddamn film—a dog fucking a woman. Can you imagine anything more degenerate? I wish I could show the film to the whole country. Wake the bastards up. Let them see what we are all coming to! I'm not normally a crusader, but doesn't someone have to start sounding the alarm? If that ten isn't sufficient to cover my bill, just say so. Money means nothing to me."

"Well," Winston hesitated.

"Plus, of course, you got more coming when you leave. Don't worry about it."

Marty Gero stumbled out of the cab and up the steps and Winston followed. Inside, wall-to-wall soft pink carpet, pinker than the man's brightly flushed face, but still somehow managing to be in good taste. Gauguins, Picassos on the walls, baby grand piano music sheet still open, winding stairs leading to the upper floor. Music had started playing somewhere, mysteriously, automatically, the moment Marty switched the lights on. But where was the toilet and did the guy have anything to eat in the house?

Before Winston could ask questions, Marty Gero had pulled a screen down over one of the walls and had begun setting up the movie projector, selecting and adjusting a film, stubbing out cigars, sipping brandy, moving at a tremendous almost chaotic clip, sweating, as though propelled by some strange inner anxieties to get everything done instantly, otherwise he might look up and find Winston had gone, that he was alone.

Lights darkened and the screen took on life. Winston was suddenly captured by the smiling image of an extremely beautiful girl, fresh-looking, blonde and blue-eyed, innocence personified. Looked like something just out of college, well-bred, best background and all, everything. . . . Now in barefeet she walked along a beach, going towards a cabin. . . . Suddenly she ran briefly, childishly, into the surf, coming out soaking wet, her flimsy clothing clinging to her long limbs. . . . Young breasts ripe, straining to break free. . . . One of them almost having broken free. . . . While she smiled, wide fully generous mouth, freckled face. . . . Skipping now along the beach, Ideal Calender Girl, TV Ad Girl, the girl next door embraced in dreams, the ultimate promise, the final prize. . . .

Then she was inside the cabin, alone, smoking, restless. She stared out the window, towards the sea, touching her breast shyly. . . . Poor girl—alone, unloved. . . . Wanting to caress someone, wanting to be caressed by someone. . . . But she had no one. She was alone.

Except for the huge monster of a dog who had just appeared outside the door, its endlessly long red tongue dripping saliva and heat. But she hadn't seen the dog yet. Now it pawed and scratched the door, whining to get inside.

The poor girl was frightened. Who was it? *What* was it? As frightened as any virgin would be. Timidly, she opened the door. Oh, it was just a nice big doggy. Nothing to fear!

Except that the nice doggy was already trying to stick his nose under her dress, pawing her, grappling with her. She fell to the floor, dress rising, suddenly terrified of the nice big doggy. For the dog was not only sticking his nose between her legs but now the long red tongue had darted out, flicking along her thighs. . . . The flimsy dress got pawed off. Should she run,

47

crawl to the door, and try to escape? But however she moved, the dog was on top of her. Now the dog had his paws hugged around her waist. As she desperately attempted to crawl away, the long frantic red penis found the spot it had been searching for. Faster than any human penis it zipped in and out of her. . . . While the poor girl though terrified couldn't help but gasp with pleasure.

"Disgusting! Disgusting!" Marty Gero said bitterly, but still watching the film intensely. "You are a cab driver, you meet a lot of people. You should tell them what is happening. Surely when the people wake up, they'll take some kind of action. But my God, in the meantime, why should I attempt to maintain my standards? Everything is falling apart, so clear any fool should see it, so why should I hold on, concern myself? If I can't beat it, perhaps I should join it, like so many others, sink, go along with the stream. Why should I care what happens to me anymore?"

Despite himself Winston had been so carried away by the fresh innocent beauty of the girl, he forgot hunger, that he wanted to urinate, everything. As the dog hunched into the girl's lovely body, sexual excitement fought his disgust and excitement won. His own penis now stood out so stiffly he had to adjust his sweaty pants to give it further room to expand.

What seemed more or less like an accident Marty Gero's hand also brushed against him.

Then it was clearly no longer an accident.

Marty Gero couldn't seem to remove his hand. It trembled, fumbling for Winston's zipper, while Marty Gero's tone became almost hysterical with disgust, "You see? Now you see what it is doing to you, too? Rousing our basest instincts! But the city is choking on its own shit, filth, so why should we resist? Let the walls cave in. How can we swim against the stream? My wife is in Florida. No one cares anyway. No one will know. Do with me whatever you wish. But no violence. I can't stand violence. I know you hate me but the world is full of hatred. I don't care anymore. If I choke to death, who will care."

Winston drew back in shock, outrage—but still there was his hardened penis to contend with, and maybe the loss of a large tip as well if he didn't appease this bastard. . . . .And what the hell was the harm in letting the sonofabitch do a blow job

anyway? Charge him another ten, twenty bucks. . . . But Good
Lord, what the hell was he thinking. Would he go through a
thing like this, too—for money? He should punch this character
in the nose and get out of here. . . . Still, he no longer moved.
He found himself watching the dog and the girl again. The girl
now blowing the dog, eyes closed rapturously, while the dog
blew her, and while Marty Gero lifted not only his penis out of
his pants but his balls, licking first the funky sweat under the
balls, and then gasping and trembling and trying to take the
whole prick into his mouth.

"I got to piss. . . ." Winston mumbled. "Listen. . . ."

Marty Gero's tone was choked, breathless.

"Piss. Piss! Do anything! Piss on me!"

Winston didn't know if he was coming or pissing, but
suddenly he let out a great flood, bloating Marty's cheeks, some
of it spilling upon the soft pink carpet, perhaps both coming
and pissing as the beautiful All-American girl moaned and came
as well, the dog now fucking her from the rear again.

"Don't stop!" Marty Gero said huskily. "Please . . .
Please. . . ."

But Winston pulled himself away from the warm greedy
mouth. Sexual arousal diminished, disgust rushed back over
him. How could he have allowed this to happen, all for a few
bucks more, this degenerate bastard who would burn at the
stake all other degenerates! He had a desire to kick the man
away from him, smash the hands still reaching for him.

"Pay you more!" Marty Gero pleaded. "You want to get paid
more? Another ten? Twenty? Money means nothing. Where is
my wallet?"

In the excitement, crawling and swilling and squirming to get
out of his own pants, which were still half-way down over his
plump pink buttocks, Marty Gero must have dropped his
wallet. But Winston hardly listened to Marty. He was absolutely determined now to get out of there. Then he spotted
the wallet, lying near the edge of the sofa in the glare and the
shadows from the screen. Tell Marty? Tell Marty that he had
spotted the wallet? The thought crossed his mind, but fled so
swiftly it hardly registered. He stepped closer to the wallet,
concealing it, while Marty Gero in all of his nervous and pitiful
tension crawled around on the pissy rug feeling for it.

49

"Maybe you dropped it in the cab?" Winston said, his mind already jumping ahead and not only remembering the crisp green bills he had glimpsed in the wallet but trying to imagine and counting the amount of the bills. "Listen, I'll run out to the cab and see if it is there." Stooping and scooping up the wallet and palming it, while poor Marty, back turned, butt turned, peering through his round white glasses, crawled around in circles. "I'll be right back. Meantime, why don't you put on another one of those swinging films."

"No. No," Marty Gero protested. "I'll find the wallet." Then he saw that Winston was at the door. "Well, hurry! If the wallet isn't there, I don't care. I have more money upstairs. What do you want, another thirty? Tell me and we can go upstairs and get it. People should be happy. I can bring the projector upstairs where we can be more comfortable. You're right, I'll change the film. Disgusting people reduced to sleeping with animals! I have one here, film of two nice fellows together."

"Right," Winston said.

Then he had the door open. He got out quickly and slammed it. The clean fresh night air embraced him. But though he was tremendously relieved to have gotten away, to be free of Marty Gero, plus having the wallet, he nevertheless found himself nagged by a question as he rushed towards the cab. Had he been right to flee now? Always best to quit while you're ahead, right? Still, he couldn't keep himself from wondering: how much more money would Marty Gero have had upstairs?

four

He jumped into the cab, turned the motor on, but in his haste, he pushed down upon the gas too forcefully, and the engine choked off. He gripped the wheel. Had he flooded the goddamn motor? My God!

Marty could have heard him trying to pull off. Probably hear him now attempting to get the car started again. The motor gasped, sputtered, failed to catch. Keep cool, he warned himself. But it was tough to remain calm. He kept turning his head and watching the door, feeling like a common thief in fear of being caught.

But still no Marty at the door. What was he doing, calling the cops? Did he dare, degenerate bastard! But the cops wouldn't see that; wouldn't care about that; would only see Marty rich and white and right, and him a bum and nobody, a nigger robbing people in this beautiful neighborhood.

Well, maybe he could still jump out of the cab and run back in and give Marty his wallet back? Tell him, the only reason he had attempted to start the cab was to warm the motor up? Yeah. But who in the hell would believe that?

Then some of the tension fled. The motor sputtered but caught again. It was holding. But before he could whip the car into gear, the side window shattered, splintered into several fragments, and part of the glass came crashing out. The sound stunned him. Now he saw Marty Gero, almost upon the car, racing around the shrubbery from some side exit to the house. It was almost comical the way he stumbled, attempting to get in front of the car, his face distorted by rage. He was holding his pants up with one hand, while with the gun in the other hand he tried to take aim at the car again.

51

Another zigzagging splintering of glass appeared in the front window shield. Winston was so numbed he stared at the glass and the bullet hole for a second, unable to digest the danger he was in. Did Marty actually mean to kill him . . . ? Over a few hundred bucks in the wallet? Rich guy kill somebody for that? But then there was Marty's face again. He had succeeded in getting in front of the cab. Winston could see Marty's pink lips trembling, his eyes those of a mad-man behind those round silver glasses. It wasn't the money. It was much more that Marty Gero was after now.

"Black nigger, stinking bastard!" Marty screamed. "Stop damn you or I'll kill you, kill you!"

Winston shivered, hesitating. Every nerve in his body urged him to whip the car into gear, push down upon the gas, and knock Marty Gero out of his path. But then suppose the car didn't knock Marty free and he was forced to run over Marty? Commit a murder? Or suppose he wasn't fast enough in getting the car going, and Marty began shooting again?

He clutched the wheel, staring back at Marty. Crazy sonofabitch seemed to be waiting for him to make a move, almost hoping he'd make a move. Hell, he'd give the perverted bastard his goddamn wallet and get the hell out of here! Make up the lost time elsewhere.

"O.K. goddammit," he shouted. "Put down that gun and I'll give you your fucking wallet!"

Marty Gero kept the gun pointed at Winston's face and came around to the driver's side of the car. His face was an angry red blob; but what further unnerved Winston was to see tears swimming in Marty's blue eyes, eyes that now gazed at him with absolute hatred.

He was nearly incoherent. "To think I trusted you! Invited you into my house! When all the time you were planning to betray me, humiliate me! There I was thinking you were more intelligent than the other niggers, and a gentleman! With me you could have had everything, now you have nothing! You are a crude, uncouth, dishonest man! If I hadn't been drinking, I would have seen that. From the instant I got into your cab, you were trying to rob me! Then when you saw I was drunk, you took advantage of me. Humiliated me, forced me to do things I never would have done otherwise. Get out of the car! I want my property back, but I am also going to call the police."

"Take it easy, Man," Winston said. The gun kept wavering before his face, as though deep down, deeper than even Marty knew, he still wanted an excuse to use the gun, needed one. "I'll give you your wallet back. Here, take it!" He flipped it out of the cab, but Marty didn't even bother to catch it. He kept the gun pointed at Winston.

"Don't try anything! Don't attempt to play me for a fool again! Now my bag in the back of the car."

"Bag?"

Winston turned his head and saw that Marty had forgotten his plastic bag he had been so eager to get out of the cab earlier and into the house.

"Then," Marty ordered, "I want all my money back. Every cent!"

Winston was reaching for the bag, but then a quick spurt of anger went through him despite the danger of the gun.

"All your money back? What do you mean? Man, you owed me for the fare for bringing you up here . . . and the tips. Goddammit, you owed me the tips, too!"

"I don't owe you a penny!" Marty exploded. "Everything you got from me, you took by force, deceit. I should shoot you this moment! I don't care. I could kill you and then I could kill myself. I have never been so humiliated in all of my life. Utterly debased by an animal like you! I *should* kill myself! But I don't have to. I can blow your brains out and the police will give me a medal for ridding this beautiful city of the scummy likes of you! Don't provoke me! Give me my bag, *all* of my money!"

Winston's entire body had tensed. Sure, give him the bag with the filthy crap inside, fake pussy, fake dicks, who needed that crap anyway. . . . But goddammit, return the bread he had lost all this time earning? Even stooping so low as to allow the punk to blow him, putting his degenerate mouth upon his penis, maybe giving him some kind of venereal disease or something. . . . Going through all of this and now to give the money back?

"Listen, Man, I'll give you your bag but. . . ."

"No! Everything! The bag *and* my money as well!"

Winston brought the bag slowly from the back of the cab, his mind burning with resistance, leaving his body cold, sweaty, as though he were in greater danger now than before of being shot. Because how in the hell could he return the money, all this time wasted; instead of having increased his bank account nothing added, nothing! He had already lost the wallet, and now to be forced to lose what he had rightfully earned was too much.

Perhaps he could con Marty a little, get him to put away the gun? He straightened in the seat, holding the bag, forcing a smile.

"Maybe, Man, I wasn't trying to run away at all. Maybe I was just trying to park the cab out of the drive so that I could come upstairs and look at that other swinging film."

Marty Gero gazed at him searchingly, but then an even greater rage suffused his cheeks.

"Lying nigger! Never will the likes of you ever deceive me again! *I know you now!* All you niggers stick together—robbing, stealing, destroying the cities, the country! If you had been a decent man I might have helped you get a decent job, my private chauffeur or something. Now I am finished with you! I don't need the cops, nor my friends to help take care of you, I can do it myself. I am not so weak as people think. But enough of this crap, talking! Give me my bag, my money, now!"

Winston sighed. He knew the wisest thing was to give up everything and be done with it. Perhaps this mad man would let him go; chalk up the night as a loss, one of those unpleasant experiences he'd have to learn from. . . . But by now he couldn't think rationally. His entire life-line had become tied to a dollar, the number of dollars in his bank account, and the withdrawal of any of those dollars, either actually in the account or ear-marked for it, seemed to threaten his very life. . . .

Even as one part of himself cautioned: give up the bag, give up the money, another part of himself had already begun to move desperately. With his right hand, out of sight of Marty, he fingered the bottle into which he sometimes used to urinate. But could he bring the bottle up and smash it into Marty's face before Marty fired? Perhaps he should attempt to thrust the door open and knock Marty off balance? Or better still, why not fling the bag out quickly and then jump out and subdue Marty before the gun went off? Nothing seemed guaranteed, or possible. He only knew if he was going to act, he must do it instantly, otherwise, Marty might begin to sense his thoughts and shoot him anyway.

It looked hopeless. He was thinking, never was he going to get beyond fear and move, when he must have moved, not even knowing anymore that he was going to. He could already see Marty Gero stepping back, trying to get the pistol re-focussed around the bag he had just flung at him. And even then his thinking hadn't quite caught up, for his other hand gripped the bottle and the bottle had also moved; yet it seemed to him his thinking went no farther than the barrel of the gun swinging back to face him. He still felt numbed by fear, since the bottle seemed to be moving like molasses, a million miles away from Marty's face.

But the next thing that registered was Marty reeling backwards, clutching his mouth, blood spraying from his lips and teeth, while the gun went off like a cannon momentarily deafening him.

Then, still moving, dazed, he had flung the door open, and Marty was upon the ground, lying near the fountain, the brightly lit green water a gigantic halo above him.

Breathing harshly, he stared at Marty, ready to continue the attack. Now that the rage in himself had been unleashed, he had difficulty curbing it. Sonofabitch! he thought. Trying to cheat me! Putting that fucking pistol in my face and . . . and . . . But dead? A number of the front teeth smashed out. . . . Bloody mess oozing out of his mouth. . . . Dead? A new thread of fear began swelling, numbing him again.

He leaned closer to Marty. No. Not dead. But breathing crazily.

Get out of here. Cops show up now, there would be worse trouble than before. . . .

Hastily he picked up the wallet and shelved it into his pocket. He jumped in behind the wheel, and found that Marty's flailing arms must have knocked the bag back into the car. He reached for it to fling the bag and the crap out when the barking of a dog somewhere penetrated his consciousness. Security guards? The homes were so isolated from each other around here he couldn't be sure. Still he felt panicky. He pressed down again upon the accelerator more forcefully than he knew he should. But though the car spun and screeched upon the gravel, this time it took off. Outside of the winding drive-way, Winston forced himself to drive slower through the quiet streets. Once he spotted a patrol car up ahead and he turned and went in the opposite direction. After a time, he was lost, but he kept on driving. It didn't matter as long as he was putting distance between himself and that place. Then he found another entrance to the highway and took it. He drove blindly. But he soon spotted the George Washington bridge glittering in the night and he knew where he was. When he arrived at the exit to 125th Street, he took it. He didn't stop until he was in the middle of Harlem, where he felt safe.

On a darkened street, he opened the wallet, fingers trembling in anticipation. Three $100.00 bills. Two $50.00 bills. Four $20.00 bills. Three $10.00 bills. Two $5.00 bills. And four $1.00 bills. How much? Total of $524.00. Plus the tips he had gotten. Not bad. Sent his bank account back over the $4000.00 mark. Yeah, not bad for a night's work.

Still, for some reason, he was vaguely disappointed. All the crap he had been through! Should have been more.... And suppose Marty Gero died, could he be traced? Or suppose Marty Gero didn't die and tried to track him down? Which meant he had to spend some of this money to try and cover his trail. He could end up after all with this fucking night leaving him in a hole, plus in future danger.

He continued to search the wallet, maybe some secret compartment with more cash hidden. But all he found now were a batch of credit cards, membership cards to clubs, and a check for $237.00. He'd be stupid to tamper with these. Well, throw it all in a garbage can. Let happen what will....

On second thought, he wiped all prints off the wallet and shelved it into a mail-box. Maybe if Marty got those cards and things back he'd decide to forget tonight. Perhaps be afraid that his sex life would also be exposed if he didn't forget? Yeah, could be a good reason to hold onto the plastic bag. If Marty came after him he could dump this fake dick and fake pussy on a court-room table, and any judge would have to take a second look at Marty Gero. Leave Marty's fingerprints all over the crap.

He opened the bag gingerly. Again he was disappointed. One of the bullets had ripped into the huge wax penis and knocked it all out of whack. Well, hell. But there should still be a lot of Marty Gero's fingerprints on it, and as crazy as it seemed maybe it had been this false prick that had deflected the gun and the bullet and saved his life. Wasn't that a bitch. He kept going through the bag. At the bottom of it he spotted a package he hadn't noticed before. Tied securely, dirty white string, wrapped and tied over and over, a definite effort to keep the package secured. More crap? Careful to leave Marty's fingerprints, he unwrapped the package. Exactly. More crap. Possibly some kind of Spanish Fly. White powdered stuff. It was said you put it upon the tip of your penis and once you got inside a woman, she'd practically crawl a wall . . . so good it was. . . . But of what use was it to Marty Gero? Or how did it work on a man. . . ? Perhaps it wasn't Spanish Fly after all, but some other kind of aphrodisiac?

Winston hesitated, then lifted the package and sniffed cautiously. Nothing. He sniffed again, staring at the substance. A faint burning began at the tip of his nostrils, lanced up and nearly watered his eyes. He leaned back, a suspicion stealing over him. But he felt nothing more yet. He decided to take an even bigger sniff. This time the burning in his nostrils was stronger. After a few seconds a series of brilliant lights began to explode before his eyes. The top of his head felt lighter, and he could feel tension, at first resisting, then swimming in waves away from his body. Sonofabitch . . . he thought. Some kind of a drug? What? Cocaine? Heroin? Or one of those psychedelic acids? He knew so little about drugs. He had no idea which, but he was convinced it was a very powerful drug.

Although he felt light-headed, super-cool, and wanting to smile at nothing in particular, there was another thing he was convinced of, too. Whatever it was, it was undoubtedly worth a lot of money.

How much? $5,000.00? $10,000.00? $20,000.00? Or even more?

But he hated drugs. It was a thing he felt very strongly about—hated seeing drugs being pumped into Black neighborhoods, capturing children before they knew what life was all about, destroying the minds of an entire Black generation. Sometimes he was convinced that the dumping of the drugs might be a governmental policy, or that at least the government did not want the drug traffic stopped. Drugs dulled rebellious minds, kept the ghettos quiet from insurrection: like when the

Western Powers had dumped opium into China. Once the people were hooked they hadn't had to worry about revolts and revolutions anymore.... How otherwise explain why the government didn't stop the drug traffic?

So no matter how much this goddamn junk was worth he didn't want any part of it, couldn't be a part of it, destroying helpless children ... victimizing his own people. The only reason he didn't toss it into a garbage can immediately was because he figured he should throw it away where no one would find it, use it, right? Drive to the Hudson River and fling it into the Hudson. That many more children saved.... So what if the goddamn junk was worth $20,000—$40,000—or maybe even $50,000 bucks, he didn't want any part of dealing with it. It would be about the lowest a person could sink. And even if he didn't hate drugs he'd be a fool to try and hold onto it and sell it anyway.... Get caught with the junk and he'd certainly be in trouble. Best thing to do was get rid of it, this minute. If he opened the package and scattered it in a garbage can, wouldn't that do it? No one could use it.

He saw a couple of garbage cans up the block but he still didn't move. Instead, he finally started the car. He pulled away from the curb, convinced he was headed for the Hudson River. He wanted to be absolutely sure the drug would be lost forever and wasn't the river the best place in the world to lose it?

five

Patricia Wallstone had a horror of taking New York subway trains. It was like diving into an unclean pool, never sure how she'd come out again. Somewhere in the City some unknown children wanting to be known, wanting to be listened to, had crudely, garishly, painted their lives upon most of the trains; and the trains rumbled into sight like wounded monsters, bleeding an array of red and yellow and green and blue scrawls, every conceivable color, every conceivable message: JG is HIP!; THE DEAD BROTHERS; THE SCREAMING FALCONS; FUCK YOU AND YO MAMMY TOO!

The passengers themselves seemed like those young people who had done the writing, the painting, now grown up—still pleading for attention, for someone to call them, ask for Dottie, Sam, *me,* someone. Except that their faces were more tightly closed now, tensed; bodies weary, eyes wary; many of them already shattered but keeping on with a sort of belligerent desperation, not yet left behind forever at those faraway stops where the trains came from. . . .

Pat Wallstone went down the grimy steps to be enveloped by the fetid air, surrounded by tired sweaty people, staring people, sick-in-the-mind people, outraged people, perverted people, hard-working-down-to-the-bone people. At this stop, mostly Black people, but a few whites. Those few whites who still had not yet escaped to the world of taxi-cabs, automobiles, or away from a passage through Black worlds altogether.

Pat waited for the train, trying to keep herself composed, but everything made her more nervous this evening. Outwardly, she no doubt appeared composed and sure of herself—a slim, neatly dressed black girl, in a white blouse and dark green skirt, with a very youthful night black face, lit up by large luminous dark brown eyes. But inwardly, more or less as usual, she was going off in several directions. So many things seemed to be wrong, though there was no single thing she could put her finger on. Was she failing in school? Why hadn't she got up the courage to ask for more money for all the work she was loaded down with on her part-time job? How long would she continue to have to lie to Gru and fend him off? Was she really making any progress with Winston or deluding herself, and if so, or if not, would it be wise or unwise at this point to tell Winston that her monthly "friend" hadn't visited her yet and that she was already eight days over-due?

Most of the questions were vague, leaving no more than small pockets of anxiety. But the pockets seemed to expand at the slightest excuse, opening up great vacuums, into which even greater anxieties could rush.

At the moment, she was sure she was being stared at, critically. The suspicion winged into her already delicate security and left her self-conscious. She wanted to whip out a cigarette, do something with her hands, or find a spot where she could go unnoticed until the train came. But often these days when she thought she was being stared at no one was looking at her at all. Yet today she was positive it wasn't her imagination. Perhaps people had a genuine reason to stare, especially the men. Against her better judgment she had worn the green skirt. It was much too short and perhaps even her blouse was too sheer. . . . But she had on a bra so where was the problem? The skirt, of course, was Winston's fault. She would have felt more comfortable in slacks but he liked her in skirts and dresses. He thought her legs were beautiful. And she believed so little in her beauty to attract and hold him, and was so pleased when he found anything at all about her attractive, that she caught herself always wearing what she thought he wanted her to.

The train roared into sight and ground to a stop. She got on. She took a seat but realized almost at once that it was a mistake to sit. Eyes zeroed towards her knees. An old grey-haired man, a younger brown-skinned guy with an Afro, a red-headed freckle-faced white boy. . . . Excepting the old man, pretending they weren't looking. . . . Should she stand up? Uncross her legs? Burning with self-consciousness she did neither. She fumbled inside her handbag and brought out the newspaper Winston had asked her to bring him. She held the paper before her eyes and stared at the words. If the men still gazed stupidly at her knees she wasn't going to allow herself to be concerned about it. And she really should read the paper, keep up with what was going on in the world, as Winston was always telling her. But the words upon the paper made no sense yet, for her mind had now veered towards Winston. As usual she could almost see his face, hear his voice, as though he was right there in the subway car with her, blotting out everybody, everything, by the intensity of his presence. On the phone he had seemed to ramble irritably, but never admitting that he wanted to see her. Never, as always, willingly giving her much of anything of himself, as if to give in to feeling was a kind of weakness he couldn't afford and even felt threatened by. Sometimes it was a great strain to extract a response from him, to push him towards a show of affection.

Finally, she had said, "Do you need me, Winston? Do you want me to come to you?"

His silence had lasted so long she'd thought he'd end it by saying, no. No, he didn't need anyone. Never admitting he needed anyone, even those times when she knew that he did.

Then he had said, "Well, bring me a paper."

It was exasperating. Like as if the only reason he wanted her to come to him was to get a paper, as if this was all he would or could allow her or himself to believe he wanted. Not even asking her to bring the paper, telling her in the same gruff and irritable tone, ordering her. It was never ". . . Would you please, Pat, do this or that . . ." or ". . . Do you mind, Pat, doing that or this. . . ." It was always *do it.* Sometimes he ordered her to do something and she'd forget. Deliberately? Maybe her way of telling him, Please ask me nicely, Winston. I'm a person, too, you know, even if I am not as smart and clever as you are. Show me a little consideration and I'll do anything for you and you know that.

Now she tried to force herself to read the paper, get her mind off Winston. She had to keep up more with current events. One day she had had a moment's trouble remembering who had been the President of the country just before they had elected this new one. And Winston had stared at her in astonishment, gazing deeper into her secret fears, like she must be the dumbest, most stupid person in the world, and the proof of it was out in the open now.

"Listen, don't you ever read the papers, watch TV news?" He was really furious. "Aren't you concerned about what's going on in your own goddamn country?"

"Sure I do!" she said, defensive. "But why should I worry all the time about all of that stupid stuff when I got so much else to worry about? And whoever is President or in Congress or all that, it's all the same, ain't it? I don't see it making any difference to us!"

Winston was so annoyed, he jumped out of the bed, pacing the floor in disgust, locking her out, always locking her out when she crossed him, displeased him.

Though it embarrassed her, she found herself swallowing her pride and getting up out of the bed, also. She paced right along with him, touching him and trying to tease him, coax him into coming back to her.

"Okay. Okay," she had said. "Now you know how dumb I am! Right? I haven't bothered to read newspapers much, except about fashions, stuff like that. So you're right! You have every reason to be disgusted with me! I am disgusted with myself! But . . . but . . . from this day forward, I'm going to read a newspaper every day! Maybe two! Why not three! Maybe even four if I can find another one! You can test me. Ask me questions about politics and all that stuff and I intend to know. Everything! I don't blame you for being ashamed of me."

"Oh, for Christsakes!" Winston said in exasperation, trying to pace around her, both of them still nude, trying to keep his eyes away from her. "It's not a matter of . . ."

But she always knew when he had weakened, opened back up to her again. She slipped herself into his arms, trembling slightly, hoping that she wasn't wrong. . . .

"If you don't hate me, then please kiss me."

"My God," he said. "You're about the most impossible chick I've ever known!"

But he kissed her, and after that she had him back with her all over again.

Sometimes he was even gentler, sweeter, after silly spats like that; yet there were other times when there remained a deeply buried and resisting part of him that she didn't win back altogether, and that she wasn't always sure she ever would.

The newspaper headline concerned again the Washington Diplomat, the big shot guy Winston had gotten messed around over on the plane. The autopsy revealed the possibility of the Diplomat's neck having been broken *before* the car crashed, and the newspaper was still asking why hadn't the police found the chauffeur and the blonde actress, Trina Swan. The article continued in the middle of the paper and Pat's gaze zipped from the sales ad at Bloomingdale's and Macy's, back to the article and then back to the ads again. She found that she had paid $2.16 too much for a pair of slacks. Absolutely, unmistakably, the same identical slacks she could have gotten for less! It always upset her, finding that she had shopped badly, like she had been taken advantage of, especially now when she needed every cent to get through school. And as for that chauffeur and false blonde girl, it was rather clear. . . . She remembered the chauffeur as having been a fairly handsome guy. White women were resorting to all kinds of tricks these days. No sooner did a Black man start to get himself together, fight his way upwards, not even as high as Winston, and there they were, exposing their breast, legs, white smiling all over the place, and grabbing everything they could. As far as she was concerned, when they found the chauffeur they could be sure they'd find the blonde. . . . She looked at a blouse. No bra type. But she had a suspicion Winston wouldn't like it. In some things he was pretty old-fashioned and if he made up his mind he didn't like something you couldn't change him, not one bit.

Something smelly and creepy was now sitting beside her. She sensed rather than saw a man trying to press his leg against her thigh. She had tensed up, staring at the paper, unseeing. Then she felt his fingers, dangling above her bare shoulder. She stood up, angry, embarrassed—but was it her fault? If she hadn't worn the dress. . . . When the doors slid open, she walked out. She needed to change to the Local anyway, but hadn't meant to do so until Fifty-ninth Street, Columbus Circle. . . . Now it would take her longer to get to Winston's stop. Well, let him be angry, she thought. "Black people always late," she could hear him say. "Be late for their own goddamn funeral! Why don't you start out a half hour earlier, Pat, then maybe you can get off this CP time?"

So be angry, Pat thought. I don't care! You're always angry with me anyway, she could hear herself telling him, about this or that, or that and this and any old thing. Up there and safe in your apartment while I have to fight the subway and come to you! Well, maybe one day you'll whistle and I won't hear it. There are other fish in the sea!

She paced the platform, surprised at the sudden depth of her anger. Then it vanished, almost as though she had suppressed it, leaving her feeling vaguely guilty, uncertain. Who was she kidding? Minute she let Winston go, somebody else would grab him, and then where would she be? Never in her life had she met anybody like Winston, a Black man who knew what he wanted and allowed nothing to stop him from getting it. All the Black men she had known before, even including Gru, had been defeated, accepted a compromise, or lived from day to day from one big dream to another, dreams that slowly wilted before reality. Ending up in the post office or cooks or porters or waiters, working eight hours a day to make other men rich. While Winston intended to be rich himself. "No one ever got anywhere working for another man," he always said. "You got to take a chance. Go out there for yourself." And going out there for himself, too. Except sometimes he seemed so fanatical about it, cruel, ruthless. . . . Upset her, frightened her. . . .

Still, she'd be crazy if she didn't hang onto him as long as she knew she had a chance. And often these days she sensed she was getting deeper into him than even he, himself, knew.

Pat paused at a broken vending machine, glass shattered, slots for gum, candy ripped out, the pennies, nickles, dimes disappeared, the machine unrepaired forever now, like most of the vending machines and public telephones, vandalized throughout the City.

Through the fragments of glass she could barely see her reflection, the dark oval face and large dark brown eyes, topped by a boyish Afro. As she pulled out her comb and touched her hair, a couple of more worries zeroed in. The other day had she allowed her hair to be cut too short? The guy had begun cutting and hadn't known when to quit. And what was Winston going to think when he saw that not only had she had her hair cut again, but that she had also had an extra hole pierced in her ears? Or would he even notice, the hair or the fact that she was wearing a double set of earrings? Could be so preoccupied by "business" he wouldn't notice anything.

Except her hair, maybe. She always thought her hair was as thick as some kind of wire, but he liked to touch it. Preferred it natural to a wig. She had shopped like crazy to find the beautiful wig she had worn to meet him at the airport, but it had turned him off.

"Don't you like it?" she heard herself say.

"Well."

"Come on! I spent my lunch money for weeks. But if you don't like it?"

He decided to be funny.

"Can you get a refund?"

"Don't be silly!"

"Yeah. Well, It's okay. However.... Nevertheless.... Etcetera . . . and so on. . . ."

"Which means you don't like it?"

"Not really."

Finished with the fun.

She was doing her lips, had shadowed her eyes a bit more, when it got creepy behind her again. Mostly whites at this subway stop and the few Blacks, more subdued, hidden behind cool stares and frozen faces, seemed to be conscious of it.

She turned swiftly and stared into the blue eyes of the red-headed freckle-faced boy. Had he followed her from other train? Had he been the creepy one sitting beside her, fingers easing towards her breast? No. She was getting a different reaction, a different vibration from him. In fact, all the creepiness went away and she simply felt tensed, hostile, often a feeling that came automatically when she was in the presence of whites these days.

The young man was staring at her apologetically, embarrassed. Two red spots colored his freckled cheeks. Even though she was tensed against contact, she noticed that he was dressed decently, that his golden hair had been recently combed, flowing down neatly to touch his collar but not too long, and that instead of a freckled-faced sex hungry boy he might be closer to her own age.

"Excuse me," he said, his voice shaky with embarrassment. "You don't know me . . . but I've seen you on Campus. I just want to say it's nice, it's great, it's always great to . . . to . . . see you."

When she continued to stare at him stonily, half-frightened, uncertain, the color grew deeper in his cheeks.

"I'm sorry," he stammered. "But it was a surprise . . . and . . . great to see you. . . . And well . . . thank you. Excuse me . . . see you again sometime."

Abruptly, awkwardly, he turned and went up the steps.

She let out her breath.

Well, what the devil was that all about? Still, why had she been so uptight? Some guy from school, most natural thing in the world that he should say hello, even though she didn't remember ever seeing him. But had that been all he wanted, just a desire to say hello? Then why so nervous? Like maybe from a distance he had been watching her on Campus. . . . Well, he wasn't really bad looking, now that she thought about it. And he had seemed like a rather decent kind of guy, too. Despite herself, now that she felt less tense, she found her spirit lifting. Wait till she told Winston! No matter how hard she tried to ignore it, she knew very well that Winston didn't always sleep alone when she wasn't around, so who knew—she might start playing the same game herself.

"Oh, I ran into this fellow from school . . ." Could hear herself say. "Quite handsome guy, white boy, you know. And can you imagine, he came up to me and admitted that he had noticed me for a very long time! He was so shy and sweet that I listened to him, but of course I don't take such things seriously."

Slip it into the conversation like it meant nothing, like maybe she had so many admirers Winston had better watch out, sometimes don't think about business and winning so much, but think about her at least half as much as she thought about him. Slip it to him, remind him that she wasn't exactly a zero and he should understand that.

Except that she'd better not say the boy was white. Really blow his stack behind that, she knew. Like he felt he was in a battle with the white world all day and then at night would have to battle against the image of a white man in his own bed. But what about his white bitches? Pat thought angrily. The gall some men had! She knew very well Winston had been involved with white women, though she had no definite proof of it. So how did he think he could do what he didn't want her to do? Maybe she'd have to see about that!

Two lights appeared down the darkened tunnel, getting brighter, and then the Local emerged and came to a halt. It was crowded and she pushed her way in and backed against a wall, so that no one could get behind her. Almost every day some perverted man attempted to press himself against a woman, get himself a dry screw. Women were often so frightened, they simply stood there and took it. A few braver women would jab their heels into the guys' feet, elbows into their ribs. . . .

Her back to the wall, she didn't have to be brave or humiliated. She only had to look out for the front, and right before her luckily not a man but a Puerto Rican woman with a baby. Cute baby, plump as it could be, with fat little cheeks, and black sparkling eyes. The mother looked harassed, tired, bloated by misuse and defeats, while the baby smiled, tried baby-talk, spittle dripping happily from its lips, full of life, promise. . . . Pat smiled and a rush of warmth went through her. The warmth became a longing, an ache.

"Why don't you want a child?" she had asked Winston.

"No time."

"And if I became pregnant?"

"Don't."

She bit her lip, looked away from the baby. She almost wanted to cry. A man wouldn't meet her eyes, sitting comfortably in one of the seats. Bastard wouldn't get up and allow the poor woman and the baby to sit. Sometimes she was stunned, people in the City, all over the world, seemed so inconsiderate, cruel.

Yes, perhaps Winston would have stood and allowed the woman to sit, but then he would have taken advantage of the woman in other ways. Charging high rents in those slum buildings he had bought from that guy, Bernie Stein. Dispossessing, Evicting. . . .

One day she had heard him on the phone angrily telling Donald, "Give them another week. Then get the Marshal in there and put their goddamn furniture in the streets! And, listen, don't bother me with this petty bull-shit! If tenants don't pay, use the normal procedure!" Slamming the phone down, irritated, furious with Donald, who never seemed to learn anything fast enough, with poor Black and Puerto Rican tenants, but maybe most of all furious with himself. Still, he wouldn't slow down, wouldn't allow himself to care, as if now he couldn't slow down or allow himself to care. He went right on amassing mortgages, bank accounts, more buildings, whatever he could get his hands on. Watching him "doing business," he took on an attitude that was so ruthless and cold-blooded, he seemed almost like a stranger to her.

There was especially one day of "business" she had witnessed when she had jumped into the car with him and Donald and Gru that she'd never forget. It was a few days after he came back from Europe, and he hadn't yet closed down his office in Brooklyn. She had used some excuse to get by the office, making sure she'd get there before Winston left for home. She found him sitting on the edge of a desk, speaking impatiently to Donald and Gru, his tone barely concealing contempt, and perhaps a strange kind of fear, too. Fear that he was falling, falling, and had no one around that he could depend on to help him regain solid ground. He was outraged and puzzled—how could Gru go to the expense of setting up an office with ten phones and costly paneling everywhere, and four extra desk spaces that no one would ever use, and indirect lighting and carpet on the floors, and a goddamn Caddie sedan whose motor would hardly turn over—go to all this expense but forget to renew a lia*bility insurance policy*? How in the hell could Gru explain this? A bathroom ceiling had fallen on a child. Didn't Gru know what the fuck that meant? A law-suit for maybe as much as $100,000 bucks! And what smart lawyer would settle for much less? Tie up all of his property, everything, a wipe out! And this was only one of the problems Gru had allowed to crop up.

So she was there when the tense silence descended between them, wanting to talk brightly about this or that, about how she had gotten eighty-five on an exam and wasn't that pretty good for an old woman, eh? But she said nothing, intimidated by the tension and the silence, and since she didn't know what else to do when they stormed out and piled into the car, she got in, too. Donald was driving again, nostrils quivering with anger but not quite daring to express it, Gru smoking airily, blowing smoke rings, like good God why did Winston make such a big fuss over this small crap, already dreaming of some bigger deal in case Winston went broke, Gru who would set up an "office" on Park Avenue if he got the chance, even if there was nothing to buy or sell, and no one in the office but Gru himself and his phones and his dreams. . . .

Donald didn't even attempt to disguise the problem he was having getting the Caddie into gears and at red lights the sound of the brakes was also nerveracking. But soon they were in a section of Brooklyn, Williamsburg or somewhere, on a street one of the worst she had ever seen. All the buildings looked as though they had been through a war, bombed, assaulted by flame-throwers, half of them torn down or falling down, gutted, vacant lots strewn with garbage, fat green flies rushing towards the car and bouncing against the windows, Black and Puerto Rican children yelling and running after the car, junkies milling about the corners, older people sitting nervously in door-ways.

Donald brought the Caddie to a halt before one of the buildings.

Winston looked out at the grimy structure as though he could vomit.

"Is this it?" he said.

Donald seemed almost happy to tell him, "Yeah."

Though he owned it, there was the possibility Winston had never seen the building. It was just an address, a figure on a piece of paper, part of one of those "packages" she always heard him talking about on the phone. He stared at the building, —broken windows, uncollected garbage, people crowding the stoop—, with an expression of both distaste and embarrassment.

"How old is the child that got hurt?" he asked, strangely chastened.

"Man, what does that matter now?" Gru said impatiently. "Since you insisted on coming down here, we better get on in and see what we can do. But I still think it's a waste of time. Man, what the professionals would have done in a case like this would have been to wait for their lawyer to call, and then sit down with the lawyer and make a deal. Lawyers are only

69

interested in paying their own rent and eating anyway. We could have given the cat a few thousand bucks for himself and gotten this whole thing settled."

Winston's face had hardened. He wasn't any longer listening to Gru. "Okay," he finally said, abruptly. "Let's go in." Then he seemed to notice her for the first time that day. "Pat, wait in the car."

But she didn't. Afraid both maybe of the neighborhood and what was going to happen to Winston inside that building. She got out. She followed them, feeling hostility all around, conscious that she was dressed better, ate better, lived better than most of these people ever would, trying not to feel guilty about it, still afraid. Winston and Gru, in their natty Summer suits, pushed their way past the people on the stoop, like some kind of Lords, Kings, like the way only White people used to do. Donald in his sport shirt waved hello to a few people. They knew him, and though he was the one most often down here pressuring people to pay rent, no one seemed to dislike him, and Donald was pleased that they knew him, and especially that they didn't seem to dislike him, or if they did dislike him had better sense than to try and do anything about it.

Up rickety stairs, beer cans, cigarette butts, sour smells, a Black man lying drunk, shattered, defeated, on the second floor landing, a couple of kids playing around him, not even seeing him anymore.

They halted before a garishly painted green door. Winston wet his lips, his face ruthless with tension.

Gru pounded loudly upon the door.

"¿Quién es?"

"Landlord!" Gru shouted.

A brown-skinned, timid-faced, Puerto Rican man cracked the door and then opened it wider.

"Come in. Come in. I have just this minute returned from the doctor with my daughter."

"How is she?" Gru interrupted, strolling into the tiny two rooms apartment boldly, briskly, possibly to show Winston how to solve this thing, now that they were here, get it done with. "Hi, there!" he called to one of the little children. There were about six of them, crowded here and there around the cheap furniture, the mother perhaps the short fat sad-eyed woman standing near the stove. "You kids look okay to me! No one seems hurt at all!" He tickled a little boy under the chin, who looked as if he was about to cry, run away.

"No, Señor," the man said. "My daughter who is hurt is now sleeping."

The man led them to the small crib next to the window. The child that had been injured lay there with her tiny lips still puckered as though she had cried herself to sleep. A bandage covered a spot to the upper left side of her face, above the ear, where her curly black hair had been shaved. It was a relatively small bandage, but who could really tell how badly the child had been hurt?

Winston stared at the child, perspiration beading his forehead. He seemed stunned, one of the first times she had seen him when his mind wasn't working, racing, planning, plotting.

Gru stammered, but blustered, "Well . . . er . . . Well, I mean, it doesn't look as if she's hurt that badly!"

"But you never know with a child!" she heard herself exclaim.

Winston turned slowly and looked at her sharply, icily, and she caught herself. Now she could see that he was getting himself together and that his mind was beginning to race and work after all. Whose goddamn side was she on? his cold gaze seemed to say. This child could topple him.

He ceased staring at her, his face hardening again. What sympathy that had softened it for the child was now vanishing. His eyes behind the tinted glasses had begun to dart about like animals in a trap, surrounded by enemies, strike first, at someone, anyone, at her, too, or he would be struck down forever. . . .

Still Winston was silent, as though a part of himself was still numb, paralyzed. There didn't seem to be any way out. Except do the right thing. Take care of the child. Perhaps it wouldn't cost him everything. After all, wasn't it only fair that he should face up to his responsibility to the little girl?

It was Gru who kept talking, putting his arm around the father's shoulder, comradely, voice syrupy, speaking confidentially, "Look, you seem like an intelligent man. Why don't we sit down and hash this thing out and see if we can't work out some kind of a deal?"

The father shrugged Gru's arm from around his shoulder. "What do you mean, Señor? A deal for my daughter's life? This is a serious matter. Have you a child who cries away her pain before sleeping?"

Winston mopped his face, turned his back and walked into the bathroom. She followed, feeling helpless, torn between concern for Winston and sympathy for the child and the child's poor family. She wanted to say to Winston—even if you go broke, have no money at all, nothing, I will love you anyway, Winston. I'll stop school and get a full time job and we can both work very hard and start all over again. But he didn't look around at her again, everything closed out but that desperate worm in his brain, win at all cost, squirming, frightened now, but the more vicious, always the more vicious when he found himself threatened, trapped.

Winston gazed at the great gaping hole in the ceiling from where the plaster had fallen, then at the leaky shower, broken tile, tub full of clothing to be washed, the gaudily flowered shower curtains, roaches rushing to conceal themselves within the walls. The others followed him to the bathroom, crowding the door, Gru annoyed, disgusted with the father now; Donald with his arms folded across his chest, not asking for any trouble but ready if some damn fool was crazy enough to start something.

Suddenly Winston seemed to come alive. A faint smile flashed across his face but she doubted if anyone noted the smile but her. It was that brief; then it was gone, but she knew what it meant. The desperate little animal in his brain had possibly glimpsed a way out. Despite herself she felt a flush of excitement. Though she considered what she called the worm in Winston's brain something basically evil, destructive, she nevertheless found herself stimulated when Winston was caught up by it. A sort of intense glow came over him, made him seem more alive, vital, than anyone she had ever known. The glow reached out and warmed her, caressed her, almost sexual.

Winston swung about and stared at the father dramatically.

"Okay," he demanded. "What kind of game are you playing, fellow?"

"¿Señor?"

"Come on, Mister!" Winston said fiercely. "You've been deliberately and systematically destroying my property, causing an accident to your own child, and now expect to blackmail me into paying you for it!"

"I don't understand," the father said uncertainly.

"He doesn't understand," Winston mocked, his tone harsh, even outraged, looking at Gru. "You hear him? He doesn't understand!"

"Well," Gru hesitated, trying to see where Winston was coming from. But Gru didn't understand either. Perhaps no one did, not even Winston himself, especially Winston himself. Desperation had simply pushed him to attack. And it was possible that even he was not exactly sure what he was going to say or do next, sensing only that he must continue his offensive at all cost now that he had started it.

She didn't think anyone but herself saw Winston hesitate. A flicker of self-doubt or a stall for time while he got his thoughts together? Then all the ruthless fire in him seemed to get concentrated again.

He swung about and pointed to the shower curtain rod attached clumsily to the wall with an emphasis so intense, it was as though he was bringing everyone's attention to a ticking bomb. "If you don't understand," he demanded of the father. "Then who put this up?"

The father bristled.

"I did, Señor. But not to destroy property! I call your office to have my shower fixed, but though I pay rent no one comes. No one ever comes to fix anything, only to collect money. So I fix it myself!"

"And weakened my ceiling in the process!" Winston accused. "Effecting a . . . a . . . structural change without the permission of the owner. Causing plaster to fall!"

"Right!" Gru caught on, cleared his throat. "Right! Not only willfully and criminally--and it is criminal, let there be no doubt about that—defacing property without the owner's express permit, but fraudulently claiming—and it is fraud, in case you don't know it—that the owner is at fault for an accident that in fact you brought about with your own hands! In all of my years in business—and I go way back, I've done business with some of the biggest boys you can find Downtown, in the City, in the State, Professionals! *I'm known,* I know what I'm talking about—in all of my business years I don't think I've ever seen anything worst than this flagrant, outright criminal attempt at

73

blackmail, undermining the very foundation upon which justice and truth must stand and prevail, if we are all to survive!" He paused for breath, then added, "And . . . and . . . after all, aren't we all Black and Puerto Rican here?"

"Precisely!" Winston cut in. Sometimes Gru didn't know when to quit once he got wound up. "Yes, you are correct, Mr. Gru," Winston went on, his tone suddenly conciliatory. "But I am sure the gentleman here is beginning to realize that it is not he but us who have been wronged. And, of course, I could sue. It is my right. It is my property that has been damaged, but I am not an unreasonable man. . . . As you so aptly put it, Mr. Gru, we are all Black and Puerto Rican here. And poor. So why should we fight each other? Now I am willing to work out a compromise. If claims are dropped against me, I see no reason to press claims against anyone else!"

Angrily the father looked from Gru to Winston.

"But I am guilty of nothing! I fix my shower. For many months before this the ceiling was ready to fall. Always a leak up there but nobody comes to fix! You know in your hearts this is true, Señores. And my little daughter was in the shower when the plaster fell. It is lucky she is not blind. This thing cannot be my fault. I have telephoned my lawyer and he has said justice is on my side!"

Winston hardly looked at the father, staring instead at the ceiling now, eyes averted, totally concentrated. Clearly the installation of the curtain rod would have had little to do with the plaster falling. Yet would logic as simple as this effect Winston's attitude? Undoubtedly not. In a moment he climbed upon the edge of the tub and began measuring the distance between the rod and the gaping hole, using his hands dramatically. Then he climbed down and shook his head somberly, wearily.

"Okay, Donald, dash out to the car and bring in the camera."

"Huh?" Donald mumbled. "Camera?"

Donald didn't pick up; he stared at Winston.

"No. Wait," Winston said, frowning. "Maybe I can explain it to the gentleman this way. Cameras don't lie," he told the father quietly, patiently, only faintly exasperated. "Now when we take these pictures into court, any judge is going to start thinking about cause and effect. Get that? Cause and effect. Now our claim is that you—perhaps not intentionally, you seem like a decent man—caused the accident. Your claim is that our negligence caused it. Sir, what I am trying to tell you is that any fair-minded judge is going to laugh your lawyer right out of the court-room when we present . . . well, our evidence that . . ."

"That is incontestable, irrefutable!" Gru cut in. "Evidence that no judge, or even jury, can deny! In fact, this reminds me of a case I was involved in several years ago. . . . Now I'm not a lawyer, but I know my law—ask any of the big boys still around and taking care of business and they will confirm that— We came into court with pictures and the judge instantly spotted the shabby dastardly attempt at blackmail, and not only exonerated me and my people—people that I was at that time representing in my capacity as Business Consultant—but fined the Plaintiff right on the spot for daring to sully his court-room by bringing in such an insulting and shabby case!"

"But justice is on my side!" the father exclaimed again, so angry he could hardly get his words out. "When I see my lawyer he will surely understand what to do about this!"

Winston's thick black eyebrows rose a trifle. He exchanged a swift glance with Gru but almost as quickly concealed his thoughts.

"Oh," he said, his tone deceptively matter-of-fact. "You didn't meet with your lawyer yet?"

"How can I get all things done? I have been so busy with my poor daughter, that you would insult! But I have been well advised of my rights, Señor, by telephone and I shall see my lawyer tomorrow!"

"If you insist," Winston said, with a show of indifference.

Then he pushed past everyone and went back into the combination living room, bedroom, and kitchen. He removed a toy from a chair and sat down at the cheap dining table. He mopped his face again and then brought out his pen and finally found a scrap of paper. Remarkably calm, nothing betraying him except the perspiration dripping off the tip of his nose, he began to put down and add up a column of figures.

Everyone had followed him and now stood around him uncertainly, almost embarrassed. Finally Gru made a great show of being democratic too and sat down in one of the chairs, trying vainly to ignore a baby roach crawling not very far from his sleeve.

Winston said nothing. A child whimpered. The mother stirred a pot on the stove. The father was still ready to fight, but who was there to combat in all of this silence? Donald had his arms folded across his chest, glaring at everyone, but mostly at Winston. Where in the hell did Winston get off, putting him on the spot about some goddamn camera!

Winston had filled up the piece of paper with figures. He leaned back, and pointed slowly to the paper as though it contained irrefutable conclusions, was as sacred as the bible, and though written by Winston himself he had been only a sort of instrument in putting the figures down.

"Okay," he said quietly to the father, again with barely a hint of exasperation. "Sir, allow me to try and reach you in another way. You sue me, the maximum you can sue for is about ten thousand bucks, you know that, don't you?"

Did the father know that? Hardly. Did Winston? If $10,000 was the maximum, what had happened to the $100,000 mentioned at the office? "All right," Winston went on. "So suppose your lawyer pushes his luck and asks for a few thousand more, what would you get? Even if I was a rich man and could pay off, your lawyer would screw you out of one half of it, and the rest you'd have to pay for medical bills. But I will not pay off. I don't have the money. I'll have to declare bankruptcy and then what will you get, nothing! Plus, of course, I shall be suing you for having driven me to bankruptcy. I got down here in black and white where I got the legitimate right to sue you for $18,000. Destruction of property, intentionally or not; the anguish I've been caused because of your false claim. But don't get me wrong, why should we be vindictive with each other? Why bring in lawyers at all? In the end, the lawyers are going to grab all the money and leave us with nothing! Sir, I have a proposal here that should satisfy both of us. I don't sue you, you don't sue me. We work out a mutual agreement. Are you willing to listen to my proposal?"

The father gazed at the paper with angry suspicion, hesitated, then said emphatically, "No. I see my lawyer."

"Sir," Winston frowned. "At least have the wisdom to . . ."

Gru jumped up, declared belligerently, "If he doesn't want to listen, I'll go out and get the camera myself!"

"No. No," Winston said. "Take it easy, Mr. Gru. We are all civilized here and prepared to be reasonable!" Then he turned to the father. "Are you a Welfare recipient, Sir?"

"Yes," he admitted reluctantly.

"Good," Winston said, promptly. "Another reason why you should hear me out. Now here is what I can do for you. First, I agree to withdraw my suit against you and, of course, I'm willing to put that in writing. Second, I shall arrange for all medical expenses to be paid for the child. Third, if you will also put in writing that you have no intent of suing I'm prepared to make you a cash settlement."

"How much?" the father demanded cautiously.

Winston hesitated. She watched him anxiously. At least $5,000.00 she thought. At least be a little fair to the people.

"Well, let me see . . ." Winston said. "How much cash do you have on you, Gru?"

"Forty bucks," Gru said.

"And you, Donald?"

Donald mumbled that he had about seventeen dollars.

"And . . . er . . . what do you have, Pat?"

"Six dollars," she said, embarrassed. But what was he getting at?

Winston shrugged, regarded the father warily, apologetically.

"Well, I have around a hundred. Looks like we have only about a hundred and sixty-three bucks between us."

"And this you think I take for my child's accident!" The father was livid. "Never!"

"Wait. Wait," Winston held up his hands. "Take it easy. Did I say that was my final offer? However, Sir, you must be prepared to bend a little, too—compromise. Now here is as far as I can go. $163.00 in American cash, responsibility for the child's medical bills, withdrawal of my suit against you—and you're saving money there, too—you got to figure that in—plus, I'm going to give you this apartment for three months rent free, three months when you pay no rent at all, nothing!"

The father stared at this offer for a couple of seconds only and then rejected it also angrily, "No. Never!"

Winston's brow furrowed, as though he was suddenly angry himself, or faking it.

"Sir, I don't see how we're going to do any business! Okay, go to your lawyer. You will come out with nothing. Zero! I'm trying to be fair. Now here is my final offer. Instead of three months rent free, I'm going to give you six, six whole months! And to show you what kind of guy I am, I'm going to write you a check for an additional $100.00 bucks. Now how does that sound?"

The father glanced briefly at his wife but she said nothing. Apparently he was calculating the rent money he would save, the original amount of cash and the extra hundred bucks, weighing it against all the mysteries that would confront him in dealing with lawyers and judges and courts, and perhaps thinking if he didn't take some kind of offer he could end up with nothing as Winston had said.

"Not enough," he said, but his anger had weakened. "Also, my rent is Welfare, two-party check."

"Doesn't matter," Winston said at once. "We'll cash the checks and give the money back to you. And hell, okay, I'll give you two more months. That means eight months rent free!"

"No," the father frowned. "For this rat-trap, not worth it. I think I still see my lawyer."

"For Christsakes!" Winston's anger was suddenly almost real. "What do you want? What more can I give?"

The father hesitated.

"Well, one year rent free. No, no, *two* years rent free! Three hundred dollar check and the cash and the medical bills!"

Winston's anger vanished, but he kept cool, shaking his head as though the father was now asking the impossible.

"Ten months rent free," he said. "And a two hundred dollar check."

"No," the father said firmly. "At least one year and one half rent free and a two hundred and . . . and . . . fifty dollar check!"

Winston's shoulders sagged, as though he was beaten. "You drive a hard bargain," he said. "Are you sure you will not come down a little more, at least meet me half-way?"

"Never!"

78

"Okay," Winston conceded tiredly. "I know when I have to take a loss. Now if we can write up an agreement and we both sign it. . . . Mr. Gru do you have a piece of paper?"

One of the few times Gru didn't have his note book and paper with him. Donald didn't have any paper either; nor she. Winston ended up writing out the agreement on a couple of lined sheets from one of the children's school tablets. He signed that he wasn't going to sue the father and that he agreed to all the other terms and then it was the father's turn to sign that he wasn't going to sue and that he agreed to the terms.

The father took the pen, but the mother came out of her stony silence and said, "I don't trust this."

"What?" the father said, holding the pen. Then he said, "Shut up. What can I do?"

But he kept hesitating before scrawling his name and Winston had to practically guide his hand towards the paper to get the signature down. Then Winston collected all the cash and wrote the check, and shook the man's hand firmly, solemnly, earnestly, still implying the man had gotten himself a beautiful deal.

Outside, safely away in the car, he laughed, but strangely without joy, as though he was even depressed.

"My God, poor people are such damn fools! How can they ever win?"

* * *

As the subway slowed for her stop, Pat smiled at the baby one last time. She had wanted to take her handkerchief and wipe the spittle from the child's tiny beautiful mouth, but she had been afraid to do it. The gesture could have been misunderstood, frightening the mother. The mother thinking she meant to harm the baby. People were so distrustful of one another in New York. You said, "Good morning" to someone and instantly the reaction was, "What are you after?" checking to see if his or her wallet or pocketbook was still intact. No one friendly anymore; each person living in his own frightened and isolated little world.

She was pleased that the baby's bright black eyes followed her and that the baby waved and waved and even squirmed around in the mother's arms and watched her as she got off the train, sorry to see her go. When she waved back this time she saw that the mother was even smiling, also.

Up out of the subway the fresher air met her and she sucked in a deep and grateful breath of it. Trees lined the wide street, angle parking before the upper income apartment houses. Before the entrance to the building where Winston lived she saw one of the blue-uniformed guards, holding a giant police dog on leash. The dog's malevolent eyes regarded a youngster walking slowly past the building, perhaps too slowly. For except for the fact that the youngster carried what seemed like a violin case, he didn't seem to belong to this street of well-dressed, affluent-looking people; dirty levis, old tennis shoes, and above all a black youngster when most of the tenants in the area were white. . . .

She always felt a bit guilty when she entered the building, and yet at the same time a kind of pride that her man lived up there somewhere at the very top and that she had the right to be admitted without anyone staring or challenging her.

The guard recognized her and nodded respectfully. The dog dismissed her as okay, still watching the young boy who had paused at the subway entrance. He had suddenly bent heavily at the knees as though just then having been jolted towards a deep sleep. He lingered there for an instant before bouncing alert again; then looking around himself in frustration, he disappeared into the subway.

She entered the vestibule and buzzed Winston's bell, waiting for what was always the shock of his voice over the intercom, thinking: the kid probably stole the violin somewhere or perhaps his poor struggling mother had sent him to take violin lessons and he had spent the money on drugs. . . . Sad when drugs had captured so many young people. Someone trapped by drugs in almost every black family in the City. Made you angry, want to blow your top. Especially when everyone knew who was dumping drugs into the country. "Big shot white criminals," Winston had said. "And they get away with it because they pay off everyone, all the way to the top. . . ." Sad. Older folks getting rich, while dooming children. That boy hadn't looked sixteen years old. Hadn't lived at all yet.

But where was Winston?

"Yeah?" the voice finally came down from the twentieth floor, gruff, cautious.

"Me," she said. "Pat." Thinking: Well, still not in a good mood, right? The way his voice sounded. Well, why had he agreed that they should see each other today then? Because she had persisted? No, probably not. She sensed it had something to do with the Jew, Bernie Stein, the guy he had bought buildings from and who he kept talking about again lately. Some new deal he was about to get into, a deal that would solve everything, put him back on solid ground again. . . . Except that it seemed Bernie Stein's lawyer had called and broken an appointment.

The door buzzed and she entered. Spotlessly clean lobby, murals of white doves and blue lakes and deep green forests. The elevator opened soundlessly, closed without sound.

She tried to relax. But the closer she got to Winston's floor, the greater her tension. Sometimes she thought she should end this affair, and never see him again. Always when she thought she had just about won him over, had beaten down all resistance, and could be completely sure of him, she found him wiggling away from her again. It forced her to fight harder, kept her in a strain, sometimes even planning conversations she would have with him before she saw him, so that she wouldn't run the risk of boring him with idle chatter.

It was exhausting, kept her nerves on edge. But what could she do? If she dropped Winston there were a lot of Sisters and certainly white chicks that would snap him up before she was even halfway out of his bed.

She got off the elevator, tension pushing her towards a kind of anger. If Bernie Stein hadn't broken an appointment with him today, would he have agreed to see her this evening? Substitute for a business appointment, how was that supposed to make her feel? Upset because of Bernie Stein, he needed her to be close to him. But maybe she was being unfair? Could be one of those times when he wanted to see her, for her, no motives, except just needing her, loving her . . .

She pushed the bell and heard the chimes echo inside. After what seemed like an endless time he opened the door.

Before he could say anything she found herself closing her eyes and going into his arms. For a moment his response was tentative, almost reluctant, then he held on to her as tightly as she held on to him.

six

The first time Winston had met Bernie Stein he realized how very little he knew about "business." The meeting came on the same day he also met Patricia Wallstone. Gru, whom he had known for a few months, brought her to the Contract at Bernie Stein's office. It was a crazy, exciting day; first to meet the sharpest business man he had encountered so far, and next to find himself face to face with a girl who seemed like everything he had ever secretly longed for. Almost immediately he was sure he had finally found what he had nearly lost hope of ever finding, what some men called their Eena, or even their Lorelei. To him he believed Pat Wallstone might be his Black Princess at last.

That she was Gru's girl presented a problem. At first. At that time he still had a very deep respect for Gru. He had not yet heard the term—among many others— applied to Gru by some of Gru's closest friends and associates, "Long on promises, but goddamn short on performances!" It took time to see through the bluster, the projected self-importance of a guy like Gru. Especially when Gru seemed to fill his own desperate need so well: a man who appeared to know *everything* about business when he, Winston, though he had now struggled and humiliated himself to get money, still didn't know what to do with it, how to invest it wisely. It was Gru who found this first "package" of buildings. Bernie Stein was selling off some properties and buying others. Gru had known Stein for a number of years. They went "way back together . . ." according to Gru. So, Gru said, he knew for a fact Stein was very eager to sell, was reorganizing his own packages. If Winston hurried and got into this thing right now, he could pick up ten or twelve buildings and save a small fortune. Gru, of course, would act as "Business Consultant," and no Real Estate broker would be necessary either. Gru would act as Broker also. He was going to cut all the corners, save Winston money. And since Winston had met no one else who appeared to know half as much about business as Gru, he began to go along with Gru, taking Gru increasingly seriously, even though he had moments of doubt.

At lunch with Gru, expensive East Side cafe, Gru's choice, Gru puffing on a tiny brown cigar and putting more figures upon the massive sheets of paper he had already filled with other figures, diagrams, charts, projections. . . .

"Yeah, yeah, that's it!" Gru finally said, eyes bright and dreamy with excitement. "Got this problem solved! Instead of $213,000 total price we're going to beat Bernie down to $202,000! It'll save you $11,000 bucks! How do you like that?" He poked Winston with his elbow. "Old Gru is still pretty sharp, right? Didn't lose my touch yet, huh? And, Man, this is just the beginning! On top of this package, in several months, I'll have you picking up another one. And on top of that package, we'll stack still another! Pyramid this thing all the way to the top! That's the way the Big Boys do it. And before you know it, I'll have you knocking at the door of the Stock Exchange, going Public!"

"Listen," Winston cautioned, "I just want to be sure to come out of this thing with a decent income. I want to relax a little now, take life a little easier."

"Then relax!" Gru stated. "We'll sail through this Contract with Bernie tomorrow and then go for a quick Closing and after that you can take off. Grab yourself a plane and go to South America or Paris, anywhere. Live it up! And don't worry about a thing while you're gone. I'll take care of business. That's my speciality. I used to have an office with seven salesmen under me. I could walk into a bank and on my signature alone pick up $5000.00 bucks. But, of course, I had this little problem. . . . People envied me. That was the crux of it. Otherwise, I'd be on Wall Street by now. You have nothing to worry about. By the time you come back, I'll have the second package of buildings lined up!"

The waitresses were all very beautiful in the cafe and scantily dressed and Gru joked with the waitresses and smoked his tiny brown cigars and looked around himself expansively. Other business men, all white, ate quietly, occasionally speaking in low tones of possibly even greater deals.

The check came and Gru was just a bit embarrassed. But not for very long.

"Er . . . I'm a trifle short on cash. Take care of the bill and I'll leave the tip."

Left a quite generous tip, making sure the girl saw it, capturing her smile and thanks. Then he led Winston out as though he, if not Winston, was already worth a couple of million bucks, was part of the world of the "Big Boys."

The next day, at that first meeting with Bernie Stein, both Gru and Bernie were late; Gru out of an incurable habit; Bernie Stein, as Winston learned later, out of pure strategy.

At that time, Bernie Stein's office had still been located in Brooklyn, in a forty family building with several stores and offices on the first and second floors. Gru had said that this was one of the buildings that Bernie Stein owned, and Winston was impressed by the elaborate front, but once inside he found that the building was old and seedy. The elevator creaked to the second floor where Bernie had his "Closing Room." Once inside the room, Winston shook hands with the two lawyers, his own and Bernie Stein's. He also acknowledged the introduction to Bernie's secretary, thinking that the Closing Room as well looked small and shabby for a man who was supposed to be as rich as Bernie Stein. Yet wasn't that the way the rich did it? The more you had, the less you needed to show it off. Poor people bought Cadillacs, the rich rode around in Volkswagens.

He took a seat and regarded the other three surreptitiously. They sat around the long second-hand-looking table that dominated the room. Bernie Stein's lawyer, who had introduced himself as Jack Golden looked as bummy as the inside of the building: dirty white shirt cuffs, cigarette ashes upon the lapels of his cheap suit, finger-nails needed cleaning, but the figures he was now making upon the yellow scratch pad were neat, precise. On the other hand, Jonathan Johnson, who always referred to himself as E. Jonathan Johnson, was impeccably dressed, severe conservatively cut grey suit, with a perfect conservative tie and matching handkerchief fluffed from the breast pocket of his coat. He was a good friend of Gru, and Gru had recommended that Winston use him as his lawyer for this deal. "He's sharp, Baby!" Gru had said. "Real sharp. He knows how to handle these Jews! Of course, I know law myself but I don't have a license to practice, otherwise we wouldn't need Jonathan. Well, you'll see how sharp Jonathan handles this deal!"

Now, however, Jonathan kept glancing at his watch, the bright expensive gold only a couple of shades lighter than his golden brown skin. He had small restless eyes, set deep in a broad forehead, an aquiline nose, and a thin sullen mouth. Clearly he didn't like being held up like this. His time was valuable.

Later, after Winston had become so deeply involved with Jonathan and Gru that it was too late to make a change, Winston heard someone say that Jonathan "looked like somebody who had stolen his college education and then turned around and pawned it in order to buy his law degree!"

However, now, he knew very little about Jonathan and felt vaguely intimidated by him, resentful. Hardly had Gru introduced them the other day when Jonathan had inquired, "Mr. Gru tell you about my fee? I come expensive, you know. Now I don't care how you got your money, held up a bank, numbers, pimped, I don't want to know the details. I represent you in this deal with Stein, you get top service, I get paid. That's it."

Talking about a fucking fee before he had even done anything! Winston thought, arrogant bastard. Nigger with a little education and trying to look down on him. Well, maybe this was the kind of cat he needed to beat Bernie Stein.

The secretary was also silent, filing her nails, bony white knees crossed. Except that she wore an excessive amount of mascara and lipstick, she wasn't too bad to look at. Especially the bright skinny legs. Though skinny, they tapered beautifully. At one point he had the curious feeling that she was aware that he had noticed her legs, and that she was supremely confident that her legs were attractive. But she showed no resentment that he had been looking at her, perhaps had even been staring. In fact, instead of pulling her skirt down, she began to swing one foot slowly. A swift wave of heat went over him and he looked away.

He had been so concentrated on money, money, money the last few months, years really, that he hadn't had time to relax with a woman as he had wanted to. It had been all hit and miss. If a relationship threatened his advancement, or didn't contribute in some way to his advancing, he broke it off, no matter how painful it was to him or the other person. And a couple of times it had been painful. . . . But now it would be different. The worst was over. With this investment he'd be able to sit back and take life easier, travel, find the woman he needed so badly, make a home for himself and for her, far above the ghettos from where he came.

The girl unzipped her purse and took out a block of gum, placed it daintily into her mouth, and began chewing. When he glanced at her knees again he was surprised to see the edge of her panties. Didn't she know? An easy screw? he wondered. Maybe after the Contract was over he could casually strike up a conversation with her. Celebrate. Get rid of some of this goddamn tension. Thin as she was, but with legs like that, she'd probably be quite exciting. But she still didn't glance at him. She filed her nails as though there was no one in the room but herself.

"Where in the hell is Bernie?" Jonathan demanded.

Jack Golden squinted over curls of cigarette smoke.

"Where's Gru?" he returned the challenge. Then added, "Patience. The Prima Donnas should show up at any moment."

"Well, I have another appointment," Jonathan said. "I'm giving them another ten minutes."

Gru showed up first, sweeping in lordly, chuckling away Jonathan's impatience, introducing Patricia Wallstone.

Winston stood up, staring at the petite black woman, smooth black skin, oval girl-like features, with large dark eyes glowing with curiosity. Instantly he was impressed by her, so much so he was suddenly nervous, off guard. He mumbled something about Gru having mentioned her and in a soft shy girlish voice she said Gru had mentioned him also. He hadn't yet released her hand, which she had offered at the introduction. Now she flushed slightly, but kept staring back at him, too. Finally, he released her and moving awkwardly, held a chair for her to sit

87

and then he sat, still gazing at her profile. A fullness was in his chest and he was conscious of his pulse racing, almost apprehensively. Was it possible? *His woman* at last? He couldn't believe it. He knew he also stared at her now to detect some flaws, something that would lessen the intense and almost painful attraction he felt for her. But so far he saw no flaws. . . .

The secretary stirred, shifted in her chair, and this time when he glanced at her, he thought he saw her smile briefly before she looked away. Was he correct? Probably. Perhaps she would notice him now, feeling the challenge of another woman in the room. But though it was pleasant to be sitting between the two women, the secretary was no longer of any great importance. In his mind it was already the difference between a quick and perhaps interesting screw, and someone that could mean a real involvement, commitment. The question was, how ready was he to get himself involved, even though a few moments before he had been day-dreaming about just such an involvement? And even if he was ready, what made him think it could be with Patricia Wallstone? Wasn't there Gru? Also, maybe there was still some serious and hopeless flaw in her even though he hadn't seen it yet.

Bernie Stein came in then, hardly had everyone gotten settled. His entrance was so well timed, it was as though he might have been responding to a secret signal. Winston was surprised to see him hobble in on a crutch. Still, a wave of intensity and power seemed to radiate from him. He had shrewd blue-grey eyes, a fighter's heavy jaws and yet a warm full mouth that wore a faint friendly smile. But soon his bushy grey-black eyebrows contracted and he frowned and complained after he shook hands with everyone and hobbled to his seat. "What a day to do business! I'm really in no condition to get anything done today." Agonizingly he sat, clumsily adjusting his great paunch, placing the crutch where he could get it if he needed it. "Young fellow," he looked at Winston. "I wish you had sufficient money to buy all of my buildings. I'd sell everything! Take off. I'd gladly take off and find myself a place where there's sun the year round, and live out the rest of my life sensibly."

"I didn't know you had had an accident," Gru said sympathetically. "We could have postponed this meeting."

"No. No," Bernie said. "The show must go on. The race must be run whether the old horse is in shape or not. Nothing serious. Getting into my car, rushing to an appointment, and of course in this business you are always rushing, rushing, rushing—I got side-swiped by a truck, that's all. Lucky it was a small truck. But I didn't get my X rays back yet, so I don't know exactly what's wrong. I've been having a few headaches."

Even Jonathan was a bit sympathetic.

"If you want an adjournment," he said, and he glanced at Winston, "I suppose my client and I can hold this thing up until next week."

Bernie held up his hands.

"No. No. If I don't get through this evening, serve me right. I should already have retired from business. What more can a man do with two million that he can't do with one? Besides, I got Jack here, and I hope Jack is in sufficient shape to look out for my interests today."

Jack Golden continued to squint through the curls of smoke of another cigarette he had lit. Rather than being seriously concerned about Bernie, he seemed ever so faintly amused. Cigarette ashes dropping upon his lapel and coat sleeve, he added more figures upon the yellow scratch pad.

"Well, let's get this show on the road," Jonathan finally said. "Now I haven't had adequate time to brief myself on the exact nature of this deal, so I will have to play it by ear as we go along."

Jack Golden, who apparently was thoroughly briefed, shrugged.

"We are ready."

Gru cleared his throat as though he was about to address an audience of a couple hundred people. "Gentlemen . . . and . . . er . . . ladies. Allow me a few words before we get down to the nitty gritty. I think my expertise, especially as regards this particular deal—and the fact that I am acquainted with both parties concerned—puts me in the unique position of seeing to it that this deal works smoothly and to the interest of all parties concerned. However, I would like to begin by saying one thing to you, Bernie,—and I am truly sorry about your very unfortunate accident,—but my associate, Mr. Winston and I, have gone over the figures on the twelve buildings. Your asking price is $213,000, with a minimum down on Contract of $10,000. Well, I'm reluctant to drive a hard and nasty bargain, especially taking your condition, but my associate and I feel—and we feel strongly about this, make no mistake about it—feel that not only is the asking price excessive but the down payment on Contract is unreasonable as well."

"O my God!" Bernie buried his face in his hands. "Jack, I thought you and Gru had come to some kind of terms on the phone. I thought the asking price was already settled, down payment as well. And now this! My God, I figured this was going to be a bad day."

Jack Golden was unmoved.

"Gru, we talked about $213,000 on the phone. What's the problem? What do you want to do, steal the buildings?"

Gru held his ground.

"Your figures are off. The rent roll you're projecting doesn't make sense. In fact, right this minute you got a sewage back-up in one of the buildings over in Williamsburg. I had one of my boys check it, and three tenants have already fled the building. C'mon, Jack. You know I don't go for no bull-shit. I've been around. I know this business. This is, Gru, remember!"

"Terrible!" Bernie moaned. "We didn't get started yet and already we got this problem. Jack, I don't know what I hired you for. You could have spared me this."

Jack stubbed his cigarette out and lit another. In the same dry unemotional voice he told Gru, "So we'll get the sewage fixed. We'll have a maintenance crew out there tomorrow and take care of it. What do you want, an affidavit to that effect?

"I want to talk final price, down payment!" Gru insisted. "You know me, Jack. And you know you're way off base!"

Bernie shook his head.

"For Heaven's sake, Jack, give them a couple of thousand off the asking price, but keep the down payment *firm*. After all, we all must compromise a little. I'm in no condition to sustain this kind of bickering today. I'm getting a headache already."

Jack looked at Stein disapprovingly.

"Lower the asking price? Are you out of your mind? You are very near the bottom line, already."

"Doesn't matter," Bernie groaned. "So I'll be driven to the poor house. Forget it. Forget it. Lower the asking price a few thousand."

"Not a few," Gru hesitated. Then pronounced, "Eleven thousand!"

"Eleven!" Bernie's mouth quivered. He stared at Gru. "You got to be kidding!"

"You see," Golden said dryly. "Gru is out for blood today."

"No more than five," Bernie exclaimed. "Five thousand off, and that's it!"

"Eight!" Gru hazarded, and then seemed to muster up an added firmness. "And that's where we stand!"

Bernie regarded Jack Golden imploringly.

"Talk sense to him, Jack. You going to sit here and allow me to lose my shirt? What have I done to deserve this? Or maybe this is what I get . . . get for doing business on Monday. We shouldn't have made the appointment for today. Isn't it well known, Jews are the worst business men in the world on Monday, give away their last dollar in order to start the week off on the right foot! Otherwise, why do I even sit here and consider the loss of eight thousand bucks?"

"It's Tuesday," Jonathan said impatiently, the first time he'd been able to get a word in so far.

"Tuesday?" Bernie mumbled. "Really? Well, now you see how badly I have been hurt. Even got the days mixed up! The hell with it. Gru, take it, take it! Six thousand and five hundred off and let's get on with the deal. But, of course, we got to have the full down payment. If I'm losing my shirt, at least bend over a little and compromise."

Gru hesitated again, then finally chuckled magnanimously.

"Okay, Bernie. I'll go along with you. But if you weren't a sick man, I wouldn't back up an inch. You know me!" Then Gru leaned over and whispered to Winston. "Beat him out of six thousand and five hundred. Not bad! And I'm going to beat him some more a little farther on down the line."

Winston nodded, but felt strangely numb in the pit of his stomach. Suppose the property wasn't worth $213,000 in the first place, so what was Bernie Stein really losing?

If Patricia Wallstone hadn't been sitting there near to him, diverting some of his attention from the business going on, he had the suspicion he might be deeply depressed at the moment. Always he became uneasy and attacked by self-doubt when caught in a situation he didn't understand, and had to submit to being led instead of leading. Now he felt more nervous than usual, threatened by a nagging fear. There was so much to lose, and he did not know the terms of the game being played on this new level. Though fascinated by Bernie Stein, he felt himself small, inadequate, and even stupid in the face of him, because if Bernie Stein could carry on business this well as a sick man, how utterly formidable he must be when well.

Also, Winston sensed that he had now arrived at that level of existence where only an occasional poor person ever got to; a poor person who scraped and saved all of his or her life, or "hit it lucky" with the lottery or numbers, but suddenly having the money and ready to cross the line from the have nots to those who have, and who still lose.... Lose because of improper advice, business counseling, shabby representation, and more often than not was flung all the way back down to the bottom again.

Though one part of himself was more or less captured by Patricia Wallstone, there was another part of himself intensely focussed on Bernie, on Jack Golden, on Gru, on Jonathan who hadn't contributed very much of anything yet. Focussed on them, absorbing, learning, desperately trying to pick up everything he could, almost as if he knew if he didn't hurry and learn the name of this new game he could be losing right now when on the surface it seemed as though he was winning. Still, towards Patricia he found himself pretending a sort of indifference to the business that was going on around them, partly, he knew, to disguise the fact of his own ignorance and, foolishly, to impress her with the attitude that he was accustomed to handling business deals of this nature every day.

As the others droned on with the negotiating, subsiding from the high points, giving the lawyers time to put it all down in complex and legal language, he lowered his voice and questioned Patricia, probing into her like some over-anxious detective, at once hopeful and dreading what he might yet find hidden in the depths of her personality.

She seemed pleased to ignore the business going on. But she spoke so shyly, haltingly, and in a voice so soft he could hardly hear her.

"What?" he said.

"I said.... I mean, I'm not a real nurse. Not a registered nurse. I'm a...." And she flushed again, as though she was confessing something shameful about herself. "... a practical nurse. Lot of cleaning and everything. Not much. But I've been thinking of going back to school to get a degree, and get my RN license."

"Great," he said.

"But I don't suppose I've felt properly inspired."

"Well, why not start feeling properly inspired?" he said playfully, but ended up with his characteristic intensity. "Get in there and get everything you can!"

"Maybe I will," she said.

"How long have you known Gru?"

She seemed suddenly embarrassed about that, too.

"Two . . . almost three years."

"Long time."

"Yes."

"Where are you from originally?"

"Virginia. Small town.''

"And you like New York?"

"No. Not really. But where else is there to go?"

"Well, I hope you don't mind my talking to you, asking you so many questions?"

"No. But what sign are you?"

"Sign?"

"You know . . . what month were you born?"

He told her November and the date.

"Oh. Oh." she said. "Scorpio."

"Is that bad?"

"No. Terrible. I mean, I'm a Libra and a Scorpio is just terrible."

"You mean, well, the two signs sort of go good together?"

She wouldn't meet his eyes.

"Something like that."

"And Gru? What sign is Gru?"

He thought she wasn't going to answer at first and then she said, "Sagittarius. Almost a Scorpio."

"Does that go well with a Libra?"

She hesitated again.

"Well, I don't think I'll answer that."

But he knew: Gru might be a real first class professional in business, but there was something missing between Gru and his woman.

He relented, sat back, and tried to keep from staring at her after that, the slim neck, the big eyes, the full soft mouth. She wore slacks with an orange blouse with a neat little bow above her bosom and though he couldn't see her legs, he was almost positive they'd be as slim and well-formed as the rest of her. But maybe not, he told himself. Maybe her legs will be too skinny or too fat, and I'm already wasting my time.

Also, why did she speak so shyly, in that little girl voice, and why did she seem to be so easily embarrassed? In a way her shyness and a certain soft vulnerable quality about her was charming, but was it real? Sometimes people put on all sorts of attitudes to cover up their true personalities. . . . And what he wasn't sure he found charming, even though he liked the sound of it, was the little-girl tone of her voice. If the tone was not an affectation, whose little girl did she still think she was?

Furthermore, what about Gru? How in the hell did he dare go after Gru's woman even if he wanted to when it was Gru he needed to help him learn this new level of doing business? Maybe it was going to be too damn complicated.

Jonathan pushed some more papers before him and instructed, "Sign here."

Winston pretended to read the papers for a moment, but nothing made sense and he signed, hoping again that Jonathan and Gru knew what they were doing.

The Contract lasted for a couple of hours with Bernie crying out as though he was about to collapse at every concession he had to make. Gru was in his glory. Whenever he thought Bernie had been driven to the wall, he became magnanimous, generous, chuckling with satisfaction.

"Oh, hell, Bernie," Gru said at one point. "Take it! You want the mortgage to read ten years, you got it. Hell, we can live with it!" Gru concluded with a magnificent dismissal of the problem, chuckling again, saying in an undertone, "No problem. Hell, we're going to have most of these mortgages refinanced anyway, then we got our bread back, home free!"

Jonathan was less sure. He glanced at Winston. "You sure you want to go for the ten years? What it means is, you're going to have a balloon on your mortgage in ten years, and you'll either have to pay up or lose out."

Gru was irritated.

"Look, Jonathan, I know what I'm doing. The mortgage can be six years, five years, even three years—what do I care? Man, do you think I mean to stand still with this property? I mean, allow Winston to stand still with it? This is nothing but the foundation upon which to build. Right, Winston? We've already talked about that. Let me handle this. I know what I'm doing."

Winston okayed the balloon, whatever the hell a balloon was. He okayed everything else, too, signing it all, struggling against the apprehensive feeling in the pit of his stomach.

Finally it was over, everyone agreeing to have a quick Closing, Bernie Stein recounting the $10,000 Winston had put down, not even, apparently, taking Jack Golden's word for it that the amount was correct. Then Bernie picked up his crutch and hobbled over and shook Winston's hand warmly, exuding good will, his injury almost forgotten.

"Young fellow," he pumped Winston's hand, "you're getting yourself a great deal. You're going to go far in this business. In a few years I'll probably have to come to you and borrow a few bucks!"

Winston smiled through it all. The secretary who had earlier, finally, pulled her skirt down, now swept by him with an air of icy contempt.

Jonathan collected his papers and stuffed them into his briefcase and came over and said, "Got you a quick Closing. But now are you sure you'll be ready with the balance of the cash? That's going to be $13,000 more, plus Closing cost and of course the balance of my fee and whatever Gru is going to charge you."

Winston was irritated.

"I wouldn't be making this deal if I didn't have the money."

Jonathan said crisply, "Just checking. Want to make sure." He left.

Winston went out with Gru and Patricia Wallstone. At the elevator, Gru exclaimed, "Well, Man, how does it feel to have in Contract a couple hundred thousand dollars worth of Real Estate! And did you see how I banged the shit out of those Jews. Man, I told you. The Big Boys get out of my path when they see me coming!"

Winston didn't say anything. He still felt numb, disbelieving. It was as if it had not been himself but someone else sitting in there watching the negotiations. Also, he didn't know what to do about Patricia Wallstone yet either.

seven

Everyone who knew Bernie Stein couldn't help but concede that he really wasn't vicious. Even Winston came to understand this. Bernie never bragged when he had gotten the better of a deal, nor did he complain when he got the worst of it. Today's loser could be tomorrow's winner. In fact, towards those with whom Bernie did business, especially the novices, the hapless Winstons who crossed his path, he developed a protective attitude. It was almost sexual, as though in winning he had just succeeded in a magnificent seduction, and now felt an overwhelming tenderness towards the seduced.

But first came elation. After Patricia Wallstone and Winston and Gru went out of the door, he sat there for a moment, eyes sparkling, cheeks flushed, as if satiated. Then, neither to the surprise of the secretary nor Jack Golden, he pushed his crutch aside and bounded to his feet.

"Cash! God all mighty cash!" he exclaimed. "You never get enough of it in this crazy goddamn business!" Without the faintest sign of a limp he walked towards the window.

Golden's sour countenance almost broke into a smile.

"On a crutch for God's sakes, you nearly over-did it, Bernie."

"Those niggers don't know as much about business as I do," the secretary said bitterly.

Bernie looked around and frowned at her.

"Listen, none of that racist shit around here. Business is business. And I just did a good bundle of business." Then, at the window, he looked down again at Gru and Winston and Patricia Wallstone leaving the building, headed for the subway.

"That young fellow seems intelligent, like a guy with balls. The only thing is he's saddled with a couple of jackasses. If he doesn't wake up, he's going to lose those buildings in six months and I'll have to take them back."

Golden and the girl joined him, watching the three.

"A lot of cash he seemed to have," Jack said dryly. "Wonder where he got it?"

"I don't care where he got it," Bernie said. "As long as I get it before someone else does. And it comes in handy. With the cash we're picking up from him, not only will it help to expand operations here in Brooklyn but it'll make easier my move over into the City. You know, it is getting damn tiresome being property rich and cash poor."

"The other two fellows were all right," the secretary said. "Gru and the lawyer, but that guy acted like he was stuck on himself, already owned the world."

"So that's why you were showing him half your ass," Golden said. "So that he could own that, too."

"I resent that!" the secretary bristled. "Bernie, I will not stand for. . . ."

"Calm down. Calm down," Bernie said. "Today has been a good day. Beautiful. What are you fighting for? Get your coats and let's find a decent cafe. Dinner is on me, and you may even splurge and order a glass of champagne."

eight

If Winston had some kind of a "worm in his brain," Pat had once felt she had an entire "stranger" inside her body. The stranger shared her eyes, her voice, her breast, her thinking, even the most secret parts of her. After a time, she seldom even questioned the right of the stranger to exist, convinced that maybe she was "normal" after all, and that maybe everyone had some kind of a stranger in them. Still, she found herself very often tensed up, watchful and uneasy, always a little wary that the stranger might surface and throw her off balance again.

She could remember a couple of times when as a little girl she had discovered that she was not always at one with herself.

She had been a "runner." Mama would tell her to go to the store for something, and instead of walking and being as lady-like as she wanted, she'd find herself running as fast as she could all the way to the store. And all the way back home. Hardly able to breathe she had been running so fast. Mama really disapproved of her running, but Mama would still say, "My, my, that was quick," a sort of compliment. Papa was even more impressed. "Girl you keep using that kinda foot-work, and after while you gon be as fast as me, unless, of course, you run into a tree first and break your pretty neck."

Since Mama's compliments came more grudgingly, she put on her top speed for Papa. A few times she almost got run down cutting through traffic, staggering into the house, at last, breathing like a horse after a race. But instead of disapproving, Papa would hug her sometimes. He would keep his arms tight about her, quiet her down, his arms around her even though Mama might be there talking about this or that.

He didn't scold her about climbing trees either or putting on boxing gloves with the little boys. He would stand there and watch her, laughing indulgently as she swung her wild "haymakers" and "uppercuts." She would put on quite a show, prancing about wildly, spitting upon the tips of her gloves, a whirlwind of energy, enough to scare any little boy half to death.

In fact, instead of disapproving, Papa sometimes joined her and the other children in their games, surprising everyone by staying at home instead of "dressing up" and going across town, where people kept whispering he had "another woman." He would strip himself to his waist and put on the gloves and try to teach them how to box properly. He showed them how to climb a tree faster, and then would lead all of them in a race across the green cow pastures.

Most of the time she "came in second." Papa was always first. When she came in third or fourth or last, Papa wasn't too happy about it. There were no compliments, hugs, nothing. She'd find herself so tensed up she could hardly sleep. But the next time he stayed home and raced with them again, she ran so hard she thought her heart would pop out of her chest. Most often then, she came in right upon the heels of Papa.

"That's my little girl!" He hugged her while she clung to him trembling, afraid she was never going to get her breath back again.

Then one day it was like her "stranger" got complete control of her. Even as she suspected she was about to make a serious mistake, she made it. She closed her eyes and ran so fast and desperately, she came in *ahead* of Papa. Collapsed upon the grass and started laughing so hard she was almost strangling herself. She couldn't stop laughing. She wanted to stop so that Papa could compliment her, hug her and quiet her down, proud to claim her as his little girl again. But before she got control over herself, the laughing had got contagious. The other children joined in, bending over double and laughing, too.

Papa, on the other hand, whipped out a cigarette and stuck it between his lips.

"What y'all laffing at like a bunch of jackasses? And you, young lady, if you knew how ugly you looked with the snot running outta your nose you'd shut your ugly face!"

End of all the laughing. You just didn't cross Papa when he got this mad at you.

He walked home with her, stonily silent at first, while she kept blowing her nose, trying to get all the mucus out of it, while it kept running like it was never going to stop.

"Not in good shape today," he finally said. "Little too much to drink last night."

Hastily, she agreed, feeling guilty all the way down to her toes that she had out-run him, and then for some crazy reason she didn't understand had even laughed about it.

Papa almost never apologized for anything and she knew it must have taken a great effort for him to say, "Hope I didn't holler at you too much. And them other kids. But ain't nothing for you to keep crying about, is it?"

"I ain't crying. Just trying to blow my nose. And you didn't holler hardly at all."

But maybe she had been crying and didn't know it, feeling uglier than she had for a very long time, and feeling that maybe she was no longer his "pretty little girl," almost before she had begun to hope, if not believe, that she might be.

All of her life she had been vaguely and sometimes not so vaguely conscious that there were other "pretty little girls" in Papa's life. Two other daughters in the State of Arkansas where he had originally come from, and occasionally visited; and right here in town still other girls, except—not counting his most recent one—they were full grown women. And they were not at all related to him by any blood.

She suspected that it had been more than his drinking that had caused him to lose the race.

Mama was always saying, her face torn up with misery, "You keep on messing around with every wench you can get your hands on, and you gon mess yourself straight down into a grave! But I don't care! I don't care!"

And it was nothing unusual these days for Papa to "mess around" all night long or two or three days at a time, and when he came home he was so tired and hung-over he could hardly stand.

No wonder he had lost the race. Also, wasn't she almost as tall as he was now? When she walked "downtown" shopping or something with him, she had become increasingly conscious of his height, and that he was much shorter than other men, other fathers. Though he had a broad chest and powerful shoulders, he was only five feet five and one half. Even when he walked with his chest pushed forward and his shoulders thrown back, he still looked short. But he didn't *act* short. Every woman they passed, especially taller women, he looked up and down, even, if a little more slyly, the white women, too. And many women looked at him, probably because of his reputation. He might be shorter than other men, but the rumor was all over town how good he was at "messing around."

So she really believed she was more embarrassed by the way he stared and flirted with other women than that she had a father who was not as tall as other men.

Of course, worst of all, he had a habit of flirting with her school mates, or at least, those girls who were only a few years older than herself. The girls giggled among themselves and stared back at Papa. They, too, had heard about him.

Then, just before she won that race with Papa, talk started going around in town that "something was going on" between Papa and a girl who had just one year ago gotten out of high school, and it was this girl who was the "other woman."

She knew this girl, tall light brown-skinned thing, with funny-looking light blue eyes, who hadn't ever done anything—like playing basket-ball or running track, and who you couldn't even imagine climbing a tree or putting on a pair of boxing gloves. She always wore pretty white dresses and ribbons in her straight black hair and sat with her knees pressed together and smiled vacantly at everything. Never saw her without a smile, and you could hardly hear her she seemed so frightened and spoke so softly.

What did Papa see in her, everyone wondered? Sick with what she thought was embarrassment, she wondered what Papa saw in the girl, too. Watching Papa who normally had women running after him now running after the girl, Mama simply ceased talking even more than usual and when she had all the housework done, she would go sag down upon the bed and soon fall asleep. Like she didn't much care if she slept forever. Saturday afternoons there was no more boxing or racing either,

unless it was with the other boys and girls. Papa put on his blue
suit and knotted his tie and she watched through the window as
he disappeared down the road.

For a very long time she blamed herself. Why had she laughed
at Papa? Why had she beaten him in the race when she had
suspected he would be angry? His new girl wouldn't attempt to
beat him in anything, and certainly wouldn't laugh at him
either.

One Saturday when he hadn't been home for several days, she
just had to see him. She couldn't believe he didn't miss her at
least half as much as she missed him. She put on the prettiest
dress she had and "straightened" her hair until all the nappiness
was out of it. She washed her feet good and put on a pair of
Mama's shoes, too. She left Mama asleep in the house and
headed across town. She passed other frame houses where once
share-croppers had lived but now were occupied by factory
workers. Papa had finally bought and paid for their house.
"Don't like being in debt to no kinda white man!" he had
declared. But the truth was Papa either had to buy the house or
get out. White people didn't like him anymore. From being one
of the "best colored fellows" white folks said they had ever
known, they now thought Papa had become "no good."

Before, Papa used to say, "Niggers ain't shit! I don't see how
God coulda made such a mistake and thrown me into the same
patch with them!"

When other black people started changing, he stopped
admiring white people, too. He talked then as if he had always
hated them the most. "Boil their honky asses in oil, is what I
say. Evil devils! Paid twice as much as I shoulda for that house
and I ain't making half as much as I ought to be making at that
factory either. But watch out, I don't keep on taking no shit
forever. My day is coming!"

Apparently, it wasn't coming fast enough. Papa seemed to
become more discontented and meaner than ever lately. Shout
at you for nothing. Reach up and slap Mama if she looked at
him too hard. Rushed into the house a couple of times and
cleaned and loaded his shot-gun, but then sat there staring out
the window. Angry with black people again. "Niggers just ain't
gon never move up outta this shit, and take charge!" Drank

more. Talked about going North somewhere. Stared at white women more arrogantly and scornfully than he ever had before.

She was only halfway across town when the high-heeled shoes began to hurt her feet so badly she almost wanted to cry. She clung to buildings for support, lamp-posts, parked cars, anything to keep herself going. But before she got to the new place where her father lived most of the time now, she had to take her shoes off. This side of town was paved almost everywhere and the concrete burned her feet, but in her bare feet she felt a thousand times better than being cramped in the shoes. Despite herself she began running. At the house she would put the shoes on again. She'd calm herself down before knocking and be so lady-like he'd be surprised when he saw her. She'd smile and say, "Daddy, I was just passing around here, and I hadn't seen you for nearly a week, so I thought I'd drop in and say howdy." And, of course, he'd smile, too, maybe dressed up still in his blue suit. "My God, girl, you done got prettier than ever! How's my little baby?"

"Fine. Just fine." Of course, she'd reply.

"Well," he'd say. "You sure look fine—too good for us to go racing. You come on in here and I'm gonna learn you a coupla more new dance steps and we also gonna have a soda pop or something."

"That would be wonderful, Papa." And she'd sit down, all lady-like, and wait til he got her a grape soda which he knew was her favorite. Then he would turn on the music and jump back, clapping his hands.

"Well, all right, my pretty little baby, let's get with it!"

And, wow, could Papa dance! Best dancer in town. Taller men and every one else just stood still, stopped dancing, once he took the floor. That was Papa. Whatever he did, he was the best, or tried very hard to be. He seemed always ready to step out in front, take charge.

She cut through a vacant lot in order to get there faster, jumping nimbly over cans and bottles and other discarded garbage. But her eyes suddenly weren't quick enough and her bare right foot came down upon a piece of glass. The glass seemed to keep rising up to meet her foot, cutting deeper, cutting so deeply she didn't think it would ever stop. She cried

103

out and fell. Flies and maggots wiggled and flew about her. A mess of garbage soiled her pretty dress.

She managed to stand, pain bringing tears to her eyes. She limped from the vacant lot, blood dripping upon the ground, leaving a trail upon the hot pavement as she continued towards Papa's new house. Her tears half-blinded her and she knew her nose was running and making her ugly. But she cried almost as much because she could not now put her shoes back on as because of the pain. Instead of being happy to see her, Papa would scold her for having cut herself.

She finally reached the house, a two story green frame, with a white fence around it, and yellow flowers in the yard. Papa didn't own it yet, just rented it so it was said, but was trying to scrape together the money to buy it.

She wiped her eyes and tried to steel herself against the throbbing pain in her foot. She went through the gate and stood before the white door. She rang the bell, her hands trembling. She touched her hair, but her hand came back greasy and filthy and she knew she must look a mess. She wanted to cry all over again.

"Papa!" she called.

There was no answer, even though she was certain she had heard someone inside.

"Papa!" she called again. The silence was now so absolute, she wondered whether she had heard anyone in the first place. It could've been her imagination, thinking that Papa was in there somewhere messing around.

She hobbled around to the side of the house and knocked on the window. Not a sound. She limped back to the door and rang the bell again. She began pounding on the door. For a moment she thought she heard whispers but no one answered.

"Papa!" she cried. "Please! Please open up. I cut myself. I'm bleeding! Bleeding! Please let me in."

Still, silence.

A torrent of tears overcame her. She leaned against the door, sobbing.

"Please, Papa. . . . Please let me in! I know you're in there with . . . with her. . . ."

She seemed to wait at the silent door, weeping forever. At last she couldn't cry anymore, as though she had cried away all tears. Now she could only gasp and moan. Then, at some point, she knew that the door was not going to be opened, not only today but never.

She finally turned away, dry sobs locked deep within her, like one gigantic pain. She limped home where she fainted for the first time in her life; home where there was Mama, at least, who washed her foot, and who later shampooed all the grease out of her hair. Afterwards, when the home-made bandages wouldn't stop the bleeding, Mama called a doctor, crying her own tears, tears that her daughter couldn't cry anymore.

In time, after the divorce, Mama married again and she went with Mama to live with her "new father" in North Carolina. He was a light, bright, almost white looking man who already had a daughter who looked much like him and who was a few years younger than Pat. The daughter was about the greediest little girl Pat had ever seen. She was greedy for food and pretty clothes, but especially greedy for affection and attention, so greedy that not only did she get everything her father had to give but soon began to demand and get most of the attention from Pat's own mother.

When the man "courted" her mother before marriage, he had occasionally noticed Pat and brought her a present now and then. Despite herself, Pat had found herself reaching out towards him, flattered almost to tears at the slightest display of attention. But once the man had Mama in marriage, he was noticeably more cool and aloof. What little affection he had went first to his little daughter and then to Mama. She turned to Mama desperately, smiling hungrily, ingratiatingly, more starved than ever to be noticed, caressed, but Mama was no longer as patient with her as she used to be. There was a deep down fear in Mama now. She had lost one man and she was deathly afraid of losing another. There were even times when Mama acted as if she loved the man's little daughter more than she did her own flesh and blood daughter.

"You is almost a grown woman now, Patty," she would explain. "And this here other young'un ain't had no mother to fuss over her in a long time. You try and take care of yourself a little bit more, cause Jesus knows I'm tired and I just ain't got but two hands."

At nineteen years of age, Pat upped and abruptly married a boy who had just turned twenty-one. And a *boy* was exactly what he turned out to be. Instead of him "taking charge" and leading her somewhere, driving away some of the misery and emptiness of her life, she found herself having to take charge and *lead him*! He was as helpless as those little boys she had beaten in those races in those days when she had run with her father.

He had dropped out of school too soon and could only find work as a janitor or porter or dish-washer, menial jobs. She tried to fire him up with ambition to go back to school but he would say, bottomlessly pessimistic: "Won't do no good. No matter what I do *they* gon keep me down! Seen in the paper the other day where even up in New York they won't let no kinda black folks join a union. And won't let black folks into the better schools either or live where they want to. What's the good of trying and trying, when I ain't gon git no where anyway!"

Aching inside with disappointment, she wanted to break down and cry. But she didn't dare, for he'd probably have crumbled and cried worse than she did.

Lucky there were no children and after three hopeless years of marriage, she gave it up. Since there was nowhere else to go, no other place to turn, she got on a bus one afternoon, choked up less with a sense of adventure than with fears and self-doubts, and came to New York City.

nine

Junior had been talking to his mother when she gave a soft almost inaudible sigh, rose up in the bed slightly and stared at him, and then sank back down again. He continued to gaze at her, trembling, believing nothing, talking even more wildly than he had before: "When I git back, Mama—you hear?—I'll have you a bigger TV than you ever had before. With color! And a switch you can change all them channels you want without gitting outta bed. Also, I ought to have a surprise for you, too. I got around them dogs the last time I was over there. So now I know how to git into the building where he lives. Make out like I'm one of them delivery boys or something and go on in through the basement. And like you said, once he knows how sick you is, I suspect he'll come running here to see what he can do about helping you. Naw, he didn't mean to hurt me. Reason he knocked me down was because he had no way of knowing who I was. . . ."

What he didn't tell her, was that he didn't believe Winston would have come to see her even if he had known who he was. Also, he didn't tell her about the gun either, the one he'd had then, nor about the new one he had now. He just kept trying to go along with her. He no longer attempted to stop her dreaming. All that seemed to be keeping her alive now was the dreaming.

She was very still upon the bed and silent, bony black skeleton-like face almost lost in the white pillow. She was often still and silent when she listened to him. If there had been a moment of doubt back there that maybe she wasn't listening in the way that she always did, it could mean no more than that he was higher than usual. . . . Everything was kind of unreal and mixed up anyway. He hadn't been able to sleep for a couple of nights, dreaming about those dogs. Not just one dog anymore, but several. All of them coming after him. He had told her he could get into the building. What he hadn't said was that though he had the other gun now he never saw in his own dreams how he was going to get out again.

He nodded towards the stove, but remembered he was heating up the soup for Mama. He pushed the spoon into the soup, surprised that he hit the bottom so quickly, almost turning over the pan. Apparently he hadn't yet ceased talking, for suddenly he could hear his voice again out there in the room, going on and on, increasingly high-pitched, like it was trying to run away from him: ". . . Didn't mean to leave you without a TV for such a long time. . . . But these junkies out here in the streets you can't trust them. Dirty low-down bums! One of them probably sneaked in here and stole our TV! But Mama, I tell you, if I catch him, I'm gonna beat his brains out! And . . . and . . . before this day is over, I'm gonna have you a TV, biggest one you ever seen!"

He poured soup into a bowl, spilling some of it. He couldn't understand why he was so nervous, hands trembling. He should be cool. Unless the stuff had been diluted again? Price going up all the time and the stuff so weak you had to keep turning on to keep yourself straight. Dudes in the streets knew he was packing so maybe nobody was trying to put anything over on him? But he hadn't picked up the gun to use on no punk pusher. And he didn't have enough extra shells anyway. Two loaded and two spare. And he was going to need that and maybe more. Nobody was going to slap him around like he was a kid and get away with it.

"Sleep?" he said, looking at her. "You want to sleep, Mama? You don't want no more soup?"

He didn't go towards the bed, just stared at her.

His voice tried to break down on him.

"Mama? You want the soup later? You want me to go out and get the TV set first, so that you can watch a show while you have your soup?" She didn't reply and he went into a frenzy of motion, putting his jacket and tennis shoes on. "Okay," he said. "You sleep. I'll be back as quick as I can.

Might have a big surprise for you. . . . Told you I know how to get up there where he . . . And . . . and . . . like you say, once I explain it to him, he won't waste a minute coming here and . . . and. . . ."

He pushed his fist into his eyes, didn't know why he was suddenly crying. He stumbled to the closet and took the old battered violin case out from under a pile of dirty clothing. He opened it briefly and checked the small ugly double-barreled shot-gun. Then sniffling, trying to stop the tears from flooding his eyes, he went out the door. . . .

ten

Right from the beginning Winston was a surprise. Pat had almost ceased believing that someone would come along one day who could and would "take charge." All the men like that seemed to be on television or in the movies, and were mostly white, or already taken by some Sister, or one of those white females who seldom allowed any kind of man half-way worthwhile to escape.

Gru, at first, had seemed like a man who could take over, help her to thread her way out of confusion, release some of the things she sensed deep down inside herself.

But Gru, a far better man than most men she had known, had soon collapsed. She began to glimpse the vast difference between what he kept promising himself he was and what he always turned out to be. After that, there were times when she had to force herself to keep smiling. She paced herself, maybe even down-graded herself, her own strength, so as to be sure of not upstaging Gru, always careful of his fragile ego. In return he sometimes lavished upon her wild bursts of affection, and even when it dwindled as another one of his great dreams faded, and he became morose and depressed until fired up again, she at least knew he was there and cared about her. Unlike many lonely women in the big frightening City, she had *someone*. . . .

Winston, on the other hand, was something else again. Instantly she was convinced that no woman or even man would ever beat him at anything. He might get slowed down temporarily, but he'd always spring free, charge forth once more. Plus, he didn't seem to be dreaming about "pies in the sky," waiting for his *number* to come in to win or for some

110

outlandish scheme to materialize. Nor had he succumbed to a low life of crime either, which so often was the self-defeating short cut many black men weakened and took under pressure, pimping off helpless women, pushing drugs to defenseless children. Instead, Winston seemed to have mastered this thing called "business," moving straight out into that strange and hostile world, controlled almost exclusively by Whites, and where thousands of people were being shattered and defeated every day, even Whites. . . .

At the beginning, however, she didn't know how much this thing called "business" could consume a man, how it could leave him so ruthless and very often insensitive. She only knew she had finally met a man who, though he frightened her a little, left her brimming with excitement.

Still, she had a very strange reaction after first meeting him at Bernie Stein's. She began to dread seeing him again. If she suspected he was going to be at a party or at a meeting Gru wanted to take her to, she found herself becoming so nervous she didn't calm down until she got to the party or meeting and saw that he wasn't there. Then she was disappointed, and wondered why she had been so nervous in the first place? It was like a kind of fear, and what was there to be afraid of? Suddenly she was almost uncontrollably anxious to see Winston so that she could prove to herself that he "didn't mean anything to her, and never could. . . ." But though she listened as Gru dropped his name from time to time, he never seemed to be where Gru thought he was going to be, and she began to believe she'd never see him again.

Then one Friday night, when she didn't dress up as sharply as she should have, she went to a party with Gru. He wasn't there either at the beginning, and she drank three scotches and sodas, getting higher than usual. Suddenly she looked up and there he was across the room. . . .

He wasn't dancing, and, though holding a glass, not drinking very much out of it either. He just stood there a little to the side of everything, almost aloof, critical. He stared at the people "partying back," at their guzzling scotch and gin and rum and bourbon and just about everything else, gnawing fried chicken, and swallowing peanuts, "letting their hair down. . . ."

She passed him and frowned slightly as if she didn't quite remember him and then she smiled a dazzling hello. When he only nodded and half-smiled at her in return, staring at her, she hurried away from him and made a point of ignoring him altogether. She clung to Gru so affectionately, trembling for some strange reason, Gru started getting ideas. She knew if she didn't soon calm down Gru would want to take her home.

Though she held onto Gru, she couldn't help but notice that Winston was finally dancing, some girl with sandy hair, and light-brown skin, who pressed herself against him as though she was already staking out a claim.

Pat downed another drink and tried vainly to keep up with the gaiety and the conversation going on around her. Then she tensed as Winston left the girl and started walking towards her.

He stopped and said, "May I?" holding out his hand. He glanced at Gru, adding as if in afterthought, "You don't mind, do you, my Man?"

"Go ahead!" Gru said generously, so sure of her, or so sure of himself. "Pat, why don't you show Winston some of these new dance steps! Man, it's about time you started breaking down and having some fun!"

It was a slow dance, and she was sorry about that, thinking he might be one of those guys who'd move in right away and try "laying in the cut. . . ." Many guys like that would pull you in so close, grind against you so obscenely, almost screw you on the dance floor. Most of the time she kept a distance between herself and people she didn't know very well when dancing, but she couldn't remember ever being as ramrod straight and distant as she was as she danced with Winston now. Though a good dancer, she kept missing steps. A third person could almost have walked through the space between them.

Winston suddenly stopped, stone still, gazing at her, his heavy black eyebrows running together in a frown. Though he didn't release her altogether, she had the suspicion he was about ready to walk off the floor and leave her. She sensed that he was attracted to her, but that he was not now very happy about it.

He made no effort to disguise the anger in his voice.

"You want to play games?"

"What?"

"You heard me."

She stared back at him, trying to get angry herself. Who in the hell did he think he was talking to her like that!

"I want to see you," he said, the anger still in his voice. "Tomorrow. I don't know why, but I do. Maybe if we see each other, we'll either get this thing started or over with."

"What thing?" she said.

"You still want to play games?"

She let out a deep breath, just then conscious of how utterly tensed she was. She shook her head, saying almost inaudibly, "No. I guess not."

"Tomorrow, then?"

"It wouldn't be fair to Gru."

"I know. But I can't think about Gru right now."

"If I see you . . . I mean . . . it will only be to talk, you understand? Maybe as you say we can straighten this thing out before it goes too far if we talk about it."

"Sure," he said.

But she didn't believe he meant it. All the intensity of his personality seemed to be already aimed at her, flowing straight at her. Even if he meant to try and stop this crazy thing growing increasingly more powerful between them, maybe he couldn't stop it himself now. But she had the feeling he didn't intend to try and stop it anymore.

"I insist," she said. "I will see you, but it will be only to talk."

"Sure." He reassured her again. "Seven tomorrow evening, okay?" He mentioned a restaurant mid-town where they'd meet, and she agreed.

And since that was settled and she was only going to talk about this thing and not get involved anyway, she allowed herself to dance a little closer. Which was a mistake. It was not like "laying in the cut" with anyone else. He wasn't vulgar, grinding against her or anything. He just held her closely, tenderly, hardly moving on the floor. She felt her body beginning to tremble and strangely she almost wanted to cry. She was relieved when the next record was a fast number. She jumped back and did her thing, "got with it," put Winston down a little, too, for to the swift, deeply throbbing Soul music he moved stiffly, uncertainly, years behind the latest steps.

Someone in the crowd urged, "Go, Pat, go!" That turned her on even more. She even had the impression that she was grinding and twisting a bit vulgarly and that though Winston wore a frozen smile he didn't approve of what she was doing at all. She wanted to stop herself but found herself going at it even more intensely. When it was over, Gru came up and claimed her with pride, putting his arm around her so that everyone would know that she was his.

"Hey, that's my girl!" He beamed at the circle of people who had watched and applauded. "Hey, y'all, sometimes I forget myself what a great dancer I got here!"

She escaped and got into the bathroom and stared at herself in the mirror. What was the matter with her? Why had she danced like that when she hadn't meant to?

When she came back into the living room where the music and the dancing and the eating and the drinking and the partying were still going strong, Winston had gone.

eleven

She had dinner with Winston twice more before he got her to his apartment. Even then he got her there because he tricked her, told her an outright lie.

The first date hadn't gone very well. She'd had doubts he was going to show up, and when he did he seemed almost as tensed against her as she was against him. Her dominant memory of the evening was that she had been whipping out so many cigarettes and smoking to give herself some kind of poise that she had broke into a fit of coughing.

Rather than being as sympathetic as she thought he should have been, he had said, "Why don't you quit?"

"What?" she said, her voice still strangled, her throat feeling like it was on fire.

"Sucking that stupid stuff into your lungs."

"Well, you don't smoke so you wouldn't understand."

"I used to. But one morning I took a long look at the cigarette I was about to stick into my mouth, and I asked myself, what kind of sense does it make, dragging smoke into my throat and lungs? It didn't make sense, so I quit."

"Just like that?"

"Why not?"

"Well, I suppose some of us do not have your great will power." Sarcastic? She suspected she had been. Because in little ways it seemed he had been observing her critically, putting her down all evening.

At another point, perhaps before that stupid business about smoking, he had upset her. She had still been feeling guilty about the vulgar way she had danced the night before, so unlady-like, like somebody who was still a stranger to herself. She found herself wanting to apologize and explain that she wasn't that kind of a girl but didn't know how to apologize or if there was anything to apologize for. She remembered she could hardly meet his eyes, so conscious was she of herself. Also, he seemed so distant and guarded against her. What had happened? Last night and when they had first met he had appeared to be very much attracted to her, but now he acted as if he could be thinking it was all a serious mistake.

Sitting there in the softly-lit cafe across from him, the silence began to echo between them. Anxiety tugged at her voice: "Sorry," she murmured. "I mean, I am sorry I didn't get a chance to dance with you again last night . . . to a . . . well, a number you might have liked better."

Should she have said that? Perhaps he'd think she was rubbing it in because he couldn't dance too hot, at least, to the fast numbers?

And why had she spoken in a tone of voice even more hopelessly girl-like than usual, her cheeks frozen in a helpless smile, almost as though she was a child again and pleading not to be judged too severely, pleading for him to come back closer to her again.

"Doesn't matter," he said, still distantly. "I am not the best dancer in the world."

"I didn't mean that. I mean, you dance very well. You like dancing?"

"Why not?" he said. "As long as it doesn't become an escape, like so many black folks use it for."

"I don't understand."

"Black folks dance and party all night, while both night *and* day white folks are running the banks, the railroads, the government, and everything else."

"Well, I like to dance," she said, almost defensively.

"Sure," he said, coolly. "So I assume."

No matter how she humbled herself, it didn't seem he was ever going to warm up to her again. Suddenly she wanted to walk out and *leave him,* escape, feeling hurt and rejected all the way deep down inside.

But after a moment he shook his head as though exasperated with himself, and then he sighed. He reached across the table and touched her cheek.

116

"Eat," he said.

"I'm not hungry."

"Sure you are. Eat."

Still, she couldn't eat very much. The food seemed to bounce around in the middle of her stomach. She was relieved when he called for the check, paid it and they went out.

The air was crisp and cooled her cheeks, but as she stood in the streets with him and waited for a taxi another kind of panic assailed her. A cab finally stopped and he ushered her inside. Where did he plan to take her? To his apartment? Well, that was out. Definitely out! Where did he get off thinking that she was *that* kind of a girl! Buy her dinner, which she'd agreed to have with him only to "talk," and now without having even talked very much, resolved anything, maybe trying to get her to his apartment, like she was some kind of a "push over!"

However, once settled in the cab, he seemed undecided, then he said abruptly, "You want to go home?"

"Yes!"

"Okay," he agreed. "As you wish."

So finished, right? Finished before it even got started. He took her home and she was relieved to be free of him. She woke up the next morning and she was still tremendously relieved. But by night fall she had begun to wonder where she had failed. How could he have seemed so attracted to her at one time and then suddenly not care about her anymore?

Sleep came badly that night. Had he found her attempt at conversation dull and stupid? She had worn a black dress when maybe she should have worn the red one, been a bit more sexy, right? Or maybe he simply didn't like women as black as she was and had really been more interested in that light, bright, damn near white chick at the party?

The next day she was so depressed she couldn't keep a cigarette out of her hand. This depressed her even more, for she'd already thought: who the devil did Winston think he was? He was not the only one who had a little will power. When she met him again, probably by accident somewhere, one thing he'd realize at once was that she, too, could do whatever she made up her mind to do and he'd see how she had quit and no longer smoked at all.

But for the moment she couldn't even *think* about quitting.

117

Until midnight she kept checking with the phone company to see if something was wrong with her phone. The operator continued to assure her that the phone was okay. It had become difficult to understand why Winston didn't call, when he had to know by now how badly he was hurting her.

He didn't call for five days, and even then didn't sound like he was very happy to be calling her. Like maybe despite himself he had thought about her, wanted to see her.

On the other hand she resented his having not called sooner and yet at the same time was fearful that she could still lose him even though he had called.

And again the date didn't go too well, though not quite as badly as before. She talked manically, blindly, about her job, about going back to school, about how maybe she'd married too young, about how she knew she had a lot of "short comings," but how she was always trying to improve herself, and he was right—dancing and partying wasn't everything, and black people had to get themselves together and be more serious and get out there into the banks and all that and everything else he'd said.

Whatever he said or she thought he was going to say, she found herself hastily agreeing even before he said it. She realized she was prepared to do almost anything to keep him from slipping away from her again, maybe even sleep with him, though she'd never in all of her life slept with anyone until after the fifth or sixth date. In fact, many a man had quit phoning her after she wouldn't "come across" after the first couple of dates. Even Gru hadn't been able to get her to "go all the way" the first two months. But Winston didn't push her. He watched her, as though sifting her words, her attitude, everything about her for meaning, as if he really wanted to believe again what he'd thought about her when they'd first met.

Also, at moments, he seemed somewhat preoccupied, but she suspected it was something that had to do with "business" rather than something against herself. Was his business going wrong? Had Gru gotten him in trouble already? He didn't say anything. Not about the business. Rather, he seemed to be making every effort to understand her, agreeing with her almost as quickly as she agreed with him.

He took her home and though she pulled back before the good night kiss could carry her too far, she was almost confident he'd want to see her again.

Then he lied to her. An outright lie. Hardly was she in the taxi with him the next time when he snapped his finger and frowned, as people do when they have forgotten something, or when they are pretending they have forgotten something. He leaned forward and spoke to the driver through the opening in the bullet proof glass, changing the address from the restaurant with the soft candle lights and little silver stars floating across the ceiling and the piano playing, where they usually went to have Soul food. So where were they headed now, his apartment? He leaned back and straightened his tie, and she knew he had just glanced at her out of the corner of his eye. Well, she had suspected it was going to be different this time, maybe even a hassle. If he had been somewhat preoccupied on the last date, he now seemed to be totally concentrated on her, the little "worm in his brain" trying to figure out how she was going to react before she did.

"Where we going?" she asked, feigning a mild surprise that he had changed the address. "A new restaurant?"

"Got to stop by my place," he said at once. "I'm expecting a long distance phone call. Don't want to miss it."

Oh, yeah, she thought. I bet! Still, she'd never heard *that one* before. And it was so simple. Maybe he was expecting such a call? And if she said she didn't want to stop at his apartment, wouldn't that seem as if she didn't trust him? Which she didn't. Not yet. In fact, maybe he could be one of those guys she'd never be able to trust completely.

Yes, one of those guys who, once he made love to her, got deep inside of all of her guarded places, would toss her aside anyway. And everything she'd opened up for him, she'd have to go through the pain of trying to close up again.

Yet she said nothing, surprised that so far she wasn't much more nervous and afraid. If he tried to get too fresh, she could still always walk out of the apartment, right?

As the taxi gained the West Side Highway, she watched him surreptitiously. If she could look straight into his eyes, she'd know if he was lying to her or not. But across the City, the evening darkness was descending and all she could see was the

119

dark outline of his profile, the firm almost arrogant curve of his full mouth, the conservative sweep of his Afro that often seemed to her to have been combed hastily, as though he couldn't always find as much time as he wanted to devote to his personal appearance.

So she sat there, aware of his arm thrown carelessly across the seat in back of her, barely touching her shoulders, and yet sending vibrations to the very pit of her stomach every time the taxi took a turn and he leaned in a little closer.

"Your phone call . . . something about business?" she asked.

"Business? Yeah." Then he sighed. "Business always business. Sometimes I don't know how Rockefeller and Vanderbilt and all those cats ever made it. Except back in the days when they were accumulating their fortunes they could steal millions before the public caught on, plus there were hardly any taxes, and also they bought themselves Congressmen and Senators and even Presidents outright."

She wasn't at all sure he was talking about what was really on his mind, but she went along with it, hearing her own voice as though it came from somebody else.

"Don't they still do that, buy up all the politicians?"

"Oh, sure. But the clever ones, today, attempt to be more subtle about it."

"And a black man . . . you think black men can ever get as powerful as those guys . . . Rockefellers and such?"

He hesitated.

"Why not? But one thing is certain, it can't be done unless some of us have the guts to try it."

"And you intend to try it?"

"Why not?" he said again.

Some ego, right? she thought. Not only did he intend to try, but seemed convinced he would succeed. Well, maybe that was the attitude it took to win. You had to be sure of yourself. That was her problem. She was not always sure of herself. Sometimes she didn't want to take things like Astrology and such seriously, but where there was so much smoke there had to be some fire, right? And hadn't a lot of things she had been unable to understand about herself become much clearer once she had discovered she was a Libra? Even the Stranger that still seemed to live deep within

120

her was less of a stranger, a little easier to understand. The reason why she did this or that, or very often couldn't make up her mind and get things done properly, was because she was trying to find a balance, right? Everyone knew that Libras were always struggling to achieve a balance, maybe even when they didn't know it. So things were clearer. Now she even knew why she was always so desperately eager to please people, to get along, to be liked, could find herself doing almost anything to win a compliment, a bit of affection—simply another burden you had to live with if you had been born a Libra, right? It was all right there in the way in which the moon rose and the sun came down and the month into which you happened to be born. Practically everything was explained—except maybe a few things. She was often surprised at her ability to say No to people when everyone knew how very difficult it was for Libras to say No. True, it tore her to pieces inside to say No, but she always mustered strength to say it, especially if someone pushed her beyond a point she couldn't allow herself to go, a point and place that seemed to go even farther than what she so far knew about being a Libra.

And of course she was going to say No tonight, too. Because if everyone knew how utterly weak and defenseless Libras often were, everyone also knew it was people like these Scorpios who would take advantage of that weakness. And no doubt about it, Winston was a typical Scorpio: arrogant, aggressive, and always ready to "take charge" even before you were ready for him to.... And further, everyone knew how ... well ... sexy Scorpios were supposed to be, hang you up, right? and might just toss you aside without even looking back at you again.

Well, she wasn't as weak and as helpless as she seemed. If he thought he could trick her by lying and deceiving her as he was doing, he had another thought coming!

*   *   *

But she still couldn't determine if he was lying. By now she had been in the apartment with him for more than a half hour and so far he had made no disrespectful move towards her. True, he had given her a drink and she had suspected before she sipped it that it was going to be extra strong, and she was right. The liquor bit at her throat and attacked the nervousness in the pit of her stomach as though there was hardly any chaser in it. Also, he had put on an album when they first came in, music she hadn't heard before, or hadn't really listened to before. It was some French singer with a lot of violins in the background and a beat beneath it very soft and romantic. It made her think how beautiful places like Paris must be in April, and how far away ugliness in the world seemed to be when you were all the way up here on the twentieth floor.

She had walked with him out onto the terrace and he had pointed out the Empire State building and she could see Central Park down below and beyond was Fifth Avenue.

Back inside she had found a chair and sat down, sipping her drink faster than she intended. As for the apartment itself, it was still in chaos, since he had only moved in a few weeks ago. Bags were unpacked everywhere, and piles and piles of books stacked in corners. The place still smelled faintly of fresh paint. But she couldn't help but notice that he or someone hadn't neglected the bed, and the green spread and the throw pillows not only went well with the color of the walls, but had been arranged and made up quite neatly, attractively.

Winston left her and went into the bathroom and she whipped out another cigarette and waited for him. She pulled the smoke deeply into her lungs. Previously this used to relax her. Now she was so conscious of swallowing the filthy smoke, she couldn't relax. Still she couldn't toss the cigarette aside either. But I'm going to quit, she promised herself. Except that Rome wasn't built in a day, right?

She regarded the windows again, the view beyond of a star-filled sky and airplanes circling and the tops of buildings, where so far there were only Venetian blinds. She thought about the kind of draperies that would go well with the windows, and then she imagined a deep green carpet for the floor. Before she knew it she had almost furnished the apartment. Be very cozy, she thought. Perfect place to do his . . . well . . . "messing around." No doubt about it, he'd probably have girls lined up outside to get in here.

The thought left her agitated and uneasy. She stood abruptly and stared at one of the pictures he had on the wall. It was the picture of a very lovely woman, dressed in a beautiful robe, and wearing a hair style of many centuries ago. Against the white background, the dark beauty of the woman seemed to glow, like some kind of an African Princess. She thought the hair-style was intriguing. Maybe she'd try it herself one day. Still, she thought, nothing could ever make me as beautiful as the woman. She wondered who the woman was.

The books she glanced at hastily. They were mostly about Real Estate, Economics, Business law, the Stock market and Politics. She realized he must read an awful lot, but the kind of books that would probably bore her to death.

She thought she heard the bath-room door opening and she rushed back to her seat and sat as though thoroughly composed. But he didn't come out immediately and the position began to feel awkward. Her throat felt scratchy and she wanted to cough. Her right foot suddenly throbbed uncomfortably in her super high-heeled shoes. It would have been great if she could kick her shoes off and lean back and not have to worry about a thing.

He came out with his tie loosened and touching his Afro into place. When he got a little closer, she could smell his cologne or shaving lotion.

"Everything okay?" he asked.

"Fine!"

Couldn't tell yet what he was up to by looking into his eyes. For one thing, with his glasses off, he squinted slightly. His bushy eyebrows came together and his black eyes seemed to be staring at her more intensely than ever. Trying to meet his eyes and penetrate his thoughts and maintain her composure all at the same time, she became more nervous and unsure of herself. She didn't want him to think she didn't trust him. She longed to please him, so that he would continue to like her, maybe even come to love her. But how could she retain his respect and, above all, her own self-respect, at the same time?

"Another drink?"

"No," she said abruptly. What was he trying to do, get her drunk? Then she was flustered. Had she spoken too sharply?

"Perhaps a small one," she said, hopelessly apologetic, in her most defenselessly soft and girl-like voice.

So predictable again, right? she thought angrily about herself. Naturally the drink he brought was stronger than the one before. She sipped cautiously, but wasn't she already feeling a bit tipsy, so what good would caution do now?

"Who is the beautiful lady?" she asked.

"Nefertiti."

Nefertiti? She didn't know who that was but he seemed to assume that she should know. She nodded her head as though she really did. Thinking: now I suppose I got to find out who she is, right?

"Dance?" he said.

Naturally. Naturally that would be what he'd want to do now. Get her up close to him. Like going according to some kind of a formula. Her today, someone else tomorrow. She knew how these New York guys worked!

If she said No to the dance, didn't allow him to get close to her, she could still be certain of beating this thing, of getting out of this apartment and going home. But why should she be afraid of herself? Why not go ahead and dance and let him think he was getting away with something? Serve him right when she disappointed him later. Men could sometimes be so childish, going through the same routine, the drinks, the music, and acting so charming in order to deceive a woman. Why hadn't he come right out and been honest and asked her? How did *he* know she would have said No?

She carefully stubbed the cigarette out, then she rose and went into his arms. Mistake again. Once more she was surprised at his gentleness, the tender manner in which he held her. She was amazed at the rich well of softness she sensed deep down in him, and even more amazed that it was opened up to her. It was as though, instead of planning to deceive her, take advantage of her, she was already someone special to him, someone more precious and fragile than she had known or believed she could ever be to anyone. What baffled her, too, was that normally he always appeared a bit aloof, somewhat unbending and stiff, and even, at times, closed away in a world that was both cold and ruthless. Now he seemed to be exposing himself completely to her, allowing her to step beyond his facade. She wished she could remain here with him in this deep place where maybe the best of him lived, and where it was so warm and secure. But how soon would it be before he pushed her out and closed himself off to her again?

She shivered and embraced him tighter. They hardly moved, the music flowing about them, holding onto each other.

"Why did you lie?" she murmured.

"What?"

"Why did you lie to me?"

"Oh," he hesitated. "That? Well, because I knew you wouldn't have come with me if I had told you the truth."

"But where are your scruples!"

He hesitated again.

Maybe he was one of those guys who had no scruples, no matter how gentle and warm she thought he was right now, maybe he would lie as quickly as he would tell the truth to get what he wanted?

"I . . . well . . . I couldn't think about scruples for . . . wanting you."

"I can't believe you. You wanted me so badly, you had to go so far as to lie to me?"

"Yes. That is the truth."

She should stop dancing with him right this minute! Nothing justified the lie he had told her, or did it? On the one hand she was flattered that he had wanted her so much that he would lie to her, but on the other hand how could she ever believe anything he said?

"You should have been honest and truthful," she said.

"Are you angry?"

"Yes," she declared. "Very much."

But she made no attempt to get out of his arms. She kept thinking: I'll stop soon. . . . In a minute I'll stop this whole thing. . . . In the meantime it felt so good to be held so tenderly, to believe that he really and truly cared her, wanted her so badly he'd go to the length of telling a lie to get her.

He kissed her cheeks, and his lips brushed her ear. She closed her eyes and tried to control some of her trembling.

All composure seemed to have melted away a long time ago. She simply felt herself floating along with the music and the feeling of his arms.

When he eased her down upon the bed, she was still sure she'd soon put a stop to this thing. Far back in her mind she was positive she had even staked out the exact line she had no intention of allowing him to cross. She supposed that was why she could allow him to fumble with her brassiere and could withstand the heat that charged through her body at the shock of his lips upon her breast. All she had to do was keep some semblance of control over herself, right? keep herself from floating so far away and feeling so good that she couldn't find her way back again.

His trembling fingers began to pull off her dress. He seemed so nervous and excited it further stimulated her and she couldn't bring herself to stop him yet. Then he peeled down her stockings and took off her shoes. Dazed, she watched him watching her, both amazed and pleased that he seemed so dazzled as he gazed and marveled at her body. Looking at her as though she might be more beautiful than she had ever believed she could be.

And then he practically ripped his tie off and his shirt and then his pants were coming off, too—while her mind said: Stop, please stop, because I'm going to have to disappoint you. But she said nothing even yet. Through half-closed eyes she caught a fleeting glimpse of his manhood, thick and swollen, lunging out of his pants.

She turned her eyes away, holding her breath against excitement. Still, when he grasped her panties, she tightened her legs, and she could sense his disappointment. But deep inside she kept saying, No, it had gone as far as she intended it to go, too far, and then she was surprised to feel her legs relaxing a little. Against a very great resistance that seemed to exist only in a corner of her mind, she felt her panties moving down her legs, and then Winston had them off altogether.

For an instant, she was assailed by an uncontrollable surge of fear, thinking: Oh, my God, I can't do this. Gru and.... But it was more than Gru. Without having made love to her yet Winston had already gotten deeper into her emotions than anyone had ever reached before. Wouldn't she be completely lost once he got past all the remaining secrets of her life, when she still couldn't be sure he wouldn't leave her once this night was all over? Up to now she at least had been "getting by," maintaining some sort of balance to her life. What would happen if he opened up all the doors and all the strangers came flooding out and overwhelmed her and she couldn't get her balance again?

His mouth came down upon hers once more. He kissed her cheeks, her neck, her arms and then her mouth again, while his fingers moved gently down her side, caressed her stomach, then slowly down and between her thighs. She almost gasped. In one motion he had begun not only to storm all the remaining closed doors, but was dashing beyond, defenses crumbling, touching her as if her body had been made only for him to discover. She believed she might still say, No, even though her body was saying, Yes, to everything. Everything.

Then she was trembling and kissing him and holding him and almost wanting to cry. If she felt so wonderful already, why should she say No? Maybe he would never hurt her and would be patient and kind and try to understand her. If she wasn't so brilliant and sophisticated and intelligent as some of the women he had known, perhaps he'd wait and see how fast she could catch up and learn and how she'd be so much better for him than any woman he'd ever find again.

Deep down inside herself she hid in her final small place, knowing that in a moment it, too, would crumble, saying: Please, if I say Yes and let you in, will you really care for me then, and promise that you will never leave me again?

Outwardly she groaned and fought back tears and hung onto him, her body moving hungrily, blindly, to meet him.

twelve

Winston ran hot water over the frozen meat to thaw it out and then chopped up the meat and some potatoes and carrots and threw it all angrily into a pot. He lowered the flame under the pot. What was so goddamn difficult about making a pot of stew? Then he unplugged the refrigerator so that it would defrost. After that, he grabbed the mop bucket and ran water into it and threw in some soap powder. He hated mopping, hated doing any kind of "housework," but he had definitely decided to mop the bathroom and the kitchen and the living room, do it all himself, plus do the cooking and defrost the refrigerator. He didn't need Patricia Wallstone—or anybody else!

He was furious. He had made an absolute decision to drop Pat Wallstone, "cut her loose."

A few minutes ago she had finally left the apartment to go to the grocery and he had thought now he could get his mind back on the meeting with Bernie Stein tomorrow. God knew he had to be ready, had to have himself completely together for this second go-round with Bernie. He had been clearly out-smarted the first time, nearly wiped out. Wouldn't he be stupid to allow it to happen again? But he wasn't ready. His mind seemed sluggish and drugged, filled with Patricia Wallstone, still numbed by a sense of her presence although she was no longer in the apartment.

She had become like an addiction. Until now he had been unable to make up his mind to cut her loose, and yet he had been convinced for some time that she was not "good for him."

A couple of days ago, instead of keeping his mind on business, he had even written down on paper all the things "wrong" with her.

1)—Too possessive and insecure; smothering him to death!

2)—A mind preoccupied by a lot of crap, the latest movies, the latest styles in clothing, and whatever goddamn song was number one on the "hit parade."

3)—Understood nothing about business—, couldn't take dictation, typed badly, and wasn't even very quick with a little con when he allowed her to answer his business phone calls, protesting: "Winston, I can't lie as quick as you can. . . . You *are* here, and you haven't stepped out anywhere! And, after all, the poor woman's pipes have been busted in her kitchen for five days and she says she has children and can't cook or nothing!" She couldn't be cool, detached. Hell, he was as depressed as she was by the poor people's problems but how could he solve everything all at once? Normally he was forced to take the phone from her and deal with the callers himself. In this case, pacifying the tenant by telling her Donald was on the way with a plumber.

And, oh, yes, what else?

Talk about men keeping women in *bed!* Well, she kept *him* in bed all the time! Which was really number (4). If left up to her they'd never get up and clean the apartment or cook and wouldn't even answer the phone. They'd lie there and starve to death! But it was not because she was that sexually insatiable; it was more because she needed the assurance of being near someone. Nothing gave her more pleasure than to curl up in his arms and sleep. He could be talking a mile a minute and glance at her and find that she had fallen fast asleep, her face unutterably contented. And he'd be alone again, unable to sleep because of *his* problems. . . .

And, yeah, the bed thing again: when they made love, WHY DID SHE ALWAYS WEEP? Not just a couple of tears—there'd been women he had known before who had shed a few tears out of sheer pleasure—but in Pat's case there was a complete breaking down kind of weeping. Her body would go into convulsions and then collapse and she would weep as though she'd never stop, clinging to him, kissing him.

He didn't know if he should be flattered or frightened.

129

"What is the matter? Do I hurt you or something?" He was forever asking, alarmed, tensing up against her.

"No. Oh, no. I just love . . . love . . . you so much! And everything is so . . . so . . . beautiful. I never believed . . . believed . . . it could ever be!"

Well, maybe it was a normal reaction? Maybe there were other women like her, but he'd never met one.

But lastly, number (5), and it was the most devastating: Pat was not only a lousy house-keeper but a lousy cook as well. She burnt eggs. She made bacon that was either too crisp or too raw. Her favorite dish was veal parmigiana. And, good God, he had to hold a smile on his face and keep assuring her how good it was, when it was really lousy! Of course, it didn't help that he didn't care very much about veal parmigiana anyway.

In any case, she'd open up TV dinners rather than get out of bed. Maybe it wasn't so much that she was a bad cook but that she disliked being alone, even in the kitchen. Bustling about the stove she'd carry on a running conversation with him and if she could hear him in the other room grunting an occasional "Yes" or "No," assuring her that he was still around somewhere, the food would get her attention and sometimes come out adequate, if not as good as it looked. Alone, she simply hurried to get out of the kitchen.

So wouldn't he have to be out of his mind to continue this stupid relationship?

There was so much "wrong" with Pat Wallstone he felt the constant threat of being pulled backwards, instead of being helped by her to move forwards. What could he say to her about Bernie Stein? She had so many anxieties of her own, when would she ever be able to see that he might have a couple of fears himself?

"Please wait, Winston. Please have patience with me. I'm trying."

Yeah.

Some Goddamn Black Princess he had found!

He dashed some water across the kitchen floor and mopped it up angrily. He did the same to the bathroom. But in the living room he hesitated. Something in the back of his mind caused him to pause. He couldn't remember how Pat had cleaned the hardwood floor—those few times she had done it.

It seemed to him she'd used a wax mop or something. But didn't you have to clean a floor before you waxed it? She always ran around the apartment in her bare feet. Maybe that was why she had to constantly wash her feet, the floor covered by the filthy wax?

But, goddammit, wasn't this whole thing ridiculous! Here he was wasting his time on house chores when his mind should be firmly concentrated on business! Irritably he dashed the whole bucket of soapy water across the floor. Hell of a thing when a man didn't have a woman whom he could trust to take care of the house.

The water ran everywhere. The more he mopped, the more there seemed to be of it. He flung the draperies all the way back so that he could better see what he was doing, thinking angrily: Why did she prefer the draperies to be closed, blocking away the world outside? So that he'd forget where he was? So that she could continue to smother him? Lock him forever into the small and limited world on this side of the draperies?

He stared at the floor. It was taking on a greyish, dingy color, losing its mahogany shine. It suddenly struck him, my God, now he knew what had been in the back of his mind. He wasn't supposed to use *soap* on the floor! Apparently the floor was treated by some sort of chemical and there was a special kind of cleaning fluid or wax he should have used. Well, too late now! Unless a couple of buckets of water would clear the soap up? Had to try that. Get it cleared up before Pat got back. Worst thing in the world would be for her to see how *he* had screwed up, when he was about to cut her loose because *she* was the one who was always screwing up!

He threw two buckets of clear water across the floor. Such a flood he had to roll his pants up. In the meantime, he thought he smelled the stew burning. He rushed into the kitchen and stirred the pot. Back in the living room he had to move the couch and chairs and tables to get at the water.

Sweating, panting, angry, he had about half of the water up when the phone rang.

He answered it impatiently. It was his Answering Service, calling him on his private line. Occasionally his business phone was switched off on Sunday, but his Service had instructions to call him at any time if something that seemed important came up.

The girl was upset. Someone had been calling and using abusive language. Also, one of his tenants had phoned three times complaining about two windows that had fallen out. The tenant said she had paid Donald the rent so why couldn't she get something fixed once in a while? Six other calls had been from people seeking apartments, but they seemed to prefer something in a "nicer" neighborhood than where Winston had his buildings. Then a Mr. Rios had called, from the Manhattan Tenants Action Committee, and demanded that Winston return the call first thing Monday morning.

"Demanded?" Winston said.

"Yes, sir," the woman replied. She always seemed rather happy to report bad news. "He said that he and the tenants . . . ."

"Okay." He cut her short. He tried to keep calm. The day already had him upset enough. But it always galled him for anybody to demand that he do anything. Ask him, yes, and maybe he'd do it. Who in the hell was this Rios anyway. . . ?

"And, sir . . . ." Answering Service said in her own peevish and disgruntled voice. "What about these abusive calls? I don't get paid to talk to people like that."

"Did the person leave a number?"

"No. He just told me—when I said you weren't available—to go . . . fuck myself, and hung up."

"Okay. If he calls back, hold him on the line, and buzz me on my private line again and I'll take care of it."

"I hope so, sir. I don't get paid for . . ."

"I said I'd take care of it!" Winston hung up. What the hell *did* she get paid for! She missed at least three or four of his calls a day. It was a lousy Service. Something else he'd have to do, change to another Service. Well, maybe one day he'd have a secretary and a decent office again and instead of doing business seven days a week, he could take off Saturday and Sunday like any other sensible business man. Crawl before you could walk and all that crap, he supposed. But, my God, how long did a man have to crawl!

He looked at the water still standing everywhere. It was discouraging. Maybe he shouldn't have started this goddamn mopping in the first place.

He still didn't have all the water cleared up when the door buzzer sounded. He went to the intercom and said, "Yeah?" even though he was fairly sure it was Pat. But he had to be positive. A couple of times Process Servers had been trying to con their way into the building, looking for him with Summonses, and also a few tenants had found out where he lived and with everyone so enraged and uptight these days you never knew what to expect.

Still he hoped it wasn't Pat yet. He stared at the water again. He figured he needed at least another ten minutes. . . .

But it was her voice. "Me," she answered gaily, apparently in the same bright mood she'd been in when she left. He buzzed her in. Often a beautiful night of sex lifted her up like that, left her with a glow, a state of happiness so intense that he was depressed when he couldn't always share her euphoria. The world was still outside, filled with menace, and even through sex he couldn't always escape that knowledge.

But with her who knew. By the time she rode the elevator up to the twentieth floor, she could be back down in the dumps again. Also, whatever *his* mood was, she'd soon change hers. If he was in a good mood, she tried to maintain a good mood. If he was depressed, she became depressed. All of her moods seemed dependent on how he happened to be feeling. The very opposite of every goddamn thing he needed! Hell, when a man was down, he needed a woman not to sink down with him but to help him come back up!

He toweled the perspiration from his face and body and attacked the water-soaked floor again. If he hurried, maybe he'd still have it cleared up. Then the bell chimed. Like an express train today. Any other time it would have taken her a million years to return with the grocery, stopping and shopping in every store window she passed.

He opened the door, feeling hostility mounting, his anger becoming so acute it was like a fist twisting inside his stomach.

She came in smiling.

"Hi. It's so beautiful out I wanted to go and run through the park! But I knew you must be hungry."

One arm holding the groceries, she came up to him and embraced him with the other. Her cheeks were warm and he always liked the faint woman smell of her and he was again amazed to note how lovely she was. A moment of confusion gripped him, vying with his hostility against her. But he pulled away and walked deeper into the room.

She was going towards the kitchen when she let out a cry of alarm.

"Darling, what happened to the floor?"

"Nothing," he grumbled. "I'm cleaning it."

"Cleaning it? With water? Oh, no! It . . . you don't do it with water! It'll buckle the floor! Ruin it completely!"

"What do you mean?" he said stubbornly. "How in hell you going to clean it if you don't put water on it!"

"Oh, Winston!" She hurriedly put the groceries down. "We got to get the water up, fast! You clean it with a special wax, a special fluid. Like I've been doing."

Deep down he knew she was right. It even seemed now he had read somewhere, in the literature he had been given when he leased the apartment, that no water should be put on the floor. But instead of his anger diminishing, it increased.

"Yeah. Well, whatever you've been doing, the floor is never clean. Otherwise, why are you always washing your feet!"

She was about to reply, then she glanced at him, felt all the rage that was coiled and ready to strike her, and her eyes dulled and grew wary. She seemed to visibly drop from the clouds, to be already cringing inwardly, as though she not only expected further blows but must be somehow guilty of whatever he decided to accuse and deserved them.

"I'm sorry," Her voice had become small and saddened. "Sorry I don't clean the floor so good. But . . . I . . . Well, I didn't know you thought that. . . ."

What the hell could he say? She already seemed so contrite, whipping herself before he had even begun to let her know that he was finished with her.

A vast wave of annoyance shook him. But today he wouldn't listen to her sad and frightened little girl's voice! Nothing must threaten his resolve. Today he'd shake himself free of this stupid relationship.

Still he hesitated, conscious of her staring at him, knowing that she might start crying in a minute. And, God, how he hated her tears! Despite himself the very sound of her weeping could tear into him more deeply and painfully than anyone had ever gotten before. Why couldn't she do things calmly, reasonably, with a bit of sophistication? In fact, maybe he would delay breaking this thing off until dinner, and then he would speak to her quietly, without anger, in a very civilized manner. Maybe she, too, would see that they were totally incompatible?

Besides, there was the floor. Shouldn't he at least let her help him get it cleared up first? But my God, was he beginning to chicken? Of course not! He knew himself. Nothing ever stopped him once he had made up his mind, right? So there was no danger of his weakening if he calmed down and did this thing a little later. And if she wept then. . . ? Too bad!

"Listen . . ." he started to say, surprised that his voice still seemed confused. Then he was jarred by the phone ringing again. Goddamn Answering Service! More trouble. Maybe that bastard who had cursed her out trying to reach him again?

Annoyance followed him to the phone, but as he picked it up he also felt a strange kind of relief. He didn't understand it. If he was determined to end the relationship with Pat, and he was sure he was, why was each delay greeted so eagerly? He frowned, confusion sharpening his tone. "Yeah?"

"Hey, my Man, how you doing! You ready for Bernie again tomorrow? You sound worried." Of all people, it had to be Gru. Well, maybe good it was Gru. Another reminder why he should break with Pat. Stabbing another man in the back. How much more of a bastard could he become? Worst of all, he didn't even feel guilty about it anymore. Why? Because he had almost ceased to respect Gru as a businessman?

"We going to take care of that sucker this time!" Gru said, brimming with his usual enthusiasm. "One thing, your buddy, Gru, never makes the same mistake twice! Don't worry about that postponement. I've checked around and the reason Bernie didn't meet with us the other day was because his new partner was out of town. Also, Jack Goldin was tied up with a lot of extra legal work, and you know Bernie never does anything without Jack. They're a team. . . ."

Sure. Winston thought sourly. Don't I know they're a team. *Now* I know.

Out there in the Real Estate world, people still came up to him, saying: "Say, you the guy Bernie and Jack unloaded those buildings on? Man, where did you come from! You got to watch those guys!" Even Bernie had felt a little sorry for him, *after* the deal; bought him dinner a couple of times. "Young fellow, you seem to have guts. Now no hard feelings, eh? In every game you got to pay to learn the rules. You're just paying a little more than most, that's all. Tell you what I'm going to do, here's my private number. You have any problem, need some advice on how to bail yourself out of this bind, you call me. I like a guy who doesn't tuck his tail and run when the going gets rough. You could go far in business."

Yeah. Sure he could go far. If he didn't get flung back downwards first. The morgue was probably full of guys who could have gone far, but hadn't.

"You there, Baby?" Gru said.

"Yeah," he said. But the truth was, he found himself increasingly impatient just talking to Gru, the churning hostility deep within himself now directing itself towards Gru. He had already made up his own mind how he intended to handle Bernie Stein this time, so what the hell could Gru really tell him anymore? Also, he was partly distracted, conscious of Pat moving uneasily about the room, mopping the floor with abrupt nervous strokes, watching him surreptitiously and trying to gauge the depth of his anger against her, already preparing to appease him, to do anything to escape being hurt by him.

He frowned and looked away from her.

"You see what I mean?" Gru said. "No doubt about it, we've caught Bernie sleeping this time, caught him with his pants down, so to speak! Well, even the best of operators sleep sometimes, even me. But, Man, Bernie done slept through the possibility of picking up $250,000. And that's a quarter of a million! A quarter of a million, you hear what I say! With that kind of bread, Man, you could donate those crappy buildings you got now to the Salvation Army! I'd say, milk them and drop them. A quarter of a million puts you into the Rolls Royce class, chauffeur up front, phone in the back, bar, TV, the whole bit! What I mean is, Baby, I don't see how we can lose this one!"

You didn't see how *we* could lose the last one either, Winston thought, but *I* lost. Thinking that the only reason he might not lose this time was because he was going to handle the deal himself, no more short term mortgages, and buildings falling apart even as he was signing his name to become the owner of them. And no more of all that legal gobbledygook that left him exposed to a lot of hidden time bombs. He had learned a little about this game, maybe not nearly enough yet, but hopefully enough to get him through this next deal with Bernie.

"We'll get Downtown yet!" Gru said. "Go Public! After all, most of the Big Boys had a few setbacks before they got to the Street!"

"Sure," Winston said. "But did Jonathan speak to his friend, the deputy Commissioner again? And don't you think we should do less dreaming and a bit more practical foot-work?"

"But, Man, it's all taken care of! Haven't I told you how far Jonathan goes back with the Commissioner? Man, they were frat brothers together and they are still drinking buddies! That's why the Commissioner trusts Jonathan completely, absolutely. And dig this, I've told you Bernie doesn't have a single Jewish connection or cracker connection, either, for that matter, in the Commissioner's office. Man, this is strictly a Black operation!"

"Yeah. But Bernie still could have spread some bread around."

"Wouldn't make sense, Man! If Bernie knew as much as we know, why would he and his partner want to get rid of the six buildings? I'm telling you only our man, the Commissioner, knows that we are right smack dab in the middle of an Acquisition! And he knows because he's got the *power* to tell the Big Boys at City Hall—and I mean all the way up to the Mayor—*how* the game has got to be played. Naw, Man, this is a Black operation. This time it's us Niggers who've got the connections and the Whites are outside looking in!"

"Hope you're right," Winston mumbled, resenting the fact that no matter what he thought about Gru and Jonathan he still had to rely on them. So far, Jonathan's friend, the Commissioner, had even refused to see him, would only trust Jonathan. And it was really Gru who had discovered the six buildings, hot for Federal money, that it seemed Bernie and his partners had over-looked—, or maybe not really over-looked, for Gru had quoted the Commissioner as having said: "I can get some Black guilt money if you guys get in there. The administration has got to throw some crumbs to the Niggers if it means to get re-elected, so I can put on a little pressure and squeeze these buildings into a Site. What do I want? Jonathan will take care of everything; but *off the top.* . . ." So maybe Bernie had realized that he was *too white* to get the money? And had decided to go for a substantial mortgage and bail himself out of the buildings the best way he could? In any case, what could he, Winston, do—except keep hoping. Whether he liked it or not, he had to rely on Jonathan and Gru to do their part, while he prepared himself to make the best deal he possibly could with Bernie tomorrow. And he certainly had to make a good deal! He had borrowed every penny he could, mortgaged the junk buildings he had to the hilt, and he still didn't have sufficient cash to take over the six buildings. . . . A fact that even Gru didn't know yet. He had already thought that either he, himself, had to postpone the Contract tomorrow or go on in there and bluff his way through. . . .

He gripped the phone, a wave of fear suddenly knotting his stomach. Sweat broke out upon the back of his hands, itched his armpits, stung his cheeks. The knots in his stomach seemed to swell up and flow into his chest, squeezing at his very breath. Was he moving head-long towards another failure? Perhaps he was never going to be a match for Bernie and the so-called "Big Boys?" What an illusion for him to even think so! Maybe the odds were too great for a Black like himself to ever really win out there in the American System? And sooner or later he, too, would be flung back downwards where he came from?

Pat took that moment to ease herself down beside him on the bed and to press her cheek anxiously against his. Apparently she hoped he'd slip his free arm around her, as he sometimes did when talking on the phone.

But instead he tensed, steeling himself against her again. He put his hand over the mouth-piece. His tone succeeded in being almost as frosty as he intended it to be. "It's Gru."

"Oh, Lord." She jumped up guiltily. She went to her bag upon the table and whipped out a cigarette and lit it. She switched on the TV, looking at him startled and apologetically

138

when the volume came on too loud. Finally, she got the sound adjusted.

He looked away from her, bottomlessly irritated once more. If she had finished the floor, why in the hell didn't she go into the kitchen and get the stew ready or something! Also, she kept saying she was going to quit smoking, well, why didn't she show some backbone and go ahead and do it!

"Well, see you tomorrow," Gru said. "And, Man, don't worry! There's absolutely nothing to worry about. I'm still hanging in there with you, and we have Jonathan and, Man, now we even got a Commissioner hooked in with us! We moving!"

"Yeah," Winston said. "Okay. See you." He hung up. Then thought: maybe he should have mentioned this guy, Rios, who had called and who no doubt was a representative of the tenants up there at the buildings he was about to get into? No, goddammit, he must break this dependence on Gru. Figure things out for himself. Get beyond the sad black bag of the blind leading the blind. He would call Rios and make his own decision as to what to do. He felt a little better, self-doubt diminishing at the thought of himself in action, by-passing the Grus, the Jonathans, and perhaps even the Commisioner who hadn't so far condescended to speak to him.

Still he sat there for awhile, staring broodingly at nothing in particular. Suddenly he was ravenously hungry, as though the knots in his stomach had all burst, leaving one gigantic hole. Why didn't she have the food ready? He could hear her now out there in the kitchen where she had finally gone but when he looked around he saw that the table wasn't set up yet. What was the big hold up? After all, hadn't he put the stew on himself? Instead of wasting time and gazing at him, she could've had dinner ready by now!

He got up abruptly and went to the bathroom and washed his face and hands. If he expected to eat, it was probably a useless gesture, since she was never going to have dinner ready anyway! He needed a shave but didn't feel like bothering with it. In the mirror, his eyes seemed stormy and black and absolutely hateful even to him. Was it possible he was being unfair to Pat? Well, hadn't he decided he was going to speak to her calmly and quietly and explain to her that they were simply not meant for

139

each other? What more could he do? She'd have to understand that it wasn't his fault if he needed a woman much more sophisticated than she was, who already knew as well as he did how to cope with the rat race outside.

Sure, he admitted, she was willing to learn but how long could he wait for her? He was aware of how backwards a disadvantaged background could leave a person. The ghettos of the country were teaming with people who had had their lives short-circuited. But, my God, he wasn't running a Community Training Program! He was having enough trouble trying to save himself.

And talking about disadvantages, he surely hadn't been born with no silver spoon in his mouth either. But she didn't always seem to listen when he tried to explain to her how far down he, too, had come from.

Outside, Pat rapped timidly upon the door. He jerked it open.

"Yeah?"

"Phone ringing," she stammered.

"Well, answer it!" he said abruptly, more sharply than he had intended. But the quick hurt that deepened the wounded look already in her big eyes only irritated him again. He pulled the door closed. Goddammit, just when he had been trying to calm down and talk to her sensibly, once more confronted by the fact that she was so goddamn numb she couldn't even answer the phone! Unless, of course, it was his private line? And, yeah, right, he had never encouraged her to answer his private line. He hadn't wanted to take the chance it would be some chick and she'd be upset.

His jumbled thoughts accepted the fact that it had to be his private line, since his business phone was turned off for the day, but now he didn't care. If a woman was on the line, maybe Pat would get so angry *she'd leave him.* Save him the trouble of terminating this thing over dinner!

He heard the faint sound of her rapping upon the door again and then she knocked a bit harder. He pulled the door open, stifling some of his hostility this time.

She hesitated.

"It's somebody called a . . . well . . . a Mr. Slick."

"What?"

"A Mr. Slick."

"Slick?" He stared at her. "Are you sure?"

"Yes. Doesn't sound like the kind of people always calling you. Sounds like some kind of a hustler or something. . . ."

Winston was speechless. A thousand things ran through his mind. Those TV cameras that had caught him debarking from the plane. . . . A Black newspaper that had run his picture under a caption: "Black entrepreneur and world Sportsman returning from his recent trip abroad to his multi-million dollar Real Estate Enterprises!" Multi-million dollar, indeed! Black press using him to jack up its own ego and the sad and battered egos of its Black readers, who wanted and needed so badly to identify with power and success. Let a Black man make a five thousand dollar investment and the Black press instantly made him a billionaire business tycoon! But how many nuts had seen him on TV and his picture in the paper and were now trying to get to him? Some of his tenants, yes, and that was bad enough. And what about nuts like Marty Gero? And the enemies he may have made on the plane itself? And now this Slick—if he could trust Pat's message—and, of course, he supposed he had to.

"You okay?" Pat asked. "Is it someone . . . someone after you . . . trying to hurt you. . . ? He doesn't sound *right* on the phone."

"Is he still on the line?"

"Yes."

"Tell him. . . . Tell him I'm not in. Tell him to leave his phone number and I'll call him back. In fact, tell him I'm in California . . . or somewhere. . . . But that you expect to hear from me long distance and I'll call him back."

She didn't move for a time, alarmed that he seemed so stunned.

"Do it," he said. "And do it right, okay?"

He came out of the bathroom after she had hung up. He went to the window and stared out at the late evening. Wafts of white and orange clouds drifted across the blue sky. All the buildings and the City itself seemed quiet and peaceful below. It was amazing that out there in the Sunday-like tranquility so many threats could rise up out of the rotten depths and aim themselves at him.

From behind him at the phone, Pat told him, "He said there

was no particular place you could phone him. Said you could find him like you found him before."

"What else?"

"Well, when I kept asking, are you sure it's Mr. Winston you want, he insisted it was. He seemed high on drugs or something. Said he was down on his luck and had to talk to you and that maybe the two of you could work out something."

"Sonofabitch!"

"Darling, are you in some kind of trouble? Is there something I can do to help. . . ?"

"Forget it," he said. But suddenly he wished very much that they were friendly to each other at this moment, or at least that he could unbend himself and be friendly to her. Right now he seemed threatened from every direction. Never would he be able to out-maneuver Bernie, and the Whiteys beyond Bernie who owned the City, the country. His phone could be tapped and the bastards who had been guarding Vanderpool on the plane could already have tossed his name into some computer, pushing buttons, and if they were destroying and killing each other all the way up to the top, of what importance would be his destruction? He didn't wish to think again about an enraged tenant who might attack him the moment he stepped outside his door, or about Marty Gero who he was sure would never forgive him even if restrained from attacking him by the fear of his own self-exposure. But most of all, he didn't wish to think about Slick, a sonofabitch he had almost pushed out of his mind, forgotten.

Pat came up off the bed and moved towards him. But instead of being able to unbend, he found himself growing more rigid. A wave of new anger swept over him. What the hell could she do anyway? In fact, if he told her the truth about Slick, she'd probably turn against him also. But how in the hell did she suppose he had climbed up out of the gutter? You didn't crush your way up through all the rot and come out smelling like perfume!

She came close to him, big eyes bright with concern, searching his face, but stopped because she couldn't help but feel the intensity of his antagonism. She didn't know what to say. On the one hand he wished she could find some word that

142

would help him unbend, but on the other he wished she'd turn, go, leave the apartment and he'd never see her again.

"That guy . . ." She finally mumbled, whipping out a cigarette and dragging the smoke in so deeply he knew the smoke had to be hurting her. "He . . . he . . . didn't seem like anybody you would know. But if it is trouble, why don't you tell me? I know I'm not much help. But when you don't even take me into your confidence, it's worse. How can I ever learn to be of any help to you if you always . . . always lock me out?"

She was right, of course. Perhaps sometimes he didn't give her much of a chance. Maybe he should try one last time to explain to her what was bugging him. Maybe this time she'd understand better than she had before?

But how to explain to her that he, too, could sometimes be afraid, ripped apart by self-doubts, when he knew very well that she didn't believe he was afraid of anything. She needed to believe for her own strange reason that he was so strong and "all together," that he could go out there in the world and slay all the goddamn dragons seven days a week, twenty-four hours a day.

Well, hell, yes, he could slay one or two dragons but what the fuck did you do when they kept multiplying and coming after you!

Everything had been so imperfect in her life, he suspected she desperately needed to see him as "perfect," or whatever it was she imagined perfection to be, maybe like one of those phony characters in cool Summer suits sitting on the decks of rented yachts and sipping scotch and sodas for ads in *Life* and *Ebony* magazine. And yet for his own reasons, maybe out of a need as peculiar as her own, he knew that he had not always discouraged her in this unblemished and childish view of himself.

Preachers had their flocks; entertainers their followers; Gurus packed stadiums; most everyone had someone—following. Well, he supposed that he had Pat Wallstone!

Yeah, Pat whose greatest fear would never be that he might be defeated and destroyed, nor that she'd probably never become the First Lady at the White House, but a fear of that

143

which obsessed her the most: *the loss of love.* . . . If she had love, she seemed to believe that everything else would work out just fine.

So what the hell could he tell her? Well, he'd still try this one last time. . . .

"Slick," he began, not quite looking at her though superconscious of her presence. "Yeah, Slick. . . . But, first of all, why should you be surprised that all of my associates are not . . . are not members of some Ivy League? A lot of people I know now are worse crooks than many of the people I met years before. What would you say if I told you I'm just about to piece off a Commissioner? A guy who is sworn into office and is supposed to uphold the law and look out for the welfare of the people! Slick is a bum but what is the Commissioner, and other dudes in high places ripping off the public? I mean, how in the hell do you think people who call me are *supposed* to sound?"

She made an effort to say something but he cut her short, his voice rising despite himself. "I've told you that I, too, have lived among the goddamn garbage cans of this City. But you can't seem to get rid of the idea that I came charging in out of *nowhere,* riding a white horse and all that crap! You don't really listen when I tell you how goddamn rotten the game is. I'm not always proud of what I have had to do to win—and may still have to do—but you should at least listen when I tell you I don't intend to allow anything or *anybody* to stop me. Why should I? What the hell do I have to go back to? When I was a kid, the people in my building would say, 'Hey, kid, my toilet won't flush. Yo ole lazy daddy don't never fix nothing good, and you is the super's son, so if we paying him we paying you, too, right? So git yo ass on up here and clean up this shit!' "

He stared out of the window, furious.

"Bastards," he said. "Themselves caught so low on the economic scale that to 'get on Welfare' was not only their sole salvation but had become their only ambition. And yet if I was their flunky, where was I? At sixteen, I escaped—I put my age up and went into the army. *I thought I had escaped.* But, right, there I was surrounded by shit-houses and garbage cans again. The highest rank most Black guys had been able to obtain was Corporal or Sergeant, excepting a few Lieutenants and even fewer Captains. The higher it got, the Colonels, the Generals, the *whiter* it got. For those of us caught at the bottom of that pyramid, it was either cut your own balls off and shape up or face the guard house. For a number of us, the army became a shuttle from garbage cans to the guard houses. The battle is a bit more even now, but why can't you understand what a misfit I must have been then?"

"I do understand, Winston. I . . ." She moved in a little closer to him, her big eyes gazing at him anxiously. But it seemed to him she was only looking for an angle of weakness; something that would tell her his rage had diminished and she could move in even closer.

"Do you? Or are you only *saying* that you do? If you understood, you wouldn't be so surprised that bastards like Slick can still reach up out of the gutter and phone me. You'd know, too, how it was when I got out of the army. *Nothing* had changed. Except that the Generals now wore civilian clothes. And except that now, instead of army latrines, they had a whole country full of shit houses to be cleaned. But I was still naive. There was the flag and apple pie and all that crap. I kept putting in application after application for jobs I was never going to get. Then I began to see that even if I put on a white shirt and was allowed into the banks, my function was always going to be to *count* the money rather than *spend* it. Still, though I'm sure it must have crossed my mind, I didn't begin *sticking up* the banks or cracking people over the head and mugging. I was lucky. I had an inheritance. $697.00. Not much, right? A pittance! But most Black parents are never able to amass even that much to leave their kids. Yeah, certainly not much, but it helped me to keep alive while I got myself together; while I slowly adjusted to the fact that if I didn't hurry and find a way to beat the system, almost, you might say, *get around* the system even as I punched my way up through it, I was going to be destroyed. . . ."

He paused, still breathing furiously. He was aware he hadn't said much of what he had meant to say. Yet he was partly disgusted with himself. Instead of allowing himself to be carried away, almost as if he had been evading the subject, he should have told her bluntly *everything* about Slick. If the affair was

145

finished, why should it matter if he retained her respect? It should be a pleasure to tell her those things that would repell her.

He could sense she had stepped in so close she could touch him. He glanced at her and saw that tears had dampened her eyes. The thought crossed his mind that even if he told her the worst about himself, she might not like it, but she still wouldn't leave him. Right now, she seemed to want no more than to share in his pain, to share whatever it was that bothered him now, or ever would.

"You poor darling," she said.

He shuddered. He looked away from her. Why did the concern in her voice seem so suspiciously close to pity? It was as though in his outburst he had revealed a weakness about himself he hadn't known he had, and surely had never allowed her to see before.

"Don't say that." He whirled back towards her. "You . . ." He had difficulty finding words. Even the suspicion that she might look upon him, however briefly, as just another sad and defeated Black man was intolerable. "You haven't understood a single thing I've said!" He pointed out the window. "The poor darlings are *down there*. The goddamn Lieutenants and the Captains and maybe even a number of Colonels! And I tell you, before I'm finished a few Generals may look upwards and can't see me either. So don't give me that 'poor darling' business. I'm sick of niggers wallowing in self-pity. I'm sick of *victims*! We got to strike back. Crush our way up through the crap, that's all!"

"I just meant . . ."

"Forget it! Why didn't you set the table yet? You intend to let the stew burn up?"

* * *

Sitting at the table, he fell into a gloomy silence. The outburst hadn't done anything but left him feeling drained. Nothing was solved, and he was still faced by the task of breaking this thing off with Patricia Wallstone.

She moved about the table as though the very air was composed of delicate glass, and the slightest wrong move on her part would cause everything to break and come tumbling down.

She set the table, put a plate of stew and rice before him, all the while watching him apprehensively. It was as if she suddenly knew that no matter what she said, no matter what he said, nothing was going to unbend him, and knowing that she had begun to sense what he really intended doing today. . . .

Still she tried. She adjusted the TV where he could see it as he ate, even though this meant she'd have to turn her head and strain to see it herself. Then she went and put on an old cotton dress that she sometimes wore when she was working around the house. He had once told her she looked "sexy" in the dress: body moving freely beneath it, legs bare. . . . But now he was only annoyed. As she sat, he looked away from her, stared at the TV, dipped into his stew.

And as for the stew, it was about the worst he had ever tasted. Meat not only as tough as leather but tasted like it!

Why didn't she complain? Why sit there like a dummy and not rub it in? Undoubtedly, he had done something wrong when he put the goddamn stew on the fire. It had cooked too fast or something. . . . Well, what was he supposed to have done, wait for her to come back with a TV dinner!

He chewed angrily. She kept dipping bravely around the edges of her own stew, swallowing with difficulty and glancing at him surreptitiously. When the heavy silence persisted between them she hesitated, then ventured, "Well, stew not bad . . . could've cooked a little bit more . . . maybe . . . but . . . but . . . really not too bad."

He grunted.

"Tastes okay to me."

"Oh, me too. I didn't mean to say it didn't. I just thought maybe I should have cooked it a little longer. I mean, I know you like things well done and . . ."

He grunted again, his attitude so chilly, her voice trailed off. He knew how profoundly he was wounding her, and he sought to will himself towards an even greater coldness towards her, so that he'd cease being concerned that she was being wounded. Recently it had gotten so every time he hurt her in some way, he seemed to feel the pain almost as much as she did, like maybe he was already tied to her more deeply and strongly than he really knew. All the more reason he should get out of this thing, and get out fast. Keep it going and allow her to continue to hang around and worm her way into him, and he could wake up one morning and it would be too late, find himself trapped forever.

He manifested a great interest in the TV while he gathered his thoughts. One of those old phony movies was coming to a thunderous conclusion: a number of Foreign Legionnaires were bravely blazing away with muskets and cannons, defending themselves against a horde of attacking "natives. . . ." Then, amidst a great deal of bugle blowing and a final false dash of white courage, all the "natives" lay dead and destroyed across miles and miles of white sand. . . .

She turned her head and pretended to be absorbed in what he was watching, though clearly she wasn't interested. The news came on and the news almost always bored her, but she gazed at the screen intently.

The international crisis again: Gold, the dollar, the pound; inflation and devaluation; and everyone scrambling all over the World in search for oil and copper. Quoting: ". . . Once the sun never set on the British Empire, now the sun could hardly find Britain, let alone the Empire. . . ." And America? Worlds were falling apart. . . .

Yeah, something else to annoy him, leave him uneasy. Just when he was about to learn how to cope and carve himself a piece of the pie out of the rich and powerful Free Enterprise USA System maybe the whole goddamn thing was about to come apart and crumble. An added reason why he had to move faster, get *his* while the getting was still good.

The White House shrouded in solemn light flashed onto the screen, and then the camera went into the Senate, where everyone stood and applauded, hundreds of white faces, some even whistling. A new man had finally been found to replace Vanderpool. . . .

". . . In the meantime," the Newscaster said. "The FBI and local New York Law Enforcement Agents stormed into a Harlem apartment early this morning, and though one suspect was shot, Leroy Brown was believed to have escaped. . . . The suspect," A Black face was flashed onto the screen, and he sensed how all at once Pat became interested but his own interest was also heightened. ". . . before dying, denied knowing Leroy Brown. He claimed he had shot back at the Law Enforcement Agents because he had thought they were after

148

him, even though he hadn't done anything illegal, but wasn't sure he could prove he hadn't.... Apologies have been extended to the parents of the dead man.... It has still not been ruled out that Brown, former chauffeur to fallen Diplomat, Vanderpool, was not the suspect who fled the apartment. Law Enforcement Agents are working on the theory that the former chauffeur could have had links to a Black extremist group, though proof to support that theory has not been found so far.... Now a look at the latest score of the Dallas football game, following this announcement...."

She turned to him her eyes blazing angrily.

"You see! You see what they do! Broke in and shot somebody down like a dog, when the man wasn't guilty of nothing!"

Her breast heaved with indignation. Though her anger was genuine, he suspected it was also a needed release of tension, maybe even a part of it an anger she would have liked to direct at him, but was afraid to.

Her little girl voice had all but disappeared and her tone was husky with outrage.

"Why don't they track down that ... that white tramp! When they find her, they'll find the chauffeur, and I bet she helped to plot the whole thing, she and them other white crooks! Howcome they so mean to us, blame us for everything? Don't we have feelings? In school my professor looks all over me when I know an answer to a question, but the minute I don't put my hand up and he think I don't know the answer, he pops the question at me every time! Embarrassing me. Don't they know we got feelings?"

He had to look away from her.

He knew her so well, so very well, all the way down to the very core of her feelings, and they were delicate feelings. All she asked for was to be understood and respected a little and loved. He knew that she was truly concerned about the chauffeur and the man who had gotten shot, but he was even more aware now that she was torn up inside and afraid because she didn't always know how to cope with him and had probably already sensed deep down that this thing was just about over between them.

He heard her voice, breaking a little, her anger still struggling to support it.

"... One of them ... can you imagine! ... even came up to

me on the subway.... A . . . a . . . creep . . . following me. I
mean, not really a creep . . . but . . . but . . ."

Then she was crying.

He couldn't escape the sound of it. At first she just sniffled
and swallowed and then a gasp of pain welled up deep from
within her chest. When he looked at her, her face was flooded
by tears, her big eyes wide open and gazing at him.

Suddenly her voice was more pitifully small than he had ever
heard it before.

"Please," she said. "Please don't hurt me, Winston."

The sound wrung at him, cutting so deeply, a rush of
emotion escaped his controls and rose up with such force to
meet hers that tears were almost pushed into his own eyes. My
God! he thought, this is ridiculous! If I don't stop this thing
right now, clearly I'm never going to be able to stop it. He
struggled to regain his most ruthless attitude. But she came out
of the chair and around the table and onto his lap, weeping
more uncontrollably, holding onto him. Despite himself his
arms went around her. After all, what the hell difference would
another day make? He still knew himself. He could always
break this thing off tomorrow. But even as he tried to
understand it, he was surprised to find himself not only
caressing her tenderly but holding onto her trembling body
almost as hopelessly as she held onto him.

thirteen

Someone watched him. A man sitting at the wheel of a battered lavender El Dorado. Pimpmobile. Stone gone. Hub caps ripped off and huge gashes in the paint along the side and hood of the car. Two windows were shattered and barely hanging in there.

Junior circled around the building again, avoiding the dogs and the guards, and came back and the El Dorado was still there. But was the man watching him or the building? At first he had thought maybe the guy was some kind of Security. Like the dogs seemed to already know what he was thinking, so they had brought this dude into the show. But how could the guy be anything like Security? He was a messed-up looking dude, sitting there behind the wheel wearing dark blue sunglasses, and as beat-up looking as an old junkie. Trust him with Security and he'd rip the whole building off. Also, a guard had already taken a suspicious look at both the car and the man, and yesterday one of the dogs had jumped at the car and barked. The man had driven away and come back and parked on the other side of the street. So if the man wasn't watching him, he was either hanging around for someone to come out of the building, or he was planning some kind of a rip off.

Junior crouched again between two other parked cars and tried to vomit. Dry rasping sounds that he attempted to keep quiet. Very little came up, except that the mucus was still streaked with blood. Like that for a couple of days now. Maybe he had punctured a vein or the shit was eating out a lining somewhere deep within his stomach?

151

But what did he care? Once he had finished what he started out to do, what did he care? If he still didn't have to look out for Mama, he wouldn't care at all if he suddenly fell over and never got up again.

He gripped the side of a car and clung to his violin case, gagging, snot running out of his nose. He'd fixed himself up only a few hours ago. Did he already need to do it over again? It used to be only once a day. Now it seemed like every time he looked around he was strung out. . . . Pretty soon maybe he'd have to fix himself up every ten or fifteen minutes?

But I'm okay, he thought. I can cut this shit loose any time I want. It ain't as if I'm like one of them no good thieving filthy junkies that can't quit.

A shadow fell across the sun. Before he could look up, a cruel hand grasped his neck and pushed his face towards the ground. Panic seized him, vying with the pain. Motherfucker! he thought. Sonofabitch had caught him again. Slapped him around once like a kid, and now had him again. . . . Or was it one of the guards? But he didn't hear a dog barking. Frantically he tried to get the violin case open. But the hand began to choke him, as though it didn't care if it broke his neck. Then whoever it was wrested the violin case from his hand and ordered, "Get up, junkie!"

He lifted dazed eyes and looked at the dark blue sunglasses. The man had a cruel heavy mouth and seemed to wear a red rope around his yellow neck.

"Get up and get over in the car." The man indicated the battered lavender El Dorado. "Don't gimme no shit." The voice sounded like voices Junior had heard before; devoid of all feeling, rasping, cold, as though all the music had been eaten out of it.

The man didn't remove his hand, pushing Junior into the car. Once settled inside, the man both watched Junior and the entrance to the building across the street. He removed his hand but sat as though he was ready to pounce again.

"Now, punk," he said in his cold musicless voice, "How come you been watching me?"

"Watching you?" Junior blurted. "I ain't been watching you. *You* been watching me!"

"Don't gimme no lip, you little junkie punk. I been coming around here for two days and every time you been watching me!"

"You're another junkie!" Junior said. "Don't call me no junkie, I ain't down with no habit!"

"With your nose running," the man said contemptuously. "And you smell like you been sleeping in shit! How you sound, you little junkie punk fool!"

Junior was forever stunned when anyone lumped him with or dismissed him as just another common junkie. Sure he joy-popped now and then and here and there, when he got so blue nothing in the whole world seemed to be going right anymore, but how come people couldn't see the difference? He wasn't so stupid he'd ever let no shit get control over him. Even Mama worried, fearing that he, too, might weaken and go down. But she needn't worry. He hated the thieving junkies as much as she did.

Now this dude was accusing him of smelling when it was the dude, himself, who smelled. Once fine-beautiful-clothes all filthy and wrinkled like the man had been sleeping somewhere in the streets, too.

"You smell your own shit!" Junior said furiously. "I know it ain't me!" If only he could grab the violin case, get it open, and either this dude would let him go or he'd use one of the shells and bust his ass wide open!

Without even a change of expression, the back of the man's hand snaked out and rapped Junior across the mouth. The other hand was balled into a fist, prepared to strike with the same casual cruelty. Now Junior saw that what had seemed like a red rope around the man's neck was some kind of a scar, like somebody had held the man and tried to saw his neck off.

Junior spat blood from his split lip and gazed at the man, trembling with hatred, but he was also partly frightened. More than ever he needed the shot-gun. . . .

"Now, punk," the man said. "You speak to me with some kinda respect. Every motherfucker in town is trying to speak to me with no respect these days. Shit, don't you know I used to own two pairs of wheels, a Lincoln *and* an El D! And I had four broads, *white* broads, working for me on the East side! Now some punk like you speaking to me with no respect!"

The man breathed angrily, nostrils flaring.

"I could drive down the street," he said, "in either one of my cars, and dudes would be lined up on the corner waiting for me to get there. They waited in the rain and in the snow, one day or two weeks, and I'd drive up and say: any complaints? Every nigger in the crowd, spics and whiteys, too, would fall over each other saying, Naw. I coulda been six months late and there still wouldn't been no complaints. Punks like you just don't know who you talking to. . . ."

The man gritted his teeth, pinched his nose, sniffled angrily.

"Yeah, in them days everybody knew Slick. I was almost as big as The Duke and Sugarman, and dudes like Snake and Spanish Red I didn't even speak to no more, with their jive assed fifty dollar bitches, when no bitch I had dared put less than a hundred dollar bill in my hand."

Junior's thoughts left the shot-gun temporarily. Relief rushed over him. Lucky he hadn't lunged forward and grabbed for the violin case as it had flitted across his mind to do. If this dude was really Slick, it would have been the last move he'd ever made. But how could this be Slick? This bum? This Junkie? Since he was almost too young to remember, he had heard about the great Slick, and the Duke and Sugarman and Spanish Red and all the other super-cool dudes with their fine hogs and women and vines. Every young stud, including himself, tried to talk like, walk like, dress like, Slick and the other great dudes. Once he had even spotted Slick's lavender El D cruising through his block in Bed-Sty, but young dudes had thought he was making up a story when he told them about it, like he was telling them he had glimpsed a movie star or something.

But how could this filthy junkie bastard be Slick? And yet it must be. Now he remembered the rumor about the scar. It was said that a couple of Spanish Red's boys had jumped Slick over a broad or something, tried to cut his head off, but Slick had shaken himself free and shot both, holding his neck in place with a handkerchief. And, Man, got no more than a suspended sentence. Pieced off the judge. And the Duke himself and Sugarman had come to court and welcomed Slick back to the streets.

"Bitch," Slick said, almost as if talking to himself. "I just married an evil black bitch, that's all. Married her before I got into the life, got hip. Had two kids she wouldn't let me see no more because I started putting bitches in the streets and because I sniffed a little shit every once in a while. Well, I should've put *her* ass in the streets! What was wrong with my money? I made in one or two hours what she picked up in a whole week wearing that fucking white blouse and sitting behind a typewriter and answering phones all day! When I went up there to beat her ass again, she had everybody in the block turned against me. Some of her jive ass relatives and friends had even put up signs: SLICK AIN'T SHIT! I drove into the block and they all had bottles and bricks. Even the goddamn kids against me! And the first one who threw a brick was some jive turkey who was supposed to be a minister! Well, I shot him. I shot him. I wished I'd killed the sonofabitch! Dude can't make a decent living anymore without going through a lot of changes. Well, they were all in court, the whole block, look like she had all of Harlem there, and even though I'd gotten a little taste to my judge, I got five years and the pressure forced the judge to put my bail so high, it took the Duke and the rest of my buddies three months to get me back to the streets." Slick exhaled bitterly, a bitterness so intense the blood had darkened his face, swelling the reddish rope-like scar around his neck. "Yeah. Three months! And by then Spanish Red and Long John had moved in on most of my ends. And you think that bitch would let up, would realized she'd fucked over me enough? Naw, you ain't never seen such an evil broad. Everywhere I go she liable to pop up, or she got somebody watching me. Even when she don't pop up, I keep seeing her anyway. . . . Some shit! Even getting so whoever I'm talking to, I can't stop thinking it could be somebody she and them fools she got on her side done sent. Till I saw you wasn't nothing but a stupid junkie, I figured you, too, was somebody she'd put on me. . . ."

"I don't care who you are," Junior said. "Don't call me no stupid junkie!" But Junior kept staring at Slick, still stunned at how once Slick had been such a big shot but was now nothing.

"Well, that's what you is," Slick said. "And she wouldn't have bothered with nobody like you nohow."

"Just because she kicked your ass and you ain't nothing no more but a common junkie yourself, don't make me one!"

"You better button up your fucking lip or I'm gonna go up side your head till you can't see good!"

"Okay," Junior said. "Okay. Just gimme my case."

"What's in it?" Slick looked at it as though he was going to open it. "Some kinda guitar or horn?"

"Yeah . . . a . . . a . . . horn."

"What's it doing in a guitar case? Where you steal it?"

"I didn't steal nothing. It's my horn. I play some time. . . ."

"Junkie like you? You can't even stand up straight. You steal it in that building across the street? That's why you hanging around here to steal something else?"

"Naw . . . Naw. . . . I'm waiting for. . . . I'm waiting for somebody. . . . Now gimme the. . . ."

Slick snapped the case open, stared at the sawed-off shot-gun. Junior grabbed for the gun but Slick got his huge fingers around his neck again and squeezed.

"What's this shit? Lying to me. You trying to play me for a fool!"

"Sonofabitch!" Junior gasped. "Gimme. . . !" And he tried to both punch and kick Slick in the balls but Slick was too powerful for him to break free.

"What you got it for, a stick up? Now hold still, punk, or I'll break your neck!"

"Got it. . . . Got it to kill somebody! And I'll kill you, too!"

"Kill who? Somebody over there? Who paying you? Don't give me that shit, nobody would pay a punk like you to do nothing. Tell me the truth. If you done stuck somebody up, where is the bread?"

"I didn't stick nobody up!"

"You lying punk. Where is the bread?"

Slick bent Junior's head towards the dash-board and began to search him. A guard and a dog passed across the street, and Slick paused for a moment, but though the dog turned and stared briefly, the guard didn't look around. A white man and a woman were leaving the building and the guard was speaking to them. Slick continued his search and took Junior's cheap wallet. Two dollars in it, which Slick instantly pocketed, and then a wrinkled picture fell out and Slick stared at the Black man getting off the plane. Junior struggled more violently then ever to break free. Slick rammed his elbow into Junior's stomach and swung his face around.

"What you doing with this picture? And don't lie to me, punk!"

"I told you," Junior panted. "I'm going to kill him and I'm going to burn your ass up, too!"

"Kill him for what?" Slick demanded. "Somebody paying a punk like you?"

"Nobody paying me nothing!" Junior said. "He is . . . he is . . . my old man." And tears suddenly jumped into his eyes. "No good bastard! No good just like you!"

Slick eased up a little, saw that some of the struggle had drained out of Junior. He was trying to keep from crying. But Slick watched Junior more intently than ever, as though sensing a score of some kind.

"What's going down, kid?" Slick even faked a bit of sympathy. "He throw your ass out?"

Junior caught the sympathy and found himself reacting to it despite himself. Though he succeeded in stopping himself from crying, everything pent up in him still wanted to burst out.

". . . .Kill . . . kill him cause I hate him!" he blurted. "Cause he . . . he . . . messed over my . . . my. . . ." But it was very difficult to bring himself to mention his mother. Also, he could sense that Slick's sympathy was false. And even if it wasn't he didn't wish to lower himself by accepting sympathy from a no good bummy dope-fiend. Still he sniffled and couldn't quite stop the words from tumbling out. "Had . . . had . . . her waiting . . . and she . . . didn't even have a television to watch. . . . Some dirty rotten junkie had even stole that! . . . .waiting for years . . . while he rode around up there in airplanes. . . . Left her to die . . . with not one penny . . . when he owns all kinds of businesses and stuff . . . and worth millions."

"Left who to die? . . . .Millions?" Slick said.

"Maybe even more. But what business is it of yours? You gimme my gun and I know what I'm going to do."

Slick caressed the gun, watching Junior.

"So he's your old man? Well, I'll be damned. Yeah, living all high and mighty. Real slick bastard, but had to be slick to think he could get away with out-slicking me!"

157

It was Junior's turn to stare at Slick.

"What you mean?"

"Well, if this is your old man, kid, I know the bastard. Yeah, I know him."

Junior continued to gaze at Slick. Though he hated his father, how could someone like Slick, the common junkie that Slick was now, know someone as important as his father? Suddenly he was swept by a wave of confusion.

"You don't know nobody!" he said violently.

"Don't I? Well, wait till he comes out of that building. No. Maybe not . . . Maybe we better figure this thing out real good. . . . Get away, and come back. . . . Together. There might be some bread here for both of us."

"How you know him?" Junior demanded, still disbelievingly.

"He crossed me once. That's how I know him. And nobody crosses Slick that I don't remember real good."

fourteen

Several days before he met Slick, Winston had been both
fired from his cab driving job and had had his hack license
suspended. Fired! The very thought had left him terrified. The
flow of savings into his bank account stopped! One moment
feeling secure and that maybe he was slowly winning and the
next moment the world shifting from beneath his feet again. He
moped about the tiny kitchenette apartment where he lived
then. Couple of mornings he dreaded getting up. What was the
use? Breakfast or dinner had become like a plate of worms that
he listlessly picked over and tried to digest, longing only to go
back to sleep. His spirit sank so low he ceased spraying, and the
roaches began to take over the apartment again.

It wasn't even an apartment but two small rooms, chopped
off from the rooms of other tenants in the rooming house, and
the bathroom was in the hall.

It seemed to him he spent most of his day staggering from his
bed to the bathroom and then back to his bed again. Sometimes
he got into the toilet and sometimes he didn't. One of several
neighbors was already in there. Though he ate less than ever,
guarding every nickel he spent more than ever, the cheap food
or tension cramped his stomach and he had developed a severe
case of diarrhea.

And even when he got into the bathroom, it would smell. He
would close his eyes, offended by the odor of strangers,
shakened by the fact of knowing that the diarrhea was probably
as much psychological as physical, a vast sense of insecurity
ripping him apart. Nigger being crushed forever, ground back
into place, at the bottom of the giant white pyramid, sick with

doubting himself again, not only losing a belief in victory but that he would even be able to survive.

And when he left the toilet, the foul smell would follow him. Who knew what disease, crabs, and maybe even syphilis he could pick up?

He hadn't met Slick yet. He didn't know that Slick existed yet, at least not by name. He wasn't sure what he was going to do until Friday came again and he had to go to the bank and make another Withdrawal. Sweating, reluctant, coughing nervously, he felt almost as though it was his blood he was withdrawing from the bank. He made out four withdrawal slips, trying to take out the least possible. $20.00. $30.00. $40.00. $60.00, but tore all the slips up. He knew he would need more. Finally, almost nauseous, he withdrew $75.00; the distance increasing between himself and his goal of $10,000. He realized that at this rate he could soon be flat broke again.

Anxiety attacked him that evening and destroyed sleep, cutting off escape into oblivion. His nerves a frazzle, he got up and ended up in a cheap gaudy men's store on 125th Street. When he came out of the store he wore a bright green jacket and green shoes with heels so high they seemed to add another four inches to his already considerable height.

He felt like a fool. Utterly ridiculous. He longed to return to his little apartment and sleep, throw the jacket and shoes away. Figure out how he could get himself another job. But the people who passed him on the street didn't give him a second glance. In fact, a number of people, especially the teenagers, were dressed as he was.

He threaded his way past the street merchants, wigs, cheap jewelry, burning incense. From the record shops, music flooded the street, and kids as young as five and six years old, stopped, gyrated, dipped, stomped, wiggled and then caught up to their approving parents. Now that he had decided on a course of action he felt better, except that he kept coughing nervously, as though he had picked up a virus somewhere.

He made it nearly a block in the green shoes and then it seemed as if his feet were about to come apart. The shoes were built in such a way he seemed to be walking on his toes. He tried to keep going, to ignore the pain, but he suddenly knew he'd never be able to make it to 117th Street and Lenox

Avenue in the modish shoes. Take a taxi? My God, he thought, another dollar disappearing right there! Plus, he'd have to tip. At least, fifteen cents.

Confused, he limped towards the entrance of a newly built office building and sat down. The building rose high into the air, a miniature version of the tall glassy buildings Downtown, the only one of its kind in Harlem. He decided he'd take his shoes off, and then rip his handkerchief in half, and stuff the toes of the shoes and maybe that would alleviate some of the pain.

The evening hummed around him. The people of Harlem thronged the street, shopping, going nowhere and yet everywhere within the confines of Harlem. The outraged voice of a street speaker sifted across the street: ".... racist white fascist pigs!" Occasionally someone paused and marveled at the tall new building, but went on. A taxi drew up to the entrance and a white man leaped out, followed by a portly Negro chewing on a cigar. The white man rushed through the glass doors as though he couldn't get off the street fast enough. The Negro, clutching his own briefcase, followed almost as swiftly.

He had some trouble ripping the handkerchief in two, and when he looked up again a bummy-looking character had sidled up and sat down opposite of him. Layers of dirt caked into the skin and bruises upon his forehead and tip of his nose where he must have fallen. A bottle of wine protruded from his pocket. On a pair of pants slick with grease and slime, a safety-pin held the man's fly in place.

"Drink, Bro?"

"No," Winston said, irritated. "Beat it!"

"Just trying to be friendly, Bro. If you needs a knife to cut that, I got one, but it ain't sharp much. . . ."

"No. I got it."

"Say, you know you ought to have a prescription for that cough. Seem like you might have TB or something. Sodium petroleum gerolelum is what you need!"

"Yeah?"

"I got my Doctorite from up there at Harvard. In the Pacific I was promoted on the Field . . . put in charge of thirty tank regiments . . . came out a Colonial."

161

Winston glanced up again into the man's mad red eyes.

"Colonel," he said impatiently. "And I suppose you also mean, Doctorate."

"That's what I said," the man stated. "Rite . . . Reet . . . Rate. Anyhow, I only practice medicine a little here and there. I travels mostly now." He leaned towards Winston, a gust of foul breath clogging the air. "Hush, hush, stuff. Secret. Push a little bitty button up there in the plane and I wakes up music playing and sliding down into my pool. Womens all around brings me my breakfast. I got a card blank. Guns and all. If I shoot, you're dead, that's all!"

"Great."

"What you say? You calling me a liar?"

"Man, I'm not calling you any fucking thing."

The man jumped to his feet, stood unsteadily.

"Okay, Bro, that's it! That's it. You've pushed your luck too far! I got to take you in. You're under arrest!"

Winston finished his shoes.

"Beat it, Man."

The man clutched his pants, reeled, proclaimed, "By the power invested in me, I hereby declares that the party of the first party is to be remained for thirty years and a day, as the first party of the said party has been found guilty of all charges, and you is the first party!"

Just then a husky Black Guard came racing out of the building, club in hand.

"Keep moving, you bums! How many times I got to tell you, don't hang around this building!"

Winston bristled. But he supposed he did look like a bum. . . . He put his shoes on and stood. One day, goddammit, no one would ever mistake him for a bum.

The "doctorite," the "colonial," the play-boy secret agent, was shouting at the guard; "Hold it! Who is your commanding officer. How come you don't know the code? You're under arrest, too! This minute! Shape up or ship out!"

The guard kept slicing the club into his hand.

"Now I don't want to break no heads. But you brothers better move, and I mean now!"

Winston glared at the guard. But what could he say or do? He hobbled onto the streets. With the split handkerchief in each toe, the shoes felt a little better but not much. He'd simply have to take a cab.

He saw a gypsy cab and hailed it. At least the meter started off with less than the fleet-owned cabs. But before he could give his destination, the Wine-O came reeling up: "Fink! Traitor! Desertion in the face of the enemy! I gives you a reprieve and what do I get? You thinks you too good to drink with me? I hopes you coughs your head off!"

"Stupid old fool" the driver said, watching Winston like maybe he was thinking how he could make something extra out of this trip.

"Yeah, 117th and Lenox."

The driver made a U turn.

"Mind if I make this without turning on the meter?"

"How much?" Winston asked suspiciously.

"Oh, about a buck fifty. What do you say?"

"I say let me out of this goddamn cab!"

"Take it easy, Brother. All right. A buck then, okay?"

"Seventy cents, including the tip!"

"You crazy? I got a family to support. How can I make it riding fares around at a rate like that?"

"Eighty-five cents," Winston compromised.

The driver sighed wearily.

"I'm glad I don't get many fares like you. Man, I'd starve to death! Okay, eighty-five cents, but I hope you have change, because I don't have none."

Ripped off anyway, Winston thought. When the cab pulled up at 117th Street it was either sit there and wait until the driver went and got change for a dollar bill or forget the extra fifteen cents.

He thrust the buck through the slot in the bullet proof glass.

"Keep it," he said sourly.

"Why thank you, sir, thank you."

"Yeah."

He got out.

And then there they were. Junkies everywhere. Dominating the street, men and women, young people and old people, milling around, waiting, like herds of cattle, hundreds of them. It was one of a number of spots where they massed in the City, flowing in to connect with pushers, fanning out again to "score," to get money no matter how for the next "fix," rip off an apartment, a small store, some lone person strolling through the City streets or parks, trading rings and watches and TV sets and furniture and suits and shirts and anything and everything for another shot of dope, for a moment of escape from whomever they were and from what they might have once hoped to be. . . .

He edged around the bulk of the crowd, both repelled and depressed more than ever, coughing uneasily. He also realized he was afraid of the junkies. Suppose he asked the wrong question or did the wrong thing and aroused their mistrust? Somewhere he had heard that the junkies would surround you and stick a blade into your back and walk away, leaving you to lie where you fell. . . .

But though a few junkies stared at him, there seemed to be less suspicion than when he had first driven by in the cab several weeks ago and got out and rather naively began asking questions. Even in his old work clothes, he had no doubt appeared to be a square, a john, or perhaps even an undercover policeman.

Still he had found out what he wanted to know. Some guy called Duke controlled this area, in conjunction with an Italian who ran the Village, and a Spanish guy who was in control of East Harlem. Who was in charge above them wasn't clear. . . .

And he had also found out that he was suddenly rich! The stuff that he hadn't yet thrown into the river but kept telling himself he was going to throw into the river was heroin. Even as he discovered the value of the heroin, he continued to tell himself he was going to throw it into the river. Through asking questions, it at first seemed he had an amount worth at least $20,000. Then after more questions, he figured the heroin might be worth $40,000 to $50,000. Still later, it seemed as if the stuff could be worth as much as $60,000!

My God! he had thought. But the sudden riches were useless to him. Never would he stoop to peddling drugs, destroying his own people! More than the idea of drug taking, he despised drug pushers. Parasites living off the blood of already wounded black communities! Murdering children. Arresting dreams. . . .

But suppose, just suppose, before he threw the junk away, he sold a bit of it Downtown? Make a one shot deal, pick up the several thousand dollars he needed, and then he would be out of it, home free. . . . After all, he'd only be selling it to the children of those who had brought it into the country in the first place. . . .

Feverishly he had driven the cab through all the likely drug infested Downtown areas, but so far it had been impossible to find a connection. Vice was much more hidden. What a congested Harlem lived with out upon the streets, the whites Downtown hid behind closed doors. . . .

What was he to do?

Nothing.

Except fling the crap into the river.

Still, he had hesitated—uncertain, tempted, agonizing, despising himself for hesitating, for even thinking of selling the drugs, but unable to squash the bright promise of thousands and thousands of quick dollars out of his mind.

And that was where he was when the boss of the cab company had called him into the office: "Say, fellow, if we don't get rid of you, you going to steal this company broke! And any other cab company will have to be completely nuts to hire you!"

And then his hack license gone. Maybe he was already being blackballed. . . ?

A horribly old shattered-looking black woman in a dirty blonde wig had begun to follow him as he circled the crowd. Her battered mouth offered him a smile. Needle marks blistered the back of her hands, and he supposed she had the hideous idea of exchanging sex for drugs.

Grimacing, the shoes hurting his feet again, he forced himself to move faster to get rid of the woman. He crossed the street, going North, then stopped. Maybe he was rushing away from the mass of junkies less to get away from the woman than that he was afraid to continue to do what he had started out to do? He coughed indecisively, a brief pain flashing through his stomach again. He was alarmed, hoping he wasn't about to be attacked by a re-occurrence of the diarrhea. Anxiety pushed him into action. The first junkie he spotted who looked a cut above the average in intelligence and appearance, he followed, hoping the addict might also be a pusher, perhaps one of Duke's boys, who could tell him how he could make contact Downtown.

The man went into the Chinese restaurant, where business seemed to be jumping, with other addicts, and perhaps even a few non-addict customers, going in and out.

Winston followed, the steamy greasy smell assailing his nostrils. But the sound of the man's voice arrested him, further depressed him.

"C'mon, Man," he heard the man whine, speaking to a Chinese or Japanese who stood behind the cash register. "This here ring is pure D gold. Was my grandmother's ring, Man. And her mother before that. Whatcha mean I can't get $10.00?"

"Five dollar. Five dollar. Finish talk," the Chinese or Japanese said, contempt barely concealed.

"Well, throw in a dinner, Man," the man wheedled. "I'm hurting, Man. You know I'm one of your steady customers."

"No dinner," was the reply. "Five dollar. Talk finish."

"You goddamn fucking gook!" the man suddenly shouted. "I fought your ass in the war! Who won, me or you? You act like *I* lost! Ain't that some shit!"

"You go," the Chinese or Japanese said, calmly, impassively. "Or I call cops, kick your ass good and hot."

The man crumbled, shivered, threw the ring on the counter, whined again.

"Okay. I'll take five."

"Finish talk. Good." The Chinese or Japanese gave the man the five dollars, but then did what probably kept him in business in the area. "You hungry? Very good. You get bowl stew. You good customer."

Community relations. Good for business. Good for Chin and Chan. . . .

For Winston saw now that the restaurant was one of the Chin and Chan outlets. Counter and stool arrangements always the same, from front to back one straight line for quick assembly-line feeding, specializing in chitterlings, pig feet, ham hocks, stews, rice and greens, sweet potato pie and root beer. Chin and Chan had started out several years ago with one hole-in-the-wall cafe in Harlem and the last Winston had heard Chin and Chan now had sixteen, excluding five in the black areas of the Bronx. He didn't know how many outlets Chin and Chan had in Brooklyn and the Queens. He didn't really want to know. In a way, the knowledge would be that much more painful. . . .

No doubt about it, such a chain of restaurants could have been his, once. But he had lost nearly all of his first $5000.00 trying to get started. He had thought, why not a restaurant, however small, but spic and span clean, no roaches, flies, good quality food, with a motto of: "Bringing a little of Downtown Uptown?" It had seemed like a good idea and he had rented a spot on Eighth Avenue above One Hundred and Twenty-Fifth Street. He had fumigated and painted and polished the place up, and set up a menu of shrimp cocktails and lobster and tossed green salad and ice cream and apple pie. He hadn't worried when Chin and Chan opened across the street. . . .

"Niggers over there eating cats and dogs," one of his "better class" customers said. "I've always appreciated the finer things of life, myself, and I make it my business to get Downtown occasionally to catch an opera."

Well, maybe he had had a few of the Blacks who went to operas, but Chin and Chan had had the masses. . . . Where he used to hang the sign, "A little Downtown Uptown" now hung a sign saying: "Chinese laundry." It wasn't clear whether Chin and Chan owned that, too, or not.

The man accepted the bowl of stew so slavishly Winston could hardly conceal his disgust. He would have liked a root beer himself, but rejected the idea and walked out. Anyway, he didn't relish drinking out of the glasses. Junkies were notoriously filthy. . . .

And yet he was surprised to notice more than an occasional junkie in the crowd who was as clean and robust looking as any square or average citizen. Maybe they were the ones still telling themselves they weren't addicts yet, he thought. . . . Telling themselves they hadn't joined the defeated mass of junkies, but were caught here temporarily, desperately needing the support of some kind of crutch, some kind of relief, until they could find strength to go on with their lives again. Most of them not knowing they had found all they were ever going to find, not knowing until they attempted to break the habit, then knowing but still not believing that this was where they'd always be.

It was frightening. How could he, himself, be sure that the hellish life of an addict wasn't still in store for him?

He saw the black blonde again smiling grotesquely into the face of a junkie who looked like a Puerto Rican. At least now he was free to move unobserved through the crowd until he spotted a pusher. He was crossing the street, heading South again, when a kid of about thirteen years old sidled up to him, scratching his cheek anxiously, a bloody fingernail mark down one side of his face. . . .

The boy shook and shivered like a little lost animal.

"Four bucks. . . ." he said, tugging at Winston's sleeve and bringing him to a halt at the curb. "Four bucks is all I got now, Man. Somebody has gotta gimme a break."

Winston stared at the boy's dirty fingernail digging again into his cheek. Evidently the boy thought that he was a pusher. . . .

He hesitated, feeling sorry for the boy, feeling a sudden helpless outrage at whatever or whoever had brought the boy to this condition. But what could he say? He had noted that about one fourth of the junkies that milled about the streets were less than twenty years old.

"I don't have anything, kid. Why don't you go . . . go home and . . ."

"Cause I'm short with four bucks? Cause I didn't have enough the last time?" The boy looked like he was going to cry. "You don't want to deal with me?"

Winston made an attempt to walk away from the boy, but the boy hung onto him. Other junkies were beginning to stare.

"Ask anybody," the boy pleaded. "I'm good for it. I know how to git some more bread. . . ."

An older junkie detached himself from the crowd and shuffled over. He was a big man, broad shouldered, with the powerful chest of a boxer, but his eyes were as haunted and desperate as those of the boy.

"Who is he?" the man asked the boy. He didn't exactly look at Winston yet. Two other junkies broke away from a group and came over.

"One of the Duke's boys," the boy said. "He going to gimme a break."

The man put his dulled, almost blankly white staring eyes on Winston then.

"You one of the Duke's new boys?"

Winston hesitated again.

Was it wiser to say he was or that he wasn't?

"Not exactly," he said. "In a way, yes."

The vacuous white eyes gazed at him, filling themselves up with suspicion.

"You is or you ain't?"

Winston coughed uneasily, glancing briefly at the other two junkies. Had he been so stupid as to allow himself to be maneuvered into danger? The other two were smaller than the bigger man and perhaps a few years younger, but they, too, had the same brutalized zombie-like appearance. One had just nodded but now he jerked upright and blinked at Winston.

The boy looked up at the big man.

"He's gonna git the Duke to give me a break, Mr. Luther," the boy said, his nails pushing deeper into the sores on his cheek.

The big man, Mr. Luther, ignored the boy.

"I said, who is you?"

"I'm waiting for the Duke or one of his men," Winston said. "But he's late."

"Late?" Mr. Luther said, and smiled. Or at least he suddenly grimaced. Then he looked at the boy. "Fool, he don't work for no Duke. He don't even know the Duke."

"Maybe he forgot," the boy whined. "Maybe he forgot, Mr. Luther."

"Forgot the Duke ain't no later than usual?" Mr. Luther said. "Late but ain't never late?" Then Mr. Luther, almost in slow motion, pointed to a car parked in the bus stop. Winston saw three white men sitting in the car. "They been waiting two hours," Mr. Luther told Winston. "And you just got here. You reckon they think the Duke is late?"

"Late but ain't never late," the boy parroted. "Maybe he just forgot. . . ."

Winston felt a surge of relief as he noted the three white men. One was in uniform and he figured the other two might also be policemen, sitting there in the unmarked car.

But what were they here for, to arrest the Duke? Perhaps so. But it didn't matter. Now he could at least try to get to the policemen if the junkies decided to attack him.—Except that the policemen seemed unconcerned with the milling junkies, trading stolen goods, huddled together in groups, maybe even shooting up. . . . Someone could still stick a blade in his back or jab him with an over-dose and who'd be the wiser or even care?

"Forgot?" Mr. Luther repeated. "And supposed to work for the Duke?"

Winston coughed uneasily again.

"Well, I didn't exactly say that...."

The boy, too, shook his head and moved away from Winston, digging even deeper and more desperately into his cheek, while he stared at Winston defensively, his young voice suddenly as hostile as Mr. Luther's. "Trying to put a hype down on me! Well, he *acted* like he knew the Duke!"

Another junkie ambled over and stared at Winston. Mr. Luther pointed again at the unmarked car.

"If you ain't with them, who you with?"

"Ain't he got nothing?" the new junkie demanded.

"Nothing," the boy said.

"Okay," Mr. Luther said triumphantly, indicating a white Cadillac with white balloon tires and a custom-built front that came past the light and double parked. "There's the Duke now. He ain't gonna like nobody trying to put a hype down around here."

The man climbing out of the Caddie wore what seemed like a jump-suit, a deep V cut in the blouse exposing his hairy chest and the bright jewelry that hung around his neck. The suit was a shock of colors: about two-thirds white and a third bright red. It was trimmed in blue, as was the wide-brimmed floppy white hat. Winston had heard that pushers and pimps took pride in "setting the style for the future." But the outfit struck him as being something out of a circus....

Also, for some reason, he had expected the Duke to be a younger man, but the guy who now stood outside the white Cadillac surveying the milling junkies had to be in his early forties, at least. And instead of being a handsome man, the black face had a greyish unhealthy tint about it, as though long ago marked by late night hours and a feverish pace of dissipation. The cold brown eyes protruded somewhat, flicking about with a harassed and almost furtive suspiciousness. But perhaps the addicts who stared at the Duke with respect and awe saw no more than the stance that the Duke had adopted, which was aloof, *cool*....

The junkies advanced towards the Duke like parishioners towards a preacher, constituents towards a politician, and the

Duke raised and spread the palm of his hands and they all stopped and kept a respectful distance.

"Hey, Duke, what's happening, Man? Howcome they busting so many of your boys?"

"You remember me, Duke? You remember me when. . . ?"

"I'm hurting, Man. . . ."

Some of the voices called fawningly, some no doubt faking awe.

The young boy broke away from the group around Winston and tried to claw his way through the crowd to get closer to the Duke. His young voice was almost hysterical.

"Duke! Duke!" he said. "My name's Willie. . . . They say you planning to use younger dudes, cause they busting your older boys. . . . My name's Willie, Duke!"

"C'mon," Mr. Luther told Winston. "Now we'll see just how good the Duke knows you!"

Winston found himself pushed before the Duke, who was saying to the crowd, palms upraised again, "Keep cool. Keep cool. All my regular boys will be back out here in the streets as usual, otherwise, I'll have somebody else out here. . . ."

From the unmarked car, the policeman in uniform was trying to get the Duke's attention.

"Tell him, over here," the policeman shouted to a junkie.

Winston suppressed a fit of coughing. At a signal from the Duke he suspected that these desperate dope addicts would rip him to pieces. But what could he do? He knew he didn't dare wait. He had to make some kind of move. . . .

Shaky with fear, he suddenly pulled away from Mr. Luther and rushed forward and slapped the Duke on the back, whispering desperately, "Man, I got something for you!"

The Duke's right hand went inside his blouse so fast, Winston didn't think it was going to stop. Then the cold brown eyes regarded Winston, as though Winston had to be out of his mind. The Duke brushed his clothing where Winston had touched him.

"Keep your hands off me, nigger!"

Winston was frantic, conscious of Mr. Luther, the crowd behind him.

"But, Man. . . . I . . . I . . . got something! Some shit . . . some . . . some . . . boss shit!"

The Duke didn't blink.

171

"What you coming to me for?"

"Because. . . . Because . . . you're the big man! You're the boss, right?"

The Duke continued to gaze at him. Then abruptly he said, "Wait here."

The junkies made room for him and he walked over to the police car.

But Winston didn't wait. He kept as close to the Duke as he could, following him to the car.

The white man in plain clothes sitting in the back seat rolled the window down.

"Hi, Duke, baby, don't see much of you lately. You eating high on the hog."

"Am I late?" The Duke said.

"Oh, no," the white man replied, hastily. "No. No. But there are people who would like to see a little more of you these days."

"My boys always take care of my ends. I'm a busy man, you know."

"So busy, you don't read about inflation?" The white man lit a pipe and regarded Duke good-naturedly.

"All you had to do was get the word to me," the Duke said, his tone begun arrogantly but suddenly ending in a sort of whine, as though he was angry but didn't dare show how angry he was. "Instead, I get pressure."

"We did send word," the man said affably. "But you're so high up there these days, Duke, the word doesn't seem to reach you."

The Duke shifted his feet and stared at the white man with something close to hatred, but again his voice shuttled between arrogance and a whine.

"Okay. So we got inflation. What kind of inflation we talking about?"

"No kind," the white man smiled. "Nothing so urgent we got to talk about it here. When you drive off, we may just drive off after you. . . ."

The Duke drew himself up, and some of his anger came through despite himself.

"I want all of my boys back on the streets. How can I take care of business, short-handed? Young punks I got to teach from scratch. Then when they ain't careless, they steal."

"Nothing I can tell you," the man shook his head, unmoved. "Everyone's got ... well ... personnel problems. Not a thing I can tell you, not here, except that. . . ." Then the man looked at Winston. The pipe became very still. The smile that hadn't been in his eyes, now even left his lips. "Who is he?" he demanded.

"Who?" Duke said.

The cold grey eyes continued to regard Winston suspiciously. "Him?"

The Duke glanced around in annoyance.

"Just some nigger with some shit. . . ."

"Yeah?" the white man said. "You know him?"

The Duke whirled and glared at Winston.

"What the hell you said you had for me, Man? I told you to wait!"

Winston hesitated. Were the white men the law ... or what?

"Something. . . . Something I found. . . ." he stammered. "I used to be a cab driver. . . . In my cab. . . ."

"What?" the Duke demanded impatiently. "Coke? Heroin? What? Shit, don't waste my time, Man!"

The white man seemed to be suddenly impatient, also.

"Better let one of your boys check him out," he told Duke, warily. "Who ever you got left. . . . Sometimes we get a little busy, too."

The Duke scowled. He said, "Yeah," like he had made the decision rather than the white man. "Hit the corner round a 113th Street and 8th Avenue and ask for Slick," he told Winston. "And listen, I guess you know I don't allow no niggers to waste my time!"

Winston frowned at the insult, but he kept his voice level.

"What place? What address?" he asked.

"No place," said the Duke. "You just keep standing on the corner and asking for Slick."

Then the Duke turned back to the white man, dismissing Winston.

fifteen

For three long days Winston waited at street corners, asking junkies where he could find Slick. It was really stupid, since he was increasingly convinced he'd never be able to go through with what he had planned. Anything was better than allowing himself to become a party to mass murder. And that was what the whole drug scene was about: *murder.* That child digging into his bloody cheek, who but murderers, the most degraded people on this earth could be held responsible? It was confusing to see how far he had already slipped towards that degradation. The only thing that kept him from despising himself altogether was his intention to persuade Slick to peddle the drug not Uptown but *Downtown.* Exterminate the white children of those who would exterminate those children who looked like him! But the sheer intensity with which he clung to this idea worried him. Maybe it was but a rationale for being unable to stop himself from going through with the drug sale. . . ?

Still, he had almost not come in search of Slick today.

And even when his resistance wavered and he finally decided to try one more time, he had made a deal with himself. If Slick didn't show up within two hours, he would keep straight to the river and dispose of the crap. Before leaving the apartment he had emptied and washed two roach spray cans and poured the stuff into the two cans, retaining a small bit of the drug as a sample in a piece of tin foil. Another can full of roach spray he had not emptied, but put it along with the other two cans into a shopping bag. On top of the cans he had placed a stale loaf of bread, a package of wheatena and a can of pork and beans. He hoped that cops or narcotic agents would assume that he was just another poor black man who had been shopping, and that Slick would come quickly so that he could rid himself of one of the cans and as quickly get away and dump the other.

Now he stood huddled in a door-way at the corner of Eighth Avenue and a Hundred and Fourteenth Street. Chilling, windwhipped sheets of rain lashed the buildings around him. A number of people, mostly junkies, huddled in other door-ways. A clock inside the poolhall indicated he had already been waiting two hours and twenty minutes. Twenty goddamn minutes longer than he had promised himself! Why didn't he leave? Why did he keep stalling? A deal was a deal. And it was a deal he had made with himself.

The chilly rain whipped at him, depressed him further. He broke into a fit of coughing, hawked and spat but nothing came up. To hell with it! He would leave now. Something would come up. He'd find another way . . . another job . . . something. And at least he'd be able to sleep nights. Except that it could take him another ten years of sacrificing and saving before he even glimpsed again the bright places where he wanted to go. . . .

Confusion gave way to despair and pushed him into the rain. He headed for the subway at One Hundred and Sixteenth Street. He had almost gained the entrance when a lavender Cadillac made a U turn and pulled arrogantly to the curb, splaying water.

A heavy jowled, lemon-yellow face, with light tan concrete-hard eyes, and a thin cruel mouth looked out at him. The Cadillac had all the accessories: TV antenna, custom built front, balloon wheels. The man wore a lavender flop hat, and a string of diamonds glittered around his neck.

"You the dude been looking for me?"

Winston glanced from the man to the subway entrance, then back to the man again.

"Yeah," he finally said, almost unable to contain his anger at having been forced to wait on street corners and in the rain.

"Get in," the man ordered. "I'm Slick."

Again Winston hesitated, glancing at the entrance to the subway. Once in the car, that would be it. How could he back out if he got that far?

"You getting in, Man?"

175

Winston coughed and clutched his package, but he went around and opened the door and climbed into the car beside Slick. The stereophonic was going and at each note of cool jazz music psychedelic lights flicked and flashed throughout the interior of the car. Thick leopard skin upholstered the seats. Inside, the garish comfort pushed away the chill and the rain.

"Is I late?" Slick asked.

Winston bristled. Here went that shit again. Apparently some kind of status crap among these hustling clowns, who even when they were late weren't considered late. He sensed that he was expected to say, no, but suddenly he was so outraged he couldn't control himself.

"You're fucking right you're late!" he said. "And, Man, I haven't been waiting in all that rain to hear no bullshit."

He was ready to get out of the goddamn car.

Slick surprised him by laughing. Or at least what was meant to be laughter, a raggedy metallic wheeze, as though the sound was being squeezed through his teeth. Above the diamonds lacing his neck, Winston now noticed a vivid red scar. The diamonds ended in an S shaped brooch of other diamonds at the base of Slick's neck.

"You cool," Slick said. "Now I know you ain't no punk. But you is also lucky. . . . If you had been waiting for the Duke, he might have kept you waiting for a week, months. He operates on his *own time.* Yeah, he's up there closer to the top than I is, but where I'm gitting. One of these days I might not show up at all, but who's going to say I is late? Now what you got for me? You already done took up a couple hundred dollars worth of my time!"

"Don't tell me about your time," Winston bristled again. "I got the same as I told the Duke, some boss . . . well . . . er . . . shit."

"How much?"

"What?"

"Pounds?"

"I don't know. But about this much." Winston tried to indicate the amount he intended to sell to Slick by cupping his hands. Then he pulled out the sample and Slick tasted it, savoring it.

A flicker of greed momentarily brightened Slick's cold light brown eyes. He pressed on the gas and whipped the car around in another U turn. At the waist of his lavender trousers, Winston thought he noticed the imprint of a pistol.

"That much, eh? You got it on you?"

"I ain't *that* stupid," Winston stated, but he clutched his package, suddenly uneasy. If Slick had shown up any other day but today he wouldn't have had all this crap with him. Suppose for some reason it got rough, and he had only a tiny pen knife with which to defend himself? But why should it get rough if he was willing to sell, and Slick was willing to buy? Even hustlers must have some kind of code they respected in doing business.

Slick speeded up and surprised Winston by making a left turn into the park.

"What you got in the bag?" he said.

Winston hesitated.

"Grocery. I had about given you up, so I shopped and was headed home."

"You cool. I'm going to stop by one of my pads and pick up a thousand bucks, and if the rest of the shit is as good as the sample the bread is yours."

"You out of your mind?

"Okay. Three thousand."

"Look, Man, I've already found out the value of the stuff I got. Now do you want it or do I find somebody else?"

"Okay. Okay. Six thousands bucks and that's it. The shit might be valuable but there is changes I got to go through and people I got to see before I git it to the streets."

Winston hesitated again.

"Ten," he said. "Ten thousand bucks."

Anger suddenly rose and muddied Slick's eyes, darkened his heavy yellow face.

"Motherfucker, you must be out of *your* mind!"

"Okay, nine, then."

Some of the anger eased out of Slick's face.

"Man, you sure got a lot of nerve. I'll give you eight. Now don't press me!"

Winston felt almost compelled to keep on pushing it, and he had to control himself. After all, wouldn't $8,000.00 added to what he already had in the bank put him into a position to go where he wanted?

"Okay," he agreed. "But what about an extra hundred . . . well . . . an extra two hundred for all that time I spent out there in the rain?"

Slick grunted in irritation, but suddenly he shrugged.

"Deal, Man. Now let's shake on it before you ask for something else. Shit, you come on like some kinda Jew."

Winston shook the moist flabby hand, laced with diamonds. Goddamn. $8,200.00! Added to his bank account better than $12,000! Jesus, now he could really get going! Buy himself a couple of buildings. Do his own maintenance and superintendent's work, and after a few years buy more buildings. In time he might accumulate an entire City block. . . . Or more!

But what about getting Slick to agree not to resell the drugs Uptown? Why hadn't he mentioned that to Slick yet? Well, hell, he'd go into that before the deal was finalized; once he saw the color of Slick's money.

Slick pressed the big car forward, leading the line of cars winding through the park, nipping lights. The City was grey with rain and scattered black clouds still dominated the evening sky. Slick surprised him by coming out of the park on the East Side at 72nd Street. He was even more surprised when Slick stopped the car before one of the canopied apartment buildings.

"Wait here," Slick said, getting out. "Keep an eye on my short. Some evil jealous motherfuckers been trying to git to me lately."

The doorman in a gold and green uniform rushed forward with an umbrella, a fake white smile nearly concealing distaste. Slick allowed himself to be shielded from the rain and walked towards the building as though he owned it. An elderly white lady holding a small frisky white dog on a leash scrambled out of Slick's path.

Winston watched him disappear into the building, wondering if Slick really lived there. As far as he knew it was an "all white area" and Blacks still couldn't rent an apartment in the vicinity whether they had the money or not. He thought it ironic that someone like Slick had penetrated the area when hard-working, so-called "respectable" Blacks still weren't welcomed to enter the front doors.

Keeping an eye on the entrance for Slick's return, he took the roach spray can that was meant for Slick out of the package and put it into his pocket. He wished he could get rid of the other can of junk right this minute but people could be looking out of windows and already watching him and the car with suspicion. Even if they didn't know what was in the can and he dropped it out of the car, it could provide an excuse for the cops to be called, if for no other reason than to accuse him of littering. . . . Anyway, he'd get rid of the can as soon as he finished the deal with Slick. What a relief it was to know that very soon now this whole rotten business would be behind him, like an ugly dream.

It was another ten or fifteen minutes before Slick came strolling back out of the building in his lavender suit and hat. Once more the doorman jumped to attention, following Slick to the car, holding the umbrella. Slick took his time, pausing and staring at the car, pointing at the right fender indignantly. The doorman was all red-faced and apologetic. What looked like a $20.00 dollar bill appeared in Slick's hand, and he proffered it towards the doorman, but just as the white man reached for it, the bill fluttered towards the sidewalk.

At first he thought Slick had accidentally dropped the bill, but then he saw the sadistic smile on Slick's face as he got into the car, leaving the doorman scrambling after the bill in the wind and the rain.

"Sonofabitch don't watch my short. I come out here one morning and some of these johns done drug a knife at least twenty times across my fender. Saying it musta happen somewhere else. Where else? Who else but these honkies is going to try to fuck with me?"

Slick pressed on the gas and the car plunged into the traffic.

"When I first moved in every honky in the building nearly had a heart attack," he said. "My whore could lease the apartment, you understand, but when I showed up they all started making excuses not to even take an elevator if I was on it. But I caught a bunch of them one day, coming from one of their square-assed parties or something. Me and my whore squeezed on the elevator with them, and in a minute my whore looked down and whispered I'd forgot and left my fly open. Man, I just stood there for a second and then I said: 'Well, bitch, zip it up!' She didn't like it, all them other crackers around her and watching her, but what could she do if she didn't want her ass whipped right there on the elevator? She reached them lily-white hands down and did the zipping."

179

Slick charged around the slower moving cars, then continued with bitter satisfaction.

"And that wasn't all. It crossed my mind I oughta make her take my joint out and lick it a couple of times, right there before them motherfuckers! I might have done it, too . . . if they had said one word to me. I might have made even one of *them* lick it!"

Slick took an abrupt right turn and sped towards the lights and then made a left turn. Winston was suddenly aware that all the while Slick had been glancing warily into the rear-view mirror.

"Cops been stopping me every time I look around lately," he said. "Running up my over-head. Greedy sonofabitches!" He took another sharp turn, still peering into the rain, his hard little muddy eyes both wary and harassed. A sudden flash of angry frustration clouded his broad yellow face. "Yeah, and then some jive mothers slicing up my short, like they following me around town, and just waiting for me to park and get out. I thought for awhile it was Spanish Red and some of his jealous dudes still trying to mess with me, and I was ready to burn some ass. But even the Duke said he can't see how come Spanish Red would stoop to some little shit like scratching up my wheels. Well, maybe the Duke is right and that honky doorman is right, too—then who is it that don't know no better than to keep trying to fuck over me?"

"I wouldn't know," Winston said, though he realized that Slick seemed to be mostly talking to himself. He sought to curb his own uneasiness, beginning also to gaze apprehensively out into the rain. He knew the sooner he hurried and finished this deal the better, because what if the cops caught him in the car with this sonofabitch right now?

" 'Course, you wouldn't know. All you know is that you just want to join the *mess over Slick club* and over-charge me for some shit. Well, okay—enough of this yakety-yak! I done already gave you too much of my time. Let's go and pick up your shit."

Winston hesitated.

"I haven't seen your bread yet."

Slick scowled. But he slowed down and pulled out a large roll of bills. He separated a smaller roll, already wrapped with rubber bands, from the wad.

Winston suppressed a cough but his voice was suddenly firm.

"One thing I got to ask . . . where do you do your . . . well
. . . pushing?"

"Where?" Slick was puzzled and irritated. "Anywhere."

"Well, if we work out a deal I don't want any of the stuff
you get from me pushed Uptown and I don't want any kids
involved with it either," Winston began, but ended somewhat
lamely. For how could he force Slick to do what he wanted
once Slick had the stuff? And no doubt a promise from
someone like Slick would be meaningless. Still he went on,
"You see, we shouldn't . . . well, Man, we shouldn't be a party
to destroying our own kids. But the white bastards, now maybe
that's something else. They brought the crap into the country in
the first place. Do you see what I mean?"

Apparently Slick didn't. His little cold brown eyes seemed to
be straining to understand what Winston was talking about.
Obviously, where he should or shouldn't do business, had never
crossed his mind before.

Slick scowled again.

"Man, you beginning to talk like my old lady. Evil black
bitch! Shit I make more money in a day than you kinda johns
do in a year! But she comes on like my bread don't spend.
Hanty bitch done even turned my own kids against me. I go up
there to see her and them jive relatives keep telling me ain't
nobody home. Well, one day I caught her ass on the way to
work and went up side her head in the middle of the street.
Think that would learn her some sense? Bitch started visiting
half the precincts in New York trying to git me behind bars. But
when your bread is as long and green as mine, what chance a
simple bitch like her got? So the cops pick me up and drag me
in before some judge, but I'm back out in the streets in ten
minutes!"

"Well, don't you see," Winston tried explaining. "She's trying
to protect your kids from the . . . from the consequence . . . of
the life you live. After all, Man, you're not exactly a salesman
of household appliances, you know."

"Don't give me that shit. She ain't trying to do nothing but
join the *mess over Slick club*. But I know how to handle her ass.
I found out this unlisted number she's got and I called her up
and I said, 'Bitch, you got two eyes in your stupid head and
what is they good for?' " His grin was a grimace. "She didn't

say nothing; and I said, 'That's right, bitch, don't say nothing because if you keep fucking with me pretty soon not only you ain't going to say nothing but you ain't going to be able to *see* nothing either!' " He paused, even the grimace vanishing. "Well, she knew where I was coming from. She knew for a ten dollar fix I could have some junkie catch her in the streets and dash a bucket of lye in her face. It shook her. She got the message. But ain't that a bitch, some simple stupid nobody chick, trying to mess over somebody like *me*!"

Winston gazed into the rain, the traffic surging about them, a feeling of acute depression settling over him. It was useless to try and get through to somebody like Slick. The guy had almost become some kind of an animal. Totally immoral. Vicious. Ill educated, pushed outside the bright mechanized world of the City, of perhaps the entire country, he had become completely degraded in attempting to form his own world to live within the American system. But what about himself? If he went through with this deal, wasn't he somehow reduced to the same level as Slick? No, he told himself. For him it was only a one shot deal. . . . And he wasn't going to even sell all of the drugs, right? Just a part of it. So this certainly wouldn't put him into the same category as Slick, would it?

Still, he wished he was out of the car. Or had never gotten into it. Then perhaps he'd no longer be thinking about making the deal at all.

Slick had turned up First Avenue, still checking the rear-view mirror occasionally.

"Okay, Man," he said impatiently. "You want me to keep straight up town or what? Where you got your shit, at your pad?"

"No." Winston paused. "Not my pad. I mean . . ."

"You mean, you got some jive-assed family and you worried about going there and letting them see you riding around with me," Slick sneered. "How you sound!"

"I didn't say that."

"Yeah. Simple-minded turkeys used to be happy to see me coming, with the new threads I sport every day, and the wheels I'm one of the first to change each year, but now some of these simps look at me like *I'm the one* who's been kicking they asses all day!" Suddenly Slick was genuinely puzzled. "What you simps see wrong with my bread? I ain't got no kids working for me that don't come up to me begging to work. And, shit, I was always willing to buy my own kids anything they wanted, and I warned them don't fool with no drugs. Don't be like all them other stupid punks. So what's everybody trying to mess over me for?"

"Well, Man, I'm trying to explain. It's not just your kids, it's all the kids that . . ."

"I ain't no adoption agency!" Slick declared. "People's got needs, and I supply them needs. Some want drugs, and I give them that; some want whores, and I give them that, too. But how come you so worried? Before that mean black bitch and me fell out, I'd tell my kids what to do and kick they asses if they didn't do it. I'd say, don't do as I do, do as I *say*! If you scared of your kids getting into some shit, then you ain't got your kids more scared of you than what you don't want them to git into!"

"It's not a matter of my kids," he said in exasperation, wanting to cut the conversation, get on with the goddamn deal, if he still really meant to go through with it. "I don't have any." But then he paused. He frowned at a memory nagging at the back of his mind. A memory that seemed to connect with the young drug addict boy digging dirty fingernails into his bloody cheek. It was not so much the horror of the drug addict boy himself resisting memory as it were the faint and faded memories stirred by the boy. Somewhere in Central Park more than thirteen or fourteen years ago, near a pond where many children had been playing and laughing, a young boy, just beginning to walk, had stretched out his arms and come toddling towards him. . . . He could almost remember the mother's sad young black face, but beaming at that moment with pride as she watched the boy stumbling, falling, but getting up, and still coming towards him. . . . There was another shadowy memory of the night he had drunkenly picked her up at some party or dance, overwhelming her feeble protests, and slept with her in her tiny lonely kitchenette. Stifling a sense of guilt, he had never wanted to see her again, to be in any way responsible for her sad and vulnerable existence. Then he had met her by accident and she had told him about the boy. "He's yours . . ." she had said. "But I don't want to cause you no

183

trouble or slow you down. I can see how ambitious you is. You don't have to do nothing about him or me. I'll take care of him, and then maybe one day when you get on your feet and win all them things you want, you'll come back and be real proud of him. . . ."

He had felt a very strange reaction to the boy, a yearning, almost like a desire not only to claim the child but a wish that he could rescue the mother. But he had finally—and perhaps conveniently—decided that the girl, because of her sad and lonely life had become demented, and was falsely blaming him of having fathered the boy. He had pacified her quickly, saying whatever came first to his mind, and then got away from her, and the child.

A couple of times in later years he had thought briefly: my God, suppose the child had really been his? But he had pushed the thought out of his mind. What could he have done for a child, still trapped at the bottom himself and making one mistake after the other in vain attempts to fight his way upwards so that he could at least breathe? If he'd been almost swamped by the battle of merely looking out for himself, the added weight of the sad lost girl and the child would long ago have buried him forever. After several years, he was still in such a strain to move forward, upwards, there was neither time, nor desire, to look back and even remember anymore the young mother smiling with pride and the boy toddling across the grass and reaching for him. . . .

". . . I said, what you going to do, Man?" Slick demanded. "I got other business to take care of. Shit, you said you ain't got no kids, so what you hung up about where I deal or don't? It's all the same to me. I can get rid of the shit on Fifth Avenue. Everybody trying to unwind and getting high today. One of my lawyers even walks into court every day stoned. But me, personally, I don't shoot up. That's for them third rate punks in the street. Me and the people that's tight with me don't go for nothing but the best, and a little coke ain't never hurt nobody!"

"So you'll peddle the crap Downtown?"

"Man, that's what I just said! Now where's the shit?" Slick held the roll of bills up again. "I got my bread. Where we got to go, cross-town?"

"No," Winston said slowly, his voice leaden. "I got it on me."

"On you?" Slick almost side-swiped a car. "Man, you crazy? You mean we been driving around and you loaded with shit? And *Downtown* to boot!" Quickly he whirled the car to the curb and stopped, switched off the motor, and they sat there within the gaudy interior, rain coming down all around them. "Man, you seem like an intelligent cat. . . . Don't you know if some Honest John cops had stopped us, we could've been in stone trouble! Where's it at?"

Winston coughed dryly into his hand, staring into the rain. It was useless to tell Slick the reason he had brought the stuff was because he had also meant to throw it away. Wordlessly he proffered the roach spray can, but didn't release it as Slick grabbed for it.

"My money," he said.

"Sure," Slick said quickly. "But I got to check to see if this is still boss as your sample. You sure you cleaned this can out good? Something else! I never would've thought of using a roach spray can. But if it ain't cleaned good you could have somebody running around and shooting up roach spray."

Distrustfully, Winston held onto the can while Slick stuck his finger in and dabbed a bit upon his tongue.

"Hmmmmmmmm. Yeah. Okay." He tossed Winston the roll of bills and Winston released the can, wanting to get out of the car as fast as he could and as far away as he could get. But then he hesitated, and began taking off the rubber bands to count the money.

Slick became agitated. His hard little eyes rolled about almost in panic.

"Man, there's a cab. You better jump out and grab it. The cops could still come down on us any minute! And as long as you're in my car this shit is yours, dig?" He started up the motor again. "Me, I don't know you. Shit, I'll go into court and swear I never seen you before. You just some hitch-hiker, who jumped in at the light, when I wasn't looking! Me, I'm a religious man with a family. How did I know you was a drug pusher? You better grab yourself a cab and split, Man!"

The sense of panic hit Winston and nearly succeeded in pushing him out of the car. But, fingers sweating, the muscles of his stomach clinched so tight it was difficult to breath, he continued to count the batch of dirty bills.

Then a blinding surge of anger released his breath. The first three bills were $500.00 bills. Then there were several fifties. Some twenties and then a number of $10.00 bills. All total, less than three thousand dollars! A sucker roll! And he was supposed to be the sucker.

He turned on Slick slowly. He didn't know what he was going to do, what he could do. Earlier, he had thought he had spotted the imprint of Slick's gun in his right pocket. But he knew fucking well he wasn't going to get out of the car without his money. Especially after all the shit this hustling clown and the other hustling clown, Duke, had put him through!

Slick suddenly surprised him by leaning over the wheel and laughing his hissing animal like laugh.

"What's so goddamn funny?" Winston demanded.

Slick continued to hiss, wiping tears from the edges of his cold little eyes.

"Now, no cause to blow your stack, Man. Any dude stupid enough to be carrying all this shit around on him, ought to be stupid enough to go for any kind of okey doke. But you cool. And there ain't nothing to git uptight about. How do I know where you at, till I see where you coming from?

Winston was furious. He thought of the pen knife in his pocket, but what good would that do against this sonofabitch? What amazed and infuriated him most was that Slick didn't seem to feel that he should be angry at all. It was simple: if you caught a sucker, you bumped his head. It was all part and parcel of taking care of business.

Now, however, Slick's laughter had ceased. He pulled out the larger roll of bills again and extracted a portion and started to count himself, but then he suddenly stopped. He shelved the bills towards Winston.

"Here, you count it." His tone was irascible, ragged with impatience, as though it was not Winston who had been affronted but himself who had been betrayed by Winston's not being the sucker he should have been. "You keep staring at me like you still don't trust the way I do it."

Winston took the money but realized in doing so, it left Slick free to *watch him.* Perhaps to move his hand into his right pocket? And outside there was no one, the streets were deserted. Nothing could be seen except the faint grey bug-like crawl of traffic and the cold yellow lights of project buildings. Shrouded in the interior of the car by the rain, anything could happen and no one would see or care.

Normally he was very good at counting money but now his fingers moved clumsily, while a part of his mind remained alert for any sudden move Slick might make. Especially towards his right pocket. He was already thinking: If he moves, I got to try and swing the bag of groceries and hit him in the face. If I'm lucky the can of pork and beans will catch him just right, between the eyes maybe, stun him and give me enough time to jump out.

But Slick made no move, at least not towards his right pocket, and another thought crossed Winston's mind. Since the sonofabitch had tried to cross him, why shouldn't he cross Slick? Hit him in the face with the pork and beans anyway and try grabbing for the whole bank roll? If he ran in the opposite direction to the traffic, it would be very difficult for Slick to catch him. And the total bank roll could very well be over $20,000. Twenty thousand! Yeah. Blood money. Squeezed from the lives of people who could least afford to lose it. A bastard like Slick deserved to be ripped off.

"Hurry up and count, Man!" Slick said. "Shit, you keep on wasting my time."

Winston exhaled a deep breath. He realized his thoughts hadn't been merely idle. His entire body had become tensed and alert the moment his mind began to toy with the possibility of escaping with *all* of the money. But it would have been a stupid thing to try. Slick would have the gun out before he got very far. Also, because Slick was an unprincipled bastard why should he be the same? He had made a deal, repellent as it was, and he'd stick by it. In fact, there was even a legitimate way—if anything like legitimacy could be applied to the whole ugly scene—that he could probably get the balance of Slick's bank roll. . . . All he had to do was break his own promise to himself and offer Slick the rest of the drugs. In the other roach spray can there was an amount of the stuff even greater than in the one Slick had. If he was already getting $8,200.00, the balance of it should be worth at least another $10,000 or $12,000.

The beating of his heart accelerated and he wanted to cough. The leaden dejection he had experienced before pressed down upon him again. Was he really thinking of breaking his own fucking promise to himself and selling all the shit? My God, at what low point was he going to be able to stop himself? Finally he had got himself to accept the sale of $8,200 worth of the crap, but how in the hell could he ever justify selling all of it? God, he had to hurry and get out of this goddamn car. . . .

But he had now made a serious mistake. Struggling to resist further temptation, his mind had dipped away from Slick momentarily. And it had only taken Slick a second to move. And the gun hadn't been in the right pocket, after all. It came from somewhere else, somewhere inside the jacket where the money had been, or from his waist. And the barrel of it looked larger than anything that could have fitted snugly into the right pocket anyway.

Slick's laugh this time contained an edge of bitterness. He stared at Winston indignantly. "Greedy motherfucker!" he said. "You wouldn't take what I first offered you, would you! You coulda had a couple of grands in your pocket and been long gone. But, naw, you want a whole $8,000.00. And then some! Even an extra $200.00 stick-up! How you sound! You greedy sonofabitch, now you don't git nothing! Just push my bread back to me, and real slow, and open that door and git your ass out into the rain. And you lucky. You lucky I don't blow you away, some jive john like you trying to out con me!"

Winston's mind went absolutely cold, thoughtless for an instant. Instead of being overwhelmed immediately by fear, it was as though he had been jolted several notches deeper into the well of his own bleak depression, perhaps to the very bottom of it. And there lived the slush of fatalism that couldn't always be outdistanced. Like knowing that no matter what he did, how hard he tried, he'd never be able to climb up out of the pit in which he lived. The cards were already stacked against people like himself. It was a fact he should have accepted and adjusted to long ago. The tight airless ghetto cage into which he had been born would be where he was destined to die.

The sense of fatalism ripped at his spirit, threatening to crush him altogether. But then his mind, as though wiggling out from beneath heavy stones, began working, slowly, fueled by small bursts of anger at his own helplessness. Was he to wake up tomorrow at the same point where he had awakened today, and yesterday, and all the days before. . . ? Was he to go back to his little room and stare at the yellow plaster peeling across the ceiling? Lying there shattered and knowing he'd never be able to lash himself into another despicable attempt to sell the rest of the drugs, even if he escaped with it. Lying there and perhaps so demoralized he might even begin using the shit himself. . . .

He shuddered. How could he get out of the car with . . . *nothing?* It seemed to him he was confronted by two choices, each offering a kind of death. If he got out of the car, of what use would it be to wake tomorrow? And if he didn't get out of the car, how long would it be before Slick shot him?

Fear, however, had forced him to move despite himself. He realized that he had placed the money onto the seat and that he had partly opened the door. The rain sprayed in and touched his cheeks, like drops of ice. He could almost see his own mind chasing through the cells of his brain. Banging desperately against closed doors, looking for a hole, a crevice, something onto which to get a grip. But instinct was running faster than his mind. Even as his mind still struggled against being trapped, he found that he was already in motion.

He seemed to be frozen outside the windshield and watching himself. From the bag he took another one of the roach spray cans and though Slick tensed, Slick watched him, too. He loosened the cap and then he pushed the door further ajar and held the can out into the rain.

He didn't even look at Slick but heard himself say in a bleak and doomed voice, "You got the gun, Man. But do you know what I have in this other can? Twice as much crap as you already got. You shoot and I'm going to drop it into the rain."

He was aware that Slick was surprised he hadn't scrambled out of the car at once and started running. He was also aware that Slick didn't believe him at first about the additional drugs. But there must have been something in his voice, echoes of fatalism, of someone who simply didn't have very much more to lose, and he knew that now Slick was beginning to believe him.

"You flipping your lid, Man? Whatcha mean you got some more shit? You think I'm going to swallow that jive? If you got more shit, how come you been holding out?"

A bit of Winston's confidence rose, but his tone remained guarded

"Because I wasn't sure I was going to like your way of taking care of business. Now can you blame me if I had doubts?"

"This little gun here? Shit, Brother, it don't mean nothing. Naw, you was right in the first place to look for me rather than some petty hustler out there in the streets. But what did I tell you: How do I know where you is, till I see where you coming from? Reason I was thinking about throwing your ass out of the car was because you kept on knitting with that little shit, even grabbing at two little hundred jive-ass dollars and all that. But now if you got more, we can get into *big money.* You won't be wasting my time. Look, here's my bread. Now let me see what you got?" Slick placed the gun on the dash-board, where no doubt it could be grabbed again instantly. "See, we don't need no gun between us."

Winston knew he was still being watched carefully. He also knew that if Slick would pull a gun on him for $8,200.00 worth of drugs, Slick would certainly shoot him for twenty thousand dollars worth.

"Man, don't spill it." Slick said anxiously. "That stuff is worth gold."

Cautionsly Winston attempted to gauge the weight of the can held out into the rain. Was it the heroin, or was it the roach spray? It could be either one. But by the weight of it he thought it most likely the spray. If so, there might be another way out. But suppose he was wrong and it wasn't the spray? Well, he'd be in even greater trouble. For suddenly he knew precisely what he was going to do. His finger found the spray trigger. . . . He brought the can in slowly, but then swiftly pointed it directly at Slick's eyes and sprayed.

A healthy dose of the spray spewed into Slick's face and eyes. Slick was caught between reaching for the gun and protecting his eyes. Concern for his eyes won and snarling with pain he covered them, but soon freed one hand and fumbled wildly for the gun. Winston unscrewed the cap of the spray and dashed all of it into Slick's face. Slick screamed, knocking the gun to the floor, trying now to kick Winston. Winston tightened his grip on the bag of stale bread and pork and beans and the other can of drugs and began beating Slick beside the head, his rage growing with every blow he struck. He heard his own voice hissing with anger, hatred. ".... Goddamn ... degenerate ... sonofabitch... ! Murdering children ... blind your own wife.... Pimping off the backs of black people ... no morals ... nothing.... Rotten ... animal. ...!"

He cursed Slick with an outrage so intense, he knew he was also striking at something about himself, the low level to which he had watched himself descend. If he hadn't been willing to sell the drugs, Slick and he never would have crossed paths. He wanted to pound Slick until Slick was wiped out of existence.

Trapped by the steering wheel and the pain searing his eyes, plus the edges of the pork and beans can striking his head, Slick could do nothing finally but try and cover himself. One side of his forehead had been opened and blood ran down and joined the purplish scar ringing his neck. Perhaps he had even been blinded by the roach spray? Winston caught himself. Of what value would it be to kill Slick? Another dupe, another fool, another casualty of the System, for beyond Slick was the Duke, who was more intelligent, and beyond Duke were those who really pulled the strings of power, the ones who pimped off the pimps and pushers, with pink-cheeked blue-eyed daughters in finishing schools, who golfed on the week-ends, and who lunched with men who owned seats on the Stock Exchange. . . .

Kill Slick and kill what? Nothing except that part of himself that had tumbled down into the rotten places where the Slicks lived.

Frantically, he gathered up the money. All of it. The rain washed over him and he ran in the opposite direction to the traffic. Then he cut across the traffic and took a side street. The can of drugs he had retrieved was in his hand. As he ran, he unscrewed the cap and spilled it. Then he took the other can out of the bag and also emptied it. The white powder dissolved quickly under the impact of the rain.

He wasn't sure how long he ran. When he looked up he realized he had crossed Madison Avenue and was headed towards Fifth. Drenched and exhausted, he hailed a gypsy cab. The driver eyed him suspiciously. He surprised the driver by tipping him fifty cents when he got out. Then he went upstairs to his apartment and collected the few things of value he had, leaving those things he no longer wanted in the middle of the floor. He hurried out with his battered suit-case and caught another cab. In less than an hour he had checked into the Hotel Hilton. It was a relatively modest room but the best looking room he had ever had in his life.

From thirty-nine floors above the City he looked down. Tomorrow or the next day he'd look for an apartment in a decent neighborhood. He wasn't too worried that he'd ever see Slick or the Duke or people like that again. The life he intended to lead would be far and remote from their lives.

Looking out the window, the bright lights of the City shimmering in the rain, the sound of the snarling traffic far away and beneath him, he felt an elation that almost left him giddy.

He clenched his fist and said aloud: "Okay. The handicaps are over. Now let's see if I can win this goddamn race!"

sixteen

Donald cursed under his breath. He had spotted a parking place, but the old Caddie back-fired and groaned and refused to increase speed. A bright new blue Buick rushed in and took the spot. All around him loomed the glass-walled office buildings. Park Avenue stretched before him. Throngs of white business men with briefcases rushed through revolving doors; hordes of women sat at typewriters beyond the glass walls. Cars crowded the Avenue. A few limousines were double-parked, with chauffeurs waiting inside. Donald knew he could drive all day and still not find another parking place.

Winston sat beside him, so concentrated on his own thoughts he hadn't said anything yet. Still he exuded tension. Like he was set to sprint from the car and tackle the whole City.

Gru and Pat were in the back seat. Pat had sat back there reluctantly. She looked as intense and concentrated as Winston. And yet, she seemed somehow happier than usual. . . .

The car continued to back-fire and Donald had to race the motor again to keep the engine from choking off. A couple of people seemed to be staring at him, at the car, amused.

Donald flared.

"Somebody give me some money so I can park this crate! I ain't going to be driving around all day looking for a place to park!"

Winston frowned, stung briefly out of his thoughts.

"What's the problem? Okay. Let us off in front of the building." He tossed Donald a five dollar bill. "When you park, meet us up at Bernie's office. Fifty-second floor."

Donald urged the car across the street. Winston jumped out at once, not even looking back. Gru hesitated and then patted Donald's shoulder. "Don't worry, Baby. If this deal go the way I'm calling it today, we'll soon be riding around in a choice piece of rubber. Shit, what do I keep telling you about Real Estate? Yesterday Bernie had his office out there in one of his crummy buildings in Brooklyn. Now he's here on Park Avenue!"

Donald grunted, watching Pat catch up with Winston. She didn't even try to conceal it anymore. . . . Though it was clear Winston hadn't been eager for her to come, he had said nothing, as though all of his energy was needed to deal with Bernie and he didn't have anything left with which to oppose Pat.

Donald was surprised to see him slow down and take her arm. The gesture was strangely protective, even if done absently. Sometimes, Donald thought, gazing after them as they went through the door, women like Pat astonished you. They could appear so weak and helpless, but they hung in close, picking at *your* weakness. And you had to be made of stone not to cave in at one point or the other. Maybe Winston didn't even know himself yet what was happening. . . ?

". . . . And got a partner who's worth at least fifty million!" Gru was saying. "How can Bernie lose with partners like that? Man, I keep telling you there's a gold mine out here in the streets! So you failed your Broker's license examination, well didn't the big boys fail a few times before they got their first million? Shit, you're wasting too much time on your gig at the post office, that's all. My advice is to cut the post office loose and come on out here in the streets, *full time!* Look what I'm doing for Winston. By following my lead, he can walk out of this building this afternoon in control of a deal that could very well net him more than a quarter of a million dollars!"

Donald nodded, frustrated. Money flowed all around him and he had nothing. He couldn't seem to get started. And always Gru made it seem so easy. What was wrong with him that he couldn't catch on to how to make the big money? And not only that, he hadn't even been able yet to pass the Real Estate Broker's examination.

Gru gathered up his briefcase and notes.

"Okay, Home. Go park. But be sure and come back to the meeting. I want you to see how the big boys take care of business!"

Gru got out, clutching his briefcase. He joined the other business men going into the building.

Donald gunned the motor and was about to take off when a patrol car eased up beside him. One of the policemen rolled down a window.

"Get that heap moving! Get it off the streets before I run you in!"

Donald glared. But the cops didn't wait for his angry reply. The patrol car moved off, speeding up the Avenue. That's right, Donald grumbled. Why don't you git them other cars off the street, too? Traffic was backing up. In the distance, he thought he could hear the beating of drums and wondered if it was some kind of a parade going on.

It took him twenty frustrating minutes to find a Parking lot that wasn't filled. By the time he got back to the Avenue, the entire area seemed to be in a bedlam. The drums had grown louder and now there were trombones and trumpets and people yelling and singing. From the windows of office buildings, people waved and shouted, flinging streams of paper.

Irritably, Donald elbowed his way through the crowd. He wished he could have found a bar and had a drink before going up to Bernie's office. But the bars in the area all seemed crowded with white business people, and, seeing no black faces, he felt self-conscious about going in.

The drums got louder and now there were sirens sounding everywhere. The traffic was almost at a standstill. He wondered what the hell was going on? He still had about a half a block to go before he'd get to Bernie's office.

Suddenly the crowd parted, good-natured and laughing, and he caught a glimpse of something white and blurred. . . . He couldn't believe his eyes. It happened so fast he wasn't sure what he had seen. A cheer went up all around.

He pushed his way through to get a better view of the Avenue. The man beating the huge drum didn't have a stitch of clothes on. Nor did the others. Some of them were on roller skates and bicycles. Occasionally one of them dashed through the crowd or hopped into the moving van that was up ahead of them.

Donald was astonished. He had been reading about all of this crazy kind of stuff lately. Full grown men swallowing frogs and gold-fish, and climbing telephone poles in the nude. People running through church naked. And a woman caught parachuting out of an airplane down in Washington somewhere, wearing nothing but a pair of white boots. Looked like everybody was losing their minds or something!

Yet Donald, too, now stared at the women, though he couldn't help but notice the others also, four or five men and even a couple of kids. All had signs painted over themselves: DOWN WITH BIG DADDY! FLY ME TO THE MOON. STREAK TO IMPEACH! And of all things, a black man was there on the edge of the crowd, naked as the rest of them: OFF WITH THE RACIST MONOPOLISTIC IMPERIALISTIC PIGS! The drummer beat wildly, the woman's breast rose as she lifted the trombone and gave a raucous blast. A few bystanders frowned and muttered, "Shame!" but mostly everyone applauded.

From up above a woman's shoe came flying from one of the windows. It landed in the streets. It was followed by a pair of sheer light tan panty hose. Men and women looked up and roared their approval, the men cheering the loudest. A strange smile suddenly crossed one man's face and he ripped off his shirt, snatched down his pants and underwear, and careful not to lose his briefcase, ran out and joined the other marchers. Stalled motorists honked their horns but less in irritation than excitement. The youngest-looking, prettiest woman was a red head who wore a ski mask; she rode one of the bikes. Occasionally she jumped off the bike, mooned the crowd and then jumped back on. Nearing Donald, either she tripped or someone tripped her. She went sprawling almost at Donald's feet, a huge YES! painted across her stomach. Beads of perspiration trembled upon her white freckled body. . . .

Donald was stunned. Even when someone helped the woman up and she got back on her bike and soon disappeared into the moving van, he could still see her, inflamed upon his imagination.

Suddenly it was over. The marchers jumped into the moving van or disappeared through the crowd. The police had arrived, looking as red-faced and as excited as everyone else. Apparently they hadn't been trying very hard to make an arrest. A sense of sexuality still floated through the air.

"All right! All right! Move back!" the policemen shouted. "It's all over."

The crowd responded good-naturedly, dispersing. Donald rubbed his neck and scratched his sweaty armpits, trying to re-orient himself. But it was difficult to keep his eyes off the women sifting through the crowd. Most of them, though white, seemed to be unusually attractive. In each of them there appeared to be a little of the nude woman who had sprawled in front of him.

He wanted to go on to the meeting at Bernie's office but now he had a craving for a drink more acute than ever. Strangely, some of his self-consciousness had disappeared. As he drifted with the crowd, he passed a bar around the corner. He strolled in and stood at the bar in the dimly lit rich-looking interior.

The people were laughing, talking about the marchers. Even the conservatively dressed people who sat at the tables were listening and laughing as though they couldn't believe their ears.

"Soon," someone said, "I wouldn't be surprised to see them invading Congress, and then the Senate. Perhaps to win the next election candidates will have to vie with each other in mooning the White House itself!"

"Hey, you see that fellow jump out of his car and run after the rest of them!"

"Was that where he came from?"

"Jeez!"

"Yes, with a pecker like that he should've kept his clothes on!"

Donald wore a cautious grin. But the white folks weren't taking any notice of him, although he was the only Black person in the bar, as far as he could see. The bartender served him politely enough, and he finished his scotch quickly and then had a beer. A woman at one of the tables with two men looked a little like the red head and he started sweating under his arms again. It dawned on him—and it made him feel a bit old-fashioned—that he had never slept with a white woman, except a whore in Chicago, the first big City he had hit when he came out of the South. It had been such a lousy screw he hadn't been very interested in white women after that.

But the red head stayed on his mind and not only did the pit of his arms irritate him but his crotch had begun to itch. His mood soured again. Goddammit, if he had money like Winston or Bernie he could do anything he wanted! Take him a trip over there to Europe and try out one of those French broads! But, shit, he didn't seem to be getting anywhere. With Winston he got a percentage of the rent he collected at the buildings, but lately he was even having a hell of a difficult time collecting. Every sonofabitch at the buildings challenging him: What about repairs? Repair this! Repair that! The old buildings were falling apart. And people blamed him because he was the one who took the rent. Winston held onto a nickel until the buffalo hollered, alloting little for repairs. Yeah, he was always getting the blame!

And play the numbers he couldn't win. The Lottery seemed fixed, he always missed by so much. Some people had all the luck. Maybe he was the kind of guy who'd never win anything. . . .

Lately he watched every black face behind the wheel of a car and studied also the black faces of men he passed on the streets, thinking that his luck might change. The newspapers and TV had announced a $10,000 reward for information leading to the whereabouts and capture of Leroy Brown. The cops had shot up a place in Harlem but apparently the bastard had gotten away. Well, if he saw the sonofabitch he'd grab him by the collar and push him up against a wall. Tell him, ". . . either cut me into some of the bread the big shots are paying you or I'm going to turn your ass in and get the reward!" He had no reason to like the goddamn chauffeur anyway.

Donald took his wallet out and almost succeeded in paying his bill and getting on to Bernie's, when he felt he just had to have one more drink. Irritably he ordered another scotch. He didn't like himself when he had decided to stop and yet kept on drinking. The bartender must have caught the note of surliness in his tone; the man glanced at him sharply. Sonofabitch!

Donald thought. Fuck with me and I'll turn this place out with all you white motherfuckers! But the bartender served him and went back to his conversation with the other white people.

Donald scratched his sweaty crotch again, feeling uncomfortable, seeing that he was still sexually aroused. He remembered that white actress that had been at the airport. Working around big shots, maybe the chauffeur had been screwing all kinds of women, including the actress. . . . But how was it that she had gotten away and they were still after the chauffeur? And what about the big guy who had been bossing the actress around? So far the newspapers hadn't said anything, almost as if the big guy hadn't been there. It was strange. Unless information was being withheld until the case broke, as the cops did sometimes on TV shows. . . . In the meantime, there were pictures of Leroy Brown everywhere; also a few of Trina Swan, very sexy looking, in her scanty bathing suits. . . .

Donald had one more beer and still brooding, walked out. He hoped Gru wouldn't give him no shit about getting there on time. "Niggers always late! Man, that's why you can't make it!" Gru who was never on time himself! Well, he didn't want to hear that shit. Early or late everything he did always went wrong anyway. Winston seemed to be advancing all over the place, picking up on the way white folks did things, while he hadn't even been able to pass his goddamn Broker's exam. It wasn't easy to admit that he simply might be slower than the Grus and the Winstons and the Bernies. Yet he remembered that very often jokes were told in his presence, and though everyone laughed, it took him an uncomfortably long time to figure out why he should join in. . . .

Donald found the building and caught the elevator and went up. The elevator expressed to the thirty-fifth floor and then became local. He got off at the fifty-second floor with his ears still popping.

He crossed a thick blue carpet that led him towards a door that said, McMANN & STEIN. Red and yellow flowers decorated the reception room, and upon one of the white walls hung a huge picture of a ship sailing across a peaceful blue sea. A middle-aged white woman glanced up from a typewriter questioningly, like maybe she wasn't sure whether he wasn't the delivery boy or something.

Donald flushed.

"Er . . . I'm with Mr. Winston's party."

Did she seem surprised? But then the phone rang. She picked it up and nodded him absently down the hall. The receptionist was far from pretty and old at that, but Donald nevertheless wanted to look back. He still couldn't shake the image of the red head out of his mind.

But now he had another problem. Which door? He had passed several doors but so far didn't hear voices. In fact he didn't hear anything. The world up here seemed as soundless and white as it was antiseptically clean.

Then a door popped open at the end of the corridor and a woman carrying a tray appeared in it briefly. He heard her mutter, "Damn!" and then she disappeared back inside the door. Had she seen him? Who was she cursing? Also, it seemed to him he had seen her before. . . Out there in Brooklyn where Bernie used to have his office. . . . Yeah, he was sure, one day he had seen her coming out of Bernie's building. He had been out there trying to borrow a repairman from Bernie's maintenance foreman for Winston. He had thought he was wasting his time. Why should the Jew do Winston any favors? They never did anybody any favors. And Winston would do anything to save a nickel, like a Jew himself.

Now he paused outside the door where he had seen the woman, more sure than ever that it was the same woman he had seen out at Bernie's. He and the black foreman had watched her coming out of the door, high-heeled, slacks so tight it seemed a wonder her skinny buttocks weren't cut in half.

The black foreman winked.

"Bernie's secretary. Best piece of ass in all of Brooklyn!"

Donald hadn't been in the mood to talk about anything except getting a boiler repaired and getting those goddamn tenants off his back.

"Too skinny," he had said. "Man, I like meat. Besides, I had this white broad in Chicago and talking about a lousy piece of ass. . . ." Still he had watched her swing a scarf about her hair and drive off in one of those small convertible sports cars.

He hadn't seen her since. Also, he had been surprised that the Jew had okayed the loan of a repairman. Looked like Winston had all the luck; even the Jews bending over backwards and trying to help him.

He rapped tentatively upon the door. Were the others in

there? When no one answered, he turned the knob and walked in. At least, he could ask the secretary. . . .

A massive mahogany desk dominated one side of the room and next to it was a bar, a glittering array of bottles and glasses. In another corner was a couch, complete with pillows and a neatly folded bed-spread. Beyond was a small kitchen and he thought he could smell coffee. Instead of an office, the place seemed like an apartment. Tenants that he had to cope with would think they were in paradise if they could live in a place like this.

But where was the woman? Where were Winston and Gru and the others? The place seemed empty. Another door, closed, stood to the side of the kitchen. Maybe the secretary was in there?

He took a step into the room and a voice almost screamed at him, "Don't move!"

He looked around startled. He saw the secretary on the other side of the desk, crawling about on her hands and knees, and peering at the white shaggy rug. Occasionally she scratched the rug cautiously and then peered at it again. Donald blinked, wondering if he was drunker than he thought he was. Also, he stared at the way the secretary's skirt had slipped up to her skinny buttock. And even though he noted that she had a small hole in the heel of her stockings and that three of her toes were covered by adhesives for corns, her skinny bright white legs and thighs transfixed him. But what was she doing crawling around on the floor?

She looked up at him and squinted, then said, "Oh" like she was disappointed. "Who are you?"

"Er . . . Donald."

"Bette. . . . You spell that B-E-T-T-E. . . . Though no one even gets that right around here anymore. You with that guy's group?"

"Er . . . yeah."

"Well, don't move. Unless you take your shoes off and give me a hand."

"Shoes off?"

"Better still, wait there." She got up and in her stockinged feet, went into the kitchen. She came back with a tray filled with cups of coffee and sugar and milk. "Take this into Bernie

201

and them. Across the hall. Tell them if they want drinks to come and get it themselves. After all," and her voice took on an edge of anger, "I'm a secretary, not a waitress!"

He hesitated but took the tray, standing there feeling somewhat stupid. She squinted at him again. "You sure I don't know you? Haven't I seen you before?" She had a nice smell about her, too, whatever perfume it was she used, and though she wasn't built nearly as beautiful as the red head she wasn't all that bad either.

"Er . . . maybe," he said.

She smiled.

"Well, you seem like a nice guy. Not like that guy you work for. If you're not too busy, you can come back and help me."

He nodded uncertainly. Help her with what? And why did she smile like that, looking him directly in the eyes, one of her eyes almost closed? He also noticed now that she wore too much lipstick and that she had hardly any breast at all. Yet what the foreman had said about her kept turning around in his mind. He wondered how the foreman knew she was the best piece of ass in Brooklyn?

She turned her back on him abruptly and began crawling around on the floor again. She seemed indifferent that so much of her body was exposed. But what was she looking for? Had she dropped a piece of jewelry or something?

He went out, holding the tray. In the hall-way it struck him. He'd be going in there and serving coffee like some kind of goddamn servant. If he was supposed to be in there learning about business, what would they think when he walked in with a tray? He stood in the middle of the blue-white hallway undecided. Return the goddamn tray to the secretary? But he remembered how she had looked up at him and smiled. Maybe if he hurried and got rid of the coffee and got back in there, who knew? If the foreman had been screwing her, and maybe everyone else in Bernie's office, she might agree to go out with him somewhere and have a drink. On the other hand, if he took the tray back and refused to serve the coffee, he could lose a chance.

He took a deep breath and opened the door and went in where they were all sitting around a long table. At the head of the table Bernie sat near a very old-looking white man, a man so old his wrinkled white skin seemed to crawl like worms. Next to the man sat a woman who appeared to be almost as old as the man, pads of paper before her and taking notes. Then came Jack Goldin, an unlit cigarette hanging limply from his lips; and then Jonathan and Gru who seemed to be annoyed for some reason, and finally Winston, tense and concentrated, and Pat. Pat sat to the right of Winston, a pad and pencils before her also, staring at everyone with her big eyes, looking more than just a little determined to get with whatever was going on here.

Bernie was speaking, his hands caressing the air.

". . . Winston! Be reasonable, young fellow! I've told my partner Mr. McMann here what a reasonable guy you are, but you're letting me down. We could hash most of this deal out in ten or fifteen minutes, and then we could leave the petty details to Jonathan and Jack. But if we already got problems, we can be here all day. C'mon, kid, I say meet me halfway. I got a dinner engagement, and you know yourself you got to be joking to ask for access to the premises upon Contract rather than at Closing, and wouldn't I have to be out of my mind to give you a written one year heating plant guarantee. Talk to him, Jack. Tell him what he's asking is not only unreasonable but *illegal*. What are you my lawyer for!"

Jack Goldin shifted the soggy cigarette to the other side of his mouth. He scowled, "Sure it's illegal."

Winston's voice was husky with tension. "I've given you my terms. Now either we got a deal going or we don't!"

Bernie jumped up and began pacing. And for the first time Donald, who hesitated, not exactly sure what he should do with the tray, noticed that Bernie was wearing a tuxedo, black tie and white shirt.

"Winston. Winston!" he said again, glancing at his watch. "I'm missing some people who just flew in from the Coast, all the way from Hollywood. Right now they're probably waiting for me at 21. And here I am haggling over peanuts, blowing a chance at an investment that comes once in a life-time! My God, Gru can't you talk to your partner? And Jonathan, you're a lawyer, you just heard what Jack said!"

Gru stared at Winston with irritation. "Well, I've been trying to talk to him . . . but . . ."

"I'll handle this," Winston cut in abruptly. "If Bernie has a dinner engagement— well, Bernie you keep your appointment. You know my phone number. Call me when you're ready to work out a deal!" And Winston made as though he was about to get up and walk out.

"Wait! Wait!," Bernie said. "What's the matter, kid? Okay, what the hell if I'm losing a Hollywood investment, you're my friend. Never let it be said that Bernie Stein doesn't treat his friends right. Okay, you see I'm calming down, I'm trying to be reasonable, I'm even going to sit down and listen to your proposition all over again . . . hoping that you, too, will be a little reasonable. Now what more could anyone ask of a friend?"

". . . Coffee," Donald mumbled, but no one glanced around, except the wrinkled faced old man, lips still trembling excitedly, spots of color in his cheeks. He gave Donald an almost imperceptible signal with his finger, much like Donald should serve the coffee but do not interrupt the proceedings, please.

Donald blinked angrily. Even Gru didn't look at him. Gru who had invited him to the meeting to "learn about doing business. . . ." In fact, Gru didn't appear to be very happy himself about the way the whole thing was going.

Jonathan looked around absently and saw the tray.

"Black," he said.

Donald bristled with resentment. He only knew Jonathan from a distance, but he had heard all about the snobbish sonofabitch. Even Winston didn't like him.

But everyone at the table seemed to be *expecting* him to serve the coffee, and if he didn't serve it and created a scene, maybe the girl would be angry with him, too, when he returned to the other office.

Scowling, he put down a black coffee for Jonathan.

Jack Goldin shook his head, indicating he didn't want any. He was now talking, "If we could get a couple of points out of the way, maybe we could take a cigarette break."

In a wheezing asthmatic voice, the old man cut in, "My apologies again, Jack. But if you must smoke, perhaps we can have a short recess?"

"Oh, no," Bernie said. "Let's get it over with. I'm losing a half million dollars just by sitting here! I told Jack to smoke a few extra cigarettes before he got here. He is aware of your condition." Then he turned to Donald. "I'll take sugar. Thanks. God, but to negotiate with you Winston I need something stronger than coffee!"

Winston accepted his coffee without even looking up, lost in his fierce concentration. Pat seemed surprised to notice it was Donald. The pads before her were still blank but her big brown eyes continued to glow with determination. Gru took his coffee and said nothing, stirring it moodily. Apparently the meeting was simply not going as he had planned it.

With all the coffee served, Donald stood there for a second. Though his mind was partly on the secretary, he still resented that no one had invited him to sit down. Jack and Jonathan were now arguing. When Donald went out the door, he was sure no one even knew he had left.

* * *

"What are they doing in there?" the secretary called. She was in the bathroom. The door stood open. He saw that she was bent over a mirror and at the same time seemed to be pushing two of her fingers into her right eye.

Donald put the tray down and rubbed his armpits uneasily. Despite the air conditioning, he was sweating. He figured he'd probably drunk the scotch and beer too fast, and that was why he was suddenly perspiring again.

"Talking," he said. He didn't know if he dared move around or not, maybe step on her jewelry and crush it? But why did she have her head twisted around like that, pushing at her eye?

"That figures. You can come on in. I found it. What is that old bag doing?"

"Who?" he came slowly towards the bath-room, still rubbing his armpits surreptitiously.

"McMann's secretary? I guess you know I'm about to be fired. It's the first time in four years Bernie has done a Contract without me. Today he said, 'Bette, sweetheart, would you bring in the coffee,' like I was a goddamn waitress or something! I know it is McMann pushing him to get rid of me. If I wear pants, he complains to Bernie they're too tight. If I wear a dress, he tells Bernie it is too short. Not good for the image of the office. Oh, wow! And let me tell you, don't let anyone smoke or cough around here. One whiff of smoke and he's looking for somebody to fire. If you even sneeze, he looks like he's ready to crawl out of the window to escape the germs! So what the hell do I care? I can get a job somewhere else. Except that it is a dirty trick if Bernie allows the old bastard to get rid of me!" She paused, and then beckoned. "Come here a minute, please."

"Huh?"

"Hold the glass up so I can see what I'm doing."

Donald rubbed his cheek nervously but walked into the bathroom and held up the mirror. There was a spot over the face bowl where the mirror appeared to have once stood. But it must have fallen down.

He gripped the mirror and Bette moved in closer and peered into it. The left side of her thin buttock brushed against him. The sweat pricked at his armpits and began rolling down his side, cool drops against the otherwise warmth of his body. I shouldn't drink so fast, he thought. Nor so much either. Still, at the moment, he wished he had another drink. . . .

She hadn't looked around or quit talking.

". . . An evil old man," she rattled on, still squinting. "Bernie's office is still being painted and renovated, so I thought it was all right to come in here and use the bathroom, especially when the old bastard is here only two or three hours a day—comes in and makes a few phone calls or swings his golf sticks, snoops around the office and causes all of us to become nervous wrecks, and then he either curls up on the couch and goes to sleep, or goes home again. . . . Leaves his complaints on little pieces of paper for Bernie to find. . . . So naturally I thought it was okay to use this toilet. No one else here. Well, yesterday I came in and sat down and there was paint on the seat! Fresh paint! An accident? Well, you better not believe it! All the toilet paper had disappeared, too. Also, the mirror was down off the wall. You think it could have fallen by itself? Some hint, eh? No, he never does anything directly. He plays his evil senile game like a little boy! He knows Bernie is reluctant to fire me. So he goes after me in little ways so that I'll quit. . . . Hold it steady." She touched his hand to lift the mirror higher.

He had been trying to get at the perspiration prickling his body and hold the mirror before her at the same time. The itching had become almost unbearable. She pushed against him again. Deliberately? He didn't know.

Suddenly he saw that both of her eyes had become bright blue and he thought, so it hadn't been jewelry, after all. Then she said, "Sometimes I think it would be less trouble to wear glasses. Do I look okay? Are you all right?"

"Er . . . uh huh. Real good. But I guess I wouldn't mind having a drink."

She didn't move away from him. She arched her head and touched her hair and pursed her lips and studied herself. No, she wasn't beautiful. But her skinny body felt surprisingly warm and soft pressed against him. Suddenly she seemed satisfied with herself. She smiled. Then she hesitated. Finally she asked, "Do you smoke?"

"Huh?"

"Oh, wow, Man, you know what I mean. You look hip. Most black guys know what's happening."

"Er . . . right," Donald said. Still he wasn't sure yet what she meant.

"Great!" she said. She even wiggled unself-consciously against him and then turned around and took his hand. She led him towards the couch and took the blanket and then she opened the door and peered out. There was no one in the corridor. Faintly he could hear voices in the room where the others were meeting.

She led him outside and then hurriedly opened the door next to the office they had just left. He followed her inside. It was not as lavishly set up as the other office, and the oak paneling on one of the walls hadn't been finished yet. Donald watched her lock the door. He stood in the middle of the floor, waiting, tensed. Maybe the foreman had really known what he was talking about. . . .

He didn't know what he expected her to do next or what he should do. After all, the others were meeting just across the hall. . . . But she seemed to know precisely what to do. She went to one of the windows and began hanging the blanket across it. She opened the window and he could suddenly hear the faint roar of traffic from down below.

"In here." She motioned to him to follow. It didn't make much sense but he followed her behind the blanket. Maybe she thought because of the blanket and the sound of the traffic the others wouldn't hear them across the hall? "Do you have a match?"

"Match?" He had been about to go ahead and put his arms around her.

"That's okay," she said. "I found some." She struck the match and lit a thin twisted cigarette. "Dynamite!" she said. "Friend of mine in Harlem laid it on me. I can't get stuff like it. It used to be safe to go to Harlem, but these days I'm afraid of getting raped or somebody snatching my pocket-book. You got a good connection?"

"Er . . . yeah, yeah," Donald said, though never in his life had he smoked anything stronger than a cigar. She sucked the smoke deep into her lungs, sniffing it, eating it. At the same time she waved her hand, fanning the smoke that the blanket didn't catch out through the window.

"Shoulda lit up in that old bastard's office!" she gasped. "Blow his fucking mind! He come in there sniffing, he'd really have something to get to. You want it now? It's really some dynamite shit!"

Donald took the marijuana. In truth, he was repelled by it, even a little afraid of it. He was a scotch and soda man. A beer man. He had never seen much sense in fooling around with drugs.

But she watched him. And she was behind this blanket with him, so close he could smell her. She kept brushing against him and remained close to him as though it was the most natural thing in the world. If he didn't smoke, wouldn't he blow his chance?

He drew the smoke into his lungs. At first there was nothing, like a cigarette. Then he took a second and then a third deeper drag. Suddenly it was as if someone had begun to pump air into the top of his head. The traffic roared inside of his ears. Right before before his eyes Bette's face seemed to swell up and then contract again, filled with her bright red smile. He wanted to cough, but suppressed it. He knew he must appear to be as hip as she was.

"Boss, shit, huh?" she said. "Take another. It's laced. Dude I know is heavy into the coke scene."

Donald took another drag, listening to her critically. Why had her voice changed? Or had her voice changed? Suddenly she seemed to be trying to talk *Black*.... Like the young niggers in the streets.... He had to keep staring at her to see that she was still white.

"... What's he into?" he finally heard her say, as though two or three minutes had elapsed. "Is he making it with that chick? Do you see how she trots after him, like a little puppy, like she thinks somebody else wants him."

"Who?" Donald said.

"Your boss."

"Boss?" Donald bristled. "Nobody bosses me. I ain't got no boss!"

"Well, that guy."

"We work together," Donald said. He searched for words. "Associates. I run the field."

"Well, he thinks he's smart," she said. "But I know better. I know guys a lot hipper than him."

"He don't mess with me," Donald said. "I don't take no shit off nobody."

"... Because if he was so smart," she continued. "He wouldn't trust Bernie. Does he know Bernie sent Jack all the way to Washington to check out this deal?"

"... Which deal?" Donald said. "What they rapping about in there? I don't have to be in there. Let them figure it out without me." Suddenly it seemed to Donald that his own voice had undergone a change, sounding almost like Gru's, as though Gru had left the meeting and had somehow become a part of him. "... We got a couple of Commissioners in our back pocket. Even if the loan we got projected comes in short of ... of ... a million and a half, it's going to be a whole new ball-game! I mean, Rolls Royces and all that, you understand...? And I'll probably go in for Real Estate full time at that point myself."

"... Washington," she was still saying, and it seemed that either she had been talking at the same time he was, or that he hadn't yet said some of the things he thought he had just said. . . . ". . . Jack used Mr. McMann's connections down there and found out that within the next couple of weeks there's going to be a moratorium on all federal loans to the state of New York. Politics, you know. The Mayor is supporting the Democratic nominee, you dig? And so Washington is striking back at all of us."

"Great," Donald said. "I usually vote for the Democrats, too. But the last time I couldn't figure out which way. . . ." She returned the cigarette to him again. He sipped on it recklessly. Then it was her turn once more. She used the tip of her nails to keep from burning her fingers.

There was something he had meant to say but could no longer remember what it was. Or rather, maybe it was something she had said that it seemed to him he should remember, but he couldn't get that straight in his mind either.

". . . Of course," she rambled on. "If he's so hip, he should know what he's doing. But tell me something about you?" She patted her hair and smoothed her skirt. "Do you think I look okay?"

"Real good." More than ever he wanted to pull her to him and kiss her.

"Stop now," she said, and he realized that he must have already made some kind of a move, even while it seemed to him he had only been thinking about it.

She allowed her cheek to brush his mouth and then he watched her right hand move as though in slow motion. It started at his waist and then her white fingers went straight down his pant's leg, squeezing the long thick rise that ended almost at his knee.

"Oh, Wow," she said. "But that's enough."

Apparently he was trying to embrace her again. The blanket had fallen and he kicked it out of the way.

"I said, that's enough!" she said sharply. Her bright glassy blue eyes seemed angry with him. "Don't be an animal!"

Something warned him to stop but he couldn't. He was now so aroused, it was painful. What the hell did she mean, that was enough? Rubbed his prick till he could hardly stand and now she wanted to leave him with it like that! But she really meant what she had said. When he grabbed her again, she tried to kick him between the legs. A sudden spurt of fear almost stopped him. Suppose she screamed?

But she fought silently, viciously, bit his hand. He took her arm and rammed it up her back. With his other hand he pulled at her panties and heard them rip. She locked her legs together. But when he pressured her arm higher, she opened them. He had her across the desk, which was still speckled with paint, and where lay a disarray of bolts and nuts and nails and screwdrivers.

She groaned painfully.

"Wait," she murmured. "Please. It hurt."

She brought her free hand to her bright red lips and spat on her fingers. Then she massaged them between her legs.

When he rammed all the way into her, she gasped.

"Wow!" she said. "Dynamite!"

seventeen

Bette kissed Donald lightly on the cheek, combed her hair, put on fresh lipstick and went out first. When Donald strolled into Mr. McMann's office, she was already there, sipping a glass of red wine. The rest of them were also there, except Jack Goldin and Jonathan. Other than an occassional sensation of everything suddenly expanding and reeling, he felt great. He walked over to the bar and planted himself near Bette, trying to keep himself from glancing at her possessively. He knew that never in her life would she forget this afternoon.

Bernie was playing bartender, serving drinks with a great flourish and talking up a blue streak. Everyone was talking, tensions released.

". . . Winston, young fellow," Bernie called to Winston, "the offer still stands. If you get a problem, call me. . . . I need a partner to run my Brooklyn office. Don't answer yet; don't say, no. Think about it. You never can tell. You got yourself a terrific deal today, but as you know business is unpredictable. You're up today, down tomorrow! But if a problem crops up, remember I always got a spot for bright people."

Donald frowned momentarily. There was something he should remember but he still couldn't get it into focus.

He shrugged and asked Bernie for a scotch and noticed that Gru kept trailing Bernie around.

". . . You suppose they are still there?" Gru said. "I could re-arrange my schedule for the evening and dash over there to 21 with you. Hell, I've been doing some thinking lately . . . about . . . about becoming a bit more diversified. I wouldn't be surprised if there isn't still a mint to be made in film productions."

"Who?" Bernie said. "Oh, yes, yes. But have a drink first."

Bette surprised Donald by walking away and joining Mr. McMann and Pat and Winston and the older woman secretary. Donald hesitated, then reeled in the same direction.

Mr. McMann was looking from Pat to Winston, as though fascinated by both of them; or by Negroes in general today.

Mr. McMann cleared his throat and his asthmatic voice wheezed with excitement. "Yes, young man, you're a credit to your race. Now, I have interest in other properties in . . . well . . . depressed areas. . . . Perhaps we shall continue to do business? They are problem buildings, but I am sure that the tenants in these areas will respond more favorably to their own kind. . . ."

The older secretary maintained a close watch on Mr. McMann, as though to support him if his strength began to fail. ". . . Don't over-tax yourself, sir."

"Nonsense! I've never felt better! Nothing more invigorating than a dose of good old-fashioned business! Colored people . . . er . . . I mean, Black people . . . or is it Negroes?"

". . . Black people, isn't it?" the older woman asked. "He doesn't know what to call you!"

Winston was relaxed, as though he had not only run a race but was beginning to believe now that he had actually won it. His tone was amused.

"Let him call us what he always calls us."

"In any case," Mr. McMann continued. ". . . It is a pleasure to see people like you finally taking advantage of opportunities, entering the mainstream, so to speak. And I also congratulate you, young man, on the very fine and efficient secretary you have here!"

Pat flushed and whipped out a cigarette. She had almost lit it when she saw that Mr. McMann had blanched, staring at her as though he was about to crawl through the floor.

"Oh, I'm sorry," she said. "I forgot."

Flustered, she thrust the cigarette back into the pack.

Bette held the glass of red wine to the edge of her lip, watching Pat.

"But I thought you were *his* secretary," she said, indicating Gru. "That was the impression I got out at Bernie's."

213

Pat tensed up, but her big eyes turned and fixed themselves on Bette. She seemed numbed by Bette's cool gaze.

"Oh, did you?" Her lips parted in a dazzling if frozen smile. "Well, isn't that strange. . . . Out at Bernie's I got some wrong impressions about you, too—one was that I thought that *you* were *Bernie's* secretary."

Bette blinked, surprised by the cutting edge of Pat's tone. Bette turned her gaze upon Winston: "What a pity," she said. She gave her own cool dazzling smile, but a smile that seemed to be filled with some of the mysteries Donald thought she had not too long ago shared with him. Donald was sure he must be wrong. He knew what a great lover he was. ". . . Yes, a pity," she went on, "that you already have a secretary when I was about to put in an application for a job! Are you sure you're not expecting a vacancy?"

Pat's eyes grew stormy, but she maintained her smile. She gave a shaky little laugh, but her tone was suddenly as arrogant as that of the white girl's.

"Not at present," she said. "But if there's ever a vacancy, I'm sure we'll call you."

Winston had been observing Bette as though he knew her, knew her in a way that Donald didn't yet know her, had long ago come to know her.

He slipped his arm around Pat.

"She's the boss," he said. His tone was playful, but the warmth in the look he gave Pat was probably more serious than he knew. "So what do you say, Boss, to having one last drink and then cutting out?"

"Right," Pat said.

The two of them went towards the bar where Bernie seemed to be trying to get away from Gru.

Mr. McMann had been regarding Bette with distaste, staring at her as though she somehow threatened him. Now with an icy almost peevish show of dignity, he turned away from her and looked up at Donald.

"Are you also in Real Estate, sir?"

"Huh? Er . . . yes."

"This has been a most exhilarating day!"

"Be careful, sir," the older woman said.

Donald was trying to catch Bette's eyes, but suddenly she, too, walked away. He lifted his scotch to his lips, but abruptly snatched the glass away. A worm seemed to be crawling around in the bottom of the glass. He stared at the liquid. But now it was clear again. Maybe he wasn't supposed to mix the scotch with the stuff he had been smoking?

"Thought my drink was . . . ." He mumbled. "I mean, er . . . yes, Real Estate. Soon I could be into it full-time, go out there Public, and the Stock Exchange and Roll Royces and the whole bit."

Mr. McMann was somewhat puzzled but nevertheless impressed.

"Well, as I have just said to the other colored fellow . . . I mean, black fellow. . . . We are unloading . . . , that is, divesting ourselves of our interest in certain areas. . . . I say drop in any time, and we can do business."

Donald nodded. "Uh, huh. Okay. Sit down over a drink and we oughta be able to work it all out."

"Splendid!" Mr. McMann exclaimed.

"Now that is enough," the older woman said, and she guided Mr. McMann to the couch. Though he resisted feebly, he finally sat down, and soon looked as if he was about to fall asleep.

Donald looked around for Bette. She was at the bar getting another glass of red wine. He steadied himself against the wall and the room ceased reeling. As he observed Bette's skinny body, the bright white legs, the thinly chiseled restless white face, he remembered how he had not long ago overwhelmed and dominated her. Again he felt masterful and supremely sure of himself. Should he go over and make arrangements to see her tonight, or should he see her tomorrow? It was said that once you laid a white broad they practically crawled after you, pestered you to death. . . . And taking the job he had done on Bette and her reaction, he figured he'd better slow her down a little. . . . Instead of tonight, he'd see her tomorrow.

He held himself erect and strolled over to the bar.

He caught Bernie telling Winston, "Yes. Yes. Well, I should have warned you about Rios. But I tell you, young man, you will not have any trouble. Rios is a big mouth. And so is his partner, Jones. Both got political ambitions. So they have the tenants stirred up and you're faced by a rent strike! So what?

Do you think I would be selling you these buildings if I thought you couldn't handle it! Give Rios and Jones a couple of bucks and they'll keep their mouths shut!"

Then Bernie grabbed Winston's hand and shook it warmly. Winston was getting ready to go.

Donald leaned towards Bette and said in his most casual voice, ". . . Er . . . gimme your number. I'll phone you later tonight."

Bette blinked. Her blue eyes moved restlessly around the room. Then she smiled, cool and distantly. She put out her hand, and he took it.

"Thank you for a lovely afternoon," she said. "It was very nice meeting you."

Then she quickly freed the hand that he was still trying to hold.

eighteen

Junior and Slick sat in the car and watched them enter the school auditorium, where all the other people were headed. There were three of them, Winston and the pretty girl Junior had seen before and the husky guy who always looked like he was angry or drunk. Again Junior thought the girl was very beautiful. Maybe as his mother had been when she was younger. Many years ago. . . .

"Get out." Slick ordered.

"We going in there?"

"Just do as I say."

Junior got out of the car, and came around to the driver's side with Slick still watching him. It was the first time Slick had allowed him to get out of the car without keeping a grip on him, like maybe it was another stupid way Slick was testing him. But he wouldn't put it past Slick to try and run him down on the sidewalk if he attempted to get away.

His contempt for Slick had increased. But his fear had, too. Anybody who'd throw lye in his own wife's face might do anything. Slick bragged to impress you, to let you know how mean he could be if you crossed him, but some of what he said had to be true. He even admitted that the lye hadn't caught his wife in both eyes; he was bitter that passers-by had started shouting for the police. He had had to run away to escape being caught. Now he had to wait all over again for another chance.

Slick was bitter against his old buddies, also. Including the Duke. Like a broken record, he kept telling how they had all ". . . let him down." When he was down from a high and depressed, he stared into space and repeated what the Duke had said: "Get outta my face, nigger. Any dude that can't handle his bitches, and then lets some two-bit john out-con him out of some of the bread *due* me, I don't want to see. Don't tell me no shit about the nigger and a bunch of his friends jumping you when you weren't looking and spraying roach spray in your face. I got my own problems."

At moments, Slick knew he had been lying to the Duke. But it seemed almost impossible for Slick to admit that a lame like Winston had been alone when he had been out-smarted. His hatred for Winston was nearly as great as his hatred for his wife.

Sometimes, like now, Junior thought that he, too, might be able to out-smart Slick. The last time they had shot up, Slick had used a new needle, but hadn't noticed where he had dropped the old one. Slick would have to turn his head sooner or later and he had already imagined how he could push the needle into Slick's throat. . . .

He had thought to do it earlier, and afterwards waylay a grocery boy and get into Winston's building like he was delivering, and get it over with. But then Winston had suddenly come out of the door and got into the car with the other two, and he and Slick had followed them.

It was difficult to keep his thoughts hidden. He watched Slick's attention waver briefly as Slick climbed out of the car. The red rubber-like scar seemed to swell up on the yellow neck. But almost instantly the blue sunglasses turned and focussed upon him again.

They stood for a moment and regarded the people going into the school auditorium. Puerto Ricans and Blacks. A few whites, mostly elderly. Some of the people seemed angry.

"C'mon," Slick said. Slick carried the violin case and strapped to his waist Junior knew there was a small automatic. But Slick didn't plan to use either gun yet, unless he had to. For the moment, his greatest interest was to find out what Winston was into, and then cut himself in for a share of it.

Junior stumbled, and Slick tensed as though suspecting a trick.

"Watch it, punk."

"I . . . didn't eat." That was true. Suddenly he had to tighten himself against a wave of dizziness. It seemed days since he had last eaten and yet how could it have been that long ago?

"Well, you had a taste," Slick said. "With me you get the best shit. But you got to eat, too."

Junior suppressed a shiver. There was something he kept almost remembering but knew he didn't want to remember. Each day he got it fixed again in his mind that he had just left home; he held onto the picture of himself tasting the soup before he offered it to Mama as though it had happened only a few hours ago. But there came moments now with increasing frequency when he was startlingly aware that he hadn't been home for many days. . . .

". . . And you ain't going to git but a taste," Slick stated. "Not what you need. Till you learn to do what I tell you, minute I tell you to do it."

Junior dabbed his soggy handkerchief to his nose. "I don't need your shit!" he flared. "I can cop by myself!"

They crossed the street and stood before the school. People streamed by them, taking no particular notice of them. There were other junkies in the neighborhood.

"Sure," Slick said. "Without a penny, what you gonna cop? You think you on short rations now, well, if you keep giving me lip, you gonna really find out what short rations is!"

Goddamn bastard! Junior thought. Trying to break him in like he'd break in a whore. Ride on his back to get back up there where he used to be, ride anybody's back. Last night if he had had the needle he would have ended it for Slick right there. Somewhere in a Village apartment, expensive furniture and mostly coke and hashie. Faggots, and women kissing women.

"My little boy," Slick introduced him. Eyes and hands rising up from the darkness and reaching for him. They didn't want Slick; but it was Slick who collected the bread. And shot up first, too. Then, in the car, Slick took his arm and pushed a small stingy dose into it while he held his head out the window and vomited.

A tall woman passed, dressed the way they did over in Africa somewhere. Her headdress was of the same colorful material that wrapped her body. Three young dudes in black berets walked beside her. They turned with the briskness of marching soldiers and followed the woman into the auditorium.

"Git your ass straightened up," Slick commanded. "And act like you is a member of whatever is going on in there."

Junior swallowed the nausea coating his tongue. If Slick wasn't so mean and disgusting, he'd try to be friendly with Slick. Sometimes he felt he was falling and falling, as if he was never going to stop, and he wished there was somebody he could catch onto. Because if he kept on falling he suspected that after awhile he wasn't going to know who or where he was anymore. But how could he reach out to Slick? Slick seemed to be pushing him faster towards the fall.

Slick opened the door cautiously, pushed him in, and then followed him inside. No one stopped them. The auditorium was almost full, people sitting and some standing. "Upper West Side Tenant's Council" a sign read. Upon the platform sat Winston and the pretty girl and the husky guy and several others.

He and Slick walked down the aisle, looking for seats closer to the platform but there were none. They had to come back to the middle of the auditorium where they found two.

Junior pressed his soggy handkerchief to his nose again, closing his eyes tight and then opening them. But he figured he was going to be okay. He was also pleased that he had the inside seat, and that Slick sat to his left. In this way, he still had his right hand free. He felt even more reassured as he fingered the needle.

nineteen

Pat sat upon the platform between Donald and Winston and only partially listened to the speakers. Her mind shuttled away from a vague sense of unease to her favorite dream again. Lately she could almost see the house she had begun longing for, a house far away in Queens somewhere or Long Island, or in one of those places with a name like Ossining. She saw the house as all white, with a beautifully trimmed lawn and shrubbery all around it. Both the basement and the back yard would be *finished* and when she and Winston had parties, they'd use the basement in winter and the back yard when the weather was beautiful. The only problem she hadn't solved yet in her mind was whether there should be a garage for two cars or one. . . . Commuting to the City, Winston would need a car to himself, wouldn't he? And whether she continued to work at the hospital or did private duty, she'd also need a car.

But the cars didn't matter. Not yet. She'd solve that later. What mattered most was the house. Winston's apartment was okay. She really liked it, but she hadn't realized how very much she wanted a house of her own until she'd allowed herself to begin thinking about it recently. An apartment in the City simply wasn't the best place in the world to live once you had children. . . .

By now, she was convinced that she was pregnant. But she knew that this was not what was bothering her. Winston probably wouldn't be overjoyed at first but he would get used to it. She had few remaining doubts about that. It was a beautiful feeling to finally know that she could almost predict everything Winston would or would not do. She assumed that

221

this must be because for the last several days she had become confident that he loved her. From that moment in his apartment when he had built up his greatest defense against her but had ended up by holding her as though he'd never let her go, she had sensed that the worst was over. Now, except that she caught him staring at her in surprise sometimes, it didn't seem as if the "worm in his brain" intended to fight her anymore. But still she'd better be careful. Maybe she could yet make some kind of a mistake, and even though he loved her, she knew he would start resisting her all over again.

The voice of the minister or priest, a man in a dark suit and white collar, droned into her consciousness.

". . . And in the spirit of love and understanding. . . . And with His Divine guidance replacing discord with harmony, hate with love, divisiveness with cooperation . . . we can resolve our conflicts today. For aren't we all God's children, landlords as well as tenants, the rich as well as the poor. . . ? And already our prayers have brought us to the threshold of rehabilitating our community!"

"Get on with the meeting!" someone shouted. "Fuck the sermon!"

"Right on!"

Julio Rios, a very light-skinned Puerto Rican with a hint of Blackness in his hair and co-chairman of the meeting, bounced up. In a voice controlling impatience, he asked in both Spanish and English for quiet, ". . . a little respect for the Father." Roscoe Jones, the other co-chairman, had been about to jump up, too, and quiet the audience, but Julio Rios had beaten him to it. He sat back down and seemed almost unhappy at the swiftness with which the tenants obeyed Julio Rios' plea.

The Father continued, ". . . the forthcoming loan will re-habilitate the community, but only the love of God will rehabilitate the spirit. . . ."

Pat's thoughts drifted towards the house again. She imagined an evening when it had snowed everywhere. It would be cold and freezing all over the City, but when Winston came home, they would be warm and secure inside. Once they locked the doors, the world would be shut far away outside. If only she could get Winston to slow down a little. . . . He moved so fast, so desperately. The more he succeeded, the more he seemed to speed up. Of course, at that Contract at Bernie's new office she had impressed him, but wasn't that because she had forced herself to try so very hard? Maybe he'd never know how little she still understood about "business," or that she still wasn't very sure she even liked "business." Everyone seemed so insincere and ruthless. Cut the other person down before he did the same to you. She sensed that Bernie liked Winston, respected him, but wouldn't hesitate a second to take advantage of Winston. Where would it all end, with Winston gobbling up more and more buildings, until one day he, too, became like Bernie, or worse still, Mr. McMann?

She closed her eyes briefly and attempted to see the house again. But it had blurred. Something was still worrying her, something she didn't understand. . . . It went beyond the realization that she didn't know yet how she was going to get Winston to slow down. No, she didn't want him to become like those businessmen she had heard and read so much about, men who were so obsessed by business there was no longer room for love, for family, children. . . . But she believed she'd find a way to deal with that. Once Winston had a child and a beautiful home, and got this last deal over with that apparently was going to make him a tremendous amount of money, maybe he'd slow down a little himself.

So what was it that kept nagging at her? On the one hand, she felt wonderful, couldn't remember having felt so good in all of her life. And yet on the other hand she felt uneasy, a strange sense of dread. Like maybe she was going to be punished for daring to feel so happy. . . .

Was it because of Gru? Though she was sorry she'd had to hurt Gru, she should be relieved that she had finally gotten it over with. After the Contract at Bernie's new office she had phoned Gru, and they had met for drinks. She had watched him coming through the door and felt so guilty and nervous she hadn't known how she'd ever get a word out. But Gru had strolled into the lounge talking, as though he still couldn't admit knowing, or, at least, suspecting what she'd wanted to tell him for some time.

Sitting down, he ordered drinks in his lordly manner.

". . . Been meaning to talk to you, sweetheart. But I got so many irons in the fire, I can't always get back to you. In fact, I got to call Bernie in twenty minutes. . . . Hell, I may have to zip out to the West Coast in a day or two. . . . Then there's this dude I been rapping with from Venezuela. . . . People don't seem to know that there's bread being made hand over fist down in ole South America these days. I could be wasting my time here. Anyway, kiddo, I been meaning to talk to you. Hell, I've done all I could for you. You came up here straight out of the cotton patch, and I've taught you how to talk and how to carry yourself and how the big boys operate. But, hell, do you expect me to stick around and teach you forever? During the next couple of years I could be catching a lot of planes. . . . I know it is tough, but I'm just not going to have the time to see you, as I used to. I don't want to break your heart, but I got to keep on top of my deals. What the hell, don't worry, you'll find somebody else. . . . In time. . . . And with what I've already taught you, you might even be able to bag one of the big boys!"

Then he was gone. Hitching up his pants and gathering his briefcase and gone. To call Bernie. Someone. Somewhere. . . .

Tears were in her eyes and for a moment she couldn't stop them from falling. She was relieved that Gru had made it so easy for her. But most of all, she fervently wished that Gru would someday find a place, a place where he could really use his great imagination, where he could make real castles instead of merely having the dreams. . . .

*　　*　　*

Pat looked out over the auditorium again. No, it was not because of Gru that she felt this strange uneasiness. Though she was sad about Gru, she was also thankful that she no longer had to lie. To Gru. To herself. To anyone.

She whipped out a cigarette, hesitated, and then put it back into her pack. Perhaps that was it? Certainly a part of it. Withdrawal symptoms. Every once in a while, the craving became acute; had her almost ready to climb up a wall. . . .

But since the Contract at Bernie's new office she had resolved to cut herself down to three cigarettes a day, and then soon she'd go to two cigarettes and then one and then none at all. But already she had had her day's quota and how would she get to sleep tonight if she was already breaking down? She didn't know. Still she was determined to stick by her resolve.

Her gaze stopped at the young boy and the older man who

sat at his side who wore the blue sunglasses. She had noticed the boy when he first came in and had been surprised. She remembered him passing Winston's building. But this time it was the man who carried the violin. The boy's father? Well, with a parent who looked like the man in the sunglasses, it was no wonder that the boy seemed hopelessly lost and strung out on drugs.

She had watched them as they advanced into the auditorium, coming towards the rostrum, ill at ease, somehow as if they didn't belong here. Were they tenants? The man looked so brutal and bummy she couldn't help feeling sorry for the boy. Children like that didn't have a chance. Sometimes drug-addicted parents sent their children to purchase drugs like other parents sent their children for groceries.

The boy had wiped his nose and glared at the man defiantly, and then they had gone back down the aisle and took two vacant seats.

She looked away, struggling against a vague sense of guilt. Here she dreamed of a beautiful home in the suburbs and whether she and Winston should have two cars or one, and kids like that were dying all over the City. But what could she do? Sometimes she thought she should devote some of her time to one of the drug rehabilitation programs after she graduated, do something to help the kids, because if Blacks didn't start trying to save their own children, who would? But of what value would it be? What could one person like herself really accomplish against an increasing tide of lost children? It was confusing. Depressing. More than ever she wanted to whip out a cigarette but again she restrained herself.

There was a scattering of applause and some boos. The priest had finished speaking. He left the rostrum and returned to his seat on the other side of Donald and next to one of the white men.

Julio Rios jumped up again and now he spoke in Spanish, translating and clarifying some of the things the priest had said. Most of the audience listened to him quietly, but a few boos continued.

The boos came primarily from the people centered around the woman in the African dress. Pat had also noticed the tall black woman when she first entered. She had been surrounded by young Blacks and Puerto Ricans in berets. There had been something arrogant about the woman as she strode to the front of the auditorium and took a seat that had apparently been reserved for her. People had greeted her respectfully and moved aside and allowed the young fellows to sit near her. Two of the young men squatted in the aisle at her side.

Instantly, Pat had felt both envy and admiration for the woman. Strong and decisive looking women like that always awed her. She had for a long time dreamed of wearing African dress but up to now she hadn't been able to bring herself to do so. And Black women had been wearing their hair natural for years before she had gotten over her self-consciousness and tried it. Sometimes she still felt she must be the most insecure and backward Black woman left in the world. Would she ever catch up to the women, Black and White, who, these days, seemed so strong and sure of themselves? She wasn't sure. But I just got to keep trying and trying, she thought.

Julio Rios left the rostrum, and Roscoe Jones, a thin anxious wisp of a man with a raggedy Afro, but with a surprisingly strong and effective speaking voice, took over. He introduced the Councilman from the district.

". . . A man who is a friend of labor and poor people, a man who has been fighting tooth and nail to help us get our loan, and who deserves our support in the coming election. Can I get a hand for Councilman Wilkes!"

Applause, but again boos; the boos once more coming mainly from the people surrounding the Black woman.

"We want to hear the landlord!" someone yelled. "We didn't come here to hear no politics. What about the rats and the roaches!"

Anxiously, Roscoe Jones held up his hands and asked for quiet. "Please Brothers and Sisters. . . ."

Finally the hisses and the boos subsided.

The Councilman, a blond man in a handsomely tailored blue suit, strolled to the rostrum loosening his tie. He spoke hurriedly, as though to discourage interruptions.

"My friends, I know you have come here today primarily to hear your new landlord. . . . And you are rightfully impatient. . . . Therefore I will be brief. I only wish to re-emphasize that if I am honored by your continued support, and your votes send me to Congress, I will maintain the high standards of service I have always given this community. I have fought, along with your community leaders, for the government loan to rehabilitate the rat-traps in which you live. And now that loan is in the making. I have worked to maintain rent controls and against exorbitant profits for greedy unscrupulous landlords. And this fight continues! I do not have to tell you about my opponent. . . . You already know he is a man bought and paid for by the Real Estate lobby. His children attend private schools, while you and your children suffer in a pit of poverty and degradation. I fought with you against your old landlord who did nothing to maintain and repair the buildings where you live, and by God I will join with you in your battle against the new landlord if he does not provide you with the services to which you are so rightfully entitled. . . !"

"Strike now!" a man near the Black woman shouted.

"¡Acción ahora!"

"You get the vote, we don't see you no mo!"

"Where do *your* children go to school?"

"Quiet!" Roscoe Jones pleaded. "Can we have some quiet, please!"

Julio Rios sprang up again. "¡Por favor, Amigos! You will hear the new landlord soon."

But the Councilman had finished. There was some applause; but an increase in the hisses and boos.

The Councilman paused near Winston. Pat noticed beads of perspiration above his upper lip.

"I understand you know Bernie? And Casey McMann?" He said to Winston, voice lowered. "Well, good luck . . . , but push that goddamn loan, Man, otherwise you're going to have a hornet's nest around here! And let me hear from you. Anytime." Then he smiled. "Especially before November!"

"Sure." Winston nodded.

Then the Councilman went out, followed by the white man sitting near the priest. A bodyguard?

The priest now stood up also, murmuring apologetically that he was committed to another engagement. . . . In the wake of the Councilman and the other white man, he threaded his way out of the auditorium, smiling shyly at a tenant he recognized here and there.

227

Pat saw that Winston had tensed up again. But was it any wonder when all the hostility in the auditorium seemed poised and ready to strike him down as the new landlord? Yet he appeared less fearful of the hostility than whether he was prepared to meet the challenge of it. His eyes darted about the room. He had listened with absolute concentration to the priest and Councilman, a faint cynical smile tugging at his lips. He watched the interplay of jealousy between Julio Rios and Roscoe Jones, but most of all he seemed attuned to the audience. He had already identified those who had done most of the booing. Though there was a hint of desperation in his attitude, she marveled that he wasn't even more uneasy. If someone called on her to speak to an audience like this, she knew she'd collapse. She wouldn't be able to get a word out. Just thinking about it increased the nervous flutter in the pit of her stomach. But as to Winston, she had no doubt that when he was confronted by the audience, he'd somehow find a way to "take charge."

Suddenly, impulsively, she leaned over and kissed him on the cheek.

He was startled.

"What was that for?"

"Nothing. Except that I love you."

Julio Rios had just finished translating again, and Roscoe Jones was going back to the rostrum. Winston's attention was torn between them and herself. Still, he didn't yet look away from her. "Well. You're something else, you know. But just wait till I get you home! I might lock you up and keep you for a week . . . a month . . . a year."

"Forever?"

He hesitated.

"Maybe so."

She looked away. A rush of blood swept from her breast and momentarily flooded her senses. For an instant, she felt breathless and giddy. Yes, about one thing she was right. He wasn't going to fight against her anymore.

". . . And now, in a moment," Roscoe Jones said, "I shall have the pleasure of presenting to you the man most of you came out this evening to hear speak. . . . But first, I'd like to say, that both Julio and I have already spoken to him, and he seems like a sincere man, concerned with the problems of our community and the inequities we suffered at the hands of our old landlords. That is why both Julio and I feel that to continue plans for a rent strike at this time would not be appropriate. In short, Brothers and Sisters, we must continue to be vigilant against those detractors and trouble-makers who would throw out the baby with the bath-water, who are asking for revolutions on a breakfast tray . . . and who would challenge hydrogen bombs with pen-knives . . . we say . . . both Julio and I . . . that the new landlord should be given a chance. . . . And only if he fails to listen to our legitimate demands should we strike."

"No! No!" People around the woman shouted, the protest spreading. "Strike now!"

"¡Adelante!"

"We are sick of promises!"

"We don't want no Uncle Tom landlord!"

"The honkies done ripped us off and now they sending in a brother to strip us of the little we got left!"

Though most of the shouting continued to rise from the people nearest the woman in African dress, she said nothing. She simply sat there, her black face rigid with scorn, waves of uncompromising hostility emanating from her.

Roscoe Jones hesitated. "Well, suppose we allow the new landlord to speak for himself. . . ." He appeared relieved to step aside.

A moment of outright fear seized Pat as Winston rose and went to the rostrum. The boos and hisses swelled in volume. She knew that the antagonism had to be further unnerving Winston because of the force with which it pounded into her. She gripped her seat, glancing at Donald for support. But he looked more uptight and disorganized than she had ever seen him.

She fumbled with her purse. Would she be breaking her word to herself if she took out a cigarette and lit it but put it out after only a few puffs? Then she could smoke the rest of the cigarette later and she'd still be within her quota, right? She suspected she was lying to herself. She knew she wouldn't be able to stop smoking once she started. She was still resisting the temptation to take the cigarette out of her purse when she almost screamed.

The Black woman in African dress had risen, and lifting her arm, she deliberately threw something straight at Winston. The object bounced off the rostrum and landed at Winston's feet. She stared, fear paralyzing the scream in her throat. At first she thought: a bomb? Winston, too, seemed stunned. He stared at the object. No, not a bomb. It was a huge rat. Monstrous and bloated, it lay there at his feet. A gasp went through the audience, pushing against the boos and the hisses. It was clear that some of the tenants did not approve of the Black woman's gesture.

The woman had not sat down. Those nearest her clapped their hands wildly.

"Right on!"

The woman returned Winston's shocked and angry stare.

"It is dead," she stated. "But those rats that feast upon the flesh of our children are not!" Her tone was venomous, softened only by an accent that was not instantly recognizable. Suddenly, gesticulating vehemently, she repeated herself in Spanish. Then she added, "My name is Anasa Makini. There have been allusions to me. Yes, I am a trouble-maker, and I am not afraid of hydrogen bombs or politicians or secret government agents! Nor am I afraid of landlords, those whites who have fed their children by standing upon the backs of our children; or those blacks who would whiten their hearts and pimp upon the carcass their fellow whites have left! Across the world we spit into the face of dying white power; but there are some, like you, who would kiss the bloody ass of that white death. Don't give us more promises about tomorrow's loan. We want to know what you're going to do today! Don't tell us we must be patient and wait and wait again. Our children are dying now! How can you ask us to pay you money to support your dream, when you would leave us dreamless? I, Anasa Makini, cast my vote for a rent strike now!"

The applause was thunderous. And kept breaking out anew as people around Anasa Mikini rose and gave a passionate translation of her speech into Spanish. Even those who had deplored the throwing of the dead rat at Winston now seemed to agree with her. Anasa Makini sat down, abruptly, as though shaken by her own anger and outrage.

Pat found herself not only impressed but strangely confused by what Anasa Makini had said. For an instant, she had to steel herself against being swayed over to the side of the tenants. Then she was suddenly angry with the woman. Why didn't she and the tenants give Winston a chance? It was unfair to assume that Winston would be as indifferent to their problems as other landlords had been.

But was it unfair? The memory of Williamsburg and the child that had been hurt by falling plaster thrust itself into her mind. She had wondered for some time if Winston was still paying and helping the family of the little girl, but she had been reluctant to ask him, sensing that he might be annoyed if she pried. Finally she had brought it up as casually as she could, telling him how sad she felt whenever she remembered the child crying herself to sleep.

"What?" Winston had said. "Well, oh yeah, I've had to sell that building. . . ."

"Sold it? Well, I mean—the little girl—will the new owner assume the responsibility for her and her family?"

He had frowned and looked away.

"Sure. Why not? I had it written into the Contract."

"But what does that—well—guarantee, Winston?"

He had tightened up against further questions, had even seemed to tighten up against *her*. She'd tried to push the child out of her mind. It had been so much more wonderful to cuddle up to him and feel him opening back up to her again.

But the child continued to shadow her thoughts occasionally. She couldn't seem to stop herself from hoping that Winston had been fair to the little girl and would be even fairer to his tenants in the future.

Now, however, Winston said nothing. Even when the applause for Anasa Makini subsided, he kept silent. Suddenly he left the rostrum and paced across the platform and then walked back to the rostrum again. He stared straight ahead, his head bent slightly, as though in deep and honest thought. But she knew that he was really furious. She also knew that the "worm" was working like crazy in his brain. But the strategy of not speaking yet, of not challenging Anasa Makini forthwith, couldn't have been better if he had thought it out beforehand. The auditorium was now absolutely silent, all eyes watching him, faces uplifted in anticipation. Still Winston said nothing.

231

Rattled by the silence, she, too, wished he'd hurry and speak. She glanced at Anasa Makini once more and was struck by a sort of jealous and breathless wonder. Had Anasa Makini so stunned Winston that he couldn't speak? The question left her face-to-face again with the depth of the strange insecurity that the woman caused her to feel. Since she had had such a difficult time getting Winston to the point where she was now less afraid of his leaving her one day, it was always in the back of her mind what kind of woman Winston would have preferred to her? She remembered she had been so on her guard against some unknown and shadowy rival, she'd almost blown her cool at the white girl in Bernie's office. It had been a tremendous relief to see that Winston was, at least, beyond *that*. So many black men were still obsessed by white legs. . . .

But what about a woman like Anasa Makini? A challenge seemed to hang between them. No doubt the woman was as clever and as tough as Winston. Plus she was attractive. Pat breathed audibly, struggling against jealousy. Seemed like every time she thought she had a few battles won, there was something else. There she'd been congratulating herself on her stamina for not breaking down and smoking, but what a minor accomplishment that now seemed when compared to the obvious abilities of Anasa Makini. She suspected that if she didn't hurry and toughen up and "get her thing together," she could still one day lose out to someone like Anasa Makini.

Donald suddenly shifted his feet and muttered impatiently, "How come he don't . . . ?"

He quieted when, at that instant, Winston nudged the huge rat with the tip of his shoe. Turning again to the audience, the silence glued to his presence, his voice surprisingly humbled, Winston said, "Where I grew up the rats I knew would have mistaken this tiny fellow for a mouse and eaten him for lunch!"

A few titters; a bit of the hostility diluted. Then Winston's voice rose slightly, but it still retained a sort of sincere intimacy. It was as though, uncannily, and perhaps not yet knowingly, something deep within him had become tuned in to the collective feelings of the audience.

"But are we here to be buried like rats ourselves—while trading personal insults that will accomplish nothing? Or should we begin working together? I cannot be held responsible for what landlords did before me; I can only say I came from homes like the homes in which you live, and I have not forgotten the sound of your children's tears. I distrust government bureaucracies as much as you, but what alternative do we have but to fight for a government loan? *Together!* I say we should join hands—all of us—and bring decent housing to this community!"

There was some scattered applause, perhaps mostly from those who'd always applaud landlords or those who appeared to be in power, but Pat found herself nodding her head in fervent agreement with Winston and wishing everyone in the auditorium would applaud and agree with him, too. His voice had *sounded* so honest. Instead of ripping the people off, maybe Winston really was interested in helping them? Perhaps seeing all the poor people before him, coupled with Anasa Makini's speech, it had somehow affected him, too?

She frowned in anger at the people surrounding Anasa Makini who began to boo Winston. Couldn't they see how sincere he was? At least they should give him a chance.

"Strike now!"

"Strike now!"

"No more lies and promises!"

"¡Adelante!"

Anasa Makini said nothing. Coolly, she stared upwards at Winston, but as though less in triumph than to let him know that she was firmly prepared for whatever he might try next.

Winston waited. Even when both the applause and boos had ceased again, he still waited. Possibly he, too, was disappointed in the reaction. Or had the waiting now become an instinctive sense of tactics?

Then, for the first time, Winston looked directly at Anasa Makini. The challenge was vibrant between them. Pat thought she could almost see the "worm" dashing about in Winston's brain, searching for new openings, a choice of new words.

"... Anasa Makini ..." he said, staring at her. "Yes, you would vote for a strike now. ..." And then he lifted his eyes and looked out over the auditorium, still searching for words. "Many of you would vote for a strike now. What can I tell you? There isn't a landlord who wouldn't oppose such a strike. But

233

am I saying the strike is unwise? It is *unwise*. . . . And yet have I uttered a single threat? Have I said, if you strike, I will retaliate by cutting *all* services to your homes? Have I mentioned mass evictions and putting you and your children into the streets? No. Instead I . . . at this moment . . ." he paused, as though listening to some secret but compelling voice out in the audience. ". . . would like to leave you with no further doubt as to my good faith. Allow me to join you, and to join you, too, Anasa Makini—to join all of you who would replace discord with . . . er . . . harmony, divisiveness with cooperation—allow me to cast my vote. I join you in calling for a rent strike *now*!"

For an instant no one responded. Faces were silenced by surprise. Pat, too, couldn't understand it. Why was Winston asking the people to strike against himself? And yet she found herself smiling with relief and even elation as practically everyone in the auditorium began to applaud. Perhaps what had been causing her to feel so uneasy was that she disliked the idea of Winston being a slum landlord more than she admitted, especially when he had to go against so many people, with the people clearly hating him. But maybe Winston had now found a way to help the people and at the same time still win what he wanted? As the applause swelled through the auditorium, she also applauded.

Everyone clapped except Anasa Makini and the few people close to her. But even her stubborn face wore a look of surprise, though heavily mixed with distrust. Roscoe Jones and Julio Rios seemed also caught off guard by Winston's decision. But they, too, applauded, cautiously. Donald clapped his hands once or twice, nearly as though they were too heavy to hold up; then he sat again in gloomy silence.

When the applause ceased, Winston, glowing in a way she had never seen him before, added immediately, almost hastily, "Thank you. But now I hope you will appoint a . . . a . . . Committee, so that we can get on with the business of improving this community. . . . Rents . . . well, rents should continue to be paid, of course . . . but into an Escrow account . . . designated by the Committee. . . . And, yes, of course, you will have my fullest cooperation in working with such a Committee. Using the rents in Escrow, we can begin our own *mini* repair program. At the end of, say, thirty days, we could always review our progress. At that time, we may find there is no further reason to prolong a rent strike. . . ."

Pat was listening so intently she seemed to keep on listening even after her attention was abruptly shattered. Both Winston's voice and a commotion that had begun towards the rear of the auditorium crowded her senses. Someone screamed. Then she saw the man in blue sunglasses come staggering out into the aisle, clawing at his throat. The boy followed, kicking at the man, and picking up the violin case. But at that instant, watching the boy's face, she no longer believed a violin would be in the case.

twenty

Donald had awakened with one of the worst hangovers he had ever had. Also, he hadn't been able to sleep well, thinking how Bette had dismissed him. Normally he was a conscientious worker and he had checked in and punched the clock but the sight of thousands of white envelopes and brown envelopes and bags of mail yet unopened and the buzzing of machines and voices had made matters worse. He had mumbled some excuse to his supervisor that he was sick and checked out for the day.

He went to a drug store where he sat drinking malted milks and ice water. He wondered if maybe the reason Bette had played it so cool was because there were so many people around. More than likely she hadn't wanted anybody else to know her business. There were two phone calls he had to make anyway. So maybe he'd call Bette at the same time. He had to find out if Gru was coming to the tenants' meeting; and he had also definitely decided that he was going to call the police department. . . . But instead of making the other two calls first, the moment he was in the phone booth he found himself dialing Bernie Stein's office. The woman on the switchboard took the call and then there was a buzz and Bette answered. "Yes?"

He tried to pull himself together and say something that would impress her instead of mumbling, but then she said quickly, "Oh, I'm sorry, sir. But Bette is not at her desk at the moment. Nor are personal calls encouraged at the office."

She hung up.

He couldn't believe it. He felt dazed, his ego so shattered, his hands trembled. A sudden charge of anger forced him to thrust another dime into the phone. The minute he recognized her voice, he demanded: "What kinda shit you putting down? It's me! Donald."

236

"Excuse me, sir. . . ."

"Excuse me, nothing! I'm the guy that fucked you so good you had to put your hand over your mouth to keep from screaming, and now you pretend you don't know me!"

She didn't even raise her voice. It became more remote, cooler.

"Sir, if you persist, you could very well find yourself arrested as a public nuisance."

Again she hung up.

When he dialed again, she wouldn't take the call.

He sat in the phone booth, sweating, shaking. How could she reject him like that, when she had seemed to like him so very much? He didn't understand it. Maybe she didn't want him because she knew he didn't have anything going for himself, and she was more impressed by people like Winston and Bernie and them lawyers? More than ever he wished he could get something started, something tremendously impressive. But what? And how? He couldn't hit the numbers. The lottery. Nothing! And to keep hoping to run into Leroy Brown again and collect the reward was stupid. Unless . . . He remembered one of the other phone calls he had been thinking about making. He had jotted down the Emergency Police number from TV: ". . . call this number . . . information . . . leading to . . . whereabouts of . . . Leroy Brown. . . . Of course, all calls are kept in the strictest confidence."

He had thought: Suppose he called the police and told them about the big guy? Told them what he had heard and seen at the airport? There might be an even bigger reward for helping to catch the big guy. . . . And maybe once they caught the big guy, they'd also be able to track down Leroy Brown and Trina Swan. . . . Once he got some money in his pocket, he'd tell a white bitch like Bette to go to hell! Gru was talking about going down to Venezuela. Hell, with the right kind of bread he might zip down there with Gru. . . .

He jammed another dime into the phone and dialed the police number. Typewriters were going on the other end of the line and other phones were ringing. A voice that sounded so metallic and remote it at first seemed like a recording, interrupted him. "Hold it. Speak clearly! Now let's get it straight. . . ."

He tried to speak more distinctly. He began telling again

everything he knew about the big guy, concluding, ". . . but I ain't seen nothing in the papers about him. On TV neither."

There was a long silence. Then the person who had been breathing close to the phone, told him, "Wait a moment."

He thought he heard whispers. After an almost inaudible click on the other end of the line, the sound of the typewriters and phones ringing ceased. There was a faint, continuous hum, as though he had been transferred a very long distance. A new voice, a voice that seemd to be even more secure in its authority, inquired, "Your name?"

"My name?"

"Yes."

He gave his name.

"Address?"

He hesitated, then gave his address, too.

"Now would you repeat your story."

"It ain't no story. It's the truth."

"Sure. Repeat it."

Again he related everything he knew about the big guy, but this time with the eerie feeling that not only was the man listening to him intently but was carefully analyzing the very inflection of his voice. He wondered who the man was; or better still, *where* he was? He no longer believed he was talking to a police precinct. He doubted even more that the man was an ordinary policeman. He didn't know why but he had the strange vision of his words going into a room somewhere far away, a room in one of those all white forbiddingly government-looking buildings, where there were always rows and rows of computers and silver filing cabinets under bright stretches of fluorescent lights.

"Continue."

"Huh?"

"Were you alone in witnessing this occurrence at the airport?"

"No. No, sir. But I'm the one giving the information. And I'm the one who gets the reward."

"Just answer the question."

"Well, I. . . ."

"Names? Addresses?"

Again he histitated. How come the man was asking so many questions when he had already told him everything that was important?

"Continue," the man repeated.

He gave the names of Gru and Winston and addresses. But they hadn't heard the big guy. They'd only seen him. So what kind of reward were they entitled to?

"Who else?" the voice prodded.

"Nobody. I mean, Pat was in the car. And just like Winston she only saw the guy when. . . ."

"Pat? Who?"

"She ain't got nothing to do with it. And them others ain't either. I'm the one who gets the reward!"

"Name? Address?"

He gave that, too. He looked out at the counter, sweating. People were sipping milkshakes and malts and cokes and eating ice cream. He wished he could step out and at least get a glass of water. In the brief silence he still thought he heard the faint and creepy humming of machines. Then the man went on, his voice suddenly even colder with authority, "What is your relation to Leroy Brown?"

"Huh?"

"Leroy Brown?"

"Well, I ain't no kinda relation to him. And I ain't seen him since the. . . . But I ain't calling about Leroy Brown. I'm calling about. . . ."

"Just answer my question."

Donald bristled.

"Whatcha mean . . . just answer? Ain't I got my rights to . . . to . . . explain? Who the shit you think you is? Hell, I'm just as good as you is!"

The man was silent for a long time. Slowly a strange fear stole over Donald. He even found himself wishing he could take back, if not exactly what he had said, then at least the violent and angry tone of it. Maybe right now the phone call was being traced and squad cars were on the way. . . . And who really knew *why* that guy had gotten shot up in Harlem. . . . Also, hadn't Gru warned Winston to be careful after having crossed those people on the plane guarding that big shot. . . ? He gripped the phone. A surge of resentment rose against the fear he felt. His anger grew even greater against the man.

"I'm doing . . . I'm trying to do what's *right* and you act like *I'm guilty* of something!"

He was surprised that the man's voice, after what seemed like a careful pause, did not sound offended. It was no more or less icy than it had been before.

"No one is questioning your good intentions. Still, in order to complete our investigations, questions must be answered fully—and intelligently. As for the person you mentioned seeing, you could have over-looked references to him in the newspapers and on television."

"I ain't over-looked nothing," Donald said. He tried to keep some of the belligerence out of his voice. "I know what I seen and what I ain't." Yet he had the eerie feeling he was still giving the wrong answers. Why didn't the man seem more eager to hear about the big guy . . . ? Or was it that the man was trying to cheat him out of his reward?

"If you insist," the man said, abruptly. "In that case, we must arrange for you to sign a statement. . . ."

"Now?"

"The sooner, the better."

Donald hesitated once more. It irritated him to feel the fear creeping back over him again. White bastards get him in a police station or in the dungeons of one of those white government buildings and beat the hell out of him. . . . Why? He wasn't sure. . . . He even felt that maybe he was being suspicious of the man when there was nothing to be suspicious about.

"Well . . . er . . . right now I ain't got time. . . . I got to . . . er . . . pick Winston and them up and go to a meeting." Give himself time to think. Sober up, deal with it tomorrow. Maybe he'd convince Winston or Gru to come with him while he signed a statement. Not that he was scared, of course, but it might be a good idea to have someone with him, like a witness, so that he could be goddamn sure he didn't get cheated out of his reward.

A sudden change came into the man's voice, a greater sharpness: "You said, meeting?"

"With the tenants that. . . ."

"Where's this meeting?"

"Whatcha mean? I mean, what's the point about. . . ."

"I said, where's this meeting?"

Reluctantly, Donald told the man where the meeting was. Then he exploded, "What you asking all these fucking questions for? You ain't said one thing about no reward! What kind of shit is this!"

The man said curtly, "We'll be in touch with you." The phone went dead.

Donald stared at the receiver, his mind a jumble. The strange fear reached out to claim him anew. Goddamn sonofabitch! he thought. Names! Addresses! And instead of being interested in the big guy, acting like Leroy Brown himself was going to be at the tenants' meeting!

He left the phone booth, scowling. Well, maybe something was going on that ordinary working guys like him wasn't supposed to know about? Secret government stuff and all that? Yet he could still be right, and the cracker was just trying to beat him out of his reward. . . .

At the counter Donald asked for a glass of water but his tone was so hostile the waitress took offense.

"You buying something?"

"I already bought! What the water gonna cost you?"

She sloshed the glass of water across the counter to him.

Fat white bitch, he thought. All alike. Cracker on the phone. That whore, Bette. . . . He wanted more water but imagined it would be an even greater hassle to get it. Also, he still felt uneasy in the place. Suppose the phone call had been traced? He went out, looking up and down the street, partly expecting squad cars to converge towards him. But except for a cop directing traffic there was no other policeman in sight. Still, he thought, "Well, it won't be like that brother you ran in on and shot up in Harlem. Come after me, you going to have to bring some ass to get ass!"

He exhaled a deep breath. Something seemed to be boiling inside of him, demanding release. He realized that he was disappointed that no one had rode up to challenge him. It left him keyed up, explosive, but forced to contain himself.

Two blocks away he stopped at a street phone and dialed Gru's number. He had to find out what time Gru wanted to be picked up for the tenants' meeting. Also, he'd have to confide in Gru—get Gru to help him against the crackers cheating him out of his reward. . . . One thing, Gru, like Winston, knew how to deal with the crackers. Of course, Gru might start talking about a "consultant's fee," but so what if they collected the rewards for all three—the white girl, Leroy Brown, *and* the big guy.

He waited anxiously to speak to Gru but the phone kept ringing, ringing. . . .

He left the phone booth, feeling more shaky than ever with disappointment. He spotted another drug store and thought he'd go in and have another chocolate milk shake. But instead he passed a liquor store and paused. He sure didn't want to be drunk going to the meeting. In fact, he should keep trying to get rid of the hangover he had. It was the worst he had ever had. That goddamn pot mixed with the beer and the scotch and the pussy on top of that had just been too much. But what was better to kill a hangover than to have another drink? As long as he didn't have too much. . . . But even as he continued to debate with himself, he found that he had already walked into the liquor store.

* * *

Now he sat and listened to Winston. The meeting seemed interminable. Instead of his hangover being cured, his head was splitting and his eyeballs felt grainy, like someone had dumped sand into them. He crossed and re-crossed his legs. Not only did he feel like a phony up here on the platform, it was a tremendous effort to keep himself from jumping up and exploding. Or, at least, from getting up and walking back to the rear of the auditorium and collaring the man he'd been watching. At first, he had been suspicious of the white guys with the Councilman, and even a bit suspicious of the Councilman himself. Then they had left. And he had scanned the auditorium again. Bastards would have to go a long way to fool him. He was sure he could tell the difference, as most Black people could, between a white-looking Puerto Rican and a pure-D cracker any day.

Finally his attention had focussed on the white man in the rear of the auditorium. He wore a crew cut, and a dark blue suit, and even though he wore a sport shirt like most of the men, he still seemed *odd*. He sat near a dark-skinned Puerto Rican woman with a baby. He kept smiling each time the woman looked at him. But Donald was convinced there was something phony about the smile.

Where were the others? Maybe already outside leaping out of cars with guns drawn and surrounding the building. . . ?

Again he wished he had spoken to Winston earlier. He was sure he hadn't hesitated because he disliked Winston. Lately he was sometimes aware that it was less dislike than envy. Envy that Winston was so much sharper than he was, envy that Winston now seemed to be on the verge of another victory; and envy, perhaps, too, of the ease with which Winston had won the love of a girl like Pat, Pat with her shy smile and slender body and big beautiful trusting eyes, a kind of woman he didn't think he'd ever have a chance of winning.

But it hadn't been this envy, either, that had stopped him from speaking. Just as he had been about to tell Winston about the man's demanding names and addresses and ask his help in collecting the reward, Bette had flashed across his mind. He could smell her, hear the throaty sound of her voice as she thrashed about atop Bernie's desk. It was like playing a record backwards, something she had said earlier, before she had said, "No. . . ." and he had thrown her upon the desk. Then suddenly it became clear. He remembered Mr. McMann's wheezing voice and Bernie hopping around in elation; and in his mind's eye, planes winged through the sky and landed in Washington. If Bette was right, *there wasn't going to be any loan*. . . .

"You were about to say something, Donald?" Winston had said.

"Er . . . naw. . . ." He had backed off. He had continued driving around the block looking for a place to park the car. How could he mention the loan now? How stupid he'd look for not having mentioned it earlier! But he knew that he should mention it. He even knew that he would eventually; but right now he needed to get it better organized in his mind so that the delay would appear a little less stupid than it seemed.

Finally, he'd found a place to park. It had been a tight spot, and maneuvering the old car into it, he had ended up breathing heavily, conscious again of the cheap scotch he had been drinking. He could imagine what his breath must smell like. Pat had been sitting between them and he had averted his face and kept silent.

If they had sat with the people, in the auditorium, he still might have gotten a chance to talk to Winston. But the Puerto Rican and the Black guy who were supposed to be leaders had ushered them onto the platform. His only hope had been he'd soon get another chance to speak to Winston.

Now he stared at the white man again. Maybe as far as the Whiteys were concerned once they realized that Leroy Brown wasn't here they wouldn't start anything. Just a routine investigation or something. Unless they got mixed up and thought *someone else* was Leroy Brown. . . .

Everyone in the auditorium seemed to be listening raptly. Winston was now saying something about, ". . . .forming a Committee. . . ." But Donald listened less to Winston's words, than to what the words made him feel. Maybe instead of envying people like Winston and Gru, he'd have to admit there was something he didn't have, in order to redouble his effort to get it. And yet he figured he must have already had the same gifts as Winston—or Gru—at one time in his life, but what had happened? Could you become frozen, locked into limitation without knowing what was happening to you? If he sometimes admitted that he felt slow and stupid, it was also as if the stupidity had very little to do with him. It was like something that had been wrapped around him, painted or grafted onto him, like an outer skin. By now it so encased him he could very well have become permanently crippled and limited.

He frowned angrily, feeling a familiar need to strike back at something, to hammer away at what seemed like his own prison.

When the commotion began near the rear of the auditorium, the rage deep within him rose to meet it almost with elation. But he was surprised. Instead of the white man moving, it was a boy and a man in blue sunglasses. The boy was ripping a shot-gun out of a case; and in a moment the man pulled a pistol. It was confusing. Unless the white man had set the niggers up to start the shit flying? Using Black folks to kill Black folks as they sometimes did. . . . Then they'd rush in and clean up.

244

Babbling crazily, the boy was rushing towards Winston. The man kept clawing at his neck. He couldn't seem to aim the gun straight. But Donald stood, crouching, still bewildered, not sure what to do, since the white man hadn't moved even yet.

twenty-one

Everything would have been all right if the woman hadn't jumped up and thrown the big rat. He thought he heard the thud of it landing, and then it started crawling all over the stage, running everywhere, even though later the woman said it was dead.

One night, years ago, when he had the flu and was dopey with all the medicine Mama was giving him, a rat came crawling up along the cold radiator pipe, the biggest one he'd ever seen. Mama stomped at it with her bare feet. But the rat just kept on coming and leaped into his bed. She must have thought it was going to eat him up alive, the way she screamed, trying to catch it.

"It's okay, Mama. It's okay" He had finally caught the thing between the sheets and his legs and choked and squeezed till he could feel the guts oozing out.

He wasn't even upset until he saw the ugly insides of the rat, as Mama cried and cleaned it up. When she turned her back, he got up and managed to get to the bathroom.

"Junior!" she called, thinking he must have gotten bitten, too. But he was okay. Except that the puke that had been trying to come out wouldn't move from his throat.

If she'd been less concerned about him and looked out for herself, she'd quit saying it was just a scratch. After all, there'd been nothing wrong with him but the flu. And even before the rat tore off a part of her toe, she had begun to look as though she was all skin and bones. She hadn't fully trusted the doctors. She hadn't been able to believe that God could visit upon the blood of Black people an affliction that no other people could get. She bought aspirins and vitamin pills and whatever new remedies she heard about from neighbors.

One day he waited and waited for her but discovered that she had fainted and fallen down the stairs. He didn't know if it was because of the rat that was now in her or if it was because of the cells that had already been damaged in her body. In the hospital, the doctors came in and out of the ward, but they hadn't known how to help her much either.

Still, instead of thinking more about herself, she kept on worrying about him. He tried to stop her, but every moment there she was pleading with the doctors to give him more blood tests and skin tests and every test, it seemed to him, they had at the hospital.

Finally she was satisfied.

"Thank Jesus. You all right. Seems like if one of the parents is healthy, the young 'uns is got a good chance to come out healthy, too. Now do you believe me when I keep telling you about your daddy? He was as strong and healthy as one of them boxing champions."

Yeah.

Healthy and rich and surprised that a rat could even come after him. . . .

He had no desire to warn Winston, but he watched the shock and the fear in the pretty lady's face and anxiety rose in him. He wanted to tell her she should hurry and lift her feet and legs out of the path of the rat. *Don't try to stomp it,* he heard himself almost shouting at her, *because it would just keep coming.* And even if the teeth left only a small scratch upon her toe, her foot and her ankle could swell up, and then the poison could crawl all over her, and the doctors could cut and cut and wouldn't know either how to get the rat out of her. . . .

But the pretty lady didn't move, just sat, frozen. Not much bigger than what Mama used to be. He wished he could warn her not only about the rat but tell her that she should be careful and look out for herself because one day Winston was sure to desert her, too.

Then he became confused. The fear in her face had vanished and she was suddenly smiling and applauding. Almost everyone was applauding. Apparently, more time than he knew had escaped him again. He gripped his seat and listened to the applause. It was like a threat. It had been much better when he

247

could share in the hatred against Winston that had filled the auditorium. It had somehow given him support. Now he felt as though he was falling again.

Were the people carzy?

How could they trust Winston?

He gazed at Winston himself, trying to understand it. Again he had to admit that Winston looked impressive—very tall and erect, a faint smile upon his lips, his hands moving slowly to emphasize his words. When he had fantasized about his father, filling the empty place beside his mother,—much like creating the kind of picture that had been of Winston and the pretty lady as they had sat side by side not long ago—, his father had always been handsome, confident, and cool. Watching Winston, he had to admit that he'd be proud of him, if he didn't hate him so much.

He wanted to get away from the voice. People were all about him in the auditorium but Winston's voice seemed to keep coming straight at him, like the people weren't there anymore. The warm friendly sound of it—like the rap of some dude conning you in the streets, but the con sounding so cool you couldn't stop yourself from listening to it yet—pushed against him and crowded him deeper into his seat. A wave of chills quivered his stomach, like small sharp teeth beginning to gnaw at his guts. His nose had filled up. He had to grip his seat again against the sensation of falling.

Lies! he thought violently. Why couldn't everyone see that? He had the wild and angry urge to jump up and shout and tell the people what a no-good lying bastard Winston was.

"Stop the fucking squirming, punk," Slick hissed. Then Slick jabbed him sharply with his elbow, cutting at his breath.

All of Junior's rage and confusion swiveled instantly towards Slick. Goddamn short-rationing motherfucker! Still, he didn't know he was going to do it now. He just felt his trembling fingers trying to balance the needle, using his soggy handkerchief to grip and support it. At one moment he was staring at the red rope-like scar curving about Slick's neck, and then he had lifted the needle and plunged it with all of his might just above the scar. . . .

He still didn't know how far he was going to go. Maybe all he meant to do was reach inside of Slick's jacket and get the unused bag that should have been his anyway. He had ripped almost all of the lining out of Slick's coat and had the stuff before he knew he'd have to finish everything now. He couldn't figure out how he could stop and roll up his sleeve and shoot the shit inside and quiet the angry hunger in his stomach before going on with the rest of it. People heard the gurgle-like scream trying to get out of Slick's throat and they had begun to scream, too. He picked up the shot-gun. Mama, poor Mama, couldn't wait forever, either. He had to get to Winston and get it over with fast. He hoped Winston would hurry and listen to him. And he knew one thing—Winston had better not try slapping him around again.

He was in the aisle. He had pushed his way past Slick. Why did the people seem so afraid of him? He stared at the faces and wanted to explain himself. Cradling the gun and reeling up the aisle, he even thought he was explaining to the people: "...I...I...don't mean to hurt nobody. But you're listening to lies! He'll put you into a trick bag, too. Mama wasn't even well when...when...he left her to the rats! Came to see me once in the park...then Mama said he never came back again...."

The pretty lady had started screaming, too. She must surely know he didn't intend to hurt her. He didn't mean to hurt Winston either if...if...Winston would listen to him, come with him; because how long could Mama wait...? He shouldn't have promised her he'd come back and kept her waiting when he must have known he didn't intend to.

He thought he saw Winston take a step towards him upon the platform, frowning, annoyed, angry that his lies were being interrupted. Then the black eyes behind the glasses seemed to grow still, and Winston was very still.

...Something he'd said? Maybe everyone was listening after all and trying to understand and Winston, too, had stopped being a big shot for a second and was listening now. Still, he didn't lower the gun. Now that the words were rushing out, he wanted to say everything that had been bottled up inside him. "No-good bastard, is what I tell you! Left her in the park...without even a TV set.... If you didn't mean to come back, how come you had to lie to her and say that you would!"

The frown came back over Winston's face, but again faded.

The black eyes stared at him. Contempt still seemed to be in those eyes. Like when Winston had slapped him before. He tightened his grip on the gun. Then, with all the screaming going on around him everywhere now, Winston took another step towards him. Why? To try to get close enough to jump him and slap him?

He thought he heard Winston say something.

But he had tensed behind the gun. All he knew was that he didn't intend to be tricked and slapped again. . . .

twenty-two

The applause warmed him all over, exhilarated him. He was surprised at his reaction to it. It was like receiving something he'd always secretly longed for, but hadn't believed he'd ever get.

It was the *approval.* Looking out upon the Black and Brown and sprinkling of white faces, he marveled at the people's willingness to trust him, to *follow* him. Yes, they were a desperate people and might follow *anyone;* still, at the moment, they seemed ready to follow *him.*

He tried to keep his head clear. He must not allow the applause to carry him away. Already, he found himself wishing that he could really and truly do something meaningful to help these people. Maybe that had been the reason why he had caught himself voting for a rent strike before he'd been completely aware that he was going to do so.

Perhaps he *had been* carried away...? Voting against himself! But was that true? Well, not really. It was Bernie who was going to have a fit. He had pushed Bernie to writing a clause in the Contract giving him ".....access to the above mentioned premises for the purpose of implementing and facilitating the transfer of ownership one month hence (30 days)...." But Bernie certainly hadn't envisioned him coming up here and attending a tenants' meeting and calling for a rent strike. And if the strike occurred now, any time within the next thirty days, it would be not against himself but against Bernie and McMann. They weren't going to like it. But what could they do? When he met them to Close the Contract, having won the tenants over, Bernie's and McMann's position would be further weakened; he might even demand *further concessions* from them. . . . Why not? A three month moratorium on the mortgage payment, for instance. . . . But, then, why not *six months*? Hell, he could always say, "What you guys expect? Don't you know you got a rent strike going on up there at your shabby buildings!"

And he could be sure of one thing: once having felt the relief of believing they'd freed themselves of a ghetto mess, they wouldn't relish wading back in. Perhaps they should be happy *if he ever decided to pay the mortgage*. . . . In the meantime, he'd fine a way to quietly halt the rent strike after thirty days.

Beautiful, right? Lord, God, maybe he was beginning to find the key to this whole thing, beginning to understand the way the System *really worked*? If so, what could stop him now? There didn't seem to be any limits up ahead.

Psychologically, at least, he could sense he was crossing another line. That invisible line that all the "big boys" must have at one time crossed. The early Rockefellers and Fords and Vanderbilts and the others. And once you'd crossed that line what could stop you?

"Thank you," he said, acknowledging the applause. He saw with amazement that he didn't have to worry anymore about what he was going to say next. Buried deep within himself, suppressed and rusty because of lack of use, an instinct so pure he hadn't been sure he had it seemed to be uncoiling, winging out and making contact with the audience. Even before he thought of what to say he was already saying it. And both the words and the tone seemed to be exactly right, targeting the emotions of the audience unerringly. But as his elation soared, and the sense of power thrilled him, he was shadowed by a vague resentment. Whatever it was he had now, he must have had it before. But how could it have flowered in the tight and closed social order surrounding him, where weak white boys could simply skip their way to the top, while the strongest Blacks had to forever storm troop to even win room to breathe?

And he still hadn't won everyone, taking no more than the small confines of the auditorium. The goddamn woman, Anasa Makini. A couple of youths ganged around her had started to applaud but had ceased instantly when she didn't. She was going to be the problem. It was either isolate her or win her.

As he continued, looking down upon the people and smiling, ". . . form a . . . Committee," he said, thoughts of the woman flitted through an edge of his mind: Yeah, speaking to him about the Third World as if only she knew what was happening. Well, could she tell him who in all of Africa had a single Hydrogen bomb? And who controlled the gold and the silver and still most of the oil? She spoke as if tomorrow was already today. In all truth, he could tell her he didn't give a fuck about *any* system. The point was never to allow yourself to be caught at the bottom of no matter what kind of system you happen to find yourself living in! For even when Africa got the bomb, someone would control it, and wasn't it better to be one of those who controlled rather than one of those who *were controlled?*

". . . Rents. . . ." he smiled again, "Well, rents should continue to be paid, of course. . . . Into an Escrow account. . . . Designated by the Committee. . . ."

Terrific, right? Use Bernie's own money to start a repair program! And if the loan was slow in coming through, he, as the new owner, would be that much more ahead. . . .

Yes, great. Except that the goddamn woman kept staring up at him stonily, as though she could read his most secret thoughts. He suppressed a frown. For Christsakes, it wasn't as if he intended to rip off *everything.* If the loan came in around a million, the rule of thumb was the landlord got away with about 10%. Of course, some landlords went for one-third or even 50%. Then there were a few landlords who went for *all* of it. Removing people from the area, gutting buildings, paying inspectors and falsifying reports. In this manner millions of homes disappeared across the country, leaving behind vacant lots and rusty material. . . .

Hell, if he only took 10% and put the balance into the premises, he'd still be doing something for the people, right?

10%. $100,000! Well, not much; not a fortune by any means, not the quarter of a million Gru had promised, but it would at least provide a base from which he could go on to the next level—Real Estate Mortgage positions, and maybe he'd form a combine and get into Insurance, and why not Supermarkets and Funeral parlors? And then there was the more glamorous world of Record companies and TV and Movie enterprises. . . . My God, the sky was the limit!

". . . .you will have my fullest cooperation in working with such a Committee," he heard himself say, thinking: Which meant, of course, *he'd* control the Committee. Most people tended to shirk responsibility; and it was those who weren't afraid to assume it who most always had the final say.

". . . .we can begin our own *mini* repair program," he declared. "At the end of, say, thirty days. . . ." He paused, fumbled, something interfering with the smooth flow of his speech. It was like static crackling across the screen of his mind, coming towards him from somewhere to the back of the auditorium. He tried to shrug it off, clinging to the high and beautiful place where he had ascended. " . . . we may find," he went on, ". . . there is no further reason to prolong a rent strike."

He even noticed that Anasa Makini's black uncompromising face seemed less hostile. Some of the stoniness in her eyes had yielded to a faint cynical smile. Though still distrusting him, it was as if she had decided to wait and see. But what alternative did she have, if *he* won the people?

Then he felt especially betrayed by her. The commotion in the rear of the auditorium had grown, swelling upwards, attempting to claim him altogether. It was disgusting. Apparently she had organized some cheap and shabby demonstration, showing an even greater lack of taste than the rat throwing.

Women were screaming and a child had begun to cry. A few people had started running towards the exit. A bummy-looking man, somehow strangely familiar, in blue sunglasses, fell backwards against a woman and knocked her down, clutching at his throat.

But what disgusted and angered him the most was the sudden recognition of the boy. It was the young junkie bum who had attempted to stick him up. The boy he had slapped up side the head, and who had lain there near the gutter, eyes filled with humiliation and hatred. What was he doing here? A tenant? Anasa Makini must have scraped the bottom of the barrel to find the young bum, as well as the degenerate-looking man.

Yet when he glanced at Anasa Makini she seemed to be as astonished as he was at the commotion. She, like the others, watched the boy coming towards him up the aisle. The boy babbled incoherently and had a gun larger than the one he had had before. He looked like drugs had nearly flipped him out of his mind. People continued to scream, scrambling to get out of range of the wavering shot-gun.

Winston stared numbly at the boy, a part of himself still resisting being pulled down from the great heights to which he had soared. —Get a goddamn toe hold up out of the crap and always there was something snatching you back again—! And my God, he could have had the boy's ass thrown in jail; had him locked up and the key *thrown away*! But instead of the boy being grateful he had let him go free,—even feeling sorry for him and thinking the boy had a sensitive, intelligent, face—, here the goddamn bum was coming at him no doubt with some mixed up idea about revenge.

And there was another thing Winston remembered. *The boy was a coward.* Not even enough balls to pull off the hold-up he had started, let alone shoot a gun. If there hadn't been something else, something he didn't quite understand as he stared at the boy, he would have told the people not to worry. He'd taken the gun from the young punk before, he'd do it again. Or, at least, convince the boy to put the gun down, and the meeting could go right on as before. . . .

But something else held him, froze him in indecision. The chaotic state of the boy's emotions seemed to charge at him with an abnormal intensity, pushing the people into the background. It was as though he was being locked into the boy's mad babble, both threatened and claimed by the distorted dark brown face and the outraged brightness of the black tearful eyes. It was strange to see so much emotion invested in the idea of revenge. . . . For weren't boys like this slapped around and humiliated every day? Why this great fury, this bitter hatred against him? Why pick on him? He was sure the boy could find hundreds of victims much more pliant than he'd ever be out there in the City parks and streets.

But it was as though the boy had *chosen* him, especially. Why? He felt a strange unease, mixed with fear. Now he found himself straining to understand the babble, get some clue as to where the boy was coming from. . . . Suddenly, he was no longer sure he could handle the boy.

"Lies!" the boy was shouting, trying to get the attention of the people. "Lies. He'll put you into a trick bag, too! Mama wasn't even well . . . when . . . when . . . he left her . . . to the rats! Came to see me in the park . . . then Mama said he never came back again!"

Park. . . ?

Park, he thought.

"Left . . . Left her . . . without even a TV set. . . . And the rats!" And then the boy's black red-rimmed furious eyes were turned upon him. ". . . how come you had to lie to her if you knew you wasn't coming back!"

The words jolted into him. He stared at the boy, disbelieving, believing, but mostly disbelieving. That small child toddling towards him in the park, reaching for him. . . . He remembered exactly how the sun had brightened the green patches of grass. The pride with which the sad skinny young mother had watched the boy. . . . "*He's yours*. . . ."

"He's yours. . . . But I don't want to cause you no trouble or slow you down. I can see how ambitious you is. . . . Maybe one day when you get on your feet and win all them things you want, you'll come back and be real proud of him."

He still resisted it, didn't wish to believe it. Had he heard the boy right? But even if he had heard the boy right, what had changed since that day in the park? He hadn't believed the woman then, why should he believe the boy now? Yet had he really disbelieved her? It was more as if he *had had to disbelieve her*. . . . How could he have climbed to this point where at last he knew he had the key, a shot at the title of everything he had ever wanted, with her and a child clinging to his back? It had been almost too difficult to make the climb having only himself and being responsible only for himself. . . .

And a junkie! His son? Impossible! No matter how horrible, how difficult it had been, would a son of his, a boy of his own blood, have succumbed like all the other losers to putting that white shit into his veins? And yet . . . everything else about the boy seemed . . . seemed . . . almost *right*. . . . Despite the distortion of the dark brown face, the trembling skinny form, he could imagine he saw mirrored in the boy something of his own intense and desperate youth. Except that it was still . . . *almost* . . . right; but not quite right. Even if he could see some physical resemblance, never had he, himself, as far back as he could remember, been a coward. And the boy had been so chicken, so cowardly, he hadn't even been capable of pulling off a stick up; or, if he had intended to shoot, hadn't had the guts to do that either.

A junkie *and* a coward!

Impossible!

Still, somewhere deep within the regions of his mind he seemed to be already thinking: Yes, well, if you're mine—and maybe you are—I can help you now. . . . What I mean is, what could I have done for you before? Even if you had been mine. . . . Now I can help you. First, get that white shit out of your veins. Get you into the best schools. . . . Show you *where it's at*. Teach you right from the beginning where the key to all the goddamn shit is. . . . If you're mine, and maybe you are, even if you're an addict and a coward. . . .

And thinking it, he was suddenly surprised by the depth of a strange and yet very real desire to help the boy. It was an emotion unfamiliar and yet familiar, a region of himself where even Pat had only recently begun to live, but where the applause of the tenants had also touched lightly and caused him to long to do much more for the tenants than he knew he could. It was as though, glimpsing victories up ahead, a tenderness in himself that had almost been closed off by the brutal struggle of yesterdays was beginning to open back up again.

And he could help the boy. Even if he still had doubts that the boy was his, he should try and understand him. He smiled and took a step towards the boy. First, get the gun and then he and the boy could talk later. . . . Get this whole thing straightened out. . . . And once he had the gun, he'd end the meeting quickly. But right now he must pacify the boy. . . .

". . . Dying. . . !" the boy continued to shout. "I'll shoot if I have to . . . if you don't come with me . . . because you promised . . . before the rats . . ."

"Give me the gun," Winston said. "I *know*. I understand. . . ." The tenderness swelled in himself and he knew the boy had to hear it in his voice.

The boy hesitated, staring back at him, as though wanting to believe him, wanting to trust him.

But then a violent surge of distrust distorted the young face again.

Winston took another step, pleading with his eyes.

Pat screamed, "Winston, don't!"

What had she seen? What had *she* understood?

The boy trembled violently. The hysteria rose in his tone.

"You won't trick me . . . like you trick everybody else! You won't slap me again!"

The blast of the shot-gun was a shock. A ripping, a burning, began somewhere in his stomach and raced like his blood had caught fire across his chest. His hands flew to his belly in astonishment. For a moment, reeling backwards, he stared at the blood coloring his fingers. He met the boy's eyes and the boy's face seemed horror-stricken at what he had done. Then he heard Pat screaming just before the floor of the stage rose up and caught him.

twenty-three

Someone screamed so close to her it was deafening. Even as she moved out of the chair towards Winston, the screams followed her. Except now all the screams appeared to be a plea directed at the boy. "Don't! Please don't!" And it seemed to her that it was only this plea that kept the boy from shooting again.

Cradling Winston's head in her arms, she was aware that the screaming had ceased. It was her own fingers unbuttoning his shirt, her own eyes that saw the blood. It was a very cool corner of her own mind winging straight through panic and fear, commanding her: *stop the blood.* She used his shirt and when that didn't stop it, nor hide from her eyes the gaping hole where his stomach had been torn, she used her blouse. She was amazed at the steadiness of her fingers. They didn't seem to have anything to do with her, except to obey that very small cool corner of her mind. The rest of her seemed to be drowning in Winston's eyes. Though they opened and closed she couldn't help but see the shadows in them.

Strangely, the world around her hadn't stopped, nor even slowed. An instant ago, she'd been somehow aware that it was Donald who had hurtled from the stage and hit the boy and knocked him into the frightened audience. Then there appeared to be other shots. Smaller, quieter sounds, but as menacing. Shots that may have been fired all along; the sound drowned out by the awful blast of the shot-gun. Somewhere out there where the world hadn't stopped, Donald was now fighting with the man in blue sunglasses.

259

Anasa Makini was shouting, "Get back. Get back. Give him room." Some people had run from the auditorium; others were trying to get in closer to see what had happened to Winston. "His son?" Someone said. Asking who? She was surprised to be asked anything. She nodded numbly, watching the shadows in Winston's eyes pushing against the brightness.

She heard her own voice, surprisingly crisp, commanding, still several steps beyond panic. "Call, ambulance. Hurry!" But she got the impression that she had already said that before; and yet she wanted to say it again. Somewhere all the shooting had ceased. She was vaguely conscious that the boy had stumbled up from where he had fallen, and that no one had seemed to know whether to restrain him or let him go. She got the strange feeling that the people had waited for her to decide what should be done about the boy.

"No cops . . ." Anasa Makini finally said, and she noted that some of the harshness had left the woman's voice. "When they come, it might be better if we don't know what happened."

Roscoe Brown hesitated, but then agreed, "Right," more or less as if it had been his decision.

Julio Rios translated into Spanish.

The brightness pushed at the shadows and she knew that Winston now recognized her. He wore a strange crooked little smile, like the smile was trying to tell her something, like he was as amazed as she was to find that he had a son, but was even more amazed that the boy had shot him.

"Don't speak," she said. If he didn't speak, if he was very quiet, he might beat this thing, too. Then she was shocked at herself for her doubts. Of course, he'd beat this thing! It was that small cool corner of her mind that had pushed in the doubt. But this was not the hospital. Some patients simply lost their will to live, had no further reasons to live, would no longer fight. But this was Winston. It was another one of those things he'd handle. . . .

Even his voice seemed strong, sure.

"Where is he?"

"Don't speak."

"Where?"

"Don't speak, please, Winston!"

"Guess you know . . . well . . ."

"Yes. When you're okay, we'll talk about it.... But now..."

"I'll be okay.... Shot me but can't even shoot. I didn't know.... Where is...?"

"Gone. You must be quiet. I insist, Winston!"

"Gone?"

"Yes. But if you'll be quiet, I'll try to get him." She didn't know what to do. If she got the boy, would that stop him from talking? Still, she couldn't make up her mind what to do, even that cool area of her mind didn't know what to do.

"Gone...?" he repeated. She thought she saw the pain rise up and shadow his eyes again. "Where? When he can't even..."

"Shhh Winston. Please!" For an instant, she thought of slapping her hand over his mouth; but suppose he still struggled to speak, and he was so stubborn she knew he just might, and that would be worse. She'd never be able to stop the flow of blood.... "I'll try to get him—I'll try to get him if you don't talk."

Anasa Makini was a blur somewhere near her, helping to keep back the crowd. She turned to her desperately; grateful, when, instead of hostility, she thought she glimpsed a moment of tremendous sympathy in the woman's eyes. "Will you hold him, please? But please don't let him talk."

Then she was standing, panic threatening to overwhelm her. But if she quickly convinced the boy that no one intended to harm him, wouldn't he come back? And no one intended to harm him—unless it was herself. Unless, the moment she saw him, she'd be unable to restrain herself from striking him into oblivion.

The blur of people still surrounded her: shocked faces, sorrowful faces, faces merely curious. She looked about wildly for the boy. But he was not in sight. Hazily she remembered that the people had allowed him to leave and that she had heard the boy mumbling, "I didn't mean to... but he... he...," staring at the faces about him but more at her before he fled towards the door behind the platform.

She didn't want to move so far away but she thought if she rushed to the door and called she could get the boy to come back. Take him to the hospital with them if that would keep Winston quiet. Anything to keep him quiet.

The panic, apparently, was catching up with her. She was already at the door staring up and down the corridor before she knew it. But the corridor was empty. She thought she had heard the clang of a door closing somewhere. One part of her raced back to Winston, but would he keep quiet if she didn't have the boy? She ran into the corridor. She came to the door. She hammered on it. It was the men's room.

"Will you come out of ... !" She was so sure the boy was inside, and yet at first she was paralyzed by the ridiculous sign, *Men*. Even in the hospital you wouldn't walk in, though you might have seen the patient's private parts only a moment before. She kept banging on the door, and then while she thought she was still banging she smelled the pungent odor of urinals.

Near the face bowls against the farther wall, bent the boy. Tears streamed from his eyes and snot from his nose. Frantically, he jabbed a needle at the veins in his arm.

twenty-four

She came at him. Her enormous eyes ablaze with anger. She didn't seem to know or remember that her shoulders, her waist, were bare; the white blouse gone. Her breast trembled in her bra as full as Mama's had once been.

He had heard her screaming outside the door but had never expected her to come into the Men's toilet. Her face was so torn up, she didn't look like the pretty lady anymore.

He jabbed more frantically to get the shit inside. If only he could get it inside and calm himself, he could explain himself to her. He hadn't meant to shoot. He hadn't wanted to shoot. But Winston should have stopped, stopped coming at him to take the gun away and slap him. And though Winston was rotten and no-good, Mama wouldn't have wanted him to shoot, either.

But she didn't wait for him to explain, to get all the shit into his arm. She flung herself at him. She seemed to hate him both for what he was doing and for having shot Winston. One hand knocked the needle out of his arm and the other hit him in the face so hard he could hardly see. He tried to grab her hands, while at the same time still attempting to retrieve the needle. But she was like something out of her mind, hitting him and shouting at him. And for a small woman, he didn't know how she could be so strong.

His fist caught her on the jaw and she kept on spinning and then she went down. He was so torn up himself, still reaching for the needle in his mind, that he lifted his foot to stomp in her face. He could see the pretty nose caving in, the smooth black skin ripped to the bone. All the while her big dazed eyes watched him. Eyes that got mixed up with other eyes. Eyes that had once looked at him and loved him, worried about him, stared at him as he backed out of the door. Now some thieving no-good low down junkie stomping those eyes out of existence. In the flash of seeing her, he saw it all. It seemed to him he had caught the no-good thieving junkie, could see his kinky uncombed hair, his snotty face, could smell him. His foot froze above the pretty lady's face. Yet it was strange to see that it was himself who fell back against the wall; and that it was someone who still seemed to be himself who stood there shivering. No matter how hard he tried, he couldn't keep from crying.

He knew she had gotten up, was still furious at him. He wanted to say never, never, never would he kick her. He wanted to tell her how sorry he was that he had punched her. However much she beat him, she had a right, too. Now he knew. Maybe Winston had left Mama; but he had left Mama, too. For days. Maybe a week. And he knew, though it was still almost too much to know, why she hadn't risen up and taken the soup. Her eyes had no longer seen the thieving junkie going out the door, who had been no stranger, after all. . . .

He expected her to strike him again. Knew she'd strike him again. And he felt he deserved the hardest blow she could deliver.—How could he have left her there without even a TV set, peddling the TV for the shit to go into his arm—? And then, in another instant, he would have stomped and stomped the pretty lady's face. . . .

He heard her move towards him, but then she slowed. He could hear her breathing, her breath rasping, tearing at her chest. She pulled his hands from his face, roughly, and then not so roughly. He knew she watched him. But he still didn't open his eyes and look at her, just waited for her to strike him. He sniffled deep in his nose and throat and stopped the crying, except that which still ached in his chest.

Still she didn't strike him. The touch of her fingers had almost become gentle. Then she exhaled a deep breath. The touch of her fingers did not leave his cheeks.

"Okay," she said. "It is going to be okay. No one is going to hurt you."

He shivered and clutched his shoulders, tight. He knew he must not break down. But he was less prepared for the tremendous gentleness he sensed in her than he had been for her blows. And he needed so badly to hang onto somebody for a moment, just a moment.

"C'mon now," she said. Her voice was urgent. "He's not mad with you, either."

He felt ashamed of his weakness, but when she put an arm around him, he trembled again and clung to her.

twenty-five

He seemed to be trying to climb up out of a manhole. But each time he gained the surface, a massive flow of traffic bore down upon him. The lights nearly blinded him. The buildings reeled above him. A huge truck, filled with garbage—tons of broken glass and concrete and old second-hand furniture—kept making a special effort to run him down.

His strategy was to avoid being hit until he could find an opening through which he could break through and escape. But his guts were on fire and he realized he must have already been smashed into several times. Fear rose and attempted to capture him as he watched the bright lights of the truck.

It was a vast relief to regain the auditorium. The faces of people swarmed above him. For a time, he heard himself breathing harshly, as though he had run a very real race after all.

Pat held him again; but he knew that more by the smell of her, the warm comforting smell of her, than that he looked at her now. He was trying to get the boy into focus. Shivering, eyes averted, the boy kneeled near him. It was an effort to remain alert against slipping back to the frightening place from which he had just fled and at the same time keep the boy in focus.

He knew, too, that he shouldn't talk. He was aware that it was foolish and dangerous to talk. But the desire to speak had become urgent. There was something . . . something . . . he must say. . . .

It didn't seem to matter that a part of him still couldn't accept the boy. For there was one thing he knew now: *The boy was certainly no coward.* Just before the boy pulled the trigger he had seen the fire in his eyes. A kind of unyielding and stubborn determination that had both scared him at the idea of being shot and strangely excited him that the boy had the guts to shoot. At that instant, he had known precisely what he, too, would have done in the boy's place. . . .

He didn't know exactly why he continued to resist the boy. It even seemed now that it might be less because of what he disbelieved than that he wasn't sure what the boy believed, had always believed, and not understood. The urge to touch the boy and explain tugged at him, but explain what? He doubted that children could imagine the depth of the terror that could exist in adult reality. He didn't know what he could make the boy understand.

"No," he thought he heard himself say. "You'll believe I just walked off and left you. You can't imagine how I could pick you up that day in the park, and yet put you down and leave you even though I wanted to keep you. You won't understand my walking away and feeling like a part of me was dying, maybe even the best part of me. . . . Nor will you understand how utterly desperate and afraid I was; afraid that I was going to be destroyed, even though I didn't know then what it was that was attempting to destroy me. *Neither will you understand that paralyzing fear of being caught, trapped, and buried at the maggoty bottom of the American Way of Life.* Perhaps you can't understand, not yet—that the horror of being trapped and buried like that would in itself have meant, for some, like me, *destruction.* . . ."

It wasn't clear whether he had said any of this yet, or even if it was the most pressing thing *to say*. He stared at the boy's swollen face, the snotty nose, the matted unkempt hair, the black red-rimmed eyes still not quite meeting his own, eyes at once sullen, defensive, and yet which seemed to be threatened by tears. Guilt and belligerency at war; like some frightened animal waiting for punishment but who hadn't decided if the punishment should be accepted when it came. But the guilt seemed to be winning and had taken the fire out of his eyes. The boy looked like he might break down again.

So he still must not have said anything yet, and hadn't lifted his hand and touched the boy either. Far away he thought he heard sirens, and the urgency increased. Whatever he had to say, he must say it *now*. Once they got him in the hospital who

267

knew how long he'd be kept out of action. And he must say what he had to quickly, briefly, otherwise Pat was going to try to stop him from speaking altogether. Tell him, tell him, forget the goddamn shooting.... What was done, was done. He *understood*. The important thing now was to get that white shit out of his arm. Don't go down like ... like.... He winced as he remembered the young boy digging a dirty fingernail into his bloody cheek. Don't go down like so many others, like as if he didn't have anybody now.... Because, yes, he could get him into one of those top schools.... And, well, if he came out a lawyer, who would need jackasses like Jonathan? Or suppose he came out a business man? Yeah. Upon the door of one of those tall glass buildings, WINSTON AND SON. How about that! He'd teach him how the shit worked from the git-go. Give him the *key*. And, God, wasn't it time? Time for Black fathers to leave behind more than just the ability to endure; time to leave City blocks to their sons, oil wells, railroads! He'd separate the boy now from the losers, the no-balls people, the cop-outs. Set him on a path where he could easily bludgeon his way to the very top of the heap. In the meantime, have him give that white shit back to the sons of the drug profiteers. Yeah....

He began to feel a headiness at his own thoughts, a tremendous excitement. He thought he glimpsed again the high place to which he had soared earlier. But was he thinking more of what *he wanted* than of what the *boy needed*? At least needed for now....

He grimaced. The bright lights stabbed at him again. Slivers of glass seemed to whirl towards him, slashing at his guts. He gritted his teeth, but for a second he couldn't see the boy clearly. Something strange must have come into his own face, for Pat's grip tightened. He moved his tongue and tasted a warm trickle of blood. Pat dabbed a handkerchief anxiously to his lips.

"Where's the ambulance?" someone up in the crowd exclaimed.

"I'm ... I'm sorry...." he heard the boy say. "But you wouldn't stop when...." The voice was shattered. The fire gone; spirit crushed. If left like this, with nothing to shore him up, would the boy be able to keep himself from going completely to pieces while he was in the hospital?

He swallowed a salty lump out of his throat. He squeezed Pat's hand, trying to tell her not to stop him from speaking.

Then he heard the sound of his own voice, so weakened he hardly recognized it. ".... If you shoot . . . you ought to learn to shoot straight." The boy's swollen face wavered before him, but it still seemed like a handsome face, a sensitive face. He also thought he saw tears glistening in his eyes; but the boy shuddered in his effort to check them, as though he was going to hate himself if he cried.

"I didn't want to. . . ." The boy's chest heaved. "I mean, I told you I would. But I'm sorry. . . . I'm sorry."

Winston swallowed again.

"Sorry?" he said. But now his voice was a bit firmer. Suddenly he sensed that instinct, beyond anything he could clearly figure out to say, might play him true again today. "About what?"

Pat, however, wouldn't keep silent.

"Hush, Winston, please!"

"But tell him . . . tell him," he told her. "It wasn't him. It was the other that. . . ."

"Yes, Winston. Of course. Of course. It was the other. The man in the glasses who. . . ."

"He can't even shoot," Winston said. "With that white shit in his arm." His eyes found the boy once more. "You just get rid of that shit. I'll be out of the hospital in no time."

The boy didn't say anything, kneeling there, torn between attitudes. Relief and yet at the same time maybe disappointed that he couldn't even shoot.

"You hear? I said, *get that white shit out of your arm.*"

"Yes . . . well . . . Yes, sir."

"And then we. . . . And then we. . . ." But now the lights came at him from a different direction; it frustrated his defenses. He watched the glass spilling, whirling, angling for another attack, but though he tensed and steeled himself to meet it, he still didn't see the truck. He breathed deeply. There was so much more he wanted to say. But he couldn't quite remember what he had been saying. Finally he heard himself finish lamely, "Shake," he said. He attempted to lift his hand and was startled by the force of the pain flashing up from his guts.

The boy hesitated, staring into his eyes. Then, shuddering against the grip in which drugs had imprisoned him, he grasped Winston's partly raised hand, hanging onto it as though out of an almost forgotten but secret longing.

Pat's face swam towards Winston.

"I've told you to hush. Now shut up. I really mean that, Winston!" The sharpness of her tone surprised him.

He met her eyes. She was alarmed but she was also quite furious with him. Well, giving *me* orders, he thought. He frowned, gazing at her; but he realized that he wasn't in the least displeased.

twenty-six

Pat was relieved that Winston had ceased talking and yet she longed for the reassuring sound of his voice. His fingers gripped her so tightly she was in actual pain. She hoped he wasn't hurting the boy with the same steel grip. But instead of the boy's face admitting pain, it now seemed rigid in its determination to quiet inner chaos, much as if what Winston had said had had an effect upon him after all.

She listened desperately for the sound of the ambulance and thought she heard it again, still far away. White neighborhoods the police, ambulances, got there instantly; many Blacks died, waiting. . . . She shuddered and shied away from thoughts of death. She became aware that Donald had returned, and stood there breathing heavily, staring down at Winston in astonishment. He and Anasa Makini were speaking, or at least Anasa Makini had just asked him a question.

"I knocked him down," Donald said, adding guiltily. "But he got away. . . ."

"Don't worry. We'll know him if we see him again." Then Anasa Makini looked down at Winston once more, her eyes still full of the sympathy that had surprised Pat earlier. "Do you know what he planned to do next?"

"Huh?" Donald said.

"I know it is insensitive to ask. But I'll have to tell the people something. . . ." Her voice was so low Pat could hardly hear her. "He's hurt badly. And while he's in the hospital—to safeguard his interest, and ours—someone should take his place on the Committee. . . ."

271

"I . . . well . . . I don't know exactly what he planned," Donald mumbled. "But. . . ."

It seemed to Pat that Donald was looking at her, wondering if she knew what Winston had planned. A part of her resented Anasa Makini having asked the question. Couldn't it all wait? If the ambulance didn't get here soon . . . soon. . . . Her throat got choked up. She had to control herself to keep from moaning aloud. Of course, Anasa Makini was right. Things had to go on. The people were so upset at the misery in which they lived something had to be done now. Some of the faces reflected sympathy for Winston but all the same they would go back to unrepaired apartments and face rats and roaches and plaster falling upon their children.

She swallowed hard and looked up at Anasa Makini. The woman's face, with its broad nose and full mouth, seemed truly kind and the compassion was real. The granite uncompromising hardness that had been in it as she challenged Winston had all but vanished, and her dark brown eyes had softened.

"He planned to help," Pat said. "Of course he planned to help. Like he said. And . . . and . . . I suppose . . ." She looked at the boy; and then at Donald. "We can help . . . take his place on the Committee."

"That would be good," Anasa Makini said. "For all of us. And for the boy here, too." She touched the boy's nappy unkempt head lightly. "Very good for the boy here. It is always good to have a purpose."

Pat glanced at the other young men who had surrounded Anasa Makini earlier, who now assisted Julio Rios and Roscoe Jones in keeping the crowd back. They went about their task briskly but courteously, snapping about with almost military bearing.

Suddenly she was surer than ever she was going to be able to help the boy. Others now would help her to help the boy. When Winston got out of the hospital, he'd be proud. Their own son—or their daughter—would have a big brother. Before, she had been hoping for a boy; but now she hoped it would be a girl. And the little girl would already have a big brother to protect her, to love her. A big brother, something she herself had never had. . . .

272

Yes, she'd work with Anasa Makini. She was a good woman and she shouldn't have been jealous of her. She was still a bit jealous of her. But maybe if she watched carefully, one day she'd know everything that Anasa Makini seemed to know.

She caressed Winston's face, sensing that the very touch of her hand somehow kept him calm. She hoped she'd given Anasa Makini the right answer. . . . For hadn't Winston *said* he was planning to help? And hadn't he looked happy as the people applauded, believing in his sincerity, his promises? So if she helped the people, she'd be doing what he wanted her to do, right? And the boy, too, would help. The boy would learn now how to get it together and drugs had a tough time maintaining a hold on a person who had a strong sense of purpose. . . .

Then she tensed and nearly couldn't breathe. One moment Winston's face seemed almost serene and then a frown creased his forehead, and his eyes spun open. He stared at her, like calling her name. Then he stiffened and a gush of blood colored his teeth. His eyes grew wider with surprise, and what even seemed like resentment. When he opened his mouth to speak, his tongue was coated with blood.

Before she could reach past terror and find words, he gasped, angrily, "Sonofabitch!" as though still battling to ward off some treacherous opponent.

And though his eyes remained open, and seemed to be frozen in a kind of incredulity, she finally knew he wasn't seeing her anymore. . . .

twenty-seven

Donald had picked up the pistol and stuffed it into his pocket, still needing to crush someone, something. Just before he got to the junkie, one of the tenants had flung a chair and knocked the junkie off balance and the gun clattered to the floor. He had only managed to get in a glancing punch beside the junkie's head before all the people were jumping in his path and kicking and striking at the junkie for having frightened them and their children. So many people tried to get at the junkie they got into each other's path, and he had to watch helplessly as the junkie bleeding and cursing bitterly twisted himself free and bolted out of the door, a bunch of teenagers howling and running after him. It wasn't easy to restrain himself from also running after the junkie. His chest felt so full, so keyed up, he might have fired the gun if he hadn't been worried about hitting one of the tenants or their children.

It didn't help when he came back to the circle of people surrounding Winston and saw that Winston hadn't moved from where he had fallen. It got worse still when he realized, maybe as soon as Pat and the boy did, why Winston hadn't moved and why he wouldn't perhaps ever again. The woman in African dress, whom he hadn't liked at all at first, looked down at Winston and seemed as stunned as he was.

She shook her head sadly.

"What a waste!" she murmured.

He couldn't speak. If someone like Winston could be brought down like that, as sharp as Winston was but still so un-suspecting, it could happen to *anyone*.... Yet how had it happened so quickly, been so quickly organized?

Somewhere outside a blast of sirens ceased abruptly. Two white cops rushed in and the two ambulance attendants also seemed white, at first. Their sudden appearance jolted him back to the moment. He pulled his eyes away from Winston, and waited for the men, his chest so full now it was difficult to breathe. He could almost hear glass crashing, doors slamming open. Other cops following these that were inside; guns drawn, intent clear. . . .

But the two policemen in uniform hadn't pulled out their guns yet, and now he began to suspect that the two ambulance attendants might be Puerto Ricans. Even the white man he had been watching earlier at the rear of the auditorium had disappeared.

He didn't understand it; couldn't unravel it yet. Did it mean that this was all of it for today, for the moment? Or was there more of it to come, perhaps in some other form? He was aware that the boy had pulled the trigger, but who had given him the gun? He knew that the junkie had been ready to shoot *everybody*, but where had the junkie come from? And even if it all had come too swiftly for it to have been organized today, it could have been organized days before; names, addresses, all the places of meetings already known. . . .

He looked back at the crowd of people around Winston. Pat continued to tremble violently and the sound of her weeping shook him. Anasa Makini kneeled beside her, attempting to comfort her. The boy had bound up, pushed his fist into his eyes, and now stood there as though totally bewildered. Finally he sank down next to Pat, staring at her, shivering each time she gasped and moaned.

The white-looking Puerto Ricans put Winston on the stretcher and covered his face.

"No," Pat cried. "No!"

Donald had to turn his back and blow his nose. Goddammit, as smart as Winston was how come he hadn't known? How come he hadn't known what even he was beginning to know? And why should he blame himself now for having not warned Winston? He had meant to; but he hadn't imagined there wouldn't be time.

He stuffed the handkerchief back into his pocket and turned to help hold back the crowd so that the attendants could bring Winston through.

Anasa Makini tried to separate Pat from Winston but she refused to leave him and stumbled along beside the attendants.

The crowd followed and milled about the exit. The policemen had taken out their note-books to make a report but no one seemed to know anything. The attendants lifted the stretcher to put it into the ambulance. Again Anasa Makini attempted to restrain Pat, but Pat, though some of her tears had subsided, was pushing into the ambulance, in spite of the attendants' protests. The boy ceased shivering for a moment. He balled his fist and glared at the attendants. Donald thrust the people aside and stepped forward. Maybe the attendants were a couple of white sonofabitches, after all!

Julio Rios spoke up quickly, rapidly in Spanish. Then he said in English, ". . . to hell with the rules!"

People murmured in agreement.

The driver of the ambulance shrugged and got into the front seat. The boy touched Pat tentatively. When she didn't draw away, and even seemed to lean towards him, he helped the other attendant get her inside, his mouth held taut and almost successful against his own tears.

Anasa Makini got in also. She took the boy's hand and moved aside and sat him down next to Pat. Then, two of the other young men, with clean razor sharp parts in their closely cropped hair, and faces grimly serious for faces so young, hopped in.

Donald took one more look up and down the streets and climbed in with the driver. He continued to hear sirens going on out there somewhere in the City, but so far they still seemed to be far away.

"She all right?" he called back to Anasa Makini.

"She's okay. She will be okay."

"And the boy?"

"He's going to be just fine."

He felt a little better, but not much. It had been too late to warn Winston, but once everybody calmed a little he'd warn them. Because if the meeting hadn't been surrounded today and the windows and the doors crashed in, it could still come tomorrow, couldn't it? He'd warn Pat. The boy. Anasa Makini. Warn everyone who would listen. So that they would, at least, be as ready as he goddamn well intended to be. . . .

Harlem/Oululan/Toronto/Nigeria/and Harlem again.

The following interview is not to be
read without the *permission* of the
author.

Below is an excerpt from an interview with the author by J. R. Priestly, noted British Playwright and Critic.

PRIESTLY: "Mr. Wms-Forde, first of all, why the pseudonym? Was it a desire to maintain a clear distinction between your present effort and your seven other novels?"
Wms-FORDE: "Yes and no."
PRIESTLY: "Then you would perhaps agree with your critics that *Requiem* is not as well achieved as your other works?"
Wms-FORDE: "No and yes."
PRIESTLY: "Along those lines, what prompted you to agree to the publication of *Requiem,* since you have consistently refused to allow the reprinting of . . . well . . . for instance, *On the Trail of the Blonde Gorilla*?
Wms-FORDE: "Well, I was asked by an actress to clarify a scene in the film script of *Requiem* involving Patricia Wallstone. I attempted to answer her question and ended up writing the novel. I'm still not sure I answered it."
PRIESTLY: "In your approach to the novel—why did you use the . . . well . . . so-called popular, mass-audience-appeal, form?"
Wms-FORDE: "Perhaps for the same reason Faulkner, Himes, etc., experimented with the Detective Story form. Besides, I was no longer living in isolation in Oululan."
PRIESTLY: "According to a recent TV interview, one of your former associates stated that ten years ago you made thirteen attempts at suicide."
Wms-FORDE: "That's a lie."
PRIESTLY: "Were the charges brought against you subsequent to your wife's murder also untrue?"

281

Wms-FORDE: "I was exonerated. Furthermore, she wasn't really my wife."

PRIESTLY: "And yet you ran berserk."

Wms-FORDE: "Berserk?"

PRIESTLY: "Well, old chap, what would you call throwing a typewriter out of the window of a sixteen storied building?"

Wms-FORDE: "Not berserk. Everyone was burning down buildings and shooting in the streets at the time. And after all, no one was hurt. The guy's car that got hit was insured."

PRIESTLY: "Well, you are remarkably calm these days. Would you credit that to your stay in Oululan?"

Wms-FORDE: "Not really."

PRIESTLY: "Then perhaps to the influence of your recent interest in . . . uh . . . Black Magic?"

Wms-FORDE: "No and yes."

PRIESTLY: "To pursue this . . . uh . . . Black Magic. How extensive would you say the practice of it has become today?"

Wms-FORDE: "Organizationally? I wouldn't know. My experimentations are still restricted to a few close acquaintances and my family."

PRIESTLY: "Is it true that you have an Aunt who can kill a man by staring at his reflection in the mirror?"

Wms-FORDE: "That's her claim. I've never seen her do it. I don't know if she has reached that stage of perfection yet."

PRIESTLY: "To change the subject, are there any good writers left in America?"

Wms-FORDE: "Some. Killens. Baldwin. Ellison. Williams. Marshall. Guy. Wright. Meaddough. Baraka. Riley. Bullins. Morris. Deveaux. Milner. Elder. Wesley. Bond. Giovanni. Reed. Harriston. Hudson. Meriweather. Himes. Morrison. Troupe. Russell. Pharr. Walker. Tchalka. Angelou. Leaks. Clarke. Mitchell. And Bobo the Beep. Etc."

PRIESTLY: "Aren't there any . . . uh . . . ?"

Wms-FORDE: "One or two. Mailer started off with balls, but then collapsed. Pynchon, Barth and Heller are interesting. Vidal, great! The others are writing musicals or are in Hollywood."

PRIESTLY: "Um. What is your opinion of Solzhenitsyn?"

Wms-FORDE: "Zero. In the 'good ole days' Solzhenitsyn would have found himself in his glory as a Slave Owner. Besides, there are three Black Solzhenitsyns dying every hour in the U.S.A.

Furthermore, perhaps we should also be careful to reserve a tear for those sad and crippled and still unsung *white American* (and British?) Solzhenitsyns."

PRIESTLY: "Um. Um. Yes. Well, yourself? Will it be Hollywood or back to Oululan?"

Wms-FORDE: "Neither."

PRIESTLY: "London, then?"

Wms-FORDE: "No, Iran. At least for one year. Then, to West Africa and the Philippines. I'm researching a book—*The Assassination of Ulti Ultimo*. I hope to complete the book before the assassination occurs."

PRIESTLY: "The man is still alive?"

Wms-FORDE: "Yes."

PRIESTLY: "Would you care to share his identity with . . . ?"

Wms-FORDE: "No."

PRIESTLY: "One last question. Would you comment on the vast difference between *Requiem* the novel and *Requiem* the film script?"

Wms-FORDE: "For instance?"

PRIESTLY: "In the script, instead of dying, you imply that Winston goes on to amass six million dollars. Pat becomes an assistant to New York's Commissioner of Health. And it is more or less the boy, especially after the California shoot-out, who is faced by the greatest tragedy."

Wms-FORDE: "Well, to explain the difference, I suppose I'd have to write another novel."

PRIESTLY: "About the boy?"

Wms-FORDE: "Perhaps."

PRIESTLY: "Well, the best of luck to you, sir."

Wms-FORDE: "And to you. *And* England."

For the complete transcript of the above interview, write or phone:

TROISIÈME CANADIAN
or Public Relations Division
WILLIFO ASSOCIATES, INC.

212-866-0095

283

About the Author

BILY Wms-FORDE is a former lion tamer and mountain climber.

He is the originator of THE GAME OF MOTHER. He is also a reigning champion player of THE DOZENS.

The fact that a distant cousin is the sole Black Billionaire in America has no relevance to the present novel.

Bily Wms-Forde has studied Yoga, etc. He recently joined the growing International Fraternity of those who sleep with their fingers crossed.